TIGHT ROPE

SAHAR ABDULAZIZ

DJARABI KITABS PUBLISHING

Dallas, Texas

TIGHT ROPE

Copyright © 2017 by Sahar Abdulaziz.

All rights reserved. Printed in the United States of America. No part of this book may be used or reproduced in any manner whatsoever without written permission except in the case of brief quotations embodied in critical articles or reviews. This book is a work of fiction. Names, characters, businesses, organiza- tions, places, events and incidents either are the product of the author's imagination or are used fictitiously. Any resemblance to actual persons, living or dead, events, or locales is entirely coincidental.

For information contact:
DJARABI KITABS PUBLISHING
PO BOX 703733
DALLAS, TX 75370
https://www.djarabikitabs.com

Cover design by Joshua Jadon
Edited by Hend Hegazi, Layla Abdullah-Poulos, and Kayla Weir
Interior design by Papatia Feauxzar

ISBN-10: 0-9967094-8-7
ISBN-13: 978-0-9967094-8-4
EPUB ISBN-10: 0-9967094-9-5
EPUB ISBN-13: 978-0-9967094-9-1
Library of Congress Control Numer: 2017907798

First Edition: June 2017
10 9 8 7 6 5 4 3 2 1

CONTENTS

DEDICATED V
PROLOGUE VII
CHAPTER 1 1
CHAPTER 2 11
CHAPTER 3 29
CHAPTER 4 45
CHAPTER 5 53
CHAPTER 6 69
CHAPTER 7 80
CHAPTER 8 89
CHAPTER 9 105
CHAPTER 10 112
CHAPTER 11 121
CHAPTER 12 134
CHAPTER 13 140
CHAPTER 14 150
CHAPTER 15 155
CHAPTER 16 164
CHAPTER 17 181
CHAPTER 18 186
CHAPTER 19 192
CHAPTER 20 205

CHAPTER 21	215
CHAPTER 22	226
CHAPTER 23	231
CHAPTER 24	239
CHAPTER 25	247
CHAPTER 26	262
CHAPTER 27	265
CHAPTER 28	275
CHAPTER 29	278
CHAPTER 30	285
CHAPTER 31	295
CHAPTER 32	308
EPILOGUE	321
ACKNOWLEDGMENTS	**336**
GLOSSARY OF TERMS	338

Dedicated

To the Truth

Racism is Terrorism

PROLOGUE

Nour Ibrahim

SLUMPED OVER HER OFFICE DESK, head pounding from exhaustion, Nour wanted nothing more than to kick off her shoes, close her eyes, and curl up into a ball of nothingness; escape from the insanity determined to squeeze the breath out of her. Still, she resolved to stick with her self-imposed habit of sifting through and dispensing with the newest batch of emails as rapidly as possible, a laborious task, since her daily pile of hate mail had nearly doubled in size from the previous week. But that was no surprise. The more she spoke out, the more she revealed in the public forum, the more the hate came seeping through the woodwork, the way hornets swarm and nest in every space worth claiming, using their stingers to mark off their territory, asserting control and fear through a cluster of chaos.

On the corkboard above Nour's computer screen, cluttered with business cards, takeout menus, and witty newspaper comics, she'd pinned a few of the most heinous quotes. They served as a biting reminder of what would befall her, and the community, should she become complacent. One particular star—a top troll contender listed on her *One Hundred Hate Hit Parade*—earned the pseudonym "Shadow." Nour thought the nickname was appropriate since he hadn't possessed the balls to sign his real name. Then again, neither did most of her foes, preferring to employ juvenile tag names.

"The only good Muslim is a dead Muslim." *—The Glock-Doc*

"You're nothing but a bunch of raghead bitches." *—The South Never Lost*

"Times up, brown trash. Get the fuck out of America." *—Stone Wall*

"Kiss your visa goodbye, you fuckin' cockroach." *—The Texas Patriot*

Nothing but a bunch of insolent Internet warriors, more than happy to curse her out from afar, cowering behind what Nour referred to as the "new white hood" from the anonymity of a computer screen. For the most part, their attempts to scare her accomplished next to nothing, except to prove their cowardice and severe lack of originality.

For months, every morning like clockwork, Shadow's special racist rants would grace her Inbox, always addressed "Dear Black Bitch."

"Dear Black Bitch: Caught you running your mouth on the news last night, lying again. One of these days somebody's gonna shut you up for good. Who knows? Maybe it will be me."

"Dear Black Bitch: You and your kind are ruining this country. But don't worry—we're gonna make America grate [sic] again."

"Dear Black Bitch: You think you're so smart, but back in the day your kind would be stopped dead in their tracks. Somebody needs to send you and your kind to the fields where you belong."

"Dear Black Bitch: Tell me, why do you wear that nasty rag on

your head? Why not look like a real American? FYI: This country was founded on Christian principals and you Moslem [sic] radical terrorists are ruining it for everybody."

At first, Nour failed to place any significance on his line of attack, and ignored him. Much like the other hate mail, his barely made any sense—nothing but a collection of misspellings and taunts delivered in a jumble of complaints, based on a fabricated yet chilling racist worldview, and fed by a diseased and slanted mindset.

Lately, though, Shadow had become brasher, attaching small extras to his messages: "Gifts," as he referred to them in his emails. In truth, they were nothing but pilfered, creepy photos probably gleaned from web searches and then altered to fit his abhorrent rants. Nonetheless, he seemed proud to share, making it imperative to keep files on him and all the other Islamophobes and racists. The files might be used as future evidence, should Nour ever decide to take legal action. If not, this was one way to help her keep the poison contained. She remained committed to not allow threats to frighten her off from doing what was necessary but, though she'd never admit it to anyone else, his most recent "gift" had shaken her to the core.

When she'd first laid eyes on the photo, she needed a minute to digest the horrific image. Along with his customary hate mantra, he'd upped the ante, sending an attachment of a tipping headstone with Nour's initials superimposed in bold black marker. Beneath her name, he'd inscribed the year of her birth and then placed an open EM dash to symbolize her awaiting death date. However, in addition to Shadow's already devastating email, he'd added a bizarre icon of an unhappy face below her initials.

"You bastard!" Nour gasped, unable to catch her breath. *Why are you doing this to me?!* Nour paced the length of her office. *I-can't-breathe.* Clutching her chest, her anxiety hit the roof. He'd gotten in. Infiltrated her personal space.

Leave me alone! Her body broke into chills, the palms of her trembling hands turned clammy, a nerve in her eye twitched. *Think, think.* No longer just an angry voice in a string of voices, his threats winded her: a reminder that, once again, there was no safe space for her. She kicked the overstuffed file drawer closed.

Desperate to be rid of prying eyes, Nour locked herself in her office. Pressing her back firmly against the door, her pent-up panic and anger exploded. Through clenched, chattering teeth, she struggled to quiet the deep-throated sobs as her clasped fists pounded her thighs in frustration. There was no use denying that his threats landed home, draining her reserves and prodding her fear and vulnerability. While this particularly sick episode bordered on the macabre, what terrified her more was the fact that he'd gotten this close.

Nour probably should have reported the hate mail, and maybe she would have, except in past experiences the police didn't afford her black skin the same unimpeded protection that white skin routinely received. Unlike her blonder, fairer, blue-eyed counterparts, who were customarily believed at face value, her safety barely sparked a pulse with city law enforcement. Her concerns were minimized, invalidated, or flat-out flagrantly disregarded. Systemic racism and the decimation of black lives reinforced the reality that the pendulum of doubt almost never swung favorably in her direction. Her existence scarcely registered when superimposed against the powerful white backdrop of entitlement.

Nour stapled the newest threatening photo to the inside flap of the file she'd intentionally created for *His Truly*, since the Shadow seemed to be her most devoted follower thus far.

Just another day as a Black woman living in America.

CHAPTER 1

Russell J. Tetler

"**FIRED? YOU'VE GOTTA BE** kidding me—you dirty rat bastards!" Russell's heartbeat began to race. Temper flaring, he struck the locker with the palm of his hand in utter disbelief. "After all these damn years…"

It was only last week he got yanked off the floor and invited to his supervisor's office to have "a little chat."

"It's like this, Tetler. Simply put, you're just not producing. Your count is way below expectation, and what you do manage to finish on time is usually shoddy workmanship at best. Frankly, I'm disappointed."

Not trusting himself to respond, Russell sat still and speechless as his boss continued to chastise him. His hot face laden with embarrassment, he was unaware that his clutched hands were balled into a fist.

"I have to tell you, on a production line like this, I can't afford to carry anyone not putting out," his supervisor continued,

TIGHT ROPE

shuffling through paperwork strewn across his desk. "I got upstairs breathing down my neck, wanting me to thin the herd. Do you get what I'm tryin' to tell you here?"

Russell glowered at his boss with a lowered brow, his lips drawn into a tight scowl.

"Bottom line is this, if you want to continue working at this plant, you'll need to pick up the pace. I suggest that if you got a problem or need support, speak to either Julio Varga or the other guy, what's his name? Antonio something–starts with an R ... Ri ... Rivera! That's it! Antonio Rivera. Speak to one of them. I'm sure they'd be more than happy to help, but for God's sake, do something."

The morning of Russell's sacking had started off like any other. Keeping to a fixed routine, he arrived by six a.m. on the dot. And, as usual, he could be seen moseying off in the direction of his station, holding the same lunch box and thermos given to him as a gift from his wife when he'd first started working for the company years back. His last name TETLER was prominently written on the box's side with a permanent black marker.

Once he settled in, the workday proceeded as usual. As a matter of fact, Russell had been in a surprisingly good mood that day. He'd been looking forward to the extended weekend. At break time, he headed back to his locker to grab his lunch, but upon approaching he noticed an obscenely pink-tinted slip crammed into his cubby. "Whoa, that–that can't be right?" he muttered. Panic settled in, remembering his supervisor's ominous warning and fearing the worst.

"Listen to me, Tetler. Either you get your act together or you're outta here," his supervisor had snapped. "I'm serious. Trust me, right now, sitting on my desk in this exact folder—" he tapped

2

his forefinger on a manila jacket for effect "—is a list of names a mile long of guys ready and willing to jump at the chance to have your job. Don't make it easy for them."

As Russell moved in to take a closer look, he immediately realized that the mad dash to resolve the pink paper's meaning proved unnecessary. The bold heading blaring in his face couldn't be missed: TERMINATED. Russell lost it. *Son of a bitch…*

Unable to control himself, he thrashed his arms aimlessly, knocking over every chair in his vicinity. Pacing, he tossed anything that could fly—riggings, pencils, rulers. He kicked anything else at or below knee level. Shaking, Russell bleated out a litany of vile, nasty threats at anyone with brown or black skin, even pointing an accusatory finger at one particular Spanish foreman not even from his department: "You fucking immigrants! Happy now? Couldn't wait to steal my job. You and all your family, the lot of you, sneaking over the border like a bunch of cockroaches, stealing American jobs – I can't wait until they finish building that goddamn wall and kick all your asses to the curb!" Security forcibly carted Russell out, dragging him to the parking lot while he continued to struggle and cuss.

Company layoffs at the plant were happening on a steady basis for the past year or so, but until Russell received his pink slip, he couldn't have cared less. For months, he'd meander off to the side when others were let go, rolling his eyes in disgust as the stream of misery from a comfortable distance away, all the while mistakenly assuming that somehow, he'd remain protected from the carnage.

For months, tension would intensify as soon as any supervisor from HR set foot on the floor. Word spread like wildfire and worry skyrocketed. Any and all sidebar conversations would come to an

TIGHT ROPE

immediate halt while anxious eyes darted from face to face, everyone wondering the same thing: who'd be the next to go. All except Russell, that is. Somehow, he convinced himself beyond a shadow of a doubt that the company he so loyally served for decades would return the favor and show him the same allegiance.

One right after the other, week by week, workers handed termination notices either individually or in small groups: sometimes right at their workstations. More often than not, the shaken recipient would slither away quietly, already worn down by a system rigged against him. Others less inclined to submit to their fate went full mega-ballistic, tussling and arguing to the point that security stepped in and carted them away.

Personally, Russell couldn't be bothered watching grown men fall apart like a bunch of crybabies. If a ruckus broke out on his floor, he'd simply turn away, divert his eyes elsewhere, and pretend not to see or hear. This coldhearted technique worked well for him…until his number came up, and dear old Russell got the ax.

"You fuckin' cowards!" he roared. Heads spun in every direction as his former coworkers searched to catch sight of those Tetler held responsible. "Can't even tell me to my face." Russell had not even been given so much as a "thank you for your decades of loyal service" package: only a cold slip of noxious pink paper indicating his immediate termination, and the proverbial, "We no longer require your services. Do not pass GO or collect $200. Adios Amigo."

Finding employment had never been much of a worry for Russell. With little more than a high school diploma under his belt, he'd still been able to secure enough work. However, back then, having a high school degree and being good with his hands had been more than enough to get him through the door and on the payroll. But times had changed. People, politics, expectations, and required skill sets changed. Yet Russell refused. He despised change and refused to expand his abilities. Instead, he continued plugging away at the same low-end jobs, absurdly confident that all would eventually be right in the world again. *Things will get better*, he tried telling himself. *All I gotta do is wait it out.*

But like far too many, he was blinded by a system that relied on the promise of allegiance to company and country; scrambling from paycheck to paycheck until The American Dream he so loyally worshiped left him drowning in debt, robbing Mary to pay Paul. Russell prayed that Uncle Sam wouldn't take him to task.

**

Leaning back on his well-worn armchair, Russell stretched his cramped legs. On the screen played his wife's incessant crime dramas. Without asking, he reached over to snatch the remote control and switched the channel back to his much-coveted news. Since becoming unemployed from the warehouse seven months earlier, television had become one of his many vices: a cheap indulgence to nourish his banal existence. A life marked by daylight, three meals, a horde of grumbles and complaints…and, of course, his steady diet of fake news. He'd become so hooked that even during the occasional trip into town, he made sure to have the radio dial in his car turned up as loudly as possible to his favorite pontificator and social instigator's station. He listened to a popular, self-anointed patriot whose persona hinged on instilling fear and hatred into the hearts of the masses, spewing lies cloaked as absolute truths. The spokesman claimed to have the answers to solve all the country's ills, especially where the military and national

TIGHT ROPE

safety were concerned. Ironically, this former drug abusing, out-of-shape, draft-dodging, wife abusing, "ranting patriot" never served one single second in the military. Yet, his followers listened to him faithfully, swearing allegiance to his all-knowing voice of authority. "Carpet bomb the entire region," this celebrity warrior demanded, screaming at the top of his lungs into his microphone. "Give those animals something to remember!"

As he listened, absorbing each pearl of nationalistic wisdom, Russell subconsciously rubbed the hair on his course chin with his aging fingers. He was annoyed that a week's worth of growth could no longer be confused for stubble, but the start of a genuine beard. As much as he despised shaving, he hated looking like "one of them terrorists" even more—a bunch of "towel-wearing, beard-sporting lunatics," as he was quick to relay, lest anyone confuse him for being a member of that misfit, ragtag bunch.

One quick visit to the barber would remedy all that. Besides, Russell enjoyed any excuse to get out of the house for a few hours to hang out with local old-timers and bullshit over a shave and coffee. It was a great way to chew the fat, catch up on juicy tidbits flying around the neighborhood, thrash out national politics, and hear updates firsthand from the barber extraordinaire and town gossip, Clyde. The outing would do him good, and afterwards, he'd even grab some lunch.

**

The young man shifted in his chair under Russell's disapproving glare. "Can I help you with something?" Up until then, he had been sitting alone, munching on French fries and minding his own business. "What are you staring at?"

"You," said Russell.

"Why me?"

"Cause you and your kind don't belong in my country," he snapped. "I'm sick and tired of my country being destroyed by you people."

"My people?" The younger man eyebrows raised incredulously. "What the hell are you talking about?"

"Damn right. Mexicans. Latinos. Hispanics. Whatever you're calling yourselves these days. It's all the same damn thing."

The young man shouldn't have snickered, but he couldn't help himself. "Not like it's any of your business, old man, but I'm not Mexican, Latino, *or* Hispanic."

Russell rolled his eyes in disbelief. "What are you, then? A Moslem? You look like one of them Moslems. You can leave, too. Take your ass back to Iraq or Afghanistan."

Furious, the young man leaned forward in his chair, refusing to break eye contact with the old fool. While this wasn't his first time he'd been disrespected by some redneck bigot, he rose from his chair like it would be his last. Instead of replying, he laughed— hard and loud, not at all the reaction Russell intended to elicit. Russell fumed crimson red, incensed at this foreigner's audacity to mock *him*: a real, red-blooded American.

The young man crumpled the rest of his trash into a tight ball. With his tray in hand, he took four confident strides toward Russell, still seated in his chair, nursing the remains of a burger. In a tempered but resolute voice, he leaned his toned, young body over Russell, only a mere hairsbreadth away. "You're nothing but a bigot, old man," he declared, loud enough for everyone in the dining hall to hear. "And don't think that you being white lets you decide who belongs in this country and who doesn't. Fuck that.

TIGHT ROPE

Take that bullshit somewhere else, man."

Someone from the back of the eatery yelled, "Fuck you, old man."

Surprisingly incapable of replying, Russell seethed instead. *Who does this shit think he's talking to?*

Instead of walking away to dump his food tray, the young man pointed his finger in Russell's face. "You know what? I'm so sick of people like you, acting like it's the immigrants ruining this country, telling folks they don't belong. Well, I got news for you, old-timer—*you're* the one who doesn't belong here."

"You got that right," another voice shouted, this time a woman's. "Tell him!"

"Matter of fact," said the young man, on a roll, "since you're so anxious to kick out immigrants and all, as a proud Native American from the only real non-immigrant, indigenous population in America, when can I count on you getting your racist ass off my land?"

People at nearby tables and those standing in line snickered. A few laughed out loud. One beaming, older White woman—the same lady who had yelled from before—rose from her chair to give the young man a standing ovation, slapping her hands together in a slow, methodical clap. Others nodded their heads in agreement.

Russell glared at the amused faces mocking him. *That's it!* Shoving his chair out from underneath him, he stood up, snarling under his breath. "Fuck you all!" he yelled, storming out of the restaurant in a huff. "You're all nothing but a pack of festering freeloaders, polluting my country." The land that he loved, from sea to shining sea, and all that jazz.

**

When the recession hit in late 2008, life for all hard-working Americans across the country had become difficult, but the hardest slam to the gut seemed targeted at the middle class. Unemployment, foreclosed homes, stagnant wages—not to mention lost dreams and hopes for a better future—all collided into the perfect storm, building on a simmering rage not seen since the last recession took place back in the early 1970s. People across the country demanded answers as they watched their financial ruin unfold.

The poverty-stricken were left to languish as governmental policies sought to dismantle a succession of safety nets. And while many in the wealthy minority had also taken a good share of the financial hits, others not so monetarily protected felt the rich hadn't fiscally bled as profusely as everyone else. The resentment between the feuding sides swelled and overflowed into the streets.

Meanwhile, the disenfranchised middle-income folks grumbled. They distrusted the political system and determined to keep their own counsel. Others in agreement with the poor also insisted that the well-off had come out unscathed, which again only added insult to an already hemorrhaging middle class.

As a result of the fiscal bloodletting, anger grew and swelled. Nobody felt safe. The lack of equal distribution, loss of pay, and increase in cost of living created a new subclass of individuals who had played by the rules. Before this, they never would have believed that they wouldn't enjoy what they felt they deserved: their slice of the American Pie to enjoy well into a ripe old age. Subsequently, this group had proven to be the most dangerous.

Russell and folks like him became magnets of discontent. For so long, they convinced themselves that they, unlike others, were

TIGHT ROPE

entitled to retain a comfortable status quo, despite doing so off the pained backs of everyone else for centuries. Waves of irrational thinking made this lot easily duped by some of the most unscrupulous powers: groomed by fear and fed years of misinformation based on half-truths, provided by unprincipled and dishonest media channels. Out of bitterness, Russell succumbed, convincing himself that his civic and patriotic duty now required him to protect his community and wallet at any cost—and he wasn't alone.

Easily misled, Russell gravitated towards other hopeless malcontents. Folks like Russell failed to comprehend the race-baiting code behind the coercions they absorbed as gospel, while confrontational flag-waving supplanted anything close to mature debate or discourse.

Plodding through most of his days in a dull routine left Russell blissfully unaware of how susceptible he'd become to despair. He developed excessive moodiness, poor sleeping habits, and ate too much or nothing at all. Looking to other groups to blame for his failed aspirations, his inflamed temperament, coupled by a misplaced desire for payback, fueled an evil craving for retaliation. Somehow, in his discombobulated mind, somebody had to be held accountable for his misery.

As the taste for revenge rejuvenated his shattered spirit, he now knew exactly from whom to collect his debt. *And as the Lord above is my witness, I'm gonna make her pay.*

CHAPTER 2

Nour Ibrahim

BLACK, FEMALE, SINGLE, COVERED, AMERICAN, *self-identifying Muslim feminist: what other strikes do I have against me? Ah yes— lonely and utterly disgusted.*

"Damn it! Where's did I put the stapler now?" Without fail, Nour's inbox overflowed with hate mail. To compartmentalize the danger without being absorbed by the hurt, she began to sort them into file categories. To date, she'd created quite a few files labeled by intent: Outright Hate, Semi-hate, Hate Laced with Bigotry, Vile Racist Hate, Misogyny, Mansplaining, Anti-Islam, and Comedic Prejudice. Oh, and the newest file: "White-splaining," now the thickest and fastest-filling category of them all.

"You and your people are always bringing up race and dividing the country. It's always people like you, a bunch of race baiters making people hate one another."

TIGHT ROPE

"You and your people? We're the race baiters? That's rich. "Whitesplaining folder."

"I hate to break the news to you, but slavery ended a long time ago. Maybe if you weren't so caught up in your BLACKness and spewing negative talk all the time, you'd see not all White people hate you. Matter of fact, if you'd all stop screaming in our faces and blocking traffic once in a while, you'd see we're trying to help you, so stop acting like only your black lives matter."

"You think only white people owned slaves, dumbass? Know your history! And let's say, if our country was stupid enough to fall for this guilt trip, I bet even reparations wouldn't be enough to shut you people up. So how about this, I'll personally send you five acres and mule, and we'll call it even!"

Nour grabbed for the Misogyny folder, but hesitated. Second guessing her selection, she reached for the folder labeled Outright Hate instead.

Being attacked by strangers and Internet trolls wasn't the only form of aggression she faced. A few of her co-workers were just as cruel. Nothing but casual racists. This last inter-office email was a prime example, dripping with racial overtones. The last time Nour tried confronting one of the offenders, she'd been lambasted by a couple of her co-workers for being "too oversensitive," "bringing race into everything," and "always making every discussion about 'you'."

In need of a trustworthy sounding board, a kind shoulder and confidant, Nour phoned her closest friend, Rabia.

"Forget the fact that the person responsible for the emails got away with being highly disrespectful towards me," Nour lamented into the phone. "But as I tried explaining to this dumb shit why I found his email offensive, he kept talking *over* me, using that pompous, dismissive, landowner intonation he gets whenever he tries to school me." Furious, Nour snapped her pencil. "And don't get me started about what a sexist, pussy-grabbing mindless tool he is." She groaned into the phone.

"Feel better?" asked Rabia.

"I'm so sick of this. I swear."

"Did you think it was going to be any different?"

"No! Well, yeah…kind of, I did. I know, how stupid am I? But you have to understand, when I took this job, I thought I'd be working with people who were politically and socially progressive, you know, on the same side. Instead, I'm constantly backed into a corner, banging my head against the wall."

"Is it that bad?" asked Rabia.

"Worse, I'm forever defending myself, either calling them out on their bullshit or explaining to them repeatedly why they are wrong. And then, if I hit a nerve, which inevitably I do in the first five seconds, how dare I, right? Especially if it's the nerve of a white woman."

"White tears flowing, huh?"

"Like the Nile."

"Miss Ann's sensibilities torn asunder."

"Basically."

"Now Nour, you know you can't be angry *and* black, now. What happened? You missed that memo?"

"I'm not kidding."

"And neither am I—it's not like you don't know where it's coming from."

"I can still hate it."

TIGHT ROPE

"You're supposed to."

Rabia had been right. Nour understood perfectly well how white entitlement worked, but knowing didn't prevent the hurt. Privilege granted allowances for impertinent microaggressions to exist, forever "white-splaining" them away until the perceived infraction was either conveniently dismissed or dropped like a hot brick, never revisited again. *Can't ever have poor, well-meaning white folk made unduly uncomfortable. Nope, can't let that happen,* Nour thought bitterly. *They can say whatever they want, insult the shit out of me, and I'm supposed to let it roll off my back and not say boo back, but the minute they get called out on their mess, they cry foul. Bullshit.*

Besides the stress and angst that came with doing social justice work, Nour's job required her to deal with white intellectuals whose hearts were in the right place, most of the time, but who honestly believed they were in the position to impose their moral authority from way up on their entitled soapboxes. She couldn't begin to count the hours spent dodging insults, especially when one of the progressives tried explaining to her how she should handle flagrant oppression gunning for her: the kind of hate that was often too vile to indulge or wish away.

More to the point, who the hell do they think they are?

Nour spent the next half hour catching up on the latest news, switching from one social platform to the next. *The country's going nuts.* The media's steady stream of stories highlighting the brutality of global terrorism provided fodder for conversations held at dinner tables across the nation. The fear of vulnerability had many people shoving constitutional concerns to the side, demanding policies to bring back torture as a new legal mandate, along with increasing the databases of information accumulated through spying and branding. Some even screamed for state succession and supported the Patriot Act, or rallied to have the Nineteenth Amendment banned altogether. As the lines blurred between church and state, and civil liberty laws risked being overturned, Nour wasn't so sure if she had what it took to fight this fight any longer, especially when the climate of hate appeared to be growing instead of decreasing.

And then there were the outer-office, inner-community issues that Nour had to contend with. She received an email asking her, as an activist, to comment on the recent race-relations controversy within the Muslim community: another touchy often discounted subject, to be sure, and one she herself wasn't immune to.

It had hurt like hell to hear that a renowned and beloved non-Black Imam was caught on a racist rhetorical diatribe, talking about "black-on-black crime" and the breakdown of the black family. For Nour and many others, however, the streams of defenses for the Imam's railings were worse. In the aftermath, non-black Muslims seemed more apt to protect his feelings than those he'd disparaged, despite the fact that he himself acknowledged that he'd made a major mistake and warned followers *not to defend him or the mistake*. But not even that stopped the apologists.

"He had a right to say what he did."
"He was only speaking the truth."
"It's not right to criticize him in public…"

It was the same deflective claptrap: another brusque reminder that Muslim spaces were just as inundated with racism as non-Muslim spaces. They were nothing but more unsafe places in which black Muslims were forced to struggle for their humanity.

Maybe—despite the pain and upheaval the Imam's words had caused—a real and honest discussion to educate non-black Muslims about the reality of racism would finally take place, but

TIGHT ROPE

Nour wasn't holding her breath. Unlike her white counterparts, Nour had never been afforded a convenient rescue plan by a system designed against People of Color: a system which did little to protect her from the dehumanizing sting of abasement and the stark realization that, as a black woman in America, every waking facet of her life could turn into a minefield. That as a Black Muslim woman, she'd never be afforded the same luxury of shelving discrimination so she, too, could pretend that all the hate and vileness didn't exist. This simply wasn't an option. Nor did society permit her to gloss over the lack of respect or underlying danger each aggressive underpinning promised to deliver. Nour tipped her head back and briefly closed her eyes.

Emotionally spent and aching for normalcy, both of which felt brutally unattainable, Nour glanced over her mounting to do list. *You'd think I'd become better at picking my battles.* Shaking her head, she rubbed her weary eyes. *Only days away from this rally, and all I can think about is this shit ... I still need to secure vendors, get the posters made and distributed, and finish writing my own speech...I'm so screwed.* Fed up, Nour tapped the delete key and followed with a gargled, worn out, "Fuck you all."

Maybe all the sacrifice isn't worth it. I mean, here I am writing a speech, dealing with racists, bigots, and lunatics, while everyone else I know is living their lives—traveling the world, meeting people, falling in love, having families. At the end of the day, when all is said and done, will anybody care one iota about anything I'm doing? What I want or need?

Nour squeezed her heavy lids shut and rubbed her temples. The slight headache she'd nursed throughout the day had begun to throb. *Then again, how can I turn away now? Pretend to un-know the horrors and brutality that have resurfaced?* Slouching with her shoulders bowed over her chest, she rubbed the back of her neck, stiffened from the mounting stress.

Displayed on the wall over her desk hung the only personalized piece of art in a rather austere office. More of a decorative quote than an actual photo or painting, the framed piece was a gift given to her by her parents, who were dismayed about how ascetic Nour kept her workspace. The rest of the office wasn't much better, only containing the bare minimum necessities: pens, computer, a few inconsequential knick-knacks…only enough stuff to fill a single cardboard box, if that. Nothing that indicated Nour was even remotely invested in her surroundings.

Day in and out, never a break. Bombarded at every turn. Black women found hanging in jail cells under "mysterious" circumstances. Black-skinned children, shot to death still clutching toy guns or bags of gummy snacks, beaten in the back seats of police cars, cuffed and tossed about in custody vans, and even manhandled while sitting at a school desk.

Playing while black.
Walking while black.
Flying while black.
Breathing while black.
Hands in the air–
Hands by your side–
Hands where I can see them–
Hands behind your back–
Me.

All supposed infractions, fabricated by people accustomed to bending laws to support their moral indictment: death by complexion, death by association. Little did these people comprehend how their heinous condemnations motivated Nour. She was willing to stake her life for change.

TIGHT ROPE

Nour's father, a rebel in his own right, prided himself on his involvement with the Civil Rights Movement back in the late 50s and early 60s, as well as his later involvement with The Nation of Islam before it splintered off. He'd often share stories with his daughter: the good, the bad, and the ugly.

"Nothing good comes without paying a price," he'd tell her. "Many good people in those movements did good at their own peril, against unimaginable odds. Fighting for equal rights when it wasn't popular or safe, many paid with their lives. Others still alive are the walking dead, holed up in prison cells across the country."

Nour's father made a commitment to raise his child to be a freethinker. To fight the status quo, to be proud of who she was and where she came from, but most of all, to remain vigilant about what she stood for and against. "Stand on the side of right," he drilled into his child. "Speak the truth, no matter who you anger."

While many of Nour's friends spent countless hours with heads buried in magazines, blathering on about the carnival lives of Hollywood's antics, meant to distract, Nour stayed busy following in her father's footsteps. She read everything political and underground, anything she could get her hands on, to learn from the brilliant thinkers of the past. One such thinker was Audrey Lorde, who said, "When we speak we are afraid our words will not be heard or welcomed. But when we are silent, we are still afraid. So, it is better to speak."

And James Baldwin's timeless insight: "People who treat other people as less than human must not be surprised when the bread they have cast on the waters comes floating back to them, poisoned."

W.E.B. Du Bois eloquently said, "Most men today cannot conceive of a freedom that does not involve somebody's slavery."

But of course, no education was complete without the wisdom and tenacity of Malcolm X.: "I believe in the brotherhood of man, all men, but I don't believe in brotherhood with anybody who doesn't want brotherhood with me. I believe in treating people right, but I'm not going to waste my time trying to treat somebody right who doesn't know how to return the treatment."

Throughout her young life, Nour not only studied facts, but absorbed them. With every fiber of her being, she consumed the insights of those past brave souls by what can only be described as an emotional and spiritual infusion: the legacy of their collective pain, a pain so daunting, it held the power to genetically alter the subconscious of every descendant. Fraught with struggle, their experiences imprinted into the DNA of the soul: a sort of branded cell, passed on generationally.

Nour applied these lessons to better guide her through her own difficult wave of hardships. She naively believed that if she could somehow emulate the courageous social justice pioneers of the past, she'd be able to face the challenges of the here and now with the same certainty and tenacity. And while she acknowledged that with any change came certain risks and disappointments, Nour never once anticipated feeling so isolated and vulnerable, even from those claiming to fight the same battle.

But Mr. Ibrahim wasn't the only powerhouse in the family. Not to be outdone, Nour's mother, a scholar in her own right, plotted a sizable educational itinerary for her child as well. She dreamt that someday her daughter would memorize the entire Qur'an cover to cover, word for word, and become a *Hafiza*, a *Sheikha*, noble and wise—a leader of leaders. She wished her daughter to become a fierce and proud tribute to the memory of the companions of the Prophet Muhammad and the *Sahabah*, peace and blessings be upon them all.

To ensure her mother's dreams became a reality, most of Nour's adolescent weekends were spent in Qur'anic study: hours upon hours of Arabic and Islamic classes, year after year. While Nour hadn't necessarily minded the discipline, there were times she'd secretly wished to be less serious and permitted to join her friends in lighter distractions. Perhaps going to a movie or a sleepover, even occasionally sleeping-in would have been nice, but Mom wouldn't have any of it. She diligently watched over her child, grooming Nour for higher education and the promise of scholarship, all while doing her damnedest to protect her—even if that made her guilty of sheltering her a bit too much. Like her husband, Mrs. Ibrahim understood all too well how the playing field her child faced was lopsided and inherently unfair. She knew full well how children of color required additional protection to shield them from obstacles and hurdles, many with the potential to escalate into dangerous and even lethal situations.

While white parents gave their children stern lectures about being responsible drivers, staying courteous if pulled over, and to never drink and drive, Black parents were obligated to include an additional set of tips: guidelines for how to survive routine police pull-overs. When Nour got her license a few years ago, her parents sat her down to talk.

"Remember Nour, if you get pulled over, keep both hands on the steering wheel where they can be seen," reminded her father. "And never reach into the glove compartment to get your paperwork. Are you listening? Wait to be told to do anything, I don't care what it is. And even then, move deliberately slow with exaggerated cooperation."

"And whatever you do, don't resist or argue," said her

mother. "Not like that matters these days, but I don't want to have to identify your dead body on some curb over a broken taillight."

These lectures were never easy, but unfortunately necessary. Early on, children of color are also taught the importance of deciphering coded nonverbal aggression, usually in the form of unsolicited comments cloaked as compliments.

"Nour, you're such a credit to your race. Your parents must be so proud of you."

Translation: People of Color aren't that bright. Your parents really lucked out with you, Missy. They should be proud that you're the exception.

"I'm not racist. I have quite a few Muslim friends, and some of them are even Black."

Translation: How can I be a racist when I have hand-selected a few from your group and given them the privilege to know me and be in my world?

"Why do your people hate us so much?"

Translation: Can you talk to your terrorist people [because of course, Islam is a terrorist religion] and get them to stop scaring me [because somehow all Muslims are on a first-name-basis with terrorists, right?]?

How easy it is for racists to undermine me as a person, while wearing a smile plastered to their faces. Nour had worked diligently to develop skills and then apply them to her work in social change. She learned to navigate through many social intersections of people, including those who furtively opposed her. Not always easy to pull off, especially when dealing with those who'd swear on their mothers' graves they didn't have a racist bone in their bodies, yet couldn't acknowledge how being white afforded them the luxury to ignore politics or race. She had fought to find common ground to build

TIGHT ROPE

dialogue on, only to realize that reasoning with those contaminated by an ideology of hate, despite providing irrefutable logic and facts, still fell on deaf ears.

**

Organizing the rally turned out to be way more complicated than Nour had originally anticipated. Coordinating all the events, lining up speakers, filing for permits and, of course, the dreaded marketing was miserably consuming and physically exhausting. Additionally, staying knowledgeable about current local, national, and international news played a huge role in doing social justice work. Sometimes she found herself stuck behind the computer for hours, reading endless posts about someone being shot, about police brutality, tainted water supplies, global warming, Muslims targeted and threatened with registries, internment, or expulsion. The list went on while the social media stress continued to plague her.

Nour employed a variety of social media platforms to distribute a wide expanse of information. While not a blogger, her brilliance in the field of social commentary resulted in journalists seeking her out for quotes or interviews. As the demand for Nour's input increased, so did the stress. Her body began to revolt. Along with rumpled clothing, the circles beneath her tired eyes did nothing to boost her self-esteem.

Working all day, bringing work home, and then binge-eating less than healthy meals by the computer hadn't been one of her smarter decisions. Neither had the string of stolen micro-naps on her lumpy office couch. Nour attempted to rub away an itch on her nose with a tissue. Swallowing hurt. Her throat felt tight and scratchy. *Great, just what I need.*

Maybe I'll go grab something at the deli, a hot tea this time. Wiping her nose with a tissue, she quickly changed her mind, remembering what a fiasco it had been the last time she stopped at the corner grocery just to buy a roll and coffee. Instead, she'd settle for the office's overpriced swill, unwilling to compound her throbbing headache with any more racist bull.

The store's clerk or owner, whoever he was, kept eyeballing her like she didn't belong. The funny part was, Nour had been coming to this same place for the past year, and his routine never changed. Wherever she moved, his eyes followed. The grim irony that the guy was also Muslim infuriated Nour even more. Thankfully, the man's son swiftly intervened.

"*AsSalaamu'alaikum* Sister, what can I get for you today?" he asked, overly polite.

"*Wa'alaikum Salaam.* I'll take a coffee, medium, no sugar, and a roll, lightly buttered, please."

"Toasted?"

"Are they fresh?"

The cranky old man perched stonily on his stool rolled his eyes and snapped. "Of course, they fresh. What you think I'm running here, huh?"

Oh, so now he's offended. Nour rolled her eyes in return.

"Dad!" This was followed by a quick and heated conversation in Arabic with the young man's father, unleashing a zinging torrent of his own. No matter how irate the old buzzard became, he never took his beady eyes off Nour.

The exasperated young man leaned over the counter and whispered, "Sorry about that. He's…" He shook his head, trying to control his patience.

TIGHT ROPE

Nour understood all too clearly what had transpired, all too well. No amount of Arabic or any other language could cover up that vileness.

"Toasted, please."

**

Nour had been force-fed that bigotry before, and it never failed to leave a bitter and offensive taste. Her childhood was saturated with all-too vivid memories of standing in the masjid, lining up for prayer with her mother and the rest of the congregation, and realizing that until every other available space had been taken, nobody came to stand next to them. Only then, when there was no other choice left, did anyone reluctantly join them, rarely shoulder-to-shoulder, foot-to-foot. Oh, how her heart ached for her dignified mother, who pretended not to notice or care. A storm of epic proportions grew inside Nour.

She also remembered that God-awful day in the masjid, when she overheard the offensive term *abeed* casually slung about in reference to her father as he walked by a group of men. All was shits and giggles until the offenders, who swore they "meant no harm," found out that her dad not only understood Arabic, but understood what they meant by calling him that racist, pejorative term. After the verbal thrashing delivered by her father in both English and Arabic, Nour assumed those assholes would never make the mistake of using that derogatory term against another Black Muslim—at least not in public. However, when she strode past them, there was no mistaking the hatred leaching out from their eyes. As he turned his back to pray, she saw those men seething with the same inexcusable disdain that she'd be reminded of every day of her life. She'd promised herself to never ignore it.

To them, her father represented nothing more than just another "angry Black"—their appalling fallback excuse as to why there was such a continuous alienation of his family by the community. But to Nour, he was a hero and an example: one of the many reasons she fought as hard as she did today.

**

Although Nour loved the work she did and thought it important, a few of her White, female co-workers weren't comfortable with the way she expressed herself. They didn't appreciate that she had a mind of her own and wasn't afraid to use it—and since they couldn't admit that the shortcomings rested on their shoulders, they either shunned or harassed her instead. A few tried to keep her quiet by bullying her, talking over her, through her, around her... anything to keep her voiceless and ineffectual, because the problem had to be her, right?

"Why do you have to be so loud?" one female colleague asked. "Any time we discuss anything, you become aggressive."

"'Aggressive'? So, in other words, if I disagree with what you have to say, then I'm being aggressive?" Nour asked.

"See, there you go ... getting all worked up over nothing," chimed Miss Ann.

"Perhaps you'd be more comfortable if I shut up and left my opinions at the door, and learned to assimilate, right?"

"I didn't say that." She threw her finely manicured hands dismissively in the air, eyes filling with the typical crocodile tears of White fragility.

"You just did."

TIGHT ROPE

**

Cold. Nour had become so engrossed catching up on work, that she'd totally forgotten to drink her coffee. Removing her glasses, she rubbed her strained, tired eyes. The constant stress and long hours had physically and emotionally worn her out. Even sleep brought little reprieve. Every night, tossing and turning, awaking often. It felt impossible to shut it off. All those disruptive thoughts rolling around in her head, all the second-guessing about how she should have replied to so-and-so, or what more she could have done.

Angry? Loud? Aggressive? Maybe I am, but damn it, I have every right to be.

Hundreds—if not thousands—of people were expected to attend the rally. While she had spoken to large groups before, the anxiety of standing in front of a group *this* large never failed to make her stomach lurch. But she didn't have time to feel overwhelmed; she had work to do. Gathering her thoughts, she focused everything she had on writing the speech.

Slowly, Nour began to type. At first, her words fell on the page in a light drizzle, but eventually the dam used to keep her emotions in check burst wide open, sending ideas pouring downward in a rapid, fevered gush. She weaved her words concisely, dismantling false perceptions for those willing to set aside their personal defenses to truly listen and learn.

The time for change is now. As American citizens, as People of Color, as Muslim Americans, we will not allow bigotry and racism to eradicate or define our existence.

Groups from all over the world were expected to attend. Faced with pressing issues and social crises, Nour planned to address a wide array of topics: everything from police brutality, civil liberties reformation, and illegal surveillance, to the ridiculous chants from groups in support of a wall to "keep illegals out of the country." The reinstituting of waterboarding as a legislated torture tactic during times of war was also placed on the agenda. Last but not least, there were increased threats of attacks on Muslims, Blacks, Mexicans, Sikhs, gays, White allies, and anyone else who dared to publically oppose the new generation of White Supremacy.

For those who allowed their entitled existence to dismiss inconvenient truths, Nour accepted that her words would fall flat. Like vapid droplets of devaluation, itinerant anger would replace openness; deflection would steer most conversations, and the unity so strongly sought and needed to move forward would suffer once more. She continued writing.

This is our country, and despite the hate, despite the historical revisionism and vile rhetoric to the contrary, we are not going away. This country was built off the backs of enslaved Africans and indentured servants; upon lands systematically stolen with the blessing of the government, who then went on to perpetuate a legacy of broken promises and treaties on the true original decedents of this country: The Native Americans.

Nour would stand up. Resist. Yell into every microphone available if necessary. She'd put those debasers of truth on notice that if they wished to eradicate and terrorize people through political posturing, insults, and derogatory messages aimed at making non-whites the scapegoats for all the country's woes, that they would do so at their own peril. She remained determined to stand on that stage and call racists out, making it clear that treating People of Color as the perpetual unwanted foreigner would no longer be tolerated. It didn't work that way, at least not yet: not if Nour and her supporters had anything to say about it.

We will no longer be kept sequestered, unable to reach our God-given potential. We will fight for our right to exist, and we aren't asking you for permission.

CHAPTER 3

Maryam Quiñónez

NEWS OF MARYAM'S CONVERSION to Islam nearly caused her mother, Mrs. Quiñónez, to have a full-blown heart attack right on the kitchen floor. Her father wound up having to hold his wife up from falling while she proceeded to tug her arm free, only to then miraculously recover enough to storm the length of the hall screaming into her bedroom and slamming the door shut behind her. Not finished, she gave the closed door a swift kick from the other side for good measure. Less than an hour later, as Mrs. Quiñónez recited long and elaborate prayers, periodically interjecting her daughter's name while crossing her chest, calling for God's help through clenched jaw and fist, her dad and sister tried to convince her to join them in the living room to discuss the matter.

"Where's Maria?" Mrs. Quiñónez asked, wiping her eyes with a crumpled tissue.

"She's still in her bedroom," answered her husband. "Come,

TIGHT ROPE

we all need to talk."

"I have nothing left to say to *her*," she moaned loudly into her cupped hands, continuing to weep.

Dejected, Maryam remained sequestered in her bedroom behind closed doors listening to her inconsolable mother's pleas through the apartment's thin walls.

For months, Maryam rehearsed in her head how best to word her news, but as time slipped by she knew in the end *how she said it* wouldn't make a difference, not in her parent's opinion. Before facing them, she did attempt at one point to seek advice from other Muslim women with similar backgrounds to hers. Women who had revealed in passing experiencing a rough patch when they'd converted. Although they were all sympathetic to her plight, the general consensus concluded that the best course of action would be for Maryam to stay honest, not to bother beating around the bush, and to remain exceedingly patient no matter how they reacted—*but*—to expect the absolute worst.

"Believe me, you're not the first to go through this with your family and you won't be the last," explained Marwa Ortega. "It took my parents months before they would speak to me again civilly, and that was over four years ago. To this day, my father still refuses to acknowledge me in the room unless he has no choice." Marwa's eyes averted downward, her smile now a frown. This wasn't at all the news Maryam had hoped for.

After the initial shock wore off, Mrs. Quiñónez, reverted to a subtler, less obvious approach, doing whatever necessary to force her daughter to witness firsthand the hurt and devastation she had caused, not to mention the embarrassment. Every ploy got pulled out of the bag, from heavy sobbing to fanning her face with a paper plate. On one particular occasion, her outbursts were so over the top that it took two people to contain her, with one wrapping their arms around her waist while the other physically blocked Maryam from approaching. Through a rather colorful litany of yelling and accusations they somehow managed to coax Mrs. Quiñónez to another room 'away from Maria,' the admitted root cause of all her heartbreak and tears. As she was led away, her team of fervent supporters chorused their united indictment, brandishing a litany of verbal castigations meant to convince Maryam to come to her senses.

"You're trying to kill me, Maria?" her mother yelled from the other room, between choked gulps of air. "I know you are. Everyone knows it too. They see what you're doing."

Who exactly comprised "the everybody" her mother spoke of, Maryam had no idea, but she assumed it meant everyone her mother managed to corral together to listen to her sad tale of woe.

"Please, Mami," pleaded Maryam from the doorway. "I'm not trying to kill you. I really wish you'd stop saying that."

"*Aye Dios Mio*, I'll stop when you stop prancing around town looking like the Flying Nun."

When Mrs. Quiñónez's first wave of guilt trips failed to generate the desired effect, she escalated her line of attack to include a host of theatrical machinations. Crossing her chest over and over until the finale when she threw both arms high up into the air, beseeching the heavens in an octave better suited for the stage, and praying to God to intervene. "*¿Por que, por que?* Why you let this happen to my Maria! *¿Por que?* Why? Why does my Maria have to become the Taliban? Why not the terrible girl in Apartment 6B, but not my Maria! She's a good girl."

Initially, her mother's reaction horrified Maryam, the guilt tough to reconcile. Perhaps she was the reason for her mother's

TIGHT ROPE

unhappiness. Then again, her mother, who had the uncanny need to control everything and everyone, had the same excessive reaction when Maryam initially told her about wanting to become a nurse as opposed to a schoolteacher. This squabble started all because her mother's heart had been set on one and not the other. Nothing more, nothing less, and no matter how many times Maryam explained to her how becoming a teacher wasn't *her thing*, her mother wouldn't listen. Instead, she'd shush Maryam with *the look*, ignore any protests to the contrary, and continue telling anyone who'd listen how her "baby girl would grow up to be a teacher and most probably a principal of a school."

"'A nurse!' *Ay*, not this again," spat her mother sardonically. "A teacher is such a nice career. Very respectable, and we come from a long line of educators."

"Nurses are respectable and they get paid more."

"*Sí, las enfermeras son muy bonitas*, but your papi and I always wanted you to be a teacher. Nurses have to touch sick people all day."

"As opposed to being stuck in a classroom around sick children all day? How does that even make sense?"

"Not the same thing, *y cierra tu boca*! That fresh mouth of yours is going to get you into big trouble one of these days! Besides, can't you do anything I want for a change?"

"I'm not trying to upset you, Mami. I'm just not interested."

"Not interested…what? You have some perverted *interest* in wiping people's nasty *culos* and vomit all day long? ¡*Aye Que Loca!* But do what you want. You do anyway." Then she stomped off again, "*Aye Dios Mio*," mumbling a long cacophony of words, which rolled off her tongue in a flourish of full Spanish staccato.

Maryam's father never cared whether his daughter became a

teacher or a nurse. However, he insisted she have a good education and a way to make a decent living. He wasn't at all happy with his daughter's decision to convert to Islam—tore him up from the inside out. In this, he and his wife banded together, scheming up ways to try and change Maria's mind, but so far, nothing had worked.

After a while, his temper began to wane and simmer. The name change from *Maria to Maryam* infuriated him to no end. It was something he could not forgive. Hurt and insulted, he couldn't get past how all of a sudden, her birth name—her Abuela's name no less—was no longer good enough for her. However, unlike his wife, Mr. Quiñónez tended to remain quieter, less openly theatrical about how he indulged his disappointment. He preferred making snide remarks, ignoring Maryam completely or speaking to his wife in private, behind closed doors so he could get her to say and do his bidding…anything to sway his daughter to change her *loca* mind. Besides, he had a whole different set of reasons for being so irritated.

For one, Mr. Quiñónez disliked when his wife became hysterical. Not only did she vacillate between bouts of crying and screaming, but whenever she had one of her meltdowns, it usually meant no peaceful dinner for him. Oh, she'd still cook—that insufferable woman never missed making him and the children a home-cooked meal—but she'd be sniffling all the while she stirred, mumbling under her breath, and then either adamantly refusing to sit at the table after serving her family, or plopping dramatically onto her chair and declining to eat much.

Secondly, despite never being a practicing Catholic himself, by any stretch of the imagination, his daughter becoming a practicing Muslim seemed, well, sacrilegious, and an outright assault to the senses, as if she were purposely turning her back on her culture, on him, her mother, and the entire family.

Thirdly, and probably most importantly, the long, flowing scarf-rag his daughter insisted on wearing on her head looked embarrassing.

"Who are you trying to be, Maria?" he remarked snidely. "Take that stupid thing off your head and stop being *ridícula*."

"There's nothing ridiculous about it. I wear it for modesty, Papi."

"Modesty?"

"Yes, like Umm Isa did."

"*¿Quien? Umm* who? Who the hell are you talking about now, Maria?"

"The Virgin Mary. Mother of Jesus."

"*¿La Virgen María?* Then say that."

The rest of Maryam's extended family didn't much care for her new name change or look, either, and thought her conversion a fad, something she'd grow past. Some family members took bets about how long it would take before she came begging back into the fold. A few of the older cousins showed their distaste by continuing to call her only Maria or by offering her pork products, and then acting offended when she turned them down. "Too good for us, now?" Unless she remained stagnant, staying the person they felt comfortable knowing and interacting, they rebelled and made her life miserable.

For Maryam, her frustration stemmed from her family's adamant refusal to respect her choices, and in turn, respect her. While converts from every background had family or friends who continued to address them by their birth name, her family's refusal came off as a sort of "screw you" protest. Their way of reminding her to toe the line, *their line*, nothing else she did or said mattered. This went for her name change, the clothing she wore, the food she ingested, and the method by which she prayed to her Creator.

Not everybody treated her this way. Some of her closer friends tried to honor the request, but on occasion, naturally forgot. No big deal. There were also a couple of older Aunties, more friends of her mother's than actual blood relations, who interchangeably called Maria both names. Again, no biggie. One elderly *titi*, on her father's side of the family, adored the hijab so much that she always smiled and told Maryam how pretty she looked "for a nun." Admittedly a bit senile, she at least wasn't openly hostile, and Maryam appreciated the sentiment.

Nevertheless, the rest of the *familia*, mostly cousins and a good handful of friends stopped talking to Maria altogether, disgusted with what they considered her "need for attention," and under the opinion that by becoming a Muslim, she'd apparently lost her mind.

"So now all of sudden we're not good enough for you?" accused one of her aunts. "You sit at my table and won't eat the food I cooked? What, my food is poison now or something?"

"I only eat *halal* chicken."

"Ha-who-chicken? Ha-lala?"

"HA-LAL," Maryam corrected. "It means 'permissible.'"

"Permissible chicken? So now Puerto Rican chicken isn't even permissible? Only Muslim chicken is? You're all *loco*."

That happened four long and arduous years ago. Since then, mother and daughter had continued to struggle over Maryam's attire, eating habits, name change, what not to do over the holidays—you name it. But over time, like her Papi, her mother had softened a smidge. Growing somewhat more accustomed to

TIGHT ROPE

seeing her daughter prance around town draped from head to toe in Muslim garb, although at family events her mother could still occasionally be caught sharing a rolling eye revulsion with one of her many sympathizers and co-conspirators.

Maryam's father ignored both his wife's outbursts and his daughter's incessant need to wear more clothing than most modern-day cloisters. It took time, but after a while even he began to appreciate his daughter's added efforts to dress more modestly, and although he'd never admit it aloud, from a protective father's point of view, there had to be something said for that. He already had *más que suficientes problemas* over one daughter well on her way to joining the ranks of single parenthood if she didn't start cooling her britches.

Over time, and more for the sake of her mother, the rest of Maryam's family pretended to tolerate her strangeness. A few drilled her for answers, blasting her with questions, trying to trip her up.

"You know Maria, I hate to tell you, but you're going to hell as an infidel," ranted one Aunt.

"Are you into polygamy?" asked a young male cousin, not necessary pro or con but openly curious. "Because that's the part I'd handle large ... so exactly how many wives can a dude have?"

"Are you still Muslim if you don't wear the scarf?" A loaded question for sure, but purposely posed by Maryam's mother often enough in the hope for a change of heart, and always with the same desperate, pleading expression.

Maryam had learned to keep her cool, remaining steadfast despite a few emotional setbacks, hurt feelings, and crying spells, and in spite of the sporadic threats about *going to hell*, being ridiculed at family gatherings, shunned by former friends or lambasted by self-righteous community members from her parent's church who had on more than one occasion accused her of trying to send her lovely parents to an early grave.

The day Maryam officially earned her nursing degree was the game changer. Family members who assumed her conversion meant a life of oppression with no further education in sight were pleasantly surprised; delighted she earned a degree and the promise of a real future. Shortly after graduation, Maryam landed a job at a prestigious big city hospital, and made a more than comfortable salary – a dream come true for both her parents who had worked hard all their lives, sacrificing to give their children better.

Now, as a professional woman, a nurse with a comfortable income of her own, Maryam felt more than equipped to hold her head up high regardless of the familial pressures being thrown in her direction to stop resisting and assimilate back into her old life.

Outside the home, Maryam worked hard to cultivate a small but select group of new friends, other Latina and Hispanic Muslims from the community. In a way, knowing they shared a commonality felt strangely comforting. She had company. Scores of converts from all backgrounds had traveled a similar path, experienced many of the same roadblocks and struggles. Naturally, this awareness and understanding blossomed into a strong camaraderie of friendship, sisterhood, and a much-welcomed support.

Thankfully, information about Islam in languages other than Arabic and English were offered at the Masjid Maryam attended. This greatly helped those who only spoke Spanish. However, translations of the Qur'an into other languages often lacked a certain level of precision. One day while Maryam was in Qur'an class, she noticed how a single word in Arabic could contain a

TIGHT ROPE

variety of different meanings.

"So, this Arabic word really doesn't mean this exactly?" she asked the Imam.

"Exactly. Although close or as close as possible and even with the very best of intentions, the text being interpreted no longer possesses the sacred and unique character of the original Arabic," he explained. "Do you see these slight changes? They can subtly alter the meaning of not only the word, but the entire passage significantly."

Nevertheless, for many converts like Maryam wishing to live according to the tenants of Islam but unable to speak, write, or read Arabic, the interpretations and translations offered not only guidance, but solace in a familiar tongue.

On days off from work, Maryam and her Muslim friends hung out, eventually agreeing to form a small study group. Originally, they had planned to meet up at a local coffee shop, grab a bite, a cup of tea or coffee. But that idea quickly got scrapped for security reasons.

"What's he looking at?" whispered Lamia to Maryam. "Do I have spinach in my teeth or something?"

Maryam directed her attention to the man in the corner booth watching Maryam and her friends and gave him the old furrowed brow treatment to see if she could startle him to look away or at least put some shade on his gaze. When that failed to make a difference, she flared her nostrils, scrunched up her lips, and shook her head 'no.' The creep continued to gape unmoved. *This spells danger.*

"Those people over there haven't stopping staring either," offered Hameedah clearly irritated. "This is ridiculous."

"They're just trying to get a rise out of us," said Maryam.

Lamia glanced over to Hameedah who in turn eyed Maryam. No further exchange of words seemed necessary. Whether boundaries were being tested or they were at risk, the unwanted intrusion into their personal space was warning enough. The small gathering collected their belongings and left. Moving forward, the three ladies decided they were better off meeting in their homes for the time being. The escalating climate of hate towards illegal immigrants apparently extended to anyone of Hispanic or Latin culture, no matter the status of their citizenship. The added Islamophobia, dangerous side-glances, and snarky remarks were all evidently the warm-up act for what some aggressive individuals might still have in store.

Working at the hospital, Maryam came across all kinds of people, a part of the job she liked most—most of the time. Once in a while, especially after a terrorist attack, when the news stations slanted their stories enough to cause mass hysteria, certain types of patients became aggressively rude or outright hostile the minute she entered the room. On the rarest of occasions, for her safety, she had to be replaced by another nurse.

"Get this ISIS bitch out of my room!" yelled one elderly White woman, finger raised accusingly in the air, pointing to the heavens. "I know my constitutional rights. You come near me again, and I swear to my Lord and Savior, Jesus Christ, I'll have you deported!"

Since the ornery woman suffered from a severe heart issue, any jarring upset could possibly trigger a fatal outcome, so the doctor, also a Muslim (but since she wasn't covered didn't pose as much of a visually direct threat) acquiesced to her patient's outrageous and unseemly demands.

On other occasions, the callousness of bigotry presented less overtly, but was distinctly implied.

"I'm glad to see your people entering the nursing field. There's a lot of opportunity for growth, but you will have to work hard to succeed."

The other day, one of her patients barely made it into the examination room before spewing her barrage of coded questions.

"Where are you from? You speak English so well."

"Please take a seat and roll up your arm so I can take your blood pressure." Maryam focused on her task.

"I like your headgear, but why do you wear it?"

"I'm Muslim. Please remain quiet while I take your pressure."

"Spanish and Muslim, huh? You must have a death wish."

These kinds of comments drove Maryam nuts. Puerto Ricans are Hispanic, not Latinos, which means coming from a Latin American country. The term *Latino* refers to geography while *Hispanic* refers to speaking Spanish. Maryam had lost count long ago of how many times she had clarified this concept.

"I'm Hispanic," she explained. "*Spanish* is the language I speak." *Patience...* "I know, people use these terms interchangeably, but there is a difference."

The woman didn't look convinced. "Do you come from Brazil? I have a lady in my building from Brazil. I can't understand a damn thing she's saying half the time."

Maryam forced her eyes not to bulge out of their sockets. "No, Brazilians are Latinos but not Hispanic since they speak Portuguese. My family is from Puerto Rico, which is not a Latin American country but a Caribbean country."

"Well, it sounds all the same to me," replied the rudely impertinent woman, dismissively shrugging her shoulders.

But there were also kinder comments, which touched

Maryam's heart and blotted out some of the ugly and hurtful.

"Your scarf is beautiful. You look so dignified all the time."

"I have nothing against the Muslims. They've always been cool with me."

"Sorry you and your community are always under fire. I'm embarrassed to say, I used to feel the same way until I got to know a few of you."

"Do you want me to walk with you? It's no trouble …"

On her block, especially in the beginning when she first started donning the hijab and long skirts, Maryam received quite a few deadpan stares, a few off-handed comments and snickers behind her back, along with a rash of outright hostility. Old school friends and neighbors didn't know what to make of her "sudden" change of appearance not to mention the name change she expected everyone to adhere to; some took it as a personal affront.

Maryam did her best to ignore the negative comments but there were times, when tired and annoyed she'd meet the cold stares with one of her own. However, the so-called "embarrassment" her mother claimed she'd caused, became a much harder pill to swallow.

Despite all the harshness directed at her, nothing could have prepared Maryam for the onslaught of shame she carried around, knowing how hurt her mother felt by her conversion. She hadn't meant for this to happen, but at the same time, found herself in a quandary, unwilling to turn her back on her beliefs. She couldn't understand why her mother couldn't for once be happy for her, especially as the woman of faith she claimed to be. Small disagreements continued to turn into arguments, and arguments turned into colossal hurt feelings, and hurt feelings ricocheted into extended periods of time where mother and daughter barely spoke.

TIGHT ROPE

**

"Maria! Come. Help me set the table," her mother called out, the first full, noncombatant sentence she had said to her in days.

From down the hall, Maryam ignored the name slight. Whenever her mother grew angry with her, she'd revert to calling her by her birth name, as did Papi, who never failed to remind her how highly insulting the name change was.

"*No sé* —you tell me why she's doing this…this name nonsense!" snapped Papi through gritted teeth, purposely lowering his voice less his daughter hear him. "How does she expect to find a husband wearing all that stuff?"

"*Ay Dios Mio*, between the stupid clothing and her head covered like a nun…" Mrs. Quiñónez began fanning herself. "Talk to her, *por favor*. She's your daughter. Talk some sense into this *chica tonta*."

"She's more than silly—she's *loca*."

"Am I interrupting anything?" inquired Maryam as she entered the kitchen. By the expression on both her parents faces, they were up to something. Counting plates, napkins, and utensils, she set the table for dinner, making sure to lay out each setting to her mother's unique specifications.

Sunday meals were a tradition in the Quiñónez house for as long as Maryam could remember. Tia Eualia would arrive soon, along with Abuela who now lived with her full time since Abuelo passed away last year. That decision took a good deal of coaxing to make happen.

Abuela, always a proud, independent woman, lived in the same home in which she grew up back in Puerto Rico. But after her last fall, which left her wearing a foot cast for five months, she was forced to admit that living alone probably wasn't the wisest choice. Once Maryam married and left home, her absence would open up the use of a bedroom. Then Abuela would more than likely choose to come here to reside with her parents, under her older daughter's care.

"Besides Tia Eualia and Abuelita, is there anyone else coming?" she asked her mother, who busily stood stirring a pot of delicious smelling soup.

"Set the table for eight."

"Eight?"

Mrs. Quiñónez didn't reply.

"Who's the two extra settings for?"

"Stop asking so many questions. ¡*Apúrate*! Get yourself cleaned up. You look like you rolled out of bed."

"Mami? What are you up to?"

For months Mrs. Quiñónez had started her hinting campaign, this time about a man she thought would be such an excellent match for her Maria, "a church going man from a fine family, too." After last week's service, she'd spoken directly to his mother and the two struck up a comfortable conversation. Before she knew it, she had invited her and her son for Sunday dinner in the hopes she'd think her daughter equally as good a match.

"Friends from church, if you must know."

Maryam nodded, then asked, "Friends? What friends?"

Mrs. Quiñónez pursed her lips and continued the meal preparations. The doorbell rang. "I told you to hurry. Now go—*márchate*!" Swiping the napkins from her daughter's hands, she practically shoved her into the bathroom. "Go! Wash up while I tend to our guests." Mrs. Quiñónez shook her head and under

TIGHT ROPE

protest spun her daughter in the right direction. "*Ay Dios Mio*, this girl will be the death of me!"

Once inside the bathroom, Maryam studied her reflection. As much as she hated to admit it, she did look a mess, exhausted. The bags under her eyes were suitcases, and her complexion sallow. "Maybe a bit of light makeup would help cover the damage," she grumbled—*at least enough to cover the eyestrain.*

Opening the cabinet drawer, she grabbed moisturizer and foundation, and began ineptly applying both, generously.

I haven't worn makeup in a long time. She dabbed foundation under both her eyes. *Hmm, that looks better.* "Maybe a hint of blush." Maryam dug deeper into the drawer for her compact and applied the rose-blush cream to the apples of her cheeks. Then she stopped cold. *Damn, is that a pimple?* Maryam leaned over the sink to take a closer look. *Yep, it sure is.*

CHAPTER 4

Eugene Underwood

LEANING OVER THE CHIPPED BATHROOM sink, Eugene mentally prepared for what he needed to do next. Wincing, he drew in a deliberate, deep breath through coffee-clenched stained teeth, bracing for the pain once he ripped the bandage off. "One, two, three ... AH, Gheesh!" The now exposed pus-filled wound showed signs of infection. Nothing a good scrub with an antibacterial soap and a healthy dose of antiseptic ointment couldn't cure. *Stupid ... I gotta be more careful.*

Eugene flipped his hand over, checking the condition of his knuckles. Slightly scabbed and scuffed. *No surprise here.* Upon closer inspection, he noticed a line of darkening bruises forming along the inner side of one massively swollen finger. One more unfortunate casualty that comes from agreeing to work alongside another ill-prepared novice, *but hey, it's the price of doing business these days.* Eugene frowned. *Next time I'll wear long sleeves—no matter what the temperature*

TIGHT ROPE

is—and a pair of sturdy leather gloves, not that cheap shitty pair pawned off on me. Eugene had a good mind to tell Rigo where he could shove his—

"Ah! What the heck?" Another sharp pain shot clear up his arm and directly into his neck. Slowly, Eugene tried twisting his elbow, lifting it at an odd angle to get a better look, but this only pinched his neck further. *Figures.* Swollen and the size of a golf ball, his forearm throbbed something fierce. *Must have happened when I smashed into the door.*

Taking deliberate care not to suddenly jerk or move too fast, he lifted his arm only high enough to thread the swollen limb through his sleeve. "AGH!" Another pained-filled moan escaped. *I got nobody to blame but me. My fault for working with idiots.*

For the next twenty minutes, he washed and bandaged his wounds, careful to clean the grime and dead skin under his nails. Bagging his dirty clothes, he changed into something clean. He'd dump the bag on his way out.

Once fully dressed, Eugene slid open the dresser drawer where his work essentials were kept, carefully sifting through the organized pile until he located his favorite pair of leather gloves. Never one to be sentimental, he'd normally dispose of anything that could possibly compromise his freedom if caught, but for whatever reason, he couldn't let go of this particular pair; considered them sort of a symbol of his recent good fortune, and a minimal risk. In his line of work, one had to be careful and take due precautions, but in his professional opinion, better to be restricted in motion and protected using a well-worn pair of gloves than to be stuck nursing a bunch of aching results like these again.

Shoving the pair into his work satchel he grabbed an extra roll of medical tape and a few fresh gauzes. Shaking his head in disgust, he couldn't help groaning. *This old body ain't healing as fast as it used to.* All the same, prolonged regret or introspection never entered Eugene's framework. Nor did penitence.

**

Unfucking real. There's absolutely no reason this should have happened. None.

From across the street, Eugene seethed. Totally incensed as to how three hired morons who were supposed to know what they were doing, could have managed to screw up to this degree. How the hell did they botch up such a straightforward job? This level of ineptness took real talent.

Eugene correctly assumed this fouled up fiasco would only serve to make the already stubborn store owners dig their heels in harder, refusing to sell. And if this happened, his street standing as *The Cleaner* would surely take a severe, if not permanent and possibly painful hit. Certainly, not something Eugene could allow.

Word on the street was the police considered the bungled robbery nothing more than an isolated incident carried out by a bunch of young, inept thugs out to make a quick score.

Theoretically, Eugene mused, *they're sort of right.*

Somehow, and Eugene still hadn't figured out how, the exact opposite of what was supposed to—happened. What remained unclear was why? The instructions given to those three dummies weren't rocket science or anything. Matter-of-fact, the job for all intents and purposes, was dull as shit: go in, shake the old guy up, trash his store, and before leaving, make it exceedingly clear that unless he and the other shop owners on the block agree to sign their names on the impending dotted line, more of this kind of

TIGHT ROPE

"encouragement" would inevitably be in their near future.

Instead, those three imbecilic cowboys roughed up the owner like a bunch of petty-ass hooligans, tried to steal money from the cash register, and then completely forgot what they were supposed to say to him, so instead, they dislocated his shoulder.

For shit's sake—they've made him into a freaking local hero. Idiots!

Eugene flicked his cigarette butt on the ground, stepped forward and stomped it irately into the sidewalk with the heel of his boot. *What a freaking mess.* Leaning back on the corner store's brick wall, he crossed his tattooed arms over his chest and heaved a long and disgusted sigh. *I just should've done the job myself, hurt arm and all.*

Eugene lit the next cigarette. Since his time in juvie, chain-smoking had become one of his crutches, along with chewing gum, the occasional Texas Hold'em, and when the right mood struck, some explicitly raunchy consensual choking. Eugene enjoyed his women submissive and pliable.

Eugene inhaled. The anticipated nicotine rush still provided a pleasant if not hazy, lightheaded feeling. *Progress wouldn't come to a halt because of a few holdouts; that's for shit sure. Besides, this is prime real estate we're talking about here. Next time around somebody's going to have to get more than a little hurt to make these folks understand we're not joking.*

Upcoming moneymakers, wheelers and dealers, and even yuppies easily bringing home six-figure salaries considered the area directly across from the hospital—and the nearby neighborhood in general—one of the most desired areas for new trendy restaurants and businesses. Subways, busses, and freshly painted cabs completed the gentrified triangle's infrastructure, not to mention a substantial parking garage only a mere hop, skip and jump away, thanks to the hospital.

The wind suddenly picked up. *More rain.* Eugene inhaled,

lightly cupping his hand protectively around the cigarette to prevent the embers from breaking off and flying into his face, scanning the area for a place to wait out the downpour. He also needed to call the Boss.

Just then, a rush of rowdy teenage boys darted past him, jumping puddles and laughing, looking like a swarm of drenched rats. Eugene took another drag of his cigarette and watched as one of the boys, the tallest one, purposely pulled another boy down by his jacket, straight into a puddle.

"Knock it off!" screamed the boy. "Look what you just did!"

"It's just water. Stop acting like such a pussy."

Eugene stomped out his cigarette and started walking. He didn't have a particular destination in mind, just wanted to be anywhere else.

**

The locker room emptied as students rushed to class, all except for two boys.

"Give me that!" ordered Carlton, snatching the cell phone out of Eugene's grip. "You're a toad. You know that?"

"Give it back, or I'm telling."

"Tell whoever you want," mocked Carlton, "but remember this first." He slammed Eugene straight into the gym locker full force. "Now go on, runaway and tell whoever ya want, ya little pussy!"

Eugene squinted, his eyes narrowed into slits. Crouching over, he gripped his shoulder protectively knowing enough from past encounters with bullies to twist his injured side away from another pending slam.

TIGHT ROPE

"From now on, you stay out of my way," threatened Carlton. "If I catch you in my business again, I swear, you won't be so lucky next time." Carlton gave Eugene one final, less than consequential shove before turning his full attention to his newly acquired prize.

Eugene's face registered no fear. Rubbing his forearm, he stared at his attacker's back with a vacuous yet penetrating evil glare. In a sudden burst of rage, Eugene leapt to his feet, bending over at the waist. Using his head as a battering ram, chin to chest, he released a primal growl and took off running. Carlton, taken completely by surprise, was quickly pinned flat against one of the lockers. The crashing sound of Carlton's body smashing against the metal should have alerted support, but once Eugene got started, nobody could stop or deter him.

Winded and in excruciating pain, Carlton halfheartedly attempted to block Eugene's next move with one of his arms but wasn't nearly fast enough.

In a fit of fury, baring adolescent teeth like fangs, Eugene reached out and seized a wad of Carlton's hair, pulling the terrified boy in close enough to clamp his jaw downward upon his ear, cleaving a substantial piece of his lobe with it. As blood sprayed everywhere, Eugene spat out his fleshy prize.

Carlton cupped his ear, screeching out in horrific pain, begging Eugene to stop, but Eugene didn't acknowledge the boy's desperate pleas or care.

"Shut up!" Eugene roared. Without the slightest hesitation, he then lifted his knee and snap kicked the boy's head sideways with lightning speed and pinpoint accuracy.

"Now who's the pussy, huh?" he taunted.

Retracting his leg, Eugene snickered, swollen with satisfaction, but not yet finished. Recoiling his knee back to his chest he drove the heel of his sneaker into the boy's blood-soaked head, wildly stomping and kicking him into the floor with sharp disabling jolts. Unable to withstand the ferocity of pain, Carlton's body tipped over, no longer capable of pleading for mercy, much less anything else.

Eugene stepped back to admire his handiwork, satiated. Now, no longer annoyed by desperate pleas piercing the air, he casually wiped off his splattered face, chin, and neck with the back of his disheveled dirty flannel shirt. Leaning over, he retrieved his phone from Carlton's now limp, inert hand.

Nonchalantly stepping over his unconscious victim, Eugene sat on the wooden bench and resumed playing his game exactly where he'd previously left off, conquering other life forms on some far off and distant planet, impervious to the carnage lying unconscious a few feet away.

Eugene consequently spent the next twelve years in the juvenile detention center, denied early release twice. One of the initial psychiatric evaluators, after spending an inordinate amount of time evaluating the boy's mental state, noted, "Eugene Underwood presents a serious risk now and in the foreseeable future. Marked by his unpredictability, his sudden outbursts, coupled with callousness and immoral lack of empathy make him a dire and serious threat to all he encounters. During his stay, he has demonstrated a propensity for violence. His records indicate an attachment to using weapons with potential lethal force. Therefore, he poses an immediate risk. In my professional opinion, Eugene Underwood should be kept in strict isolation and out of general population for the entirety of his incarceration."

Eugene wouldn't taste freedom again until he turned twenty-two years old, and by then, he was fully prepared to play his

TIGHT ROPE

endgame for a second go around, but this time for keeps.

**

Eugene pushed END and pocketed his phone, his ear still ringing from all the shouting from the other side. One thing Eugene despised more than anything was someone yelling in his face, or in this case, his ear.

As anticipated, the Boss wasn't happy. He explained to Eugene in no uncertain terms how he "preferred his authority to be expertly applied – not performed like some circus sideshow." The Boss also made it profusely clear that, despite what the three assholes had done, he placed all blame on Eugene. And while Eugene accepted the fact the job did get royally screwed up, he wasn't about to allow anyone to call him a host of vile names, with most of them being private body parts.

CHAPTER 5

Zaid Ali

BENDING OVER, ZAID SNATCHED THE squidgy from the soap-filled pail, rushing to scrub clean the latest curses and threats defacing the storefront before the customers started arriving. This type of vandalism had become the new norm, the expected: coffee, tea, or defacement. Zaid had lost count of how many times he'd scrubbed the vile graffiti off the store's glass face and metal gate.

After September 11, 2001, life for Muslims and immigrants living in America took what can only be described as an abrupt nosedive into the abyss of hell, with each passing day becoming increasingly more difficult. Life for anybody suspected of "looking Muslim" was no picnic either. Sikhs in turbans became an unfortunate all too common target for attack, as did Jewish women and Eastern Orthodox Christians who covered their hair. As suspicions ran high, the spike in verbal and physical attacks on places of business also increased. Just last month, they had to

TIGHT ROPE

replace a snack shelf destroyed by a man sporting a red baseball cap.

Zaid remembered how the guy stood in line tapping his foot impatiently as the woman in front of him gave her order in broken English.

"And a roll, with butter, *por favor.*"

"We speak American here," he goaded. Then, without any further provocation, he picked up the mobile snack cart and hurled it full force towards the counter. Snack bags and cookie boxes flew in every direction, with a few hitting the frightened young woman in the face. "Time to pack your bags and get out of my country, you dirty spic. Com-pren-do that, senorita?"

While the country entertained the idea of registries and internment camps for Muslims, covered Muslim women made for easy targets. Not a day went by when Zaid didn't fear for his mother's safety, especially after hearing about women being spit at, cursed, pushed into oncoming traffic, kicked down steps or elbowed on buses and trains. *If anyone dares touch my mother, I swear by Allah I'm going to jail.* The majority of women like his mother faced this sort of bigotry and opposition with an implicit bravery.

When Zaid's parents came to America as a newly married couple, they did so seeking opportunity, and the promise of a better life, but upon arriving found themselves facing many unforeseen obstacles, some of which, they had believed they left behind. At the time, his father only spoke enough broken English to find minimum wage jobs. Undeterred and starting from nothing, he gradually managed to build himself up working long hours at two, sometimes three jobs to make ends meet. Eventually, both he and his wife were able to save enough money to go through the naturalization process to gain US citizenship, but the arduous, long, and expensive path depleted most of their original savings. Opening the store years later felt like a dream come true.

Many of the struggles his parents experienced when they first arrived remain a mystery, both unwilling to disclose many of the details to their son, either out of humility or humiliation. Either way, adjusting to a new home thousands of miles away from everyone they knew and loved, into a culture promising prosperity and support, but instead viewing their presence as foreign and unwelcome, proved difficult.

When in high school, Zaid witnessed how knee-jerk assaults increased whenever the news reported on another suspected "terrorist" attack. How the barely contained misdirected anger boiled under the surface, ready to ignite at the slightest provocation, whether perpetrated by a person claiming ties to Islam or not. The airwaves helped augment these fears with political panderers and apologists, all too willing to lend their voice to further alienation while decimating the facts, brazenly using the media to criminalize the entire Muslim community using catch phrases meant to trigger a manic response—much like what was orchestrated against the original Americans and those in the Black community. Coded rhetoric and plaster headlines splayed everywhere. East against West, religion against religion, and culture against culture, all while tapping into the baseless fears of the easily misled. Zaid couldn't believe how easily truth took a back seat to lies. Fast-forward to today and the utter chaos and hatred continues unabated.

When Mosque's weren't being burnt down, roving gangs got together to spray pig's blood upon masjid doors. A group of hostile old White men came up with the idea of lining up pig heads to create their version of a supernatural, crypto-Muslim partition on

TIGHT ROPE

the street, while gun shop owners, emboldened by neo-Nazism, proudly displayed seditious signs designating their place of business "Muslim Free Zones." Incendiary bumper stickers meant to insult became the new racist vehicle décor. Racist gangs enjoyed kicking women of color down flights of subway stairs or recording them being cursed out on buses, in stores or restaurants. And as crazy and as bizarre as these types of incidents were, for the most part they got swept under the rug and ignored. Like magic, they never happened, but for Zaid Ali, the nasty political discourse had hit home. No longer solely media talking points for debate, violence escalated, along with an increased, ever-widening fissure of mounting distrust. Inflammatory cartoons littered countless newspapers and the Internet. Hailed by a globally discordant media as "brave" and a tribute to "freedom of speech," while in truth, the intent behind such abhorrent creations were so much more sinister and divisive, aimed at inciting further conflict, while explicitly taking aim to mock and belittle millions of people.

But Muslims weren't the only ones under assault. As clashes from all sides escalated, other communities came under attack as well. A synagogue down the block from the masjid had a big red swastika and the words "Sieg Heil" spray painted on their door. Jewish gravestones were overturned or covered in graffiti. Church members supporting inclusion and diversity were under threat as well, told to remember their places and tongues. Even the Pope came under fire. His reputation became the target of ridicule and flagrant disrespect when he publicly denounced bigotry, comparing the behavior of those among his flock who sought to terrorize others deemed different to being the absolute antithesis to the teachings of Christianity.

The first few times after the store got vandalized, Zaid

notified the police to lodge a complaint. When he'd follow up, he'd be informed by the police "that all alleged incidents were still under investigation," however, the "artists" didn't get the memo; becoming even more daring in applying their craft, the profuse damage they'd caused now in public view. Eventually he stopped expecting results—resigned to the fact that little, if anything, would be done.

While tending to the shop, Zaid primarily kept to himself, but this didn't prevent him from catching sneaky side-glances and muffled voices conversing amongst themselves about the "terrorist problem." How quickly the conversant would avert their eyes once Zaid's deadpan glare gave them a taste of their own well-deserved medicine.

Zaid's father, on the other hand, preferred to smile through the insults like some non-confrontational, happy-go-lucky, accommodating puppet so as not to let "mere political discourse get in the way of business."

Zaid despised when his father acted this way, finding his spinelessness humiliating and disgraceful. Ironically, it was his father who once scolded him for being curt after a customer, upset about how long his order took to fill, addressed Zaid as "boy."

"Let me get this straight—this moron disrespects me and instead of being mad at him, you're pissed off at me," complained Zaid. "Not the racist dirt bag, but me—"

"All he did was call you *boy*. So, what? What's the big deal? Your problem is you make everything about race."

Seething, Zaid rolled his eyes.

"Enough already. I'm tired of hearing you complain. You're making a big deal over nothing."

"NOTHING?" At this, Zaid kicked the garbage can sending

TIGHT ROPE

litter flying across the recently swept floor.

Mr. Ali smirked. "So tell me, Mister Big Shot, what did that accomplish? Huh? Tell me!" tormented his father, defiantly. "*Ya Allah*, I don't know what's come over you. Ever since you started going to that Black masjid, you've turned into someone I don't even know."

Zaid stood his ground. "There's no such thing as a 'Black masjid.'"

"You don't know who you are anymore. Next thing, you will be walking around here with your pants hanging down like those *abeed*."

"*Astaghfirallah.*"

"What's that supposed to mean?"

Zaid slapped a bag of chips off the rack. "Meaning I don't know how you can stand there and say the same things those racist bastards say. It means I don't understand how you can take the disrespect without fighting back. They don't respect you, you know—they laugh at you behind your back. The stupid brown man with the stupider smile across his face—"

"Really? And what do you suggest I do? Get into a fight with them? Kick them out of my store? I know, I should march in the street holding a sign, yelling …" The vein in Mr. Ali's forehead protruded and pulsed anytime the man lost his temper. "Sometimes a man has to do what he has to do." With a clenched fist, Mr. Ali pointed at Zaid. "Unlike you, I'm an immigrant, and they've never let me forget it. Unlike you, I've lived through worse. And unlike you, I have a family to feed, which includes you—you ungrateful child. Now shut your mouth and sweep this mess up."

At the dinner table that evening, Zaid, still fuming, decided to take a stand by announcing his plan to join the National Guard. On a scale of one-to-ten, his badly timed declaration certainly ranked high on the chart of the most poorly received and one which would undoubtedly live forever in the Ali Family Infamous Hall of Shame.

With surprising agility, Mr. Ali leapt to his feet, ready to wrap his hands around his son's young throat and squeeze the sense back into him, but his wife blocked and pulled him off. "What are you doing, Waseem?" she screamed at her husband. "Leave him alone! Let's talk to him."

"You stupid, stupid boy!" Mr. Ali spat. "What the hell do you think that's going to do for you, *humar*?"

"Don't call me that! I'm not a boy or an idiot. I'm a man. I make my own decisions."

"Since when? *Wallahi*, you live in my home? You eat my food? You shower with my hot water? You wipe your ass with my toilet paper?"

Zaid refused to answer.

"You hear that?" Mr. Ali yelled accusingly at his wife. "Your son thinks he's a man now! Some big shot, off to play soldier. Drop bombs and wipe out families—and for what? Huh? Tell me, for what?" Mr. Ali stomped around the room, nostrils flaring. "And this is how you raised him?" He yelled at his wife, pointing his stubby finger in her face.

Zaid seethed but knew better than to respond.

Mr. Ali shook his head disgusted. "So now you want to play with guns and shoot people, like that idiotic game you play on the computer. Answer me, *humar*—for what? Oil? Land? Power?"

"At least I don't smile in their face or kiss their ass."

This last comment caused Mr. Ali to charge, but this time his wife had already pressed her body between the quarreling pair, fighting hard to keep them physically apart. "STOP IT! Both of you!" she demanded, but neither man paid her the least bit of attention.

"My people live here too," retaliated Zaid. "And for your information, Muslims have a long history of fighting for their country!"

"Ah, so you actually believe this is your country now, huh? Maybe you should go back home and learn to be a man there."

"I was born here. This is my home and that makes it my country."

"*Wallahi*—"

"Yes." Zaid refused to budge. "*Wallahi*."

"And you think being born here makes a difference to these people?"

"That's the law of this land, it doesn't matter what they think."

"Law? You have the nerve to stand there and talk to me of law?" Mr. Ali began circling the room, at one point taking off his slipper and lifting it in the air, ready to fling it at his son. "How dare you! They use their power to drop bombs on women and children, on hospitals, even schools, and they sleep fine at night. Wake up the next day and do it all over again." Mr. Ali slammed his fist on the table. "They take no accountability for their savage inhumanity but call the rest of the world 'uncivilized,' building fancy memorials to honor *their* dead, *their* heroes, while not thinking twice about burying thousands of innocent lives under mounds of rubble." Mr. Ali hurled his slipper but Zaid ducked. "And for your information, even back home the Muslim army is being discriminated against, and these are the people you want to fight for? Die for?"

Zaid stood strong. "And what about the terrorists? Who's going to stop them from destroying cities? They're killing more Muslims than anyone else and what? You don't think Muslims should join the fight to stop them?"

"Which terrorists are we talking about? The fourteen who bombed the World Trade Center? For all you know, it could have been a government inside job."

Zaid scowled. "There you go again."

"If you don't believe me, go ask the Indians. They're still stuck living on reservations trying to block pipelines being run through their water and cemeteries. And don't forget, it's the same government you want to fight for who pushed them on those reservations in the first place and are constantly trying to take it away from them. Just like in Israel where …"

"Like that, mixing the truth whenever it suits you."

Mr. Ali threw his hands in the air, his eyebrows twitching.

The war raging back home had torn many families apart and destroyed others. Four years ago, Mr. Ali's brother lost his entire family when bombs destroyed his home during the month of Ramadan. The family had lived in a city called Darayah in Syria. To avoid going out in fear of being hit by shells or shot by snipers, his brother Nadir would ride a bicycle to pick up whatever provisions he could scavenge. On one particular day, while peddling back home, the bombings started. The electricity and local phone towers were constantly being turned off, a sure sign of what was to come, making it impossible to phone home. Nadir took shelter until the shelling stopped long enough for him to continue his journey. By the time he reached his block, mounds of burning cinders and rubble were all that were left. His family, like countless others, interred beneath massive cement graves, courtesy of the Syrian

TIGHT ROPE

Army. Unable to cope, Nadir went mad, refusing to eat or leave the site of the debris, which only days before sheltered his family. Mr. Ali received word weeks later, authorities had found his brother's body splayed out across the same rubble, which now contained his family... dead from a single gunshot to the heart.

"So, what do you suggest I do, Baba? Look the other way?" Zaid's voice rose. "Forget about how these crazy-ass fundamentalists have raped Islam? How they kill innocent women and children? Behead them, bomb airports and restaurants? Shit, those motherfuckers have made being a Muslim a living hell."

"Don't curse in my house you little shit, and nobody's asking you to ignore them, but what difference does it matter if you fight alongside the same invaders who made these extremist bastards come into existence in the first place?"

Since then, Zaid's father refused to speak civilly when discussion turned to anything concerning the military, but this didn't stop his son from trampling on his raw nerves. "Oh, that's funny, coming from you."

This time, Mrs. Ali could not protect her son as her husband shoved Zaid so hard it caused him to lose his balance, tripping over a chair, and falling ass first on the floor.

"Ya Allah. Mark my words stupid boy, you will never, NEVER become a man marching behind the barrel of a gun." Mr. Ali barely able to contain his anger, stomped in one direction, then running out of space, turned in the other. In a whispered roar, he spun around, face to face with his son, leaving him one last parting ultimatum. "By Allah, if you join the military, I will disown you."

※※

His father's arguing points inclined towards the historically astute only to descend into the risibly absurd. One minute he'd go from *Islam is great, Arabic is holy—and the military is bad*, to his *America good—government bad* mantra. He had a name for everything too: *CIA swine, FBI stooges, Police are heroes, but American Muslims? Not so much. Especially the Black ones*, he'd be quick to denote. The wide proclivity of his father's logic left Zaid reeling half the time, never knowing from which direction his rants would attack. One minute his father made sense and the next he sounded ready to write taglines for the KKK.

As much as Mr. Ali built a whole pretense out of wanting freedom and respect for Arabs, he never bothered trying to hide his disdain for Black people. It sickened Zaid to watch his father bend over backwards for White customers while barely sparing a pulse or kind word for anyone Black, despite being a man of color himself. Such mind-numbing hypocrisy, and his son, who for the life of him couldn't fathom the skewed reasoning behind his father's bigotry, loathed his behavior, but remained powerless to change him.

Zaid recalled the particularly embarrassing day when the American Imam, Ahmad Hassan from the masjid he attended, came into the store. Two community members were featured speakers at the upcoming event and the Imam had personally stopped by, poster in hand, seeking to enjoin community support, but before Zaid even had the chance to offer salaams, his father began muttering under his breath racial slurs in Arabic—*about the Imam*. Most of the time, Mr. Ali would have gotten away with a rude stunt like that, but not this time. It came as quite the shocker when the Imam politely responded to his father—in flawless Arabic, no less!

TIGHT ROPE

"*Yaa akhi! Nahnu Muslimoon. Li madha laa tureedu an tusaaidoonee?*"

Stunned into silence, his old man just stomped away, leaving Zaid the humiliation of facing the Imam. "I'm really sorry. I don't know what's come over him lately. My father tends to be ... I mean sometimes he can get really ..."

"Yes, I understand. But he's still your father, brother," reprimanded the Imam gently. "Be patient with him."

"*Insha'Allah.*"

"Can I leave this here?" he asked waving the poster, the original reason for the visit.

"Yeah, no problem. I'll hang it up myself."

Embarrassed and appalled, Zaid took it upon himself to serve anyone he assumed his father's prejudice deemed inferior, which frankly, had become an ever-increasing list. Besides anyone Black, Mr. Ali's list of unacceptable included Latinos and Hispanics, women in general, and anyone appearing less affluent no matter what complexion. So, besides his being a practicing racist and bigot, his claim to fame also included being a run-of-the-mill sexist and a classist to boot. Utterly charming.

Mr. Ali habitually attended the local mosque frequented by other Arab-Americans and those of immigrant status, only a short walk from the family's apartment. Naturally, he preferred to go where he felt culturally comfortable, and where he could relate linguistically. This masjid's community housed a predominantly Arab congregation, although even under this broad umbrella, other cultures spanning the globe coexisted. However, Zaid wanted more so, in open defiance to his father's wishes, he attended prayers where many of his friends from college went; a different house of worship, located in the complete opposite direction. A masjid where Arabic was spoken in prayer, but all the *khutbahs* and lectures were said in English to be more inclusive. This change of venue caused yet another, ever-widening rift between the battling father and son.

This masjid's population consisted of predominantly Black American Muslims, although anyone wishing to attend felt welcomed. This was exactly what appealed to Zaid: the sense of camaraderie. Being born and raised in America, Zaid related to this community, and felt encouraged to pursue knowledge based on Qur'an and *Sunnah*, as opposed to being besieged by his father's menu of stale traditions and cosmetic rituals. His father and some of the older brethren tried to relegate where he prayed based on their cultural connectivity and expectations, but Zaid refused to budge. The sense of brotherhood he now experienced brought with it a fresh perspective and clarity of thought, but the decision to go came at a heavy price.

Mr. Ali found Zaid's preference a personal insult, and he became instantly agitated anytime his son dared mention the other masjid by name. This struggle about where and where not to pray—to the same God, following the same beliefs—grew out of proportion. They fought often, and viciously. Hurling slight pithy jabs or curt cutting responses, while at other times their heated disagreements turned loud and nasty. Both father and son refused to acknowledge the looming train wreck mounting right before their eyes, each too busy blaming the other. Eventually, exasperated beyond measure, Mr. Ali decided he'd had enough.

"You mind the store. I'm going to the masjid," barked Mr. Ali, walking out of the store.

"I'll lock up," said Zaid.

"No. The store stays open."

TIGHT ROPE

"What are you talking about?"

"You heard what I said."

"I have Jumu'ah too," Zaid replied, refusing to let his father get away with doing this to him yet again.

Mr. Ali turned towards his son, his face perceptively disquieting. "Are you coming with me?"

This again. Without answering, Zaid wore the same portentous type glare in return.

"No? Okay then. Mind the store." Mr. Ali left, wearing a triumphant smirk.

**

"I swear, I can't take him anymore," Zaid told his mother.

Mrs. Ali had witnessed the erosion of her husband and son's relationship for more than a few years. From the time, Zaid reached the age of seventeen, he'd begun asserting himself more, pushing the envelope on issues his father refused to relent on. The two were as inhospitable to one another in the home as they were on the job, and she didn't know how much more of the two of them she could take.

"Don't say that, *habibi*. Your father is a good man. Stubborn, sure, but you know this. He's just trying to hold onto his traditions."

"His ways? Traditions? Is that what you call it, Mama? The man acts like a racist." Zaid didn't have a chance to duck before she hurled the remote control at the side of his right cheek with pinpoint accuracy, stinging his pride more than his cheek.

"Don't EVER call your father that name, do you hear me?"

Standing erect with pursed fuming lips, and acting unfazed by her whack did little to hide the pink blotch gracing his livid face, but he would never talk against or raise his voice to his mother.

"Don't talk about your own father that way. What's happened to you? You've changed."

"You don't know, he's the disrespectful one. Anybody he doesn't like at the store he talks about. Refuses to wait on them if I'm around ... it's ridiculous!"

"So, you help those people, so what? Just do as your father tells you and you wouldn't have these problems with him."

"Problems? These aren't just problems, Mama."

Mrs. Ali studied her son's posture, wondering when he had become a man.

"He even goes out of his way to make it impossible for me to pray where I want."

"Stop. Now you're being ridiculous."

"Oh, am I? Well, today he wouldn't let me go to Jumu'ah."

"Of course not, who would watch the store if you both go?"

"No, not true. We've both gone before."

"Okay? Then what then?"

"Baba wants me to go where he wants me to pray, and when I didn't agree, he told me to stay at the store."

"You must have misunderstood him."

"See, you're doing it again!" Defeated, Zaid sighed and rubbed his forehead with both hands, baffled how neither parent understood why he went to pray where he felt closer to Allah and Islam, how going to the masjid of *his choice* had not only made him a stronger and better person, but a better practicing Muslim. This constant battle with his father about where he prayed only left him bitter.

"What? What am I doing now?"

"Defending him."

"I defend him to you, his son, his own flesh and blood, because underneath his faults he is a good man who takes care of his family; he prays to Allah, pays his *zakat*, fasts …"

"But Mama…"

"Do you understand me, *habibi*?" she pleaded, softer. "He's all I have when you go and start your life." Tears welled in her eyes. "I won't have you breaking his heart." Conversation over. His mother turned her back on her son and left him standing in the room alone to lick his wounds.

I don't have time for this. Zaid grabbed a light jacket from the hall closet, halfheartedly calling out his salaams. His damaged pride still smarted from his mother's disappointment in him.

CHAPTER 6

Nour Ibrahim

WHILE WAITING FOR HER NAME to be called, Nour averted her eyes, diverting her concentration from the waiting room glares to something more productive—playing on her phone. Well, not really playing, but reading. Catching up on posts and news missed since the last time she'd checked her cell. Much like half the population, Nour had become just as tethered to social media as anyone else. She knew it, claimed to hate it, but didn't have the time, energy, or inclination to tackle this bad habit along with everything else currently bombarding her.

Escalating incidences of hate crimes since the last terrorist attack the week before had Nour seriously contemplating canceling her doctor's appointment. Unfortunately, life wasn't this simple. One couldn't simply hide until the coast was clear because the coast never cleared. With no choice but to continue, she fought back the daunting realization that each time she stepped out of her home, she risked not making it back alive. Besides, life and

TIGHT ROPE

responsibilities didn't allow her to just call it quits and bow out. Her job's insurance company recently started demanding all employees have a yearly checkup to secure lower annual rates; a big difference from the much too exorbitant ones already paid. Scheduling yet another appointment meant time away from the desk. So, she sat waiting, ignoring the sharp pain shooting in her gut as she pretended the snarly side-glances directed at her weren't her problem.

Eyes focused on her phone, she scrolled. Nour used social media to gain a pulse from the public, and as she read, she saw clearly how people's fears resonated in their posted words. In many ways, social media had morphed into a sort of psychological Petrie dish, a semi-contained testing ground for people to meet and exchange ideas. However, many of the social media platforms also invited a convergence of emotionally depleted souls long past any decorum and dismally short on tact. Open hostilities flared and rudeness seemed to permeate endless feeds in record numbers. Any person consumed by anger or frustration now had at their disposal a place to vent snarky remarks, political memes, and contentious cartoons, adding to the parade of trivial dissertations or full-fledged conclusions. Apparently overnight, everyone and their mother had turned into either a scholar or protracted moral pontificator. On television or radio, offering up a plethora of baseless and, often times, absurd Band-Aid solutions to enormously complicated issues, they spoke, devoid of conceptual reality. Corruption-politics frayed the nerves and fed worry, while an emergence of a social apocalypse—compared by some to a volcano—readied to burst. Even office slights masked as professed gentle reminders or euphemistic corrections had become far more transparent ... much like the conversation she'd overheard only the day before.

"Promotions are back on the table." Jacob fidgeted with the coffee machine.

"That's the rumor," Greg replied, as he waited for his coffee to finish heating up. Not terribly interested, but conversationally polite.

"Yeah, but I wouldn't count on it," said Jacob, lowering his voice conspiratorially.

"Oh, and why's that?"

"Come on, you know exactly why." Jacob never missed an opportunity to play the role of office ass. "I'm telling you, Jerry has it all sewed up in the bag for sure."

"What are you implying?"

"A-A."

"Alcoholics Anonymous?"

"What? No. Affirmative Action."

Noticeably uncomfortable, Greg refused to engage any further in this stupid conversation, pretending to search for the sugar, but this did little to prevent the diehard racist from continuing. "Don't stand there and act like it doesn't exist. How do you think Ibrahim got her position?"

Appalled, but offering no rebuke, Greg mumbled a less than curt goodbye and hastily took his leave, coffee cup in hand.

Standing by the copy machine located outside of the small employee kitchen, Nour overheard the entire conversation. As Greg left, he noticed her standing there but avoided making eye contact, visually embarrassed. Unfortunately for Nour, Jacob had no such conflict of interest.

"Hey—Nour, how's it going?" greeted the two-faced slime.

"You know, Jacob. Same shit, different day."

TIGHT ROPE

**

Nour checked the time. The roof of her mouth felt dry, parched. *I should have brought a bottle of water with me ... Oh wait, I think I have some sucking candy.*

Nour reached into her bag feeling around for the familiar wrapper. Leaning over, she glanced up only to realize all eyes were fixed on her, as if a woman groping around in her handbag in a doctor's office was cause for concern.

Nour read the expressions. The squinting eyes, the tight-pursed lips. The questioning smirks. She knew them all by heart. Everything from the imperceptible flinch to the nervousness plastered across their faces, they psycho-culturally casted her in the star role of terrorist purely by the scarf she adorned, and associated her with their worst nightmares. But Nour knew that goodwill and acceptance would never reveal themselves by her taking off the hijab because for her or any other person of color, the skin she lived in wasn't removable and therefore, subsequently, neither were the seeds of hatred.

"Nour Ibrahim?" the harried nurse called, glancing directly at her. "Doctor's ready for you. Follow me, please."

Nour grabbed her bag. Standing up, she threw it over her shoulder with a bit of flare. With chin held high, she sashayed across the room and directly through the held door into the inner sanctum of the medical practice.

Nour tagged behind the nurse along the short hall, turning left into room five.

"Please remove everything but your underclothes. There's a gown on the table to change into. I'll be back in a few minutes to take your vitals. The doctor will be in shortly."

Nour thanked her, waiting for the door to close before removing her clothes as instructed. Gosh, she dreaded going to the doctor. Please pee in a cup, stick out your tongue, hold your arm out for me. How does this feel? Are you throwing up? When did this all start? Does it hurt when I press here? What about here? On a scale of one to ten, ten being the most painful, how would you describe your pain? Does it wake you from your sleep? Does the pain increase after you eat? Any particular foods? What about blood? Notice anything in your stools? Urine? Are you under a lot of stress? Are you feeling depressed? Anxiety?

The questions never stopped and her answers pretty much remained the same. Nour anticipated a repeat of the last time when Doctor Khan handed her a stack of referrals to a host of specialists. Nour shifted uncomfortably in her gown. Her belly unnaturally distended and tender to the touch.

Probably a case of nerves, she told herself. Using the palm of her hand she flattened the part of the paper gown rising up over her knees. *Why don't they make these things longer and less revealing? Could an extra foot of paper really make that much of a difference?*

Nour felt her insides twist. It hurt. A lot. Folding both arms protectively around her stomach, she wished she could be anywhere else.

Nour recently experienced sharp pains in her lower abdomen. At first it started off as a dull ache after she ate. Sometimes the cramping would wake her up out of a sound sleep. Within seconds, the pain would become unbearable and the pressure would cause her to hightail it to the bathroom as fast as her legs could carry her, still half asleep before having an accident.

Now, along with a constant barrage of sharp spasms, which

TIGHT ROPE

made her cringe and moan aloud, her weight had started to disappear overnight. No longer full figured, her body type leaned on the side of bony, adding to the already drained, worn-out sallow skin tone making her parents worry to no end.

"You need to eat," demanded her mother.

"I do. I'm busy."

"Nonsense, nobody is too busy to eat. This is what they tell themselves, but your body has rights over you, so feed it for goodness sake, before you waste away. You're already as thin as a coat hanger."

With pain and indescribable fatigue her constant companions, she didn't have much of an appetite, much less time to be sick. Perhaps today's news would accompany some long-awaited answers.

A light tap at the door, and a turning of the knob, and in entered Doctor Aliyah Khan, all four foot nine of her. While petite in stature, she was no joke. She ran a highly respected medical practice with her reputation as a patient's advocate preceding her.

"Nour! *AsSalaamu'alaikum*. Glad, you decided to bless me with your presence."

"*Wa'alaikum Salaam*, Dr. Khan," replied Nour. The two women went way back, since Nour's childhood, and although they shared a true affection for one another, this did little to stop Dr. Khan from giving her a piece of her mind.

"Explain to me why my nurse had to practically bully you into coming back?"

"She didn't actually bully—"

"You think we have time to babysit you?" Dr. Khan asked, with the tiniest of smirks peeking out from her lips. "Ah, I see now," she said, pulling a form out of the folder. "You're only here because of your job's health insurance forms."

"They sent them out after I saw you."

"And here I was, under the impression that you might actually care about your declining health. Alright, be that as it may, you and I need to discuss a few things."

"What things?"

"Things–things–such as your lab results."

Nour's belly lurched. *Oh those ...*

"Your blood work indicates you're rundown, so no surprise there. Your sudden weight loss however, has me concerned. Your constant pain, stomach distention, bathroom runs ... my mind is thinking we could be looking at a few possibilities."

"Like what?"

"Well, I don't want to project, but we've already ruled out allergies. Those tests came back fine. No diabetes; your sugar levels also good. Cholesterol is fine. Here, get off the table and come next to me so I can show you."

The two women went over all the previous test results in detail. Nour listened, barely interjecting, and feeling overwhelmed with the possibility there might be something seriously wrong with her, something not showing up on the tests. "What's next?" she asked, not really wanting to hear the answer.

"You're not going to like this, but more tests, specifically your intestinal tract. I also want a CAT scan done to make sure you don't have an ulcer brewing." Dr. Khan sifted through Nour's chart. "You still have your gallbladder and appendix," she mumbled aloud. Nour didn't reply.

"How often do you have to go to the bathroom?"

"You mean pee?"

"No, but okay, pee?" Dr. Khan waited.

TIGHT ROPE

"Normal amount."

"What's normal?"

"Four to six times a day, I guess. I don't know. Depends how much I drink."

"Bowel movements?"

"Oh. Well, I used to go once, maybe twice a day, but now it's more."

"Like how much more?"

"You want an actual number?"

"An estimate will do."

"Sometimes seven to ten times. On really bad days I can barely leave the bathroom."

"Loose or solid?"

"Oh God, seriously?"

"Do I sound like I'm joking? Listen, you're wasting away on me and when my patients come in for a visit over nine pounds less than they were the last time—" Dr. Khan checked her chart, "Less than what? A week and half ago? —Then yes, I have serious concerns."

Guilty as charged, but Nour had too much on her plate right now to deal with Dr. Khan's browbeating. "What do you think this is?"

"I don't know, and I don't play guessing games. But I'm thinking these additional tests will give us an answer."

Nour nodded, not at all happy.

"I'm going to write you a referral to see a gastroenterologist. Dr. Frank. He's great, one of the best. I want him to take a look at you, run some tests, and see if we can get to the bottom of this, okay?"

"Take a look at me how?"

Dr. Khan knew what Nour meant. "I know you'd prefer a woman doctor, but he's honestly the best, and I trust him. If you want a female doctor, I can get another name for you after I ask around. It's up to you."

Nour did in fact prefer a woman doctor, but she also wanted the specialist her own doctor trusted the most. "Can I decide and get back to you?"

"No. You need to make a decision now. I'm concerned waiting will exacerbate your symptoms."

Nour pursed her lips in thought, weighing out the pros and cons in her head.

"Still waiting," said Dr. Khan.

"I'm thinking."

"I will call your mother."

"I'm pretty sure that's against the law."

Dr. Khan stared intently at Nour, not the slightest bit amused.

"Fine, I'll go see him, as long as he accepts my insurance."

Dr. Khan smiled, resting her hand reassuringly on Nour's shoulder, squeezing tenderly. "Good choice. I'll go give him a ring while you get dressed. When you're done, meet me in my office."

Nour stood outside the office, the door slightly ajar. "Yes. Wonderful. That's great, thank you … much appreciated," said Dr. Khan into the phone as she glanced towards the door, and waved at Nour to enter and take a seat.

"Yes. I agree … Oh, of course. Not a problem. Hmmm … I'll have all her test results faxed over to you today … Great, I look forward to hearing back from you, and Thanks, Ron. Love to Anne and the kids."

Perched on the edge of the proffered chair, Nour waited, anxious to hear where these next steps would lead. Different

TIGHT ROPE

scenarios running through her mind, she evaluated what might be in store for her against the limited time remaining from a full workload. Eager to hear the doctor's news and leave, she interjected first.

"I need to get back to work. I only told them an hour and a half."

Dr. Khan handed Nour the scripts, and the referral with an address. "I just got off the phone with Dr. Frank. His receptionist knows to expect your call. Make the time to see him and let him run these tests so we can figure out what's going on inside of you."

Nour understood but Dr. Khan wasn't listening. "Work is hectic right now, plus I'm scheduled to go to ah-a-a meeting this coming weekend, and there's no way I can miss it."

Dr. Khan smirked at Nour as she tried to weasel her way out of the appointment. "I understand that, but you have to find the time. If it's work, I'll write you whatever letter you need to cover your absence, but this can't wait. Do you realize as you're speaking to me you're gripping your stomach?"

Nour shrugged. *True.* Gripping her stomach had become a habit.

"No," said Dr. Khan adamantly. "With your current pain level and symptoms—not to mention your sudden weight loss—I have a good mind to admit you to the hospital right now, if that's what it takes."

"No, no. I'll go ... but–"

"When?"

Nour glowered. "This week I guess?" The face on Dr. Khan indicated she didn't like what Nour was selling. "I'll go before the meeting this weekend, or early next week at the latest."

Dr. Khan stood, walked around her desk to accompany Nour

back to the front desk. "Call me if the pain worsens. If it gets bad, go straight to the ER and have them notify me."

"What do you think it is?"

"Like I said, I don't play guessing games. But whatever it is, I want to get to the bottom of it. You're young … these symptoms you're having are cause for serious concern. Let's do the tests, see what Dr. Frank has to say, and go from there."

Nour left gloomier than when she had arrived, holding out hope the last batch of tests would have revealed something easily taken care of. She'd never been this kind of sick before, it jarred her susceptibilities, making her feel vulnerable, health-wise, for the first time. Growing up with nothing more concerning than the common cold or a throat infection to deal with hadn't prepared her for the possibility something else could be very wrong, maybe even life-threatening. *Add it to the list.*

Normally a bus ride or a brisk walk back to work would have been just the thing to clear her head, but having already spent more time away from the office than planned, she'd have to splurge and hail for a cab.

I should call Mom first.

Stepping back away from the curb, Nour pulled the phone out of her bag but became immediately distracted. Displayed on the phone screen, a part of a longer message appeared. Clicking it, she let out an involuntarily gasp. In a panic, her head spun frantically in all directions, trying to search every face in a vast crowd of faces.

Which set of eyes belonged to him?

CHAPTER 7

Doris Tetler

RUSSELL RELAXED IN HIS LIVING room, hands behind his head, eyes glued to the television, engrossed once again in the nightly news. His wife, Doris yawned. Wrapped in a blanket, she slouched on the couch, trying to block out her husband's existence.

"Get a job!" he yelled at the screen, gulping another irritated swig of beer. "That's if your sorry asses can figure out a way to pry it out of the grubby hands of them illegals!"

Russell's practice of shouting at the TV unnerved Doris to no end, hating him and his all too predictable profanities. She despised the way the tips of his hairy, enormous, aging ears turned a sickly shade of red the more he got worked up. She cringed from the tenor of his gruff laugh, which would then morph into a snort, much like escaping hiccups germinating from a flabby, sallow face. It was all rather comical to watch, in a sad and pitiable way, until such time when Russell became bored with the one-way tête-à-tête and redirect his anger to her. Currently the big, bad bully was all upset about some silly demonstration in front of City Hall, and from what Doris could gather, the moron planned to be there.

"More taxpayer money wasted protecting a bunch of loud mouths—and for what? So, they can whine and complain about not having equal rights? America is the land of opportunity, you damn idiots! Maybe if you worked harder and got an education instead of being a pack of lazy good-for-nothing drug addicts, you wouldn't find your dumb asses hung out to dry all the time."

Staring off into space, Doris tugged the blanket protectively around her shoulders. Closing her eyes, she feigned sleep. *I should have listened to my mother. She always told me Russell wouldn't amount to no good.* "Came from the wrong side of the tracks," she'd warned. "Nothing but white trash and trouble."

**

The Tetlers lived in a row house, situated one right next to the other with tiny to non-existent front yards, metal-gated windows, and antiquated cement stoops. Russell called Brooklyn his home forever. He grew up there as a child in a neighborhood not all that far from where he and Doris bought their house after getting married. And despite the changes occurring all around the city, he'd never given moving any serious consideration, although he'd be shocked to know his house would fetch triple the rate compared to what he'd paid for it back then.

This area at one time boasted a community filled with the middle working class. Up at dawn, they'd return at dusk. Mom-and-pop stores lined the blocks, all within walking distance from each other. Corner parks burst with the laughter of children and families, while local funeral parlors tended to their tears, yet they all complimented one another. Life in the city supported a certain vibrant collection of people all trying to edge out a slice of the American dream. Working endless hours at often thankless jobs, they strove to put food on the table, a roof over their heads, and if lucky, facilitate a college degree or two for the next generation.

Then gentrification slithered onto the scene, entering neighborhoods with the promise of prosperity. Practically overnight, the same mom-and-pop stores were replaced with high-end restaurants and specialized coffee shops. Where general catchall stores sold everything from hardware and batteries to footwear, jackets, and school supplies once stood, there now stood fancy boutiques overflowing with pricey esoteric clothing artfully displayed on creepy mannequins, and deliberately lit up to attract foot traffic past professionally designed windows.

Where once neighbor knew neighbor, now unfamiliar and unwelcomed faces dressed in pricey suits and carrying real leather attaché cases roamed the neighborhood, stepping out of high-end vehicles, and seen shaking hands and dispensing legal notices, sent to announce the approved pending changes. Despite the fact that some folks welcomed the transformation and money, others weren't so inclined. Many either moved away, pressured by escalating prices to rent elsewhere, while others sold off their homes as soon as the whiff of real money passed beneath their wide-open noses.

And still others, unwilling and refusing to meekly run away, put up a fight, starting first with letter campaigns and then petitions. A very few were more verbal about their mounting discontent, informing the numerous suited visitors where they could stick their offers. Russell, one of the angry, made his position colorfully clear, stating in no uncertain terms he would never voluntarily up and leave his "happy abode." "You'll have to drag me out in a body bag before I'll agree to move out of my home and neighborhood," he screamed…and he wasn't joking.

Unlike her husband, Doris never bothered adding her two cents to the brewing disagreements and neighborhood conversations, secretly all too ready and eager to pack up her memories, toss her nightmares away, and start anew someplace else. Some place without him. Maybe the *'they'* that Russell kept ranting about would do her the solid and take him up on his threat. *Get it over with already.* But so far, no such luck.

Eventually, the few holdouts sold out, as progress sprouted around, squeezing them into an eventual submission. The same levied threats and ploys hadn't affected the Tetlers, though, since they had no mortgage attached to their home. The one smart thing Russell ever did.

**

After sending off his last email, Russell smacked his lips, his mouth parched. "Doris!" he barked from inside his office, incidentally only a few steps from the kitchen as opposed to where Doris lay, tending to her current headache on the couch.

"Can you make me a cup of coffee? Put it in a travel mug for me, would ya? I've got someplace I need to be."

From the other room, Doris cursed Russell under her breath. A habit she'd grown accustomed to doing whenever her husband opened his mouth to speak.

More a demand than a request, and not waiting for her reply, Russell shut off his computer, sliding a few notes out of sight under a couple of larger papers in the drawer. Standing up to

TIGHT ROPE

stretch, he winced in pain, immediately leaning on the desk for support. Both sets of knees were acting up more than usual recently, becoming stiff if he sat too long and achy if he walked too far. Climbing steps aggravated the dickens out of them too, causing a dull, throbbing pain. Constantly rubbing, massaging, and popping pain pills were his only relief.

Slowly, Doris shuffled her way to the kitchen, passing by his closed office door. Defiantly, scrunching her nose, she stuck out her tongue. Another new habit she'd begun to regularly implement. *Inconsiderate bastard, always yelling at me like I'm his maid.*

Doris lacked height, but this never stopped Russell from demanding that his travel mugs be kept in the cabinet over the stove, and for no apparent reason either. There was more than enough space available in the cabinet below the utensils, where it was easier to reach–*But no. Why make my life any easier, right? You, selfish bastard.*

Dragging out the stepstool kept permanently in the corner of the kitchen for occasions such as these, Doris warily climbed to the second rung, refusing to take one step higher. Balancing herself on her tippy toes, she pulled the damn cabinet open, maneuvering the mug forward with the fingertips of her one free hand. *Jackass.*

This was Russell's new routine, coffee on the run. He would decide to leave all of a sudden and be gone for hours at a time. Where to exactly, she had no clue. Nor did she care. Doris treasured the promise of a few hours of uninterrupted peace and quiet, enjoyed having the house to her lonesome. His absence meant she could enjoy leisurely hot showers without Russell's inevitable banging on the door, and screaming like an escaped lunatic about her using too much hot water. It also meant a reprieve from his endless orders and flippant sarcastic remarks.

A moment later the office door sprang open. "I don't know what time I'll be home, so don't worry about making me dinner. I'll catch something while I'm out."

Doris blinked, affirming she'd heard him.

After dutifully handing him his filled mug, she shuffled back to the confines and comfort of her well-worn couch. The same couch bought less than a year after being married. The same couch she'd fallen in love with in the shop window. The same couch she'd scrimped and saved for, endlessly cutting coupons and shaving a few dollars from the food budget whenever she could manage, and the same exact couch she crumpled on the day the doorbell rang with the news: her precious, only child, George, was dead.

"Do you want me to bring you anything back?" Russell asked, more out of habit than any real concern. Doris pretended not to hear, already burrowed back onto the couch with the cushions permanently creased from years of overuse. Tugging the quilt tightly over her shoulder she didn't bother answering, acting as if she'd fallen fast asleep, while allowing her angry silence to be her riposte.

"Okay, well. I'm off then," Russell announced, trudging past, once again sporting his nasty old fishing hat and his hideous light-cream colored jacket which had seen better days. Doris cringed. She couldn't remember the last time the ratty old thing had seen the washer.

At one point in time, many years ago, Doris thought Russell a fairly attractive man. Not necessarily handsome in the traditional sense of the word, but most definitely good-looking. Tall yet brawny, his face plain, but his cheeks sported two slightly deep dimples when he smiled, making him appear rather dapper. Doris

TIGHT ROPE

had instantly fallen into heavy crush the day she'd first laid eyes on him, standing in line at the movie theater, waiting for his turn to purchase popcorn and a drink.

The two started off exchanging shy, timid glances. Then once inside the theater, they each selected seating with a direct view of the other, if one didn't count having to sneak peeks over a shoulder or a full head swivel. By the time the movie finished, Doris had already contrived an onslaught of thoughts in her head about the kindhearted looking young man, wondering his name and where he lived, but most of all, how in the world she'd ever see him again if he didn't make the move to speak to her.

As the lights lifted and people rushed from their seats into the aisle to make the mad dash out, Doris became visibly alarmed when she realized she'd lost sight of him. Panicked, her eyes darted everywhere, searching, wondering where he could have run off to in such a hurry. *Oh, well.* Discouraged and disappointed, she entered the middle aisle reluctantly to join her friends, apparently also in a rush to leave the theater.

Doris pretended to listen to her chatty friends laugh about the movie she'd barely paid attention to. As soon as she noticed him waiting for her in the lobby, leaning nonchalantly on the wall, her face immediately brightened.

There he stood, hands shoved in his pockets. His dreamy eyes followed her as she emerged into the lobby. Russell singled her with a slight wave to come over, his dimples on full display. She felt encouraged when she noticed his face breaking out into a large, invitingly warm grin as their eyes locked onto one another. Doris told her friends to wait for her outside, indicating coyly she'd be back in a minute. She'd ignored the trail of questions and giggles as she strode across the lobby in opposition to the tide of people still pushing and rushing to leave, and getting herself trampled over repeatedly. Dodging and ducking, she finally made it, but once there, her boldness abandoned her; she stood tongue-tied, like a dork. Thankfully, Russell had enough in his limited repertoire and seamlessly took up the slack.

"Russell," he said, coolly introducing himself with an extended handshake, his eyes smoldering with intensity.

"Doris," she replied, accepting his extended hand, and fighting to ignore the butterflies flopping around in her belly.

"Hello, Doris. Hope you don't mind me being this forward, but I'd like to take you out sometime. I mean if you are free and all."

Those dimples should be illegal. "Sure, I'd like that."

"How about this weekend? If you're free. Saturday night?"

Doris had already made plans for Saturday, but nothing she couldn't wiggle out of. "Sure," she said, rubbing her mouth, drawing his attention to her pouty lips. "Yes, I think Saturday works for me."

The two clumsily exchanged phone numbers and in a flash, he was gone. For the remainder of the evening Doris mulled over the sultry smooth skin of his hand in hers and swore in her heart of hearts they had shared something more intense than a mere handshake … more of a cosmic connection.

"Cosmic?" teased her friend Amy in the backseat of her father's car. "I swear, you are so weird sometimes," she whispered in Doris's ear.

Doris blushed, still grinning.

"You're reading too many of those teen magazines." Sandra leaned her head into the conversation, not wishing to be left out. "Four Sure-Fire Ways to Play Hard-To-Get," she quipped,

TIGHT ROPE

playfully thrusting out her chest and licking her lips.

"Next she'll be telling us this guy is her soul mate...the love of her life," chuckled Amy, hugging her arms, blowing air kisses and batting her eyelashes.

"Shhh," ordered Doris, cheeks flushed, but not wanting Amy's father to hear. "I can't explain it, but I know he's the one."

"From a handshake?" Sandra sniggered.

"A *cosmic* handshake!" corrected Amy, and then all three friends broke out into fits of giggles.

**

As the front door drew closed and the lock clicked securely into place, Doris popped open her eyes, a torrent of relief flooding her senses. From beneath the pillow her aging fingers groped around for the small pocketknife kept hidden. Instantly reassured of its presence, she slid it further back behind the couch cushion. Safely out of sight, yet easily retrievable *just in case* an opportunity presented itself.

CHAPTER 8

Zaid & Maryam

IN A RUSH BUT STARVING, Maryam weighed her options. Being short staffed meant a quick lunch break, which in turn, left little time to hike the extra few blocks to her favorite lunch spot even running. Maryam's next option was located directly across from the front entrance of the hospital, a corner bodega-deli, an entirely less than attractive choice because of the storeowner. He never failed to leave her feeling unnerved, following her around the store with his eyes, the grim expression plastered across his cantankerous face, watching her every move like she was some kind of thief or something. He gave her the creeps.

Maryam checked her watch, time wasted trying to decide. Hunger won out. The promise of a long evening shift at work on an empty stomach was completely unappealing. Grudgingly, she darted across the street to the bodega.

"*AsSalaamu'alaikum*, can I help you?"

"*Wa'alaikum Salaam*. Um, I'll have a turkey on rye, mayo,

lettuce, tomato." Maryam quickly diverted her eyes. She'd seen Zaid before, but their interactions had always been strictly business-like and rushed. Compared to his father, however, she'd take that any day. *Speaking of which* ... her eyes scanned over to the corner perch where Mussolini usually sat. *Empty.*

"Onion?" he asked.

"What?"

"Onion? Do you want onion on your sandwich?"

"Oh, onion? Yes, sorry. Mind's on ... stuff. No onion, thanks."

"Coming right up."

He has nice eyes ... and nice arms ... and nice ...

**

Zaid turned back to slicing the turkey. She'd come into the store before and each time he had wanted to say something, but he never had the opportunity under his father's unrelenting glare. His domineering presence put a damper on practically any attempt he made to speak with the sister, outside of taking her order, but this time Mr. Ali was in the backroom handling the bookkeeping.

"Did you say tomato?" he asked, stealing furtive glances, using any excuse to hear her speak again.

"Yes, please. Tomato and lettuce."

Zaid's mind raced trying to think up things to say to her without appearing like a total jerk, but she beat him to it.

"Are you going?" she asked, pointing to the poster. Zaid checked out her hand. No sign of a wedding band. *Damn, she's fine.*

Zaid had forgotten all about the rally. Once he had taped it on the wall as promised, he hadn't given it much thought. "I was thinking about going. You?"

"One of the speakers—this sister," she said tapping Nour's photo, "I'd like to go just to hear her."

"She goes to the masjid I attend." Zaid wasn't sure why he felt compelled to say that and immediately regretted it.

"Ah, *Alhamdulillah*."

Now this grabbed Maryam's attention, whose eyes lit up at the mere mention of Nour's name, and if Zaid wasn't mistaken, she looked almost impressed. *That's right sister, I got more to offer than sliced turkey*. Encouraged, he kept talking.

"She's an incredible speaker."

"You've heard her speak before?"

"Oh, yeah, plenty." Now he was lying. Yes, the part about Nour attending his masjid was true enough, but no, he had never heard her speak before.

Maryam checked her cell for the time.

Great. She can't wait to get away from me.

Maryam, who had been just standing there smiling and unable to reply, hastily lowered her eyes to her phone, attempting to guard her gaze, and pretending to browse her newsfeed. "*Astaghfirallah*," she murmured.

"Excuse me?"

"What?"

"You said something?"

"I don't think so," Maryam said, trying to ignore the fact her hands were shaking.

Zaid wrapped up the sandwich. "Anything else, sister?"

"No, thanks…" but just as quickly changed her mind. "You know what? I'm sort of running late. Would you mind very much if I used your backroom to pray?"

TIGHT ROPE

Zaid's face registered pure dread.

There was no missing the change. Maryam's gaze followed Zaid's glare to the curtained off backroom where she caught a set of beady dark eyes peering out directly at her and immediately retracted her request. "You know what, forget it. I work right across the street."

"Are you sure, sister?" he asked, trying to keep the doleful sound out of his voice. "I could lend you my prayer mat."

"Um, no, I'm good…thanks." Maryam looked down at her phone again. "Okay, well, I guess I'm off then."

In that instant, Zaid saw the flicker of light evaporate from Maryam's eyes, and for him, it felt like a crushing blow. Disheartened, he reached for a rag to give his hands something to do.

"Okay, well…*AsSalaamu'alaikum*," she said, offering a brisk wave goodbye, clutching her lunch and hightailing it out of the store, but not before risking one last fleeting glance back.

Zaid couldn't help himself. Just before glancing away, he caught her turn her lovely face towards his and at that moment their gazes locked together, and he knew…

**

Mr. Ali listened to the entire exchange through the thin curtain. Clearly a female voice, but he wasn't able to make out whose. After peeping through the curtain, he knew exactly who that voice belonged to: the same girl who made his son wet his pants each time she opened her mouth.

That's it! That boy needs to settle down before he gets himself into trouble. We need to find Zaid a good wife, to help him when the time comes to take over the family business. And not just any woman in a hijab either. I need to talk with his mother.

"Zaid!" He barked. "Start cleaning up. I want to close on time tonight, but first I want you to run the money to the bank for me."

Zaid, already anticipating his father's demand, had already tallied up the day's receipts and earnings. He handed them off to his father so he could fill out the bank slip. "I'll go after we close," he offered, but his dad had a different plan.

"No. Finish what you're doing. Then I want you to head straight over to the bank while it's still light out. I'll lock up and meet you back at the house."

"Why?" Zaid asked, already assuming it had something to do with the recent vandalism, but Mr. Ali continued what he was doing, ignoring him as usual.

For the next half-hour, the two men worked silently side by side, interrupted only by an occasional customer.

"Do you have everything?"

"Bank slip, money," Zaid confirmed as he swung the leather bag over his shoulder and secured the strap across his chest.

"No goofing around. Go straight to the bank and then home. I want to talk to you about something important tonight." With all the stories about muggings in broad daylight, Mr. Ali had become nervous.

"I take it that would be a *no* to me stopping for a quick lap dance?"

"GET OUT!"

Zaid bid his father a forced jovial *salaam* and left. Tired and in need of a shower, and a hot meal, and a much-desired good night's sleep, it wasn't long before the day's fatigue took over, making him move slower than usual, and instead of paying attention to his surroundings, his mind began to wander. Without realizing it, a smile snuck out. Something surprisingly enticing played around in the back of his mind...or more like *a someone*.

**

"*AsSalaamu'alaikum*," Zaid yelled, kicking off his shoes and placing them on the hall rack. His mother hated when piles of shoes were left in mounds on the floor, or scattered in the hall for people to trip over.

"*Wa'alaikum salaam*. Where's your father?" she asked from the kitchen. "Why isn't he with you?"

"He stayed at the store to close up. Sent me to the bank." *Strange*. As slow as he had gone, Zaid was sure his father would have beaten him back home.

"I called him but he's not picking up his phone."

"He knows it's you calling," teased Zaid, pecking his mother a kiss on the cheek before snatching an apple out of the fridge. "I'm starving. When's dinner?"

Mrs. Ali ignored his questions, more concerned with hers. "Why didn't your father come home with you?"

"I told you, he sent me to the bank and told me to meet him back here."

"You should have stayed with him."

"He told me to go." *Here she goes. Overreacting.* "I'm not sure why he's late."

Grabbing a sweater from the hall closet, his mother then quickly slipped on her shoes. "I'm going to the store to see what's keeping him. Your dinner's ready. You can start without us."

"Wait–stop–why are you going? He's not even that late yet."

"I know."

"Ma, relax. Just give him a few more minutes. I'm sure he's on the way."

"No, I'd rather go and meet him at the store. With all the trouble, recently…"

"Reading your tea leaves again?" he teased. Zaid adored his mother and liked to bust her chops. Reaching out, he peeled her sweater off. "You're worrying for nothing, but I'll go. I'll drag him back if I have to, but seriously, you worry too much. It's not good for your health."

"I know, I know. Thank you, *habibi*, but call me as soon as you get to the store."

**

"Mr. Ali? We'd like you to get your arm looked at."

"I'm fine, I keep telling you this!"

"At least as a precaution."

Mr. Ali snarled. "Instead of playing nursemaid to me, why don't you catch those lousy lowlife criminals."

"Yes sir, I get what you're saying," offered the frustrated junior police officer, "but you need to go to the emergency room. If you want, I'll walk you over personally."

Mr. Ali closed his eyes.

"Just let a doctor take a look at it, make sure nothing's broken."

Although admittedly his shoulder throbbed, Mr. Ali adamantly refused. "I'll call my son. He'll take me, but first I want to make sure you have all the information. I want to press charges against those *thuggers*."

TIGHT ROPE

"Thugs," said the senior officer standing nearby.

"What?"

"They're called thugs," he corrected.

Mr. Ali's face registered confusion.

"Forget it. Look, I understand you're upset, Mr. Ali. I'd be angry in your place too, but you're injured." To the junior officer he ordered, "Call EMT."

Less than a half a block away, Zaid caught sight of three police cars outside the store, their lights flashing. *What the hell?* Breaking out into a run he tried barreling through only to be stopped by one of the officers standing guard.

"Whoa, now."

"He's my father!" Zaid replied, trying to push his way through.

From the stool now placed in the middle of the store, Mr. Ali heard his son's voice. Face ashen but equally as cantankerous, he bellowed, "About time you got here."

"Let him in," ordered the senior officer.

"What happened? Are you okay?" Zaid asked rushing to his father's side, who sat nursing his shoulder with a bag of frozen peas.

"We were robbed."

"Robbed?"

"A few minutes after you left."

"*Astaghfirallah*…what happened to your shoulder?"

"Forget the shoulder. I'm fine," Mr. Ali triumphantly winked, "but those idiots were too late though, right, son?"

Zaid squinted his eyes, biting his tongue. "I'm taking you to the hospital."

Mr. Ali locked stern eyes onto his son's. "Tell me you went to the bank," he hissed.

"Forget about that for now."

"ANSWER ME."

"YES! I went to the bank. I did exactly what you told me to do, okay? Damn, dad, did they hurt you?"

"You see me holding a frozen bag of peas to my head, right?"

Zaid rubbed the back of his strained neck, his eyes darting from his father to the police officer standing nearby, who, while amused, didn't offer any info.

"One of the guys, the taller one, slammed me," indicating his upper arm, "On the corner over there." He pointed to the sharp edge of the counter. "Got really mad when he found out there was nothing left in the register but some change." Mr. Ali waved the frozen bag of peas accusingly at his son. "Now you know why I made you to go to the bank when it was still light outside."

"May I speak to you for moment?" The senior officer interrupted, looking at Zaid. "Outside." It was more of a statement than a request.

Zaid glanced back at his father, not comfortable leaving his side.

"Go, go. I'm fine," Mr. Ali told his son, but then crooked his finger indicating for Zaid to lend him his ear first. In rapid Arabic, he mumbled, "Only tell them what you have to and no more."

Zaid let out a deep groan. He had no clue what *that* was supposed to mean, but didn't have the heart to argue with the old man. "Okay."

Once outside, the officer pulled no punches. "From what I can tell, this seems like your basic robbery."

"Your basic robbery?"

"Yeah. They came for money, found nothing, got mad,

attacked your dad and left."

"Oh. I see what you mean."

"Unless I'm missing something?"

Zaid didn't think dredging up past complaints would accomplish anything so he remained quiet.

"Are you sure there's nothing else I should know?" The officer warily studied Zaid's face. "Your father mentioned the bank. Do you normally keep a set time to go or does your schedule change?"

"No set time. Whenever he sends me or if the store gets slow. Tonight, we were trying to close up early."

"Why?"

Zaid hesitated. *Shit, this was what dad was probably referring to in his little warning.* Nevertheless, it wasn't like he was going to lie either. "We've been having trouble recently. Nothing big. Just some graffiti left on the store front."

The officer checked his notes. "Your father never mentioned that. What does it say?"

"The usual stuff I guess."

The officer waited, but Zaid had nothing more to add. "Have you reported this?" he asked.

"Yeah, a few times."

The officer never let his guard drop. Under his intense scrutiny, Zaid shifted his weight to his other leg, avoiding making eye contact.

"Anything directed personally at you or your father?"

"Like what?"

"You tell me."

"Like I told you, just usual stuff." Zaid refused to elaborate. The officer waited. "Mostly scribbled gang symbols. We had an inverted swastika once." Zaid waited for him to say something, but the cop just continued to stare. "Can I go back to my dad now?"

The seasoned officer knew Zaid was lying but why? Unless he came clean, there wasn't much else he could do. "Sure, but if anyone suspicious starts hanging around, or maybe your father suddenly remembers something, here's my card. Call me."

Officer Jonathan Thorsten. "Okay, yeah." Zaid shoved the card in his pocket. "Thanks." Upon stepping back inside the store, he heard his father barking at one of the younger emergency technicians.

"Stop this," snapped Mr. Ali halfheartedly, waving his one good hand in the medic's face. "I don't need a doctor!" The old man looked drained.

"I'm calling Mom to meet us at the ER."

As the initial adrenaline wore off and the pain steadily increased, Mr. Ali didn't have much fight left, but true to form he added his last two cents. "Make sure you lock up the place good. I don't want those punks to think they can come back and finish what they started."

After a full set of x-rays, a cat scan, and one sling later, the Ali family returned home, exhausted, nerves frayed, but gratefully all in one piece. The doctor explained that Mr. Ali would be out of commission for the following few weeks. A slight tear in his rotor cuff didn't appear severe, but if it didn't have the time necessary to heal properly or became unnecessarily strained, he might require surgery in the future.

"He's going to need months of physical rehabilitation to gain back full mobility and increase muscle strength," said the doctor who then prescribed a regimen of semi-inactivity, antibiotics and painkillers.

TIGHT ROPE

Mr. Ali tried balking, but Mrs. Ali, no pushover herself, put her foot down. "Save it," she snapped. "You will do as the doctor says."

Mr. Ali's need for sleep coupled with the second round of pain killers kicking in outweighed his ability to joust. Unfortunately, it did little to dissuade him from micromanaging again. "You're going to have to be in charge of the store while I'm out," he informed his son somewhat groggily.

"I know, Baba."

"Your mother will come to help when she can, but the majority of the responsibilities will be on you."

"I know this too."

"Do you think you can handle it?"

"I'm going to have to."

"That wasn't what I asked."

"Yes, yes…I can handle it." Exhausted and needing this conversation to end, Zaid turned towards his bedroom, desperate for sleep.

"Thank you, *habibi*."

Zaid stopped mid-step. He could count on exactly one finger the amount of times in his life his father had uttered those specific three words to him. Without replying or acknowledging what was said, he kept walking, chalking it up to the drugs.

When the alarm on his phone sounded, Zaid threw the pillow over his head attempting to squeeze out one more minute of sleep, feeling as if he'd only slept a few minutes as opposed to hours. Fatigue had settled in, but with his father out of commission, there was no time to dawdle. The responsibility of the family's income now rested squarely on his shoulders and he wasn't about to drop the ball his first time out.

Without so much as a bite to eat or a cup of coffee, Zaid rushed out of the house, practically running to the store, his keys jingling around his neck under his sweatshirt. He half anticipated a barrage of more graffiti, but felt relieved to see everything looking the way they'd left it the night before, albeit disheveled inside. Nothing a quick sweep and firm wipe off couldn't fix. Less than thirty minutes later, the OPEN sign on the door promptly flipped around and business as usual commenced.

Without Baba, there to help take orders, he had to do that plus ring them up. Although working alone took additional time, the customers seemed to be okay with it, especially those who'd gotten wind of what transpired the evening before.

"Sorry to hear about your dad, Z-Man," said Ronald, the owner of the newsstand a half a block over. "Damn neighborhood's going to shit in a handbag if you ask me."

By early afternoon a collection of covered dishes arrived, along with some balloons and a houseplant tagged with a giant "Get Well" card signed by some of Dad's regulars.

"I'm sorry about your father," said Mr. Flannery. "He's a good man and a good neighbor. Hate to hear what they did to him. Nobody should have to go through what he did, those damn punks. I hope they catch 'em soon and throw their asses in jail where they deserve to rot."

As gruff and ornery and as totally obnoxious as Mr. Ali could get at times, Zaid also knew of another more compassionate side to his old man, a side he kept well hidden. Where certain customers in need were concerned, he'd apply a sliding scale. This morning, Zaid found a white envelope left near the register with a note and a few crinkled dollars stuffed inside.

"Thank you, Mr. A for always being there to help us get

through the hard times. Here's a few dollars to start paying you back. I know it's not nearly enough for everything you've done to help us, but it's a start. Feel better soon, The Kruger family."

Zaid couldn't get over how many people cared about what had happened to his father. Sure, he knew other business people, but Zaid thought those more of a passing relationship, but these folks were genuinely concerned about him. And that wasn't even the half of it; unbeknown to him and the entire Ali family, on the evening after the robbery, some of the local shopkeepers called for an emergency meeting to discuss what could be done about the disgustingly lewd and racist messages being continuously left on the Ali shop. Some voted to hire security guards, but this proved too expensive, so that was a no-go.

Ronald mentioned setting up cameras *to catch the bastards in the act*, but again, nobody had the funds or the know-how to install them, so the idea got shelved for later.

Mrs. Wells, a retired school teacher who recently opened a small boutique down the street, suggested each person take turns guarding the store. "We could do a neighborhood watch, but without guns," she said, but nobody had the energy, skills, or inclination to see that recommendation through.

Eventually, the general consensus was decided that for at least the immediate future, they'd show support as a community by cleaning the store's windows at the crack of dawn on a rotation basis, preferring to keep what they were doing on the sly and not wanting Zaid or his family to be made to feel any more upset or unwelcomed than they most certainly already did.

After the lunch hour rush dissipated, Zaid dragged a stool behind the counter to rest. His feet hurt, his lower back ached, and his eyes stung. Exhausted through and through, the lack of sleep and the mounting stress of the day had worn him thin. The prospect of doing this routine for a few more weeks seemed an insurmountable hurdle, but he swore to himself he would neither relent nor give up, no matter how hard things got. His family counted on him.

Just as his eyes started to drift closed the bell on the door jangled and startled him awake. Of all people, in stepped the beautiful woman from the other day, dressed once again in a nurse's uniform.

"*AsSalaamu'alaikum*," Maryam greeted him with a lovely, warm smile.

Zaid returned the greeting sounding less enthusiastic, but inside, euphoric. He jumped to his feet a bit too fast and wound up knocking over a few papers and a pen in the process. "Ah!"

While Maryam's eyes creased, she managed to suppress a laugh.

"Sorry about that." *Good going asshole, way to impress.*

"Are you okay?"

"Yes, fine." Embarrassment found a home under his collar. "What can I get for you today?" he asked, starting to babble. "Another turkey on rye, mayo, lettuce, tomato, hold the onion?"

Maryam appeared pleasantly surprised. "You have quite the memory. I'm impressed."

"Don't be. Comes from years of working behind the counter. Becomes second nature." Zaid blushed, wishing he'd stop babbling.

"Well, whatever it is, I'd sure wish you'd bottle it. My memory is terrible. Whatever sticks comes after hours of studying."

"You can't be all that bad. You became a nurse, right?"

"That's the rumor."

TIGHT ROPE

"In the hospital across the street?"

"More like *at* the hospital. I work for Doctor Khan."

Zaid didn't know what else to add, so he got back to her order. "Do you want anything to drink?"

"No thanks. I'm only doing water now." Maryam pointed to her travel mug. "Trying not to drink my calories."

"I don't think you have anything to worry about." The comment had slipped out before he could stop himself. *Shit.*

"Ah, thanks, I guess." Maryam blushed. "I better get going. My shift starts soon and I can't be late."

Zaid handed Maryam her order and took a chance. "Ah sister? I don't even know your name."

Maryam's smile turned unmistakably coquettish, "You're right, you don't." She left without telling him, but for all her indifference, Zaid detected something happening behind those lovely eyes.

"*AsSalaamu'alaikum*, brother."

"*Wa'alaikum salaam*, sister." *See you tomorrow.*

CHAPTER 9

Russell Tetler

RUSSELL'S HOME LIFE, NEVER a glowing portal of tranquility to begin with, became increasingly more depressing the longer he stayed unemployed and underfoot. The indignity of waiting for an inadequate unemployment check frayed the last of his nerves, the money doled out a mere pittance compared to what he used to bring home. On top of that, the payments were expected to run out soon enough. Under the mounting stress and the always-present unhappiness, Doris, Russell's wife of thirty-five years fell ill, and the severe lack of disposable income left tensions running sky high in the Tetler household.

"Piss poor timing," Russell snarled at his wife, who remained crouched on the sofa, bundled in a thick homemade quilt, running a temperature of 102.3.

Of all the time for her to get sick...

From the couch, Doris peeled off her bathrobe, flapping the front of her pajama shirt to cool her off. Two large sweat patch

TIGHT ROPE

stains underneath her armpits were visible from across the room. Russell could only sneer.

The house they cohabitated brought little solace to the suffering, lonely couple, existing within the walls of a time bomb. A cascade of memories of their George lined most of the hallway walls like loyal sentries. Each framed remembrance lead upstairs to the second floor of the family's modest circa 1950s Cape Cod. A montage of photos from infancy, elementary school, junior high and high school were fixed in their proper place, and permanently on display. Another collection of sports team memorabilia revealed young fresh faces. Proud, happy teammates stood shoulder to shoulder or on bended knees. Each child dutifully coordinated in matching school colors, all with cheerful smiling faces, innocently cheesing it up for the camera. Not a care in the world, or so it appeared.

On the landing, another grouping of photos hung. Elegant prom photos saddled next to cap and gown graduation pictures all prestigiously framed. George's high school diploma set proudly in the only expensive, professionally framed piece on the wall.

Lastly, a prominent photo of George decked out in full military attire—Russell's favorite. However, lurking behind the proud yet serious baby face lay the ominous trepidation of the pending unknown, looming thousands of miles away; the uncertainty of being sent to a foreign war-torn land filled with people from various backgrounds, customs, and languages, amassed together bearing their share of weighty battle fatigue, indistinguishable from friend or foe.

In the living room on the wooden coffee table rested a framed, glass-topped triangle box containing the same American flag used to drape over George's coffin. "An honorable keepsake," they'd explained, meticulously folded thirteen times by the honor guard before finally being presented in appreciation to the grieving parents. Each fold representing a significant purpose and meaning: symbolic of life and eternal life, in honor and remembrance, for giving in the ultimate defense of the country, and a tribute representing the bravery of the hearts which pledged allegiance to the United States of America, to the Republic, and In God We Trust. A final preserved token to honor the traditions and dedication of the nation's fallen soldiers.

Since the day of the funeral the meticulously framed flag had never been moved from the table, forever linked to the stifling grief hanging heavy in the air, as much a fixture to the memory of George as the aging collection of photographs adorning the miserable, loveless walls.

**

Russell cautiously sipped his coffee. Doris had a bad habit of brewing it a bit stronger than he preferred, but today he didn't much care. Today his mind was on other, more important details. This was the day his mission began in earnest, the day he'd plotted and planned for. The day his revenge finally found a home. Doris's strong brew hit the spot. Exactly what he needed to keep him on his toes and alert, and no matter what else transpired or got in his way, he'd need to stay sharp for his plan to work.

Before taking the train into Manhattan, Russell needed to swing by the pharmacy to pick up Doris's refill first. Lately her symptoms had worsened. The doctor agreed to up the dosage, but unfortunately, along with the relief came the unwanted side effects, which were equally as cumbersome. The original lower dosage

TIGHT ROPE

made her fall asleep a lot, unable to take care of the house, but the alternative was worse. The increased pain made Doris meaner and edgier, and harder for Russell to contend with. At least with the higher dose she wouldn't be as combative.

It wasn't as if her grumblings had gone unnoticed. The constant cursing from under her breath, the smirks or nose scrunches...Russell chose to ignore all of it. Staying sequestered in his office during most of the day helped put a healthy bit of distance between them. Lately, however, even this small measure of reprieve wasn't enough to keep Doris's mounting antagonism at bay.

Of all days, Clifford's Pharmacy seemed unusually packed. Behind the counter a new face appeared. Russell stretched his neck to search for Barry, the owner.

"May I help you, sir?" said the man with his head wrapped in a Sikh turban.

"Where's Barry?" inquired Russell, in clipped annoyance.

"He's in the back-filling scripts. I can help you," the man offered, still smiling.

Russell sucked in his breath and stared at the man. "Get Barry. I only deal with Barry."

"Yes, but I am also a pharmacist and—"

With his voice sounding pinched, Russell tried clearing his throat. "I don't care what or who you are, I only deal with Barry."

A few heads in the store turned towards the commotion. From the back room, a short, stocky, no-nonsense man emerged.

"What's the problem?" demanded Barry, unconsciously rubbing his knuckles over his scratchy, stubble jaw.

"He only wants to deal with you," explained the man. "I'll finish up in the back."

The two men had known one another for years. Russell always came to Barry's store, and for the most part, all their interactions were amiable enough, until today. "Russell…what's the problem?"

"Doris needs a refill. The doctor called it in. He's upped the dosage."

"And?"

"And what?" Russell appeared confused.

"So why didn't you tell this to my new assistant? He could have helped you."

Russell's temper flared. "If you want those kinds in your store, that's your problem, but I don't do business with terrorists."

"What the hell are you talking about now? Sonu isn't some goddamn terrorist!"

"You never know, Barry. You can't take your chances. Trust me, them Moslems will smile in your face and then stab you in the back the first chance they get."

Barry rolled his eyes and let out a disgusted gulp of air. "First of all, Sonu isn't Muslim, you old fool, he's a Sikh."

"A what?"

"A SIKH!" Barry saw Russell's face and gave up. "Ah, forget it. Give me Doris's script! I'll see if she's clear for a refill. Wait here."

A few moments passed when Barry returned with a disconcerted expression on his face. He motioned Russell over to a more private place to talk. "Listen, ah, your insurance was declined."

"That's impossible."

"I checked twice."

"Even the Medicaid?"

TIGHT ROPE

"No, that was fine, but your co-pay is higher."

"How much higher are we talking about?"

Barry showed Russell the amount on the piece of paper in his hand.

"For the same medication?" Blurted Russell, incensed.

"Afraid so."

A small line of customers began forming behind Russell.

"SONU!" Barry yelled. "Can you come to the front and take care of these people?"

Sonu walked out from the back storeroom and did as requested, ignoring Russell's glare. "I can take the next person."

"Listen," instructed Barry in a whisper. "You and me, we go back years, right? And with you out of work and all, I know things are tight right now, so I'll fill your script and renew the pain medication. Forget the co-pay this round."

Being a proud man, this charity didn't sit well with Russell. "Thanks, but I got it. Here," Russell handed Barry his bank debit card.

"It's no problem."

"No. Here."

"Are you sure?"

"Yeah, yeah, I'm sure," answered Russell gruffly. "Take it."

"Okay then." Barry threw his hands in the air in an "I give up" gesture. "Give me about fifteen to twenty minutes and I'll have it ready for you."

"I'll come back later to pick it up. I got somewhere else to be right now."

"Around what time? Only asking because we close at seven tonight."

"I'll be back about six-six-thirty."

"Yup. That works for me. See you later."

Russell left, his temper simmering, and only now more determined than ever to finish what he'd started. He had it in his power to make everyone's life go back to the way it used to be. To a better America, a greater America ... when life wasn't as confusing as it is today with everybody and their mother calling the shots.

CHAPTER 10

Nour Ibrahim

"NOUR? IS THAT YOU?"

"Only me, Mom."

"*AsSalaamu'alaikum*. I didn't hear you come in." She sat in the kitchen, swathed in her bathrobe, unwilling to sleep until her daughter arrived safely back home. "How was your day?" Her tone of voice indicated how much she didn't appreciate the late hour or her daughter's strained, pallid face.

Nour hadn't shared with either of her parents Dr. Khan's concerns. No use upsetting them until they knew for sure there was something to be upset about. Besides, her parents were already a bundle of nerves.

"*Wa'alaikum Salaam*. Sorry, I didn't mean to wake you. I had to work late."

"THIS late?"

"I lost track of time."

"You had me worried," said her mother, stricken.

"I know…I'm sorry." Nour kissed her mother's forehead. "I should have called, but I didn't want to wake you up."

"You think I can sleep not knowing where my child is all hours of the night?"

Nour smirked. "It's only nine-thirty."

"Still, I don't like you out at night alone. Too many crazy people…who knows what they'll pull these days."

Verbal and physical assaults against Muslims were on the rise, especially towards women in hijab. Mrs. Ibrahim had a right to be nervous. One woman had been kicked down subway stairs while another had been set on fire.

"Listen hon, don't get me wrong. Your father and I are proud of what you are doing, but we're worried for your safety. You've become a public figure; people know your face and this can put you in harm's way."

"I know—"

"Oh, do you? Because from where I'm sitting, you prance around like you don't have a care in the world. Like you're invincible or something, and we both know you're not!"

Nour couldn't fault her mother for having fears. Had she known about the hate mail filling countless folders back at the office, she'd have really lost her mind. "I'm being careful, but I refuse to back off. You and Dad of all people should understand."

"Don't twist what I am saying."

"Who's twisting?"

"You don't have to stop. Just take a break for a while."

"Can we not have this discussion right now?"

"Maybe until things calm down."

"Calm down? Seriously? Like that's going to ever happen."

"Nour!"

TIGHT ROPE

"I'm sorry, but you and Dad can't actually expect me to quit now, not this close to the rally. There's no putting that genie back in the bottle."

"That may be so, but remember, unlike the genie, you have no bottle. Some of these crazy people wouldn't think twice about hurting you."

As her mother spoke, Shadow's email flashed in her mind. Her mother wasn't far off. "No worries, *Umi. Insha'Allah*, I'll be fine."

Nour's father entered the kitchen, obviously pissed off. "*AsSalaamu'akaikum*. You're late."

"I already apologized to Mom."

"From now on, call your mother and let her know you're okay. Got it?"

Nour conceded, too tired to argue again.

"Stop being so damn inconsiderate. Your mother worries."

"I know. I'm sorry."

Mr. Ibrahim massaged the back of his wife's shoulders, feeling her tension through his fingertips. "A package came for you earlier," he indicated to Nour. "I put it on your bed."

Nour squinted. She couldn't recall ordering anything online.

Her father caught the look. "Bring it to me. I'll open it."

"Wait, now I remember. Probably the phone charger I ordered. Lost mine the other day."

Her parents stared at her, silently weighing out their response. "Your charger is in the living room, on the table," replied her mother curtly.

"Seriously? Oh, man, figures. Oh, well, now I have two." Nour made a show out of yawning. "Okay, well, I'm gonna jump in the shower, pray, and hit the sack. I have a long day tomorrow and

I'm past exhausted."

"But you haven't eaten." Mrs. Ibrahim went to stand. "Here, let me get your plate."

"Ah, you know what? I'll take it with me for lunch tomorrow, I promise. I'm too tired to eat right now."

Before her parents had a chance to respond, Nour scooted down the hall straight to her bedroom. "I'll see you in the morning." Closing the door only a crack, she faintly overheard the muffled sounds of her parents conversing.

"She's lying to us."

"I know that," agreed Mr. Ibrahim.

"Well? What are we going to do about it?" said Mrs. Ibrahim, terrified.

After her shower, Nour softly shut her bedroom door and locked it, then flipped the switch flooding her bedroom in light. On her bed sat the small brown paper box, her name boldly typed on the front with an obviously fake return address.

Dread spread through her as she cautiously picked it up. Shaking it slightly, she heard nothing but a faint muffled sound. Indistinguishable. Knowing she should keep the box closed and phone the police did little to stop her morbid curiosity. Peeling back the tape, she pulled it apart. Inside there was a note and a small box wrapped in red tissue paper. Slowly she unwrapped the box. Lifting the lid, she gasped, tossing the box and its contents on the floor.

Gripping her belly, she slid helplessly to the floor, crumbling to her knees, weeping noiselessly into the palms of her hands. From underneath, the chair leg where the bullet rolled, she read her name taped on the casing, written in tiny red marker.

"There's more where this came from," read the ominous

TIGHT ROPE

typed message.

Nour slid the paper into her robe pocket. As she bent over to retrieve the bullet which had rolled under the dresser, she swayed, unsteady.

I need to make prayer. Barely able to stand without shaking, she lifted her trembling arms to begin her prayer. Her knees knocked uncontrollably beneath her robe. Powerless to make it stop, she slid to the floor, terrified, and fully aware this sick cycle would only begin again tomorrow.

**

By the time morning rolled around, the fear of the night before had somewhat dissipated. Like so many before her, Nour had learned long ago to compartmentalize panic, pain, and anguish. *Fear cannot be allowed to control me.*

Boxing the latest "gift" from Shadow, she slid it as far underneath her bed and out of sight as possible. While her parents tended not to snoop—she was an adult after all—deliberately leaving it in plain sight was a sure-fire way to upset them, especially her already nervous mother.

As promised, Nour grabbed her dinner, *now lunch*, from the fridge. On the way to work, she'd stop at the corner deli and grab a coffee, and perhaps a buttered roll. Then again, the uncomfortable rumblings in her stomach reminded her how food wasn't necessarily welcomed, so perhaps just the roll instead of the coffee would suffice.

The past few weeks had been extraordinarily tough. Juggling work and organizing the event left Nour aggravated and burning the candle at both ends. No assistant meant everything on her To-

Do list remained firmly planted on her shoulders. As a result, many emails were answered behind schedule or were simply left unanswered. Crunched for time, appointments became overbooked, double-booked, or forgotten, and running late became the norm. Nour knew she couldn't continue at this pace for long before something gave and so far, it seemed as if her health, on the verge of collapse, ranked top of that list. Nevertheless, her commitment to see the rally through never wavered, except occasionally when terror invaded her heart. To all others, she appeared a staunch and shining example of one always steadfast and consistent, ready to plow ahead at all costs.

Most of the nervousness and anxiety naturally got chalked up to Shadow and his many attempts to scare her away, which were all having their intended effect.

Nour's boss, Sherri Findley entered the lobby elevator.

"Morning, Nour. Glad I bumped into you. I had planned on giving you a call later anyway." Normally the two women were about the same height, but today, Sherri wore a pair of killer stilettos that had her towering over Nour by a solid two inches.

"Morning. What's up?"

"I'd rather we talk in private. I need to go over some issues with you. Say around eleven? My office?"

"Sounds good." *This is all I need.*

From the start, Nour and Sherri's relationship had been adversarial, which was essentially the only possible kind of relationship to have when dealing with a passive-aggressive bitch who believed in her cold, icy heart that everyone wanted her job.

"Great. See you then." Sherri stuck her pointer finger in the air. "Oh, and make sure you bring the Anderson file with you. I'd like to be briefed."

TIGHT ROPE

Nour confirmed she would, and then both women disembarked on the fifth floor, heading in opposite directions.

Once safely inside the confines of her office Nour headed straight to the computer. *What emails will you have for me today, you sick, disturbed bastard?*

While the computer booted, she hung up her sweater and headed to the staff kitchen to put her lunch in the communal fridge. Running late, she hadn't had time to stop at the deli so a cup of overpriced office swill would have to do until break time. As she strode past the mail cart she heard her name called.

"Hold up, Nour, I have something for you."

Shit. "Sure, Reggie."

Reggie's thick calloused fingers flipped through the large stack of yellow envelopes. "Yup, got it. Here it is."

Nour grabbed the large envelope, heart racing. "Thanks."

"No problem. Have a good one."

Mind reeling, Nour hightailed it straight back to her office, forgetting about the coffee, and practically slamming the door shut behind her. Anxious to open up the latest delivery, she roughly tore through the seal, letting out an audible sigh of relief as she realized it contained only the templates for the brochures she'd designed for the upcoming event. With relief, she dropped everything on the desk, plopped her butt into her chair, and leaned back to close her eyes.

Ya Allah, this has got to stop. I don't think I can take this much longer.

Minutes went by before Nour sat up straighter, taking in deep cleansing breaths to alleviate her mental fatigue and better ready herself to face the day. Computer fully booted up, she tapped the key for email.

And there it was.

SAHAR ABDULAZIZ

Good Morning Black Bitch.

How'd you like my little gift? I know, I know…you're tongue-tied for words. But don't you worry, even though our little party is coming to a close, I'm sure it will end with a big bang!

Damn him.

Unwilling to be sucked into another round of tears and runaway fears, Nour blocked out the threat. She printed out the message and plopped the copy into the designated folder, forcing her mind to concentrate on her workload before she found herself out of a job. *Who knows what Sherri's discussion is about?*

During trying times like these, Nour wished her dear friend, Rabia lived closer. She could use a trusted shoulder to cry on. The two had been best friends since grade school. For over twelve years, they had done everything together, forming what they thought would be a lasting bond of sisterhood. Their friendship nourished them both through many awkward phases of adolescence. Sharing tears, successes and failures, and always at the other's side, they stuck together through thick and thin, trouble included. Crime partners to the bitter end…or so they'd said.

Then Rabia met Hashim and everything changed abruptly. While Rabia's new relationship grew romantic, and eventually culminated in marriage, her friendship with Nour took a back seat.

Now, two kids later, and another one shortly on the way, the opportunity to get together as women, as old friends, and as sisters no longer existed.

Nour contemplated picking up the phone, but then stopped. This was a ritual she'd visited before when desperate to hear Rabia's soothing, steady voice. In the past, her gentle demeanor had provided a calming effect on her, enough to help her sift through the emotions blocking her from finding solutions. Now, it seemed rather cruel that all the closeness they once shared, while technically only a phone call away, felt more like a million miles apart.

A light tapping at the office door interrupted Nour's thoughts. The knob slowly turned and the door cracked open. "Sorry to bother you," said Fran, the office receptionist, "but I bumped into Sherri. She asked me to see if you can meet now rather than later? Said to tell you she forgot about some meeting she had to go to...or something to that effect."

"Sure, I can manage it. Give me five minutes." *Why hadn't Sherri buzzed or texted me directly?* Nour didn't like the feel of this.

"Okay, cool. I'll let her know."

Nour gathered up the case folder and information Sherri requested earlier, but before leaving, she made sure to close her email.

Let's get this over with.

CHAPTER 11

THE CRAZINESS OF THE TETLER HOME

Doris

NOT LONG AFTER GEORGE'S death, Russell converted a small room in the back of the house into his office. No bigger than most modern walk-in closets, but it was enough. Sparse walls boasted a chalky light blue color, and for privacy, instead of hanging curtains over the one boxy window directly opposite to their neighbor's bathroom, Russell decided to use a set of stock blinds. Most of the time, however, to block out noises emanating from next door he kept the windows securely shut, even on the hottest of days. Regrettably for him, cheerful annoying sounds snuck through anyway: sweet giggles of young children playing in the tub or the faint luxurious groans of young parents stealing a private corporeal tryst. Any form of happiness set Russell's nerve-endings into a turmoil.

Since the dull little room barely filtered in any substantial light, Russell came up with a cheap remedy: wedging a freestanding floor lamp in the corner of the already cramped room. Ugly as sin, but a flea market find. On the tattered desk rested an old computer, a dinosaur of sorts. One of the earlier desktop models, which by today's standards didn't fare nearly as well as today's more advanced laptops, but more than sufficed in meeting Russell's meager requirements. As long as he could surf the net, read up on non-mainstream news media conspiracy sites, and send his daily hate mail, he was all set.

Doris devoted most of her free time to watching murder mysteries on their one aging television, one episode after the other. Different faces, changed stories, but murder and senseless death nonetheless. However, she only got to indulge when she wasn't fighting her husband for control over the remote. During those times, she'd busy herself in other parts of the house so as not to be available during one of his many irascible tirades.

Unlike Russell, Doris claimed no space in the house as her own except for the couch. Occasionally, she'd lie on George's bed to nap, nestling her head on a pillow which had lost her child's treasured scent long ago.

When she wasn't off napping or indulging in homicidal television, she plotted. At first, nothing earth shattering. Just small ways to needle Russell enough to make him leave her alone. Slowly, and most recently, she'd advanced to more devious methods of irking his last unhinged nerves.

Surprisingly, despite how secretive Russell behaved around her, specifically about his office, she never felt the urge to pry. He considered it his so-called exclusive domain, his 'man-cave.' From time to time she did let her curiosity coax her to *ever so slightly* move one of his belongings on or near his desk. Just a smidge, but enough to screw with his head.

Initially, Doris only messed with his coffee cup. Then, when this no longer entertained, she graduated to bolder affronts, like leaving a drawer slightly ajar or pulling out his chair, and turning the seat cushion to face away from his desk. Once she boldly opened up the small window but only a crack, knowing how the rush of cool air would irritate him.

Russell, a creature of habit, knew Doris snooped and rifled through his stuff, but ironically enough, never confronted her about it. Instead, he'd ignore her obviously ridiculous attempts to annoy him as if what she did didn't matter…as if she didn't matter. And maybe, in truth, she didn't.

Although Doris played with fire, her days of caring were gone. No longer using her energy to pretend she cared, and refusing to let Russell get the better of her. Long silent days, longer lonely nights. The days of common courtesy and open dialogue between the two cantankerous partners were long past. Their marriage existed out of pure necessity, neither one able to afford to live without the other. So, they did what many others do—coexisted. Two unhappily married lodgers cohabitating under the weight of unthinkable sadness, alongside their fading memories, lost aspirations, and intrusive but vividly haunting nightmares.

As bitterness took over and her inability to distinguish reality from fantasy set in, Doris spent inordinate amounts of time daydreaming, plotting, and preparing. All those countless hours of mind-numbing television watching about murders and death fueled her morbid imagination. *Maybe I'll stab him in the throat with my knife and watch him choke to death. Then again, maybe I'll run him a nice, hot bath, and then drop a plugged-in blow dryer in so I can watch his ass fry right up. Or, I could wait for the perfect time and give him one last hard shove down the stairs. Gosh, I'd love to watch his fat head whack each step as he plummets*

TIGHT ROPE

to his death.

Or perhaps, and this is a big perhaps, I can pray hard enough to the man upstairs that one day all of Russell's meanness catches up to him and causes him to self-combust and disintegrate like fairy dust. Now wouldn't THAT be something! All kinds of nasty diabolical goodies spun around in that tiny deranged head, egging her on while bringing her hope for a better tomorrow. But more than anything else in the world, she wanted to do him in. Knock him for a permanent and everlasting loop, and send him scurrying on his way to meet his fate, preferably six-feet below ground.

It was all Russell's fault my George is dead. If he hadn't been so insistent about encouraging our only child to run off and join the military, we coulda been two proud parents attending a college graduation.

But now, thanks to Russell, that dream and a host of others would never happen. Doris had nothing to hold in her hands but a perfectly folded flag enclosed in a triangle wood-glass box, and a bunch of dusty old photographs hanging in perpetuity ... a collection of unwelcome keepsakes and forever an agonizing reminder of her devastating loss.

SAHAR ABDULAZIZ

Russell

RUSSELL SITUATED HIMSELF BEHIND THE aged, sturdy desk, pulling his cushioned chair in as he waited patiently for his outdated desktop computer to boot up, but he didn't mind the delay or the slower connection. The time offered him the space to collect his thoughts before setting off to compose his next message. Besides, what's the rush? There were no longer any pressing engagements unless he made them, and forced retirement had become one long and empty succession of dreary days, one melding into the next.

Initially, when Russell first set up his tiny office space, he thought nothing of leaving his computer on sleep mode, but soon enough he began suspecting Doris of sneaking in and mucking about, so off went the computer after each use. Password protected, using a word certainly nobody, *especially Doris*, would have ever guessed either.

Computer booted up and ready, Russell's first task meant checking his email. He hoped one day Fat Mouth would have the nerve to write him back, but so far it hadn't happened, no matter how many times he contacted her.

Shit. Nothing but spam. The list was endless: "Quickest way to cure erectile dysfunction." "Let us help pay off your college loans." "How about a $20 Credit waiting just for you!" "Never pay for home repairs again!" "Contact us for your home warranty before it's too late!" But the one that wounded the most: "Here's a perfect gift for Dad this Father's Day."

Hmm, what kind of image should I attach to the next email? Something powerful to make my point, give her a scare. Maybe a cartoon? Nah... Clicking away on a variety of photos, time began to slip away.

TIGHT ROPE

Minutes turned into hours. Russell couldn't help it when his mind took on a life of its own, drifting from places he'd rather not revisit, faces he'd thought he'd said goodbye to long ago. *Focus, God-damn-it.*

And then an idea popped into his head. In the search engine, he typed the word, CEMETERY, all in unnecessary capital letters. A succession of photos of gravestones, mausoleums, and memorials appeared on his screen. Upon closer inspection, Russell distinguished familiar cemetery names, but as always, only ever clicked on the name most important to him, the place where his heart forever remained interned.

Subconsciously, Russell clicked on the photo showing a regimented line of headstones decorated with small American Flags, each one neatly plunked deep into the grassy earth. Russell recalled those blurred, painful days before George's funeral. All the decisions that needed to be discussed, the conversations held in hushed, respectful tones. The listing of rules and regulations to be met so as to ensure a properly prepared burial, no mistakes or glitches tolerated.

He'd committed to memory how he and Doris were gently, yet painstakingly guided through each phase, every step precisely implemented. While the Department of Veteran Affairs took responsibility for maintaining over a hundred national cemeteries, not to mention soldiers' lots and monuments, this mourning couple opted for a national cemetery out on Long Island. A bit of a distance from the city, but certainly close enough to visit by car.

On the day of the funeral, Doris left a small wreath, a unique collection of George's favorite flowers, but then they were informed that no permanent plantings would be allowed.

"No vigil lights, statues or any breakable adornments are

permitted on the grave," instructed their guide.

Without delay, once the service finished, the waiting workers systematically filled the plot from the heap of awaiting earth, conscientiously leveling off the mound with each sweep of new covering.

On the way home, Doris, glassy-eyed and silent, hugged the triangular folded flag tightly to her bosom.

"Are you hungry?" asked Russell, glancing over at his wife. She hadn't spoken a word to him in days.

"We could stop for a bite to eat at that diner you like." Russell tried eliciting a response. "Even if you have soup or something light. You need to eat."

Doris remained silent, clutching the flag close to her heart. Her eyes appeared dull and blank, staring ahead at nothing in particular, while drowning out Russell's incessant blathering.

Little did Russell appreciate how much he annoyed the woman sitting next to him, how she loathed him. How she wished she could have climbed inside the coffin and laid her body protectively next to George's, willing with all her strength for the fresh turned earth to swallow them up together and for eternity.

**

The sunlight outside the stuffy room had turned cloudy, but the blinds revealed nothing as Russell, persistent on his quest, took no notice. "Ah, there we go. Now here's what I'm talking about," Russell mumbled to himself. "That'll do just fine, yes indeed. Just fine." Russell proceeded to copy and paste the grotesque image into an awaiting email as a file attachment. Once ready, he began composing his morning missive.

TIGHT ROPE

Dear Annoying Black Bitch ... Miss me?

**

Hours later, Russell stood across the street, leaning casually into the shadows as he watched and waited. It had been a long, damp, rainy day and his old body had begun protesting hours before, especially his feet, but nothing would drag him away from this long-awaited moment. Silently, he chewed a tasteless piece of gum, the sixth piece of the evening. His restless mind conjured up all kinds of juicy scenarios about what could possibly be unfolding behind closed doors diagonally from where he hid. He speculated about how long it would be before all the players joined in the fun once Fat Mouth arrived home and found his gift. He hoped and prayed this boxed threat would cause her to tremble in fear.

Uncovering her home address had been simple. In this day and age of global information, a couple of searches revealed a plethora of information. For posterity, Russell did a search on his and Doris's names as well, but only a single entry came up: The news clipping from George's Obituary.

Admittedly, following Fat Mouth from her place of employment had been tedious, but in the end, mailing the package undetected had taken more forethought. Ironically, Doris's incessant police and murder shows had finally paid off as Russell remembered not to leave any fingerprints. At this juncture, a police presence would be a serious hindrance, but in the end, with or without them, Russell remained determined to follow through on his promises.

All the same, something inside told him not to spend too much time worrying about detection. Firstly, he suspected Fat

Mouth wouldn't go as far as to call the police. Not yet anyway. Secondly, there was nothing linking the emails or the package to him, or so he naively thought. Most importantly, he only needed a few more days before discovery became a non-issue.

But most people, despite the rise in technology and global communications, astonishingly didn't understand how relatively simple a process it is to trace an email. Once police got hold of one of Russell's emails they'd find its header. Then copy the header and paste it into a program specifically designed for tracing emails, and press the prompt, "Get Source." Every sender's Internet Protocol is associated with their computers. The address would appear and Russell's IP address would be obtainable.

After the recent tit-for-tat at the hamburger joint with the young Indian punk, Russell's frame of mind soured immensely, but now, with the package safely delivered, he felt rather accomplished and in the mood to celebrate.

Upon returning home, Russell suspected he'd find Doris out cold and sound asleep in front of a still blaring television. Her usual. But after a long day he wisely opted to honor his tired old limbs and call it a day, and as much as he despised going home to her, he didn't much like being out after dark in the city. The crime rate in the city was terrible.

**

Russell awoke, mind heavy and dazed. He'd slept hard, harder than he had in quite some time. The events from the previous evening no more than a distant, pleasant memory, now replaced with a blissful nothingness. For years, most nights inspired chilling nightmares, goaded by the same terrifying dream sequence, if one

TIGHT ROPE

could even call it that. He'd find himself night after night, stumbling blindly through the same long, cavernous, metal tunnel, each footstep echoing off the walls. Anxiously he'd call out his child's name, frantic when no answer was returned. Downward he'd plunge, but as he closed in, the pinpoint beam of light shining from the far end dragged him forward, taunting him closer with a draw so strong, pleading with him in a familiar voice.

"Daddy!" In the near distance, Russell hears his child writhe in pain. "Help me."

"George?" Russell barely stammers through his sleep induced garbled voice, "I'm coming, baby. Hold on. Daddy's coming."

Faster he runs. His sweat-drenched body thrashing under the bed covers, arms flailing violently from side to side as he tries to reach into the tunneled darkness to snatch his whimpering child and bring her to safety.

"I'm coming, George."

But as Russell reaches the end of the narrowing tunnel, the light launches another penetrating beam directly into his eyes. Blinded, he feebly wrestles to break through the penetrating rays, but soon the same light emerges, this time forming into a foggy mist-filled image. As the apparition moves closer, Russell furtively strains to make out the form. The shape mimics a human form, but the limbs bizarrely thrash about, hovering over him unattached. Without warning, a final enormous blast of light, the color of fire, erupts, blowing the apparition-like body apart. The entire tunnel combusts as hot waves of vapor burst into one final massive blazing flame, igniting the terror-filled voices screaming in his head.

"NOOOOOOOOOO," Russell wails, his breathing coming in labored spurts, releasing a desperate cry, which pierces the night. But the nightmares never change, and the outcome remains the same. His beloved child is dead.

The peaceful silence of this unusual morning nourished Russell's need for slumber.

**

At one time Russell's bitterness left him empty and without direction, but now the delicious taste of revenge fueled his desire to live long enough to see his plan through. His way of righting the wrongs which for far too long had recklessly tore through his heart, now suddenly appeared close and attainable. He could taste the stench of victory, which in his eyes would finally avenge his George's heroic death. No longer would the invasion of memories be regulated to one of thousands of headstones, lined in perfect precision on fields of tailored meadow grass. No, soon all clouded memories would be released into the continuum, free, until finally closing his eyes for good.

**

By the time, Russell dressed and made his way downstairs, he could already hear the television set to some silly talk show. Doris barely paid attention to what was on the screen, but she seemed to gravitate to the sound as a comfort, much like he did when sitting in front of his computer screen. However, the more she craved empty noise, the more solace he preferred.

Last night went off without a hitch, exactly as planned. If his luck continued, he'd have Fat Mouth wound up so tight she wouldn't know where to look or what to do next. Knowing he'd obtained both a work and home address, he assumed she'd be more cautious, but the question remained—would she contact the police? So far, he hadn't seen anyone walking with her, but this could be a ruse or a trap, lulling him into a state of complacency.

Something to keep an eye out for.

Ah! He'd forgotten! In a small bag in his jacket, he retrieved the prescriptions, leaving the contents on the kitchen counter where Doris could find them. In the past, Russell, worried about his wife's mental state, taking only the prescribed amounts of medication at the proper time, but eventually he had to accept that there was nothing he could do to prevent her from hurting herself if she made up her mind to do so.

For whatever her reason, Doris refused to take the medication if he handed it directly to her. After a while, he stopped trying. Russell wasn't sure why, exactly. He'd asked her on many occasions, but she'd simply stare through him, ignoring the caplets in his extended hand. Then she'd pour out into her palm what she required directly from the bottle…all without uttering a single, solitary word.

Closing the door, Russell situated himself behind his computer, constructing in his mind what would be his next move.

Maybe I should write her another email? Or maybe I should lay low for a while—make her think I disappeared or gave up, concentrate on my plans instead. Get the timing right. Make sure I know where to stand.

Russell thought back to when the package arrived at her house. Watched as a tall man in his late forties, maybe early fifties answered the door. Russell assumed him to be her father. This alone was cause to celebrate. The Bitch had a father, someone to mourn her death like he had with his George. Someone who will also find himself waking up in the middle of the night, body rigid, and stiff from the cold, lonely sweats, screaming out his child's name, while forced to fumble aimlessly through the remainder of his miserable excuse for a life.

Plans it is! He decided euphorically.

Months before the start of his retaliation campaign, Russell had managed to organize all of his legal paperwork: pension, life insurance, and bank information, all compiled into one large file. Now that his plan had become real, he felt obligated to ensure Doris would be taken care of financially when the need arose. This, of course, would never make amends for the loss, but perhaps it would ease her pain, the pain he knew she blamed him for.

When the time came, Russell decided to leave the folder in plain sight in George's room. He was worried Doris would fritter away the little he'd left, but then again, he'd be dead and never know.

He started a new To-Do list.

CHAPTER 12

Zaid Ali

MR. ALI REQUIRED REHABILITATION THREE times a week. Zaid's mother agreed to watch the store while Zaid escorted him over, waited until he was finished, and then walked him back home. "Making sure your father gets home safe and sound and in one piece," his mother reminded him.

At first, his father naturally put up a big fuss about being escorted, but eventually gave in under his wife's threat of starvation.

"*Wallahi*—I won't cook another meal for you unless you let one of us be there with you."

"It's your wifely duty to cook for me."

Mrs. Ali wouldn't take the bait and duly ignored her husband's childish taunts. "Sit down so I can help you put your shoes on. You're going with your son."

"I'm not a baby. I can take myself."

"And what if you fall or something? Who will know? No,

Zaid will be there for you."

"You can take me."

"You think I can pick you up if you fall on your face? All five-feet of me? Sorry *habibi*, but your son is taking you and that's final."

Mr. Ali smirked, marveling at the powerhouse of a woman he'd married, but he was smart enough to know when to stop stoking her impatience.

Uncomfortable about leaving his mother to tend the store on her own, Zaid protested, but in the end, like his father, he had no choice. Someone had to stay with the old man, but still. While fidgeting in the waiting room chair, trying to find a comfortable position, his eyes scanned the small table covered in women and health magazines, medical coupons, and pamphlets. Surprisingly, a stack of brochures about the military were also on display.

Strange. Why would these be here? Nevertheless, bored out of his mind, Zaid reached over and grabbed one. After the last argument with his father, he wasn't keen on getting caught reading, but curiosity won out.

"Be All You Can Be," huh? On the cover, smiling faces from a wide hue of complexions, all dressed proudly in pristine uniforms. The pamphlet packed a load of information into a small space in a font meant to be easy on the eyes. The glossy read showed how a career in the military offered hope, a future, and adventure for those with the patriotic balls to try.

Zaid stole a glance at his father, relaxing on the raised cot having his shoulder iced, the last step before rehabilitation ended for the day. Doctors had instructed his father to ice it three times a day at home, but getting him to follow-through consistently meant another argument nobody was willing to endure.

Zaid continued reading.

TIGHT ROPE

I could do this–if I qualify. Zaid glimpsed his father, still lying on his side. *If I signed up, Baba would flip the heck out. Lose his mind. Then again, it's my life. I can do what I want.*

Engrossed in reading, Zaid jumped up practically knocking his father over when Mr. Ali tapped Zaid on the shoulder to go. Startled, with guilt plastered all over his face, Zaid quickly palmed the brochure, carefully hiding its contents from view. His dad now stared at him like he'd lost all his marbles.

"All done, Pops?"

Mr. Ali couldn't stand it when his son asked stupid and redundant questions. Blamed this bad habit on his Americanism. The entire country's population seemed hopelessly inclined to banter about anything these days, no matter how nonsensical. Oh, look everyone, see my yummy dessert on Instagram. See my delicious dinner on Facebook. And Zaid was no better, all too quick to play the comedian filling in any silent gaps between conversations with cluttered nonsensical chatter.

"Ready to go?"

See, another stupid question. Mr. Ali rolled his eyes, grumbled something rude, turned towards the exit door, and without uttering a response began walking away.

"Hold up, Baba! STOP! Hey, slow down. Would you wait for me for a minute?"

But Mr. Ali refused to stop and kept on going, wanting nothing more than to be back in his own home where he could rest and indulge his discomfort in private.

**

The old man would never admit how tired these daily

excursions left him. Soon enough, a soft, muffled snoring filled the room.

After successfully tucking his less than cooperative father into bed, Zaid headed back to the store, anxious to relieve his Mom. No telling if those bastards would come back and finish what they'd started.

When he arrived at the store, Zaid was pleasantly surprised to see his mother anything but alone. News of Mr. Ali's attack spread quickly throughout the neighborhood. Many shopkeepers and storeowners had gone out of their way to stop by as a sign of support as well as to commiserate. Many expressed with solemnity how recently they too had felt a dangerous change in the air, openly discussing for the first time how they too had begun to no longer feel entirely safe or welcomed. Longtime customers and familiar faces mulled about, chatting, some holding tins of foil covered dishes, flowers, or cards.

"What a day. I tell you!" whispered his mother animatedly into her son's ear. "You wouldn't believe how many of our neighbors and shop keepers are still coming in to wish us well." Coaxing him over with her finger, Mrs. Ali wanted her son to follow her to the back as she continued filling him in. "So, sweet. Offering support, some asked if we needed anything. At this rate, I won't have to cook for a month."

Zaid's face registered bewilderment.

"Such nice people, *habibi*! We are so blessed."

After all that had transpired recently, seeing his mother so relaxed was honestly a nice change. Between the hate being spewed against Muslims and by extension foreigners, she'd felt under a lot of pressure, sometimes wary to leave the confines of her home, terrified she might get mocked or assaulted for wearing the hijab.

TIGHT ROPE

And she wasn't alone.

As the contentious presidential inauguration date drew closer, the incidences of racial attacks increased exponentially, and while Mrs. Ali would never give in to the threats, she remained vigilant and guarded the second she stepped out of her home.

"You know, *habibi*, it's so nice to know there are such good, kind people still left in the world."

His mother, a natural beauty, radiated when she smiled. What a shame to be the one responsible for wiping it from her face once he dropped his news on her.

**

Joining the military hadn't exactly been a long-thought out process. More like a knee-jerk response. Zaid believed he needed to feel like he was doing his part as an American citizen to protect his family. At least this was the story he told himself.

On occasion, Zaid had gone out of his way to speak with a few of the military officers who frequented the store. Initially the conversations bordered on the inane. Then slowly, as he gained more courage, he started asking a pointed question here, making a comment there. Even exchanging on occasion a few jokes to see the kind of reception he got in return. Much to his surprise, instead of being made to feel foolish, the soldiers were ingratiating. Warmly welcoming his inquisitiveness, they answered him back in as much detail as they could between placing food and drink orders, and watching the clock to make sure they didn't run late.

Zaid observed their close-knit camaraderie, their playful banter, and the obvious concern they shared for one another. He admired the how they wore their uniforms with pride, or witnessing a customer coming up to one or two of the soldiers to extend their hands, thanking them profusely for their service and sacrifice. Not at all the way he'd been led to believe by his father who held an opinion about everything and everyone, equating his son's willingness to consider military service with "joining the enemy," which Zaid thought insanely ridiculous.

Zaid wondered what it felt like to be respected instead of feared, to be considered a hero as opposed to a terrorist. Nevertheless, so far, he hadn't made any attempt to speak with a recruiter.

**

Unfortunately, at the time of the robbery, the store's cameras weren't working and Mr. Ali could barely identify the three assailants except as "those bastards." With not much to go on, there was little chance in hell of "those bastards" getting caught and brought to justice any time soon.

But Zaid appreciated the community's support, he really did. Privately, he was dumbfounded that his less than affable father had been launched into the spotlight and incredulously heralded as some sort of wronged saint. "A community activist?" *Give me a break.* But most of all, Zaid felt heartened by the kindness and acts of generosity, especially coming from people they'd shared a common space with for years. If not before, they were most certainly friends now.

CHAPTER 13

Nour Ibrahim

I stand before you, not as a leader or a knower of all truths, but as a reminder to that which lies ahead if we do not unite and face the tyranny permitted in the name of the American people, to coexist and actively work against our visions for freedom and mutual respect.

NOUR STOPPED TYPING. OUTSIDE THE clouds grew a dark gray. With the heavy promised rain, a blustery wind whipped around the city's tall buildings, leaving the air chilly and damp. Inside the workplace, the staff came prepared, wearing sweaters or long sleeves. Until now, nobody had figured out how to properly regulate the temperature.

With the door firmly closed, Nour peeled off her sweater, fanning herself with a sheaf of computer paper. While everyone else shivered, she sweated. However, any moment now, the chill would return and she'd have to throw the sweater back on. The hot-cold yo-yo routine drove her nuts.

The big rally was only days away. She couldn't believe how time flew. Groups from all over the country were expected to attend in droves. A progression of out-of-state buses would fill every available parking space in the provided lot, while city metro lines would cater to those in closer proximity. Even if everything went according to plan, the event promised to be a mad house. And while excitement in the office escalated, the mixture of stress and exhilaration translated into short tempers, shorter fuses, occasional tears, and large-scale nail biting.

As of this morning, memos were sent around the office notifying speakers and organizations the police were anticipating trouble and ready to make a militarized appearance alongside the possibility of large-scale protests breaking out. This concerned Nour, who clearly understood how it would take only the slightest hint, provocation or murmur of disruption to cause an all-out and perhaps deadly police response, and nobody wanted that.

Essentially, the crux of the notice made the police position excruciatingly clear: demonstrators blocking traffic, throwing bottles or damaging police cars were promised to be in for the surprise of their life. The last rally produced a good number of people being pepper-sprayed, hit with rubber bullets, handcuffed and dragged to the station, turning what was supposed to be a peaceful rally into a real disaster.

Each of the four-featured speakers had fifteen minutes to deliver their speech, although Nour swore she could do it in ten. Back in high school, she had been an excellent debater, enjoying the challenge of facing off with an opponent, sometimes notably arguing on topics she didn't necessarily agree with. The art of discourse provided her with the ability to size up her competition, to never display fear, to keep her temper in check—especially when

TIGHT ROPE

intentionally baited— and to never allow herself to be lured in by the opposing team's knack to sway and counterattack. Most of all, debating taught her to always come prepared to fight, notes in hand, ready to slam down the knowledge. Her uncanny knack for cramming insurmountable amounts of facts the morning of a competition kept her winning and engaged.

Outside the storm poured rain by the bucket full, pelting the windows in a succession of loud pinging sounds so profuse, droplets the size of nickels slid down the outer glass. As a small child, Nour, unlike many of her friends, never feared storms. For her, the fierce pattering sound of rain or the sudden clash of thunder mesmerized her as only the power of a strong downpour could. When rainstorms hit at bedtime, she would rush off to her bedroom to be alone. Under her covers, nestled comfortably beneath a multitude of layers, she'd listen to the raindrops pelting the window or roof, reassured by the steady rhythm, and eventually lulled peacefully into a deep and curative sleep.

Today's storm couldn't have come at a better time. Nour rose from her desk. Crossing the room, she flipped off the overhead light. Since her office window used fixed blinds, she had to pull them entirely open to get the full effect. Once the stage was set, she parked herself back down in her chair, and swiveled around to fully face the storm's lashing. Eyes closed, her thoughts wandered back to when her biggest worry hinged on getting a class assignment done on time or studying for a pressing exam. Gradually, as her mind relaxed, her memories revisited that time back in high school, the day of the championship school debate.

"In closing," Nour fixed her posture, prompted by the Coach's glare darting directly at her from across the room. Coach was notorious for making a big deal about the way all his students presented themselves during a debate. Suit, long skirt or slacks, the whole nine yards. Nour lifted her chin and continued. "It is our contention that instead of throwing people into jails or prisons where they will not get the help they need, only to be released to return a short time later, and further tax the already over-taxed penal system, the main focus should be on rehabilitation in the form of clinical assistance. Such programs would be specifically designed and intended for those suffering from drug abuse, focusing on the needs of the individual as well as the needs of their family. We believe through proper education and advocacy, as well as an empathetic healing environment, the cost of incarcerating repeat drug offenders will lessen and markedly decrease the rate of recidivism."

"She'd know. I heard that's where her mother met her father," muttered one opponent seated to her left, just loud enough.

Shaken, Nour did her best to block out the snide remarks, always followed by the usual succession of low conspiratorial snickers, hurled at her by the other team.

Nour evoked her father's advice. "Stand up straight, shoulders back, eyes dry. No matter what, never let your enemies find your soft spot; once they do, they tunnel."

"Lastly," she continued speaking through gritted teeth, "we believe it is society's responsibility to stop stigmatizing the disease of addiction, and instead support programs geared to helping those afflicted to find healthier and lasting alternatives. Thank you."

Another student from Nour's team who had clearly heard the cutting snipes huddled into Nour's shoulder protectively, squeezing her hand under the table. Leaning in, she whispered, "Ignore those losers. They're just trying to throw you off your game. We're demolishing their asses and they know it."

TIGHT ROPE

Regardless of her teammate's kind reassurances, she had been so, so wrong. Those caustic disparagements hurled *only* at her were never about competition or any school rivalry, but intentionally launched to denigrate. To vilify. Aimed unswervingly towards Nour's soul as a cruel reminder that she was and will never be anything in their eyes.

Just then a booming clap of thunder jolted Nour wide-awake. "Ahh!" she yelped, her eyes flew open in a panic. Clasping her throat, she tried to calm down, reminding herself that she was safe and alone in her office. Yet, the truth was, when at her most vulnerable, her subconscious mind would often revisit her painful history. Experiences, one after the other, crammed with denigrating and spiteful comments. Many that had drilled home for her how easily and overtly she could be *othered* and publically belittled. How then, like today, the consequences paid for such behavior were often remiss if not absent altogether. On that particular day, it had taken all the strength Nour possessed not to reach over the table and choke the life out of that feckless snit and his friends, smirking so self-importantly in her face.

**

The vetting process to be selected as a featured presenter is surprisingly competitive. Already considered a seasoned speaker, Nour had made quite the name for herself hosting symposiums on race relations, inter-faith communications and conventions, not to mention the accumulation of her many published articles known to generate excitement and controversy equally. Over the recent past, she'd even made a few guest appearances on various political news stations, talking on panels with those holding strong opposing positions. None-the-less, when the preliminary request came through, she still felt quite surprised and honored.

Faced with a discouraging array of pressing social issues to pick from, not to mention one national crisis after the next, she spent the next hour narrowing down specific points she wished to convey. She planned to deliver a concise and hard-hitting speech. No fluff. The time to cater to politically correct mantras, grandstanding apologists or White sensibilities had long passed and fizzled, especially with the last onslaught of suspicious police killings.

Luckily the coordinating facilitator of the event graciously offered her a wide berth of topics to choose from. Everything from police brutality to addressing the dangers mounting from the nonsensical chants of the un-hooded hate groups in support of building walls, mass deportation, border control issues, the reinstituting of water boarding, and all other heinous torture tactics. Last, but most definitely not least, the open attacks on all People of Color, Muslims, Mexicans, women, etc.

These kinds of events, while designed to accommodate all the presenters, also limited the depth to which she could speak on any particular topic. Additionally, no matter what she said, there would be distractors. Negative comments. People who lived to criticize, anxiously waiting in the wings to rip her apart, and emboldened to take their complaints to social media to tweet, meme or analyze her perceived shortcomings, opening her up for ridicule and derision. Nour expected this, but it hurt, nonetheless.

Daunted by the sheer numbers expected to attend, she wished there were some way to turn back the hands of time, change her mind to back out. What had started out as a great idea quickly blossomed into her becoming a target for hate mongers. Now, her

TIGHT ROPE

life had become one gigantic complicated mess. An endless parade of trials and tribulations, one unkinder than the next. And no matter how hard she prepared, she still found herself coming up short, teetering on the edge of failure.

Nevertheless, that ship had sailed the day her name and photo were plastered on all the event's flyers and billboards. Accepting the fact she was in it to win it, the time had arrived to get serious about formulating ideas and talking points. *Write the speech from the heart,* she reminded herself repeatedly, with the focus on inserting information to resonate with the masses of like-minded, proactive folks willing to fight for change. Together, the speakers would stand on this world stage discussing various methods to combat the tireless fear mongering, the many travesties of justice, and highlight the legacy of a system based on systemic institutionalized racism. A broken system inexcusably permitted and encouraged by this nation for centuries to turn a blind eye.

**

The sound of keys in the front door lock indicated Nour had arrived home. Her parents *salaamed* her in unison, but the front door slamming drowned out their greetings. Nour mumbled, "*AsSalaamu'alaikum.*" Rushing to kick off her shoes, she passed the kitchen heading straight to her bedroom. After what happened in school, she didn't feel much like talking.

"Nour?" called out her mother concerned, ready to spring into action.

Nour drew in an exasperated breath, turned and went to the kitchen, clearly agitated.

"Yes?"

"We *salaamed* you."

"And I heard you," she answered curtly, obviously upset. "And *salaamed* you back."

"You mumbled is more like it," corrected Mrs. Ibrahim. "What's going on with you?"

"Nothing."

"Something is obviously upsetting you."

"I said it's nothing! Why can't you leave me alone for once?" Nour turned and ran off to her bedroom, slamming the door behind her.

"NOUR!" yelled her mother, ready to run after her.

"No." Mr. Ibrahim rose from the table. "Let me," he said. "I got this."

Mrs. Ibrahim sank into her chair, hurt. No words between the two parents were required, both conscious of how this particular type of pain needed neither introduction nor explanation.

Nour's father had always dreaded the day when his precious, lovely daughter's gentle yet fierce fighting spirit would wish to wane, gripped by the vice of a dispirited pain, and tormented by the remnants of systemic racism, which never failed to leave its condemnation and brandishing.

Three light taps at the door. "Yes?" The voice answered amid sniffles.

"It's me, Princess."

Nour reluctantly slid off her bed, wiping her face with the palm of her hand before unlocking the door. "Daddy…" she cried, her small frame quivering. Nour wrapped her arms around her father's waist, burying her damp face on his protective chest.

"I know baby girl…I know."

TIGHT ROPE

**

Nour slowly opened her eyes. The clatter of raindrops had all but petered out. The clouds in the sky remained gray but not nearly as weighty. This storm, like so many before it, would pass once its rage exhausted.

PING

Shit, him again. I know it… The recognizable alert indicating the arrival of a new email produced within her entire body a sense of pure dread. *Can't imagine what's next.*

Nour spun the chair around to face her desk. Too lazy to stand up, she used both feet to paddle herself over. "*Bismillah,*" she mumbled, readying herself to push the email icon on her desktop. Shoulders tensed, she subconsciously gnawed on her bottom lip. She squinted her eyes and scrunched up her nose, unaware she was holding in her breath.

"*Dear Black Bitch–Miss me?*"

What kind of mind game or power trip is this? It was neither, but how would Nour possibly have known the intense pleasure Shadow took in sending his daily dose of threats or the pride-filled lump that swelled in his throat each time his red marker swiped another large "X" on the hanging calendar, marking off passing days that would bring the final standoff closer. She had to stop overthinking and just write.

Many have asked me, "Where has all the recent hate stemmed from? All the discrimination and all the manufactured and sanitized lies?" And I stand before you to tell you in no uncertain terms, what you see taking place, all these taunts, and attacks, and deaths— have always existed. Better contained perhaps, depending on which community you reside in, but never erased, never dismantled, and never destroyed.

This level of emboldened hate now displayed on our streets and airwaves isn't new, but derives from people dependent on defining their existence through a diet of force-fed revisionist history. These hateful reactions continue to lie and manifest in the hearts of so many because it feeds into their racist, xenophobic narrative. Without somebody else to blame, they'd have to own up to their own failings, become accountable for the centuries of pain and degradation they've caused, while giving up the power they desperately cling to. Historically, this level of accountability never took place...not when it was so much easier to play the blame game.

CHAPTER 14

Eugene Underwood

EUGENE GLANCED AROUND HIS APARTMENT, his latest transitory abode. Nothing more than the next seedy place to rest his head. The room contained a single-sized bed, one semi-dilapidated dresser, a card table with two metal folding chairs, and a ratty couch. The one lone standing lamp off in the corner tended to flicker if mistakenly bumped.

Since Eugene never remained in any one place for long, the monotony of sameness never became an issue. His search for constant stimulation and excitement demanded a nomadic existence. The minute anything became too demanding of him he'd simply pack up his few meager belongings and bolt. Here one day, gone the next. Don't look back and never, ever return.

Eugene relished living life on his terms. He savored calling the shots and being his own man. *Nobody tells me what to do*, he'd like to boast, although in reality, his inability to form long lasting or meaningful attachments derived from his having a severe emotional disconnect. Much too aggressive for his own good, he was easily set off. This in turn earned him the reputation as a hothead and the type of guy who would suddenly erupt in violent outbursts. In many ways, Eugene's private life mimicked his social life, in that there wasn't any. This inability to form intimate relationships with people kept him socially inaccessible. Once his immediate needs were met, he'd toss whoever it was to the side, but not before deliberately hurting them, because it wasn't any fun unless he did that.

One afternoon, after a particularly peculiar sexual encounter, Eugene became insulted when his barfly hump accused him of being "terrifyingly immoral."

"You're fucking sick," she spat, through a swollen lip encased by an already haggard, gaunt face. She was eager to hightail it out of there before Eugene had a chance to stop her. "I don't need to put up with this shit," she sputtered, dabbing her lip with a tissue.

Eugene said nothing. He simply relaxed on the bed. Propped up by a few pillows, feet crossed at the ankles, he leisurely smoked a cigarette.

"I came here to fuck, you, sick prick. Not for you to fuck me up!"

Wrapped in nothing but a bath towel, he continued to bide his time, patiently watching her melt down. The fresh blood stains smeared on the sheets amused him.

"LOOK AT MY FACE!"

Eugene took another long pull of his cigarette. As he slowly exhaled rings of smoke, he peered under his nails and began picking pieces of dried blood and skin out of the crevices, flicking them away like dust.

"I think my tooth is lose…I got a good mind to call the

cops."

Eugene remained where he was until she became distracted long enough for him to silently creep up from behind. Without a flicker of hesitation, he stabbed the woman in the neck with a penknife, practically eviscerating her esophagus. While she lay sprawled out on the floor dying, he cleaned up, casually chucking whatever needed tossing into a plastic garbage bag, including the blood-stained sheets, pillowcases, and cigarette stubs. After dressing, Eugene stood over the body, bent over and plucked the lose tooth out of the unconscious woman's mouth. "Problem solved," he said, and split.

Once successfully ridding himself of the bloody evidence, he headed to a neighborhood bar where he spent the next few hours indulging. At one point, he cheerfully informed the bartender that the next round of drinks was on him. Without missing a beat, Eugene coolly stood, raised his glass high up in the air and made a toast. "Good health and success to all."

Meanwhile, back at the motel room, the woman he'd gouged only minutes before bled out. By the time her decomposing corpse was discovered, Eugene was long gone. No, Eugene wasn't a man to be toyed with.

There was one steadfast rule Eugene followed and lived by meticulously: fuck with me and you're dead. Step on me, I'll stomp on you. Yell at me and I'll carve you open. Straightforward. Clear-cut. To the point.

In fact, the general consensus from those who knew of him was that Underwood was one scary dude and nobody to arbitrarily screw around with. And for those who mistakenly thought this warning didn't apply to them, throwing caution to the wind and crossing him anyway, well, they were promptly and efficiently—and without the slightest trace of remorse—immediately corrected.

But how exactly did Eugene get away with as much as he did, especially since he had left quite a nasty trail of liquidations stretching over two decades?

Besides his "regular guy" persona, Eugene had the uncanny knack of blending seamlessly into any surrounding. This skill provided him ample freedom from detection. His fairly unremarkable face, nondescript features, coupled with his average height and build enabled him to blend seamlessly into a crowd. Never remembered because he hardly ever got noticed in the first place. Just one more regular, run-of-the-mill sort of guy, boasting a middling facade amongst a crowd of commonplace faces.

Nothing in particular stood out about him *except* when someone either became his target or dared cross him. Then, and only then, did Eugene's calculated veneer of ordinary, fracture. Within an instant, his dreary, dull eyes turned deadly, locking unto his prey with razor-sharp precision, and usually turning out to be the last thing his victim encountered before all lights were extinguished. The stuff real-life nightmares were made of.

Being terminated from this last job meant less than nothing to Eugene, who hadn't wanted to take the stupid job to begin with. *Scaring old men and tossing a store like some petty thief—not my style. Besides, I got bigger and better-paying fish to fry*, which was one of the main reasons he subcontracted those three idiots in the first place.

Luckily, the Boss made no mention on the phone about Eugene having to return his advance, not that Eugene had any intention of forgoing his money, including paying those three miserable stooges their cut—not after what they pulled. And while he hadn't earned what he usually cleared for a job like this, it was still a whole lot better than zilch. At the least, he had enough to hold him over comfortably until something more lucrative crossed his radar, and something better always managed to show up. Nevertheless, Eugene didn't much appreciate the disrespectful tone the Boss took with him on the phone. Granted, the job got screwed up royally, but Eugene had every intention of setting things right. And if nothing else, he was a man of his word.

"Leave it alone," demanded the Boss.

"I'll take care of it."

"You and your clowns did enough. Walk away. I mean it." And the phone line went dead.

Afterwards, Eugene took a vow that if he ever got alone in a room with his former boss, he'd make sure the slimy little prick would never call him another denigrating name again...at least not with his tongue still attached to the roof of his mouth.

And so, just as with everything and everyone who he came into contact with, Eugene Underwood's life remained in a perpetual state of transience, and in reflection, maybe that wasn't such a terrible thing.

CHAPTER 15

The Tetlers

HERE LIES RUSSELL J. TETLER, Mr. Disappointment Extraordinaire.

Here Lies Russell J. Tetler, Dream Killer.

Here Lies Russell J. Tetler, World Class Loser.

Here Lies Russell J. Tetler – About Damn Time.

Doris giggled sinisterly, softly tearing out her latest epitaph ideas from a small assignment book she kept handy for such momentous occasions, meticulously folding the already undersized piece of paper until no bigger than a bulky postage stamp. Wetting her tongue with as much accumulated saliva as possible, she plunked the tiny paper wad into her mouth and swallowed, confident her habit of swallowing these brilliant compilations would ensure she'd never forget what to do when the proper time came.

Doris expected Russell back shortly. Without needing to check a clock or watch, her gut tightened with his expected arrival.

TIGHT ROPE

A tidal wave of angst joined the party. As if by some form of osmosis, her body sensed his close and looming proximity. The churning in her stomach returned, followed by a shortness of clipped breaths, and a deep-seated urge to coil under a mound of blankets and vanish. However, tonight a much-welcomed thrill accompanied the usual dreaded anxiousness. Doris had a plan, and in her modest estimation, this master plan topped all the other schemes she had ever devised.

In the light of day, Doris's so-called brilliant plan, compared to the many gleaned murders she'd seen on the television, seemed downright evil. Many of those on the shows were more spur of the moment kinds of killings, where heightened emotions caused people to react in ways they never thought possible. But not so with Doris; she'd plotted her revenge through countless seasons of her favorite murder whodunits, and for her, the time to make it happen was now. Subsequently, if she indeed followed through, and in the future, her proposed crime came under analysis, specifically by a team of therapists and third-year psychology students, they would most likely agree: these actions, while inarguably disturbed, were the actions of a severely psychologically ill individual on the brink of a total emotional and highly dangerous breakdown. Perhaps Russell should have paid closer attention. Then again, his emotional health wasn't all that great, either.

Feeling better, she tossed off her bathrobe to make it possible for her to rush about the house unimpeded. She scampered about from room to room chaotically wiping off sticky counters, picking up and disposing of trash, emptying snack bags, sweeping the main hallway, and lastly, fluffing pillows on the couch. As part of her scheme, she'd even folded up her crocheted lap blanket, resting it neatly over the sidearm of the couch. Something she normally never bothered with.

Once done, she headed straight back to the kitchen and down the small hall to the basement door. One whiff of the awful stench assaulting her senses had her nose scrunching in disdain. Flipping on the switch, the room below was instantly incased in an overly noxious light, owing to the single hanging light bulb Russell insisted on using instead of an actual light fixture. As a result, a creepy shadow materialized on the opposite wall as she descended.

Gripping the banister, she moved down the steps nervously. The creaky wooden stairs and the prospect of crossing paths with either mice or spiders scared her to death. Once she reached the floor, she sighed, her eyes darting and flitting across the room. As expected, towards the back of the open space stood a tall metal workshop cabinet, rusty from the basement's endless humidity issues. As she lifted the heavy latch, the corroded door grudgingly cranked opened. *Ah, there you are.*

Doris cautiously emptied some of the powdered contents into a different container, then returned the jar exactly to where she'd found it, being painstakingly careful not to disturb the already formed dust spot. After closing the metal doors, she darted upstairs, remembering at the last second to switch off the lights, and quietly closing the basement door. With her now semi-filled poison vessel in hand, she returned to the kitchen victorious, and ready to begin.

Rat poison, she'd found out, contains toxic chemicals extremely risky to humans. From all she'd read, it wouldn't take much to have the old fool writhing in pain. Everything from blood in the urine, nosebleeds, bloody diarrhea, hair loss, bruising, bleeding gums and lethargy could be expected. Liver failure, cardiopulmonary effects, convulsions, and even shock were on the

TIGHT ROPE

menu. Basically, what didn't kill him would make Russell wish he were dead. *Splendid!* Her intention had always been to cause him the most extreme levels of discomfort, while ensuring he ingested just enough over a short period of time to collapse his entire system.

In exhilaration, Doris switched from leg to leg, rolling her neck and shoulders, and shaking out her hands and arms like a prize fighter before jumping into the ring. *I need to play this cool for it to work...he can't see it coming, and then BAM!* Crouched in a fighting position, she punched the air. *Here we go.* Operation Kill Russell was in full swing. Doris couldn't have been more elated.

**

That evening, as Russell crossed the street, he noticed all the lights were on in his house. *What in the devil?* he thought. *Hmm, why is she still up?* He heard a series of unexpected noises the moment he stuck his key into the front door lock. *What the heck is going on?* But instead of going inside, he opted to press his ear against the door to take a listen. In no time at all Russell heard the muffled thud of feet scrambling up the stairs directly across from the front door, but then strangely, just as hurriedly, stomping their way right back down again. *What the hell is she up to now?* Through the curtains a trail of lights were turned off in rapid succession, accompanied by yet another round of heavy footsteps ascending back up the stairs. *Oh, for Christ's sake!*

On any other night Russell, wouldn't have hesitated to barge in, yelling at the top of his lungs, but not tonight. Tonight, he felt too good to allow any of Doris's harebrained antics to set him off. Besides, who cared if she entertains herself by playing with lights? He certainly didn't. Nope, tonight's adventure turned out better home came from him. *God, I would have loved to see her face.* So instead, Russell closed the bedroom door and headed to George's old room. He'd sleep in there, away from Doris's snoring, away from her unhinged night outbursts, and far away from her sickly night sweats and terror-filled moans. No, tonight he'd lie in George's bed, allowing his soul to commune with the child stolen from his life, sharing in the first faint glimmer of triumph.

After flicking off the hall light right by the door, Russell then eased the door closed firmly behind him. Whatever Doris thought she'd been up to before he came home, he couldn't have cared less. Tonight, belonged to him and George.

**

Upstairs, beneath her bedcovers, Doris held her breath, careful not to make any sudden noises. She'd purposely left her bedroom door slightly ajar so she could listen to his movements downstairs. Slipper footsteps headed in the direction of the kitchen. Then the unmistaken swooshing sound of their old refrigerator door being pulled open. A few more short shuffling steps over to the cabinet, most likely to grab a glass … the refrigerator door reopening … and then—*Oh shit, here he comes!* Doris rolled her body away from the direction of the door, pulling the comforter snuggly over her shoulder, and closing her eyes to feign sleep. She heard when Russell's hand clutched the doorknob, and waited for him to enter. But he didn't. *Why is the idiot just standing there?*

A few moments later, the door closed. *Phew! That was close.* Finding herself alone in her bed the next morning, Doris shivered despite the heaviness of her covers, energized by the expectation

TIGHT ROPE

that the next few days might be her husband's last. *And hopefully, his most painful.*

With a sudden pep in her step, she rushed through her morning ablutions and dressed, even taking an extra minute to run a comb through her short, curly, coarse, gray hair. For a split second, she'd even contemplated running a lipstick over her dehydrated, parched lips, but decided against doing so. She'd save that *for after…*

Today she'd begin to set into motion her master plan, but first she'd commemorate the occasion. In her dresser, second drawer on the right, she kept a special velvet box tucked underneath her only silk neck scarf. Inside the box, George's Purple Heart, awarded posthumously. *I can finally wear this medal close to my heart*, she decided, pinning it underneath her shirt to her bra. *This is for you, George…*

**

Downstairs, Russell prepared his morning cup since to that point, Doris had yet to emerge from the bedroom. One large heaping teaspoon of instant coffee, no sugar. He enjoyed his coffee strong, but this morning he opted for a nice dousing of creamer. In the toaster, a frozen waffle turned a golden brown. A smear of syrup and he'd be set.

Ah, she's up. The swooshing sound of house slippers crossing the wood floor above indicated she was most likely making their bed. *Their bed.* Wow, he hadn't thought of it as *theirs* in a long time. Ages. Matter of fact, Doris hadn't looked at him like *that* for many years, desire and intimacy seemingly a figment of his imagination. Had George not existed as proof of their carnal life from long ago, he'd have sworn on a stack of hotel Bibles he had imagined it.

Russell checked to see if his morning paper had arrived, pleasantly surprised to find it waiting on his stoop, housed in a plastic bag. *How many soaked papers did I have to complain about before the dimwit got the message?* Bringing it inside, he chucked it on his office desk. Juggling his hot mug and the plate with the syrup-soaked waffle, he headed to his office so he wouldn't be disturbed. He had a lot of work to do before implementing the next phase.

Patiently, he waited for his old computer to fully boot up. Mind stuck on a new idea he'd come up with on his way home the evening before, a new "gift" to send. By rote, he lifted the hot cup to his lips, cautiously slurping in those first gulps of hot brew. *Not as good as Doris's, but pleasant enough.* Reaching for the paper, he read the headline.

"Fifteen Dead at Rail Station, Islamic Terrorism Suspected" *Damn Moslems won't be happy until they kill us all.* Russell tossed the paper away, determined more than ever to finish the job he'd started. "I might not be able to get rid of all these bloodsuckers, but I sure can cut the head off this snake!" he mumbled furiously.

Search engine ready, he typed in one single word under *Images*—a word with the power to invoke an immediate and visceral response from any Black person residing in the United States. A word entrenched and laden with horrific historical and political demagoguery. A shockingly reprehensible word, found hoarded within the dark confines of every hate-mongering bastard hell-bent on destroying people based solely on the complexion of their skin.

NOOSE

CHAPTER 16

Nour Ibrahim

PICK UP...PICK UP... TWO more rings. Where are you? One more ring.

"*AsSalaamu'alaikum?*"

"*AsSalaamu'alaikum.* It's me. Busy?"

"Nour!" shouted Rabia into the phone. "*MashaAllah*! It's so good to hear your voice. What's up, lady?"

"You know, same ole-same ole. Work, work, and more work. How about you? You should be about ready to drop that baby soon, right?"

"*Alhamdulillah,* everything's good. And you're right, four more weeks. I can't wait. I'm tired of feeling as big as a house. Speaking of houses, we're house hunting."

"Seriously?" Nour fought back her jealousy.

"No more city apartments for us. Hashim found a job with a great company, but they're located in New Jersey. Instead of commuting back and forth and spending a fortune, we've decided to move to the other side of the Hudson."

"Oh wow, sounds wonderful. Take me with you."

"In a heartbeat, sis!"

Nour yearned to be with her best friend. Longed for days when they shared long chats and laughs. "Look, I know it's been awhile since we last talked, but so much is going on. I don't know where to start, but I could really use a sounding board I trust right about now."

Rabia paused. "Um, okay…"

Nour heard the hesitation. "Do you have a minute or did I catch you at a bad time?"

"Truthfully, I'm actually running late. I'm supposed to meet Hashim at his job in twenty minutes, and from there we're meeting up with the realtor."

"Oh." Nour winced as her stomach began tightening. She needed her friend more than ever right now.

"But can I call you when we're finished? It shouldn't take that long, it's just that we've tried like crazy to schedule this for the past week, and if it's not one thing it's another…and with the baby coming soon…"

Back in the day, not so long ago, neither woman would have hesitated to drop the world for the other. One always had the others back; those days were long gone. Nothing in this shifting world lasts forever. Life changes, people change, as do responsibilities and allegiances along with them.

"Sure. No problem. It'll keep until then." The cramp in her side tightened and ached, but her loneliness hurt more.

"If you're sure—" This was more a statement than a question. Preoccupied, Rabia sounded ready to hang up.

TIGHT ROPE

"Absolutely," Nour said, clenching her jaw, trying not to let her voice expose the pain she was fighting. "Take care of what you need to. We'll talk soon. Give my salaams to Hashim." The spasm in her gut burned and twisted.

"Will do," Rabia replied hastily. "I'll call you later."

Nour bolted for the bathroom.

The return call never came.

**

Nour needed to hurry if she wanted to make her doctor's appointment on time. Luckily it wasn't far, just in the building adjacent to the hospital only a few blocks away. Hoofing it would be her best bet since the buses at this time of the day were most likely overcrowded with kids getting out of school.

Changing out of her pumps and trading them for a pair of sneakers, she grabbed her bag, tossed the pumps inside, and closed her office door, mind stuck on replay, going over the long and short of the meeting. Sherri didn't pull punches or take prisoners, and despite her lack of empathy, she mercifully never beat around the bush. Never on the receiving end of one of Sherri's infamous tirades, Nour appreciated her directness from a safe and comfortable distance, but all that was about to drastically change.

"Half the time you're not here and when you are, you're in a fog," stated Sherri matter-of-factly. "Your work is late, at times incomplete, and sometimes missing altogether. Now, when I hired you, I told you this was a competitive position. If you can't hack it, tell me now. There's a line of people vying for your position."

Sharp and razor cutting…

"And don't think I'm the only one noticing. People are

talking. People in high places. And when those people talk, I listen, so what gives?"

Nour knew there was no use in denying the obvious. "You're right. I haven't been on my game recently."

"I'm sorry. You misunderstood me. This is not the part up for debate. I'm asking you why?"

Nour took a second to think about what to say and how much to reveal. With Sherri, it was always a hit and miss. "It's about this rally we're sponsoring."

"What about it?"

"All the attention it's getting."

"Which is what we want. We're in the social change business. Attention is all part of what we need."

"I know and I agree, of course, but along with the attention comes the other stuff."

"What kind of other stuff?"

"Hate mail."

"Hate mail?"

"Yes."

"You're kidding, right?"

"No, not at all."

"Is this the first time you got hate mail?"

"No."

"Then I'm not understanding the problem. Enlighten me."

"The stuff I'm getting is sick."

"Okay, again, what's the issue? It's called HATE mail for a reason. Were you expecting your hate mail to be of the nicer variety?"

"No! Of course, not. It's…I don't know how to describe it…more hateful?"

TIGHT ROPE

"More 'hateful'." Sherri made air quotes for effect. "And, so, what? Your hate mail is causing you to run scared and this is the reason why you're not producing? I'm confused."

"It's upsetting."

"It's upsetting…I see." Sherri rolled her eyes. "Listen. It's an easy fix, princess. Erase them."

"What?"

"Erase them."

Nour couldn't believe what she was hearing.

"I mean it. Get rid of all of it, especially the extra hateful mail." The resolve in Sherri's voice couldn't be ignored. "Look, do what you need to do and stop letting everything and everyone upset you." Sherri was one of those rare women who effortlessly juggled the complex matrix between being a powerful woman while fully owning her sensuality. Despite the tailored business suit attire and the perfectly executed gait, her every move embraced an elusive womanliness that demanded consideration. As she circled around her desk, she leaned-sat on the corner to be closer to Nour to make her point. "Listen, I'm not trying to be a bitch here. I get that hate mail can be upsetting." Sherri lowered her voice. "But you and I both know, as Black women, hate mail is the least of our problems."

"True …"

"Don't think you're alone, either. We all get the troll letters from time to time."

Not all of us…

"Shoot, I'd be worried if we didn't because that would mean we weren't doing our job, correct? But it's the nature of the work you signed up for. The social change business is brimming with people who either love and support us or hate our guts—and both do so with a passion. There's unfortunately no middle ground."

"Yes, but—"

"And then there's the Internet warriors. Don't even get me started on those fools. They're the kind who know it all from their comfortable, safe armchairs." Sherri rose to stand. "Quarterbacking everything. Criticizing and critiquing every single thing we say or meant to say, telling us we said it wrong."

"I know about them, but…"

"And then we have the racist assholes who hate and despise us because we exist. They'd like nothing better than to banish us brown and black folks off the face of the earth. That group of special gets super brave behind the confines of their screens and puts the rest of those losers to shame. Some seriously sick shit."

Nour wished she could leave.

"For example, Rabinowitz on the third floor. Poor slob gets gas chamber emails weekly. Did you know that?"

"He's never said anything."

"Of course not, because he deals with it, just like the rest of us."

Nour pursed her lips and almost snorted. Jacob Rabinowitz—the office mansplainer and resident racist.

"Garcia and Lopez have trolls telling them to go back to Mexico all the time."

"I thought Lopez was from Puerto Rico?"

"You think racists know the difference?" Sherri tugged then levelled the hem of her jacket. "Listen, here's my advice. Take it or leave it, but I strongly suggest you take it. Don't get upset. Don't respond. Just delete and ignore."

"I understand that, but—"

"Good. Understand it and move on. Your career here

depends on it."

No stranger to how Sherri conducted business, Nour knew her long enough to know when she wasn't bluffing.

"Hey!" Sherri snapped her fingers. "Are you hearing me?"

"I'm hearing you."

"Any more problems? Issues? Complaints?"

"No."

"You're sure now, because I don't want to have this discussion again."

"I'm sure."

"I need you on board, Nour, ready to handle your business. I have no time to babysit."

"I hear what you're saying. I'll fix this and get it together. I apologize."

Sherri stared at Nour trying to decide whether or not this admission of culpability was sincere or sarcastic. Either way, she had no more time to give to the cause. "See that you do." Sashaying over to her office door, Sherri opened it wide enough for Nour to step through, but she couldn't resist imparting one last warning. "I'll be watching you."

Where have I heard that before?

As Nour headed down the hall, her mind raced. Did Sherri mean she was watching to catch me screwing up or that she has my back? With Sherri, one could never be entirely too sure.

**

Rushing along the sidewalk, weaving in and out of crowds like a seasoned New Yorker, Nour hurried as fast as her legs could go. She didn't have time for yet another doctor's appointment, but this time she had no choice. Hopefully today's visit wouldn't take long. She still had more work to do on her speech.

She swerved adeptly past those stopped in mid-path chat and practically leaped around the mom brigade fortified behind their battalion of strollers. The endless array of welcoming aromas wafting from the many food carts lining the city street made her mouth water and stomach growl, especially as she passed the halal cart serving falafels and gyros. Those really smell so good. But with her recent stomach issues, she declined the temptation. Two more blocks and a quick right turn—and…here! One quick elevator ride to the second floor and she made it, a bit sweaty, a tinge overheated, but on time.

"Name, please?"

"Nour Ibrahim. I have a 5:30 appointment with Dr. Khan."

The receptionist, a pleasant woman in her early fifties, smiled then proceeded to check her computer screen. "Let me see…ah yes, I found you. Please take a seat and I'll let the doctor know you're here."

"Thank you." Yes, nobody's here. She despised sitting in packed waiting rooms with all eyes on her. Less than a minute later, the door to the inner office opened and a stunning covered Muslim woman dressed in nurse attire poked her head out.

"Nour Ibrahim?"

"That's me."

"Would you like to follow me?" The nurse opened the door wider allowing Nour to enter.

"Step on the scale over here, please."

"Do you want me to take my shoes off?"

Maryam glanced up from her notes. "Only if you want. Doesn't really matter. I always take a pound off to compensate for clothes anyway."

"Make it two pounds and you've got yourself a deal."

Maryam grinned. "Height?"

"Five seven."

"Follow me." Once inside with the door shut, the nurse sat near a small laptop computer and began reading. "I see you're here about stomach discomfort. How long have you had this pain?"

"For a few weeks or so."

"Does the pain shoot through your abdomen or in one particular spot?"

"Here."

"Show me where." Nour pointed to the lower left hand side of her belly area.

"Does the pain ever radiate into your shoulder or lower back?"

"Not really, no."

"Are you currently in any pain?"

"It comes and goes, kind of like spasms."

"Here?"

"Yes."

"Stabbing pain or a dull-achy pain?"

"Hurts-like-hell pain."

Maryam stood over Nour, bent over and gently pressed where her patient had indicated. "When does the pain occur the most? Night? Day?"

"Day and night."

"What about after you eat?"

"Yes, but not always with or after food."

"What about after you've eaten certain types of food?"

"Not necessarily."

"Are you able to sleep?"

"To be honest, sometimes the pain is so bad it wakes me up."

"Then what happens?" Maryam returned to her seat typing every detail being relayed to her.

"Then I have to run to the bathroom."

"Diarrhea?"

"Yes." This is embarrassing.

"Are you throwing up?"

"I have. A few times. Mostly bile." While Nour understood, this was standard medical conversation, she still felt awkward disclosing such intimate details.

"And now?"

"I feel a bit nauseous, but I haven't eaten much today."

"Do you need a pail?"

"No. Not yet anyway, but I've gotten into the habit of carrying these with me," Nour reached into her purse and pulled out a plastic zip lock bag. "Just in case,"

Maryam included that information as well. "Patient travels with plastic bags to catch vomit."

"Have you noticed any blood in your stool or urine?"

"No."

"Okay, I'm going to take your temperature. I'll need you to stay still and quiet."

Nour did as instructed, while all along wondering why this covered Muslim woman standing before her hadn't yet offered up a salaam. Then again, neither had she.

After the beep the nurse read the results. She appeared concerned. "You're fighting off an infection of some sort. Let me take your blood pressure."

A moment later, after all the stats were sufficiently uploaded

TIGHT ROPE

into the computer, Maryam stood, ready to take her leave, "The doctor will be with you shortly."

"Thank you."

But before stepping completely out of the room, Maryam vacillated, seemingly deciding on whether or not to pose one more question. "I don't mean to pry, sister, but aren't you the same woman on all the posters around town? You're a speaker, right?"

Here we go... "I am."

"The rally, right?"

"Right."

"*AsSalaamu'alaikum*!" Maryam's entire demeanor switched from professionally distant to outright jubilant. "I thought I recognized you!"

Trained from experience not to assume auto-camaraderie, Nour pressed herself rigidly against the back of her chair.

"You're so much prettier in person," gushed Maryam. "I mean, you look great on the posters too, don't get me wrong, but in person you're even prettier." Maryam's cheeks turned a rosy shade of pink. She hated when she came off giddy.

Nour shifted uncomfortably in her seat, pretending to adjust her clothes, uncertain as to how to read this sudden influx of flattery. Granted, this kind of reaction was a big difference from being called a "Black Bitch," but at least that type of attention she understood. Chatty plus compliments? Not so much.

Maryam gnawed her bottom lip, oblivious to Nour's discomfort. "I only work half-days every other Friday, so I'm going."

"*Alhamdulillah*," replied Nour somewhat curtly, again, still unsure of exactly what else to say or where this strange conversation was going.

Maryam picked up on the slight. "Sorry...I don't mean to make you uncomfortable."

"No, I'm fine."

"Here I am bothering you with all this, and you're here because you don't feel well, but I'm looking forward to going and—"

"You are?"

"I sure am! And to be honest, it's so good to hear an American sister talk. Someone I can relate to."

Well that's refreshingly kind. "Thanks."

"No, seriously, I mean it. I've read your articles, I'm on your Twitter and Facebook, and I've heard you speak before. You're great. I really admire all the work you do."

"That's kind of you to say. Not everyone shares your opinion."

"Why am I not surprised?"

Nour genuinely smiled as the two women exchanged a knowing glance. "Colorism amongst Muslims runs deep."

Maryam, no stranger herself to prejudice, shook her head in disgust. "We're supposed to have each other's back."

"Yeah, well, in a perfect world..."

"I would have thought Muslims of all people would know better."

"Some do, and they're amazing, but when you run across that other mess, well, it makes for a tough job ahead, especially when white centrality is challenged and exposed."

Maryam looked sincerely perplexed. "What about the people you work with or do I not want to know the answer to that question?"

Nour grinned. "Okay, let me put it this way—name me one

other single high-profile Black American Muslima on the stump. Athletes don't count."

Maryam leaned on the doorway, Nour's medical file in hand. Staring into her patient's eyes, deep in deliberation, finally unable to dredge up a single name. "Wow."

"Exactly. Don't get me wrong, there's a ton of strong Black Muslim women out here doing the heavy lifting, but we're just not given much recognition for it."

"That's sad to hear."

"We're all humans, trying to do our best for the pleasure of Allah, but sometimes folks fall short," said Nour shrugging.

"I know that's true..." Maryam snuck a peek into the hall. For the immediate moment, the coast was clear. She then softly closed the door for privacy and took a seat. "I'm a fairly new convert to Islam," she disclosed. "At first, I was beyond excited. Everyone seemed so warm and inviting. They had all the time in the world to speak to me about Islam and answer all my questions. I was loaned books to read, taught how to pray, and one sister even gifted me a hijab and prayer mat. So of course, being the resident newbie on the block I thought all Muslims were one big, happy family, right?"

"Right..."

"Want for your sister what you want for yourself."

"Got it."

"Exactly. Which was so completely different from what I had experienced before and it felt so good. No matter where I went I *salaamed* everyone in a hijab. Some replied, others acted confused; a couple of sisters ignored me altogether or rolled their eyes."

Nour agreed. She did know, and all too well. "Then what?"

"Well, after a while, the invitations stopped. The same people super excited about me taking my Shahadah went on with their lives, which of course, didn't include me—I'm not married."

Nour knew that was right! "Lock your doors, hide your husbands! Single hijabis are on the loose and looking to score your husband!"

Both women broke out into a fit of giggles.

"I don't know if I should be saying all this—" Maryam modulated her voice to a whisper, "but is it me or are some Muslims kind of…"

"Don't stop now," encouraged Nour.

"Okay, well, I'm not saying all—it's never an all or nothing thing— but some Muslims I've come across are seriously racist."

"You got that, right."

"And in the masjid, too."

"Yup."

"I'm serious."

"Me too! We're compromised like other groups. No different."

"It's like they see my brown skin, hear my voice, and when they realize I'm not from where they're from, all of a sudden I'm not good enough. Not a 'real Muslim'."

"Not the most welcoming, huh?"

"Not at all," agreed Maryam. "Is your family also Muslim?"

Nour nodded.

"Not my family. Every Ramadan my mother swears I'm going to die from starvation and hassles me the entire month to eat."

"I hear that from a few of my co-workers who think it's funny to make food jokes."

"It's lonely too…not having Muslim family. Take last Eid, as soon as prayer was over, everyone split to enjoy the day with their Muslim families while I spent my day organizing my closet."

TIGHT ROPE

As an American Muslim, Nour had also felt much of what Maryam now described. As a first-generation born Black Muslim, and no stranger to prejudice or to the blatant "othering," she knew what it felt like to be ignored in and out of the Masjid. Her heart went out to the beautiful kindred spirit sitting beside her.

Reaching into her bag Nour pulled out her wallet. "Here." She handed Maryam a card. "Right now, everything's pretty hectic for me until this rally is over, but hit me up afterwards."

Maryam graciously accepted the card. "I'd love to, *Shukran*!"

"*Afwan*. Me too."

A slight knock at the door startled the two new friends. "Nour! *AsSalaamu'alaikum*," greeted Dr. Khan.

"*Wa 'alaikum Salaam.*"

Maryam reverted back to efficient mode, handing off Nour's medical folder, then slipping out the room as unobtrusively as she could, but not before giving Nour a quick wink and a silent-lipped synced "*salaam*" goodbye. She shut the door softly behind her.

"So, you've met Maryam?"

"I did. New?"

"Yes. Stole her from the hospital."

"I don't remember seeing her the last time I came. Seems nice."

"She is. Good at her job, too, but we're not here to talk about her career, are we?" Dr. Khan lowered herself in the chair. "Okay. Let's see what we got." The room fell silent as the doctor's eyes scanned through Nour's file and the latest test results. It hadn't taken long before a deep look of consternation creased her face. "Slight elevated temperature today…" She continued reading. "Since your last visit, how have you been feeling?"

Nour shrugged. "Not great. My stomach is a mess and I can't

stop running to the bathroom. Achy spasms in my gut. Sometimes they hurt so bad I get winded. It makes it hard to catch my breath."

Dr. Khan flipped the paper over, searching. "Did Dr. Frank mention to you anything about having an endoscopy and colonoscopy?"

Nour fidgeted with the button on her sleeve. She'd meant to make the appointment, she really did, but with everything else going on, she'd tabled it for another time. "Not exactly."

Dr. Khan's furrowed her brow in disbelief. "Not exactly?" She sifted through the file. "I'm not seeing anything from your visit. Dr. Frank didn't happen to mention when I should be getting his exam notes and results? Sometimes he sends a copy back with the patient."

"I didn't exactly see him yet."

Dr. Khan tilted her head doing little to hide her frustration. "You can't play with this, Nour. I mean it. I know you're busy with work and whatever else you have going on, but this is serious and is becoming increasingly more so with each passing day."

This doesn't sound good. "What do you suspect? I know you don't like to guess, but at least tell me what you think this could be—"

"Well, from what little I have to go on," she said, sneering at Nour, "it's hard to say, but your symptoms are leading me in the direction of either irritable bowel syndrome, ulcerative colitis or maybe even Crohn's disease. But again, without proper test results, this is all speculation. Anybody in your family have a history of any of these?"

"Not that I know of. I'll ask my mother. Why? Is it genetic?"

"It can be but not always. Look, call Dr. Frank. Make the appointment and get these tests done. We need to get to the bottom of this before it gets any worse."

How much worse can it get? I have a racist nutcase sending me threatening messages, a boss who blames me for feeling frightened, a stressful job in an office filled with imaginary allies, two over-protective parents, and now a possible disease I can hardly pronounce. "Fine. I'll call him."

Dr. Khan smirked, raising both eyebrows, highly doubting Nour's sincerity.

"Today. I promise. Scouts honor...*Wallahi*."

CHAPTER 17

Doris Tetler

AFTER MUCH DELIBERATION, DORIS DECIDED to conceal the cylinder glass spice bottle holding the rat poison right in plain sight—*and why the hell not?* The white powdery substance could easily be mistaken for any of her other spices kept in the narrow cabinet above the stove. The label read 'Baking Powder.' Simple enough substitution, *in theory*, however the process of properly adding the Brodifacoum compound to the rest of the ingredients without contaminating herself in the process proved to be much more complicated.

Ingesting Brodifacoum is a nasty, vicious, and excruciatingly painful way to die. The entire body revolts. Even the gums and nose bleed. If all went according to plan, Russell would be in for the wildest ride of his life…or death, as the case may be.

From what Doris remembered, which wasn't a whole lot these days, Russell normally mixed the poison with a bit of Plaster of Paris, to make a thick-like cement cocktail. He'd add a smidgen of

TIGHT ROPE

cornmeal or maybe a dash or two of sugar, and a spot of milk. Once or twice she'd noticed him throwing in a few teaspoons of boric acid.

Once all the ingredients were measured and added, he'd roll the gloppy mixture into the shape of a golf ball. Then he'd leave these tempting morsels where he was sure to attract the rats and mice, especially in dark dank places downstairs. The only problem—the damn rats refused to politely die where they dined. Instead, these tiny beasts would gorge themselves silly, then roam back to their nest only to kick the bucket imbedded somewhere deep inside the walls, causing the basement to stink for months like putrid death.

The directions on the original container indicated Brodifacoum would dissolve in water. The poison was so potent, one only needed small teaspoon amounts to do the trick, but as far as Doris was concerned, this simply wouldn't do. Dying quickly was not on the docket. She wanted Russell to slowly suffer, to feel each wrenching pull of his gut knowing there was nothing he could do to stop it. Doris didn't want to shut Russell's system off all at once, but planned to sprinkle the poison sparingly onto his food and mix it in his coffee in tiny increments, much like salt. A shake over here, a stir or two over there until finally, when his body could no longer defend against the poison, the toxin would take over and he'd be left utterly helpless. Writhing in excruciating pain and gasping like a guppy for air until dead.

Doris handled the poison with a pair of dollar store plastic, disposable gloves, fully aware how any contact to skin could prove dangerous. Besides goggles to protect her eyes from floating poisonous dust particles, she also wore a paper filter mask she'd found on one of the shelves in the basement near Russell's workbench. She remembered Russell wearing them when he wanted to reduce the risk of potential skin irritation or ingestion when sanding furniture or laying poison to combat the vermin issue they'd had years back.

Turning the bottle around in every which direction, she searched for an expiration date but found none. She assumed the poison to be past its prime; fully potent or not, the toxin would still land quite a kick when the time came. Doris counted on it.

Her objective was to make Russell as deathly and as uncomfortably sick over the next few days without getting caught. Otherwise, he'd get too ill too quickly and wind up being rushed to the hospital, and perhaps saved. *Abso-fuckin-lutely not!*

No, the longer the poison stayed in his crotchety old system the better. And if Doris played her cards right, she could plan his untimely death to coincide with the third anniversary of her darling George's passing. A real *coup de grace*.

The decision to leave the jar in the cabinet in plain view and on the common area shelf didn't concern Doris in the slightest. Russell limited his exposure to the kitchen, never quite certain how to use all the mysterious cooking utensils and machinery clogging up the cabinets and closets. Only on the rarest of occasions would he make a sandwich or warm up a meal in the microwave, but even then, he'd yell incessantly at the top of his lungs the whole time.

"Doris! Where's the mustard?"

"I thought we owned a non-stick fry pan?"

"Doris, we're out of relish."

"Goddamn it, I think the bread I just bought is stale!"

The only spices Russell routinely availed himself of were the most common and recognizable: salt, pepper, sugar, and parsley. For some odd reason, Russell felt compelled to sprinkle parsley on

TIGHT ROPE

practically everything he ingested, and not the fresh variety either. Only the dry, tasteless, cheap flakes whose green color was also suspect.

Doris suspected his asinine habit came from the way his mother cooked. *Some of the blandest meals I've ever had were around that insatiable woman's table,* she recalled. *Plain. No flavor.* Not only were her meals visually unappealing, but questionable. *In his place, I would have sprinkled more than parsley on that abominable slop.*

Doris felt safe to assume her idiot husband had no clue as to the various uses of baking powder, so her intentionally mislabeling the bottle and allowing it to grace the Tetler spice shelf in all its noxious glory seemed fitting.

From what the directions recommended, both the taste and smell of the poison could be easily masked by using certain select foods or drink, so she made herself comfortable at the kitchen table and compiled a mental list of all the foods that she could sneak the poison into, using no more than one-eighth of a teaspoon at a time. *Stew … soup … his chocolate chip cookies, perhaps a smidgen in his applesauce. Russell loved applesauce. Oh, and peanut butter. I can sprinkle some under the raspberry jam and he'll never know what hit him.* Doris had already determined she'd only use the teeniest, tiniest amounts at a time, assuming she'd be able to sneak enough in without Russell becoming any the wiser. Doris smirked. *Glad, you like your coffee strong, ya old crusty bastard.*

Initially he'll feel as if he's got the flu. He'll whine and complain, be more of a pain in the ass than usual, but his deep-seeded hatred of all doctors would keep him from seeking medical attention; it would take a total collapse of his system before he'd give in. Doris couldn't help herself and shuddered with anticipation. Excited to begin, she pulled out a few ingredients from the cabinets, along with a cookie tray, and began assembling her first batch. *Chocolate chip...Russell's favorite...*

CHAPTER 18

Russell Tetler

RUSSELL NEVER INTENDED TO PURCHASE a bunch of books or paraphernalia on guns or ammunition. The need for secrecy remained paramount if this had any chance in hell of working, so he settled for conducting whatever research deemed necessary at the local library where he could pull off the shelf anything he wished to read, take a few notes and replace the reading material without anyone else catching on.

The aftermath held little to zero consequence where he was concerned. He assumed the risks going in were too high to believe he'd come out of this unscathed. Besides, carrying out his threat in an already heightened alert area like New York City would take some serious luck and planning. Not to mention a disguise.

Need camouflage.

He'd have to find something in his closet to wear to blend into the crowd without drawing any undue attention to the gun he was concealing. Law enforcement was trained to spot hidden handguns. One magazine Russell had read mentioned the "asymmetrical gait." That, he found out, was when a gun holder walked differently to compensate for the hidden weapon. Russell most likely would carry his gun tucked into the right side of his waistband. Depending on the way he secured it, it could either hinder his stride or poke out too far. To any trained cop, this would be noticeable.

No walking like I have a stick up my ass.

Russell also had to remind himself not to clip his arm swing unnaturally since the manual also mentioned how most people crop their arm too close to their body as they walked, which looks strange. He also had to remember not to rest his hand near the weapon or feel for it through his clothes; that would be a sure giveaway that he was unconsciously guarding a gun.

Dress appropriately.

Nothing screamed "shooter" like someone dressed in clothes that didn't suit the weather. Thankfully the recent cooler temperatures would allow for a light windbreaker or even a bulky sweater, but whatever he ultimately decided, how he holstered and secured his weapon couldn't be obvious.

Watch for big lumps.

Discipline and caution at all costs. Take whatever steps necessary now to ensure success later on. Without a carry permit, he'd have to be cautious not to be detected. If a cop suspected he was carrying, it could blow his whole plot, so Russell decided to give concealment the highest priority on his mental checklist.

No looking like some lowlife criminal.

This could be a fatal and premature mistake. Cops were on the lookout for terrorists, or thugs—certainly not his kind, and Russell hoped being an old White man would be in his favor.

TIGHT ROPE

Get away = good.
Death = who cares.

Fortunately, he had made no plan to outlive this undertaking. He honestly didn't care one iota what happened to him afterwards as long as in the end he succeeded. In many ways, as far as Russell was concerned, his own death was preferable to going to prison, but at the same time he wasn't going to make it easy for these lowlifes. If possible, if he could get away, so be it. But if not, well, that was more than dandy in his book, too.

Russell always enjoyed being in the library. For him, the quiet stillness of the place attracted him the most. No matter how crazy or stressed the world outside remained, once those automatic doors shut behind him, the world became a serene and more civilized place to be. His only complaint was the lack of air conditioning. Already his shirt was starting to stick to his body and this made him cranky.

Climbing the stairs up to the second level where all the adult books were kept, Russell paused, gripping the railing to keep him steady. His stomach lurched, causing a mild stabbing pain to shoot through his innards. *Maybe the coffee hadn't been such a good idea after all...* Within a few seconds, the pain dissipated and Russell continued climbing.

Between rows and rows of perfectly placed books were long glistening sturdy wood tables fitted with comfortable leather chairs. In the far corner was a door leading to a much larger room containing desktop computers for the community to use by reservation. The days of searching and sifting through countless index cards for book titles in long pull-out drawers were long gone—a thing of the past. The emergence of the Internet had libraries adopting a new and improved computerized system of cataloging books, videos, news clippings, and other borrowable materials. Only problem was, Russell had no idea how to use them.

In terms of how to properly handle a gun, well, this too wasn't second nature. Russell hadn't shot for years. In the past, he and a few of his buddies from the job used to meet up once or twice a month to shoot clay pigeons at a place in upstate New York, but rifles were the weapon of choice there, certainly not handguns like the one he planned to use. Pistols and rifles were night and day, entirely different weapons, used for completely different tasks.

When hunting, use a rifle.
To shoot the shit out of a Black, fat mouth on her soapbox, use a pistol.

Thankfully he'd purchased ammunition over a year ago, with the intention of taking up shooting as a hobby again. A new range had opened up fairly close to his house, but so far, he'd never gotten around to it. The same bullets purchased back then remained in the same box, in the same drawer, undisturbed.

He wished he had gotten to the range and gotten in a bit of target practice, but it was too late now. Time for old Russell was running out and there was still so much more he needed to accomplish. First things first, despite it being a rotten but simple job, he needed to clean the gun before using it. One of his Internet searches mentioned using baking soda. His gun was chrome, which is considered a high-quality stainless brand of silver, but it could still tarnish and get dirty. Since he'd stored his gun in his drawer for years unprotected, Russell assumed he'd find layers of accumulated dust.

Don't forget to clean the gun.

That evening after Doris went up to bed, Russell reviewed his notes. The procedure appeared straightforward enough. Two sponges and two parts water to one part of the cleaning agent.

TIGHT ROPE

Vinegar worked just as good too, but baking soda was less harsh on the chrome. Since the gun had barely tarnished, he could get away with using the baking soda.

The moment Russell gripped the handle, his adrenaline kick in. *This was actually happening.* Russell dipped the corner of his sponge into the thick mixture and began polishing. The pistol was surprisingly weighty for such a small piece of metal. Taking gentle wipes in a regular motion, he removed any dust until the area appeared spotless, careful to avoid leaving a new set of smudges. Next, he sprayed the inside of the barrel with a cleaning agent and allowed it to sit undisturbed for a few minutes longer. Lastly, he wiped the gun with the second sponge to remove all the excess baking soda missed in the first round. Once satisfied that the weapon was dirt-free, he cautiously placed it inside a clean white sock, hiding it towards the back of his drawer along with the box of bullets until...

**

Upstairs Doris slipped out of her day clothes and into her nightgown. Next, she brushed her teeth, singing the alphabet three times as she properly scrubbed each tooth, including her tongue and the roof of her mouth. Next, she ran a wide-tooth plastic comb through her wavy, short gray hair, making a concerted effort to press flat any stray strands with water.

Peering into the bathroom mirror she made half an attempt to fix her slouching posture by standing squarely upright, but after a few uncomfortable seconds, gave up and let her shoulders resume their natural droop. Finally, Doris leaned in over the sink stretching her neck to take a closer gander into her bloodshot eyes. The years of heartache hadn't been kind. Her wrinkles, large sallow pores, and dark circles told a sad and heart wrenching story. A strange cautionary tale about a deranged, middle-aged woman and a grumpy, resentful, unhinged old man, whose shared path in life crossed, then twisted. After an unimaginable loss, the couple's ill-fated travels took an even more severe turn for the worse. Now, as minutes turned into micro-lifetimes, all Doris could hope for was to have their preordained paths intersect one insufferably bloody last time.

CHAPTER 19

Zaid Ali

WHILE HIS FATHER CONTINUED HIS cycle of forced rehabilitation and rest, Zaid had the responsibility to run the shop pretty much on his own. The workload naturally doubled, but not having him looming over his shoulder would be hard to give up once the old man was back in full swing again. Nevertheless, Zaid missed his company, even if he was dour and at times blatantly uncouth.

The mornings were especially rushed and probably the hardest part of the day next to the lunch hour, but since the beautiful Muslima—the nurse with the pretty smile and large light brown eyes—came in frequently to order "her usual" it had become the part of the day he looked forward to the most.

Zaid made a point of doing her order up extra special, not that he was under the impression that she'd fall in love with him over the way he slathered the mayo. Thus far, they'd kept all chatter food related, but today he promised himself he'd try something a bit more personal if given the opportunity. Nothing over the top, but enough to drop the hint that he was definitely interested in getting to know her, despite the voices of his parent's disapproval spinning in his head. He assumed that once they found out they'd be beside themselves. Not so much his mother, but particularly his father, who had recently shared his plans to send his son "back home to find a proper bride." And in the past, Zaid would have undoubtedly complied with his scheme for the sake of peace, but that was before that sister walked into the store, changing everything.

She may not even be interested in me, he thought while restocking one of the food shelves. *I wonder if she's married? I don't think I saw a ring, but even so—she could be engaged.* A slew of unwelcome images came careening through in his head.

Zaid had been interested in a few girls in the past, but that's all they were—girls. And at the time, he was no more than a boy, so fair enough. But now things had changed. He was different. No longer willing to settle for merely a pretty face, he wanted a real and serious relationship with all the trimmings. Marriage and commitment, and a family. Zaid felt ready to take on the responsibility. *Maybe she won't want to be with a guy who works in a deli.* Her income as a nurse would surely put his to shame ten times over. But would that matter? *It might.*

For the next two hours, the morning crowds kept him and his procession of doubts and insecurities preoccupied. Not only did he have to man the food prep but the cash register as well, and it was a lot. The system used before his father's attack proved not nearly suitable to tackle the onslaught of people all giving orders in rapid succession. Everyone in a rush and out to grab a quick bite on their way to his or her prospective responsibilities.

TIGHT ROPE

"Two eggs over easy on lightly buttered toast. No, change that. Make it rye. And a coffee, light with two sugars," ordered an exhausted doctor still in scrubs.

"Coffee, super strong and black, two cinnamon rolls, and one old-fashioned," said the harried mother saddled with two fussy toddlers in a stroller.

Officer Albert, one of the regulars always came in for his usual – tea, no milk, sweet, a bagel with cream cheese, lightly toasted.

The orders kept piling up. Grateful for the business but drained beyond reason, Zaid wasn't so sure how long he'd be able to keep up the pace, but he had an idea.

"No," said his father.

"But it would only be for a few days. I promise, long enough until you're back and able to be at the store full time again," pleaded Zaid.

"No."

"But I need the help. Without you on the register, I'm running back and forth like crazy and the orders are backing up."

"You losing your hearing? I said, no." Mr. Ali refused to discuss the matter.

"How long do you want to make your customers wait in line? So far, we've been lucky, but after a while, they're going to get fed up and go somewhere else."

"Enough already! You sound like your mother."

A loud "HEY!" emanated from the kitchen. "Watch yourself before I refuse to cook for you today!" goaded Mrs. Ali.

"See! Now look what you started!" Mr. Ali looked pleadingly at his son. "A few more days. Please, habibi. I just don't trust anybody right now. I need you to do as I say."

Mrs. Ali entered the room, and gave her son *the look*. The angrier his father became, the more stressed he also became, and by extension, the more likely his mother would interject. His father he could deal with; he'd had tons of practice. But his mother scared the shit out of him.

Zaid dropped the subject but not the whining. "Fine, but if I wind up having a heart attack one of these days, don't blame me."

**

Maryam

HOW DOES ONE DRESS UP a nurse uniform? Maryam fumbled around in her drawers, frustrated and in search of any add-on to perk up her boring work attire. All she wanted was to make a good impression on the guy from the deli and get him to take notice of her, but so far all he'd seen her in were scrubs. Not exactly her most attractive look.

"Ah, now this is nice," she announced to no one in particular. "¡Me gusta!" She'd found a bright, royal blue, long-sleeve top. *I can wear this under my top. Dress it up a bit.*

Next, Maryam rummaged through her wide collection of scarves on the hunt for a soft, delicate print. Something not too busy but colorful–enough to compliment her blouse and hopefully catch his attention. So far, all she'd caught from him was her food order.

"Maryam!" Her mother called from the kitchen, purposely using her Muslim name, her newest peace offering. "Hurry up. Your food's getting cold."

Oh, no. If I tell her I'm buying out she'll freak. Maryam thought. *What do I say that won't start another round of arguments?* "Coming!" she

TIGHT ROPE

yelled to buy herself more time.

Maryam dressed quickly. *I swear, it feels as if I'm always rushing.* Despite running late, she took extra care to wrap her hijab in a more stylish fashion instead of the usually severe pulled-out-of-the-face, ready-to-go-to-work style she normally opted for. Once at the office, she'd do her usual bait and switch routine, running into the employee bathroom to retie it and tuck the fabric inside her blouse in a more suitable way. She certainly couldn't have it billowing in her patients' faces or getting in her way when she bent over to take someone's blood pressure. Not cool.

"*¡Llegas tarde! Darse prisa!*"

"I know, Mami! I'm hurrying!"

"*Esta Chica, me está volviendo loca.*"

"I heard that." Maryam barreled into the kitchen. "How am I driving you crazy?"

Mrs. Quiñónez, never bothered to answer. Instead she slammed the warm, delicious smelling breakfast onto the table. "Eat."

Maryam knew protesting was a losing battle and voluntarily walking away from this meal would certainly turn into a first-class, front row seat to Quiñónez Crazyland. Maryam didn't feel up to taking that ride.

"*Gracias, Mami.*"

Mrs. Quiñónez kissed the top of her grown daughter's head while tapping one long, mean finger on the table. "I expect you home on time tonight. I'm going to need help in the kitchen."

With a mouth stuffed with eggs, Maryam peered up. "For whaa?"

"Don't talk with your mouth full."

Maryam swallowed and wiped her mouth with her napkin.

"Sorry. What did you say?"

"You heard me. I want your help tonight. We're having guests."

"Oh God, not again."

"Stop! It's not who you think. You're going to be so happy this time. Trust me."

Maryam doubted that. "You're such a yenta."

"Who you calling a yetti?"

Maryam smirked. "Not a yetti–a *Yenta*. It's a Jewish Matchmaker."

"Don't be ridiculous. I'm not Jewish."

"I know, Mami, but it's a saying. Forget it."

"Next you'll be telling me you'll want to convert to Judaism."

Maryam drew in a deep, long breath and counted to ten before replying. "What time do you need me home?"

"After work. Didn't I just say that? For goodness sakes, Maria, you need to learn how to listen better."

Conversations with her mother mimicked talking into the wind. One could scream as loud as they wanted and still not be heard.

Past trying, Maryam stuffed the remainder of her breakfast into her mouth until every last morsel disappeared and met with her mother's roving eye of approval.

"That was delicious but I really have to run," she said, vaulting from her chair. "See you later, Mami." Maryam grabbed her sweater and bag out of the closet, and headed straight out the door. "Love you!" *Whatever she's up to it'll have to wait. The only person on my radar is*—Maryam frowned. *How ridiculous. I don't even know his name, and I certainly can't keep calling him "the deli guy."*

TIGHT ROPE

**

Zaid checked his watch for the tenth time. *She's not coming.* Attempting to blot out his disappointment, he grabbed a clean rag and started wiping off the already spotless counter. Staying busy helped. For now, the store was quiet, the usual morning rush aptly satiated and on their prospective ways. Over the next hour or so he'd prep for the lunch crowd, slicing and dicing vegetables and restocking paper goods. By mid-morning he'd be ready for the onslaught of sandwich lunch orders, most of which came in over the phone for pick up. A few years back he and his father had toyed with the idea of delivery, but after going over the logistics and added costs, they decided they couldn't swing it. Today was one of those days Zaid wished they had found a way.

With an apron tied securely around his waist, Zaid made a hasty retreat to the storeroom to grab extra produce, while still attentively listening for the tinkling of the door's bell in case anyone entered in his absence. Which of course, happened only seconds after leaving.

"I'll be right with you," he shouted, picking his way through the boxes of lettuce, tomatoes and onions. Grabbing one of each, he stuffed them into his apron's wide pocket.

"No problem," called the familiar, long awaited voice. Zaid's heart skipped a beat. *It's her.* "Um… *AsSalaamu'alaikum* Sister," he yelled. "Give me a minute."

"*Wa'alaikum salaam.* Take your time." Maryam answered,

purposely inflecting her reply with a practiced voice of calm instead of the shrill trying to escape. To keep the swarm of butterflies at bay, she looked around the store in an attempt to appear carefree and nonchalant. Pressed for time, she'd decided to order only a cup of coffee. Then make the mad dash to the office, and hopefully get there on time; Dr. Khan didn't appreciate tardiness.

Meanwhile, Zaid anxiously ran his fingers over his beard and through his thick black, hair, trying to make himself look more presentable. Satisfied, he dashed back to the front reappearing in time to catch Maryam reading the poster. Pulling the vegetables from his apron he placed them on the counter in a small pile. "The usual today?" he asked rather efficiently, diverting his eyes down to his cutting board. *Say something you fool…*

"Not today, thanks. Just coffee, light, no sugar." *Why isn't he looking at me? I knew I should have worn the emerald green scarf.*

"Coffee, light, with sugar. Coming right up." *Man, she looks beautiful in blue.*

"No sugar," she corrected.

"Huh?" he asked blankly.

"Coffee, light, with *no* sugar, please." Maryam tilted her head and smiled warmly.

Way to go, dumb ass. "Got it." Zaid busied himself with her order, all the while berating himself and trying to come up with something to say to her other than "huh?". "Um, are you still going to the rally on Saturday?" he asked.

TIGHT ROPE

"I was planning to." Maryam fidgeted with the strap of her pocketbook. "You?"

"Definitely, if I don't have to work."

"*InshaAllah*," replied Maryam, hoping her cheeks weren't giving her away.

Before Zaid had a chance to reply, the front door opened. In walked two young guys, probably in their early twenties, and loud as hell. The tall, one with bad skin headed straight towards the back to the fridge, while the other shorter, thinner guy with an obvious overbite towered over Maryam, blatantly eyeing her up. Zaid's blood boiled, but he did nothing.

A few seconds later, the front of the store's bell tinkled again and in walked a tall soldier decked out in fatigues. Mid-to-late thirties, athletic build, tall, with short-cropped hair peppered with black and gray flecks on the sideburns. His fair skin, angular cheekbones and symmetrical face gave him a commanding presence. Heading straight over to the cooler, Zaid watched him grab a can of iced tea, then join the already existing small group amassed in the front. He handed the coffe cup to her.

"No *azúcar*, right?" she confirmed.

"Nope, no sugar." Zaid answered, his focus on the beaver now ogling Maryam's ass. "Anything else?"

Maryam frowned. This wasn't going at all as she'd hoped. "You know what? I've changed my mind. I think I'll have my usual."

Zaid turned his head. "No problem." He'd never made a sandwich this fast in his life.

The two young men standing near Maryam observed the interaction closely. Zaid shot the shorter, thinner guy a warning look. "What can I get you?"

"I don't know. From where I'm standing, everything looks mighty tasty."

Zaid held his tongue but if he could have reached over the counter, he would have punched the guy square in his bucktooth mouth. "What about you?" he asked the taller guy with a face full of stubble and acne.

"Buns. I'll take some sweet buns." The short guy found that hysterical and the two slime-balls yucked it up.

The soldier in line was no fool. He caught the double entendre and he wasn't amused. Patience waning, his rugged features recoiled in disgust. Crossing both arms over his chest, he tilted his head back to take a better look at these two clowns.

Of course, this firestorm of testosterone transpired behind Maryam's back, so she remained clueless, her mind elsewhere, becoming increasingly nervous she would be late for work.

Once finished assembling the sister's sandwich, he bagged it up and handed it to Maryam. He'd have to speak to her another day. "That'll be nine seventy-six," he said to her, his eyes locked onto Lanky.

Maryam fumbled through her purse, searching for her

TIGHT ROPE

wallet.

"Forget about it, sis." Zaid wanted her out of the store as quickly as possible.

"No, I got it." Maryam handed him a ten, and waited to collect her change. She hardly glanced over at Zaid as she left, giving him barely a muffled salaam.

"Next!" Zaid tried not to appear ruffled.

The two morons exchanged snickers, both pairs of eyes glued to Maryam's ample loveliness as she stepped through the door.

"Man, I could have a good time with that *conchita*," said the shorter one.

"NEXT!" Zaid yelled again.

"I hear you, bro. Rice and beans with a falafel on the side." Stubble-face cracked up laughing.

Without missing a beat, the soldier in line barged through the two cackling hyenas and slammed his can of ice tea on the counter. First glaring at Zaid like he was a punk and then over at the two other idiots. "Shut your mouths."

"You talkin' to us?" Stubble asked, emboldened.

"Enough," warned the soldier, not close to backing down.

"Oh, yeah, soldier boy? What's it to you? You got something for Muslim conchitas?" mocked Shorty.

"Keep your mouths shut."

"Chill, bro. Not like you weren't thinking the same thing," blurted Shorty.

"Last warning."

"And whatdya gonna do if we don't?" challenged Stubble, all tough.

Taller, stronger and in a hell of a lot better shape than these two scruffy posers, the soldier edged his way over towards Stubble first. "You feel like finding out?"

Now, truth be told, Stubble wasn't beyond enjoying a good laugh at somebody else's expense, but he wasn't anybody's fool either. He knew better than to butt heads with this guy, especially after two more of his army buddies came in.

"Hey, McCormick," one said, suspiciously eyeing up the scene, and now positioning himself directly behind the two stooges, ready to throw down if necessary. "Problem?"

"Is there a problem?" McCormick asked Stubble, shooting another angry glare towards Shorty.

The two fools quickly surmised they were out-ranked and out-flanked and decided it was best to take their leave. "No, no problem," mumbled Shorty. Shaking their heads, they pushed their way through the wall of muscle, grumbling. "Keep your cool, soldier boy. Don't want you going all PSTD on me and shit. Not like we're in Iraqistan."

Shame is such a strong and alienating emotion. Under the piercing glare of the soldier, Zaid had that going on along with a large lump wedged in his throat. While not one to place blame on others, he also wasn't the kind of guy to rationalize his behavior away to make himself sound guiltless, but the damage was already done. The soldier had been right to look at him the way he had. Zaid punked out big time and felt like a disgraced turd—if there was such a thing.

McCormick wouldn't let up either. He stood firmly grounded, continuing to glare at Zaid with a look of disgust oozing out from every pore on his face. No further words needed to be exchanged.

Zaid's shoulders slumped. He'd allowed those two guys to disrespect Maryam and had done nothing to stop it. And to make matters worse, he dropped the ball in front of a guy who stood up without the slightest hesitation. *Way to go, jackass.*

CHAPTER 20

Russell Tetler

SCHOOL HAD ONLY LET OUT a few weeks before. Summer's sweltering temperatures did little to squelch the enthusiasm generated by the year-end graduation buzz still lingering strong in the air for many families. Tassels, gowns, diplomas—all the cherished markings of a completed passage of time, so sweet and yet so bitter. But for Russell and Doris, that milestone now felt rather distant. A culmination of dreams all colliding into a single, encapsulated minute in time. And as their long-anticipated momentous window slammed shut, turning forever into a yesterday, the buzz and rise of mounting tension and uncertainty permeated the Tetler household, especially as the new, significant landmark drew closer.

Boot Camp.

Basic Training.

Six to thirteen weeks of some of the most intense and rigorous training all new recruits are expected to endure.

TIGHT ROPE

Everything from the physical to the mental and emotional, each person is systematically reconditioned to think less of themselves as individuals and more as a team players, responsible for one another. Ready to function as a team to achieve success whether on land, in the air, or on the sea, all the rigorous testing is designed to make each recruit ready to face the elements of military service, while equally geared for the opportunity to learn new life and survival skills.

"Remember, it's a mind game," warned Russell. "Everyone goes through it. Hang tough and before you know it, it'll all be over."

"I know," replied George. "I remember what the recruiter said. 'Keep a good attitude even if you are getting chewed out.'"

"Hold your tongue and keep your mouth shut. If you make a mistake, don't go making any excuses. 'Yes Sir' or 'no Sir' when prompted."

"I know, Dad."

"Did your recruiter also happen to tell you arriving, on-time is considered late? Bet he didn't tell you that…"

"Yeah, he did…drilled it into us, too. About two months or so ago, when I was first filling out all the paperwork, I had to go to his office to drop off some stuff. Arrived precisely on the dot and Sergeant Connor *still* refused to meet with me. Told me I was late. I couldn't believe it! He pissed me off. Made me come back the next day."

Russell laughed, "Yeah well, in the long run, he was doing you a favor. You'll find out."

"I guess."

"Trust me, no guessing about it…" The air in the room thinned. "What are you thinking about?" he asked, measuring his words lest he be accused of being over-protective—which in truth, he was.

"It sounds dumb, but you know, Dad, by the time I'm done with all this, I'll have a slew of new skills, whether I stay in the military or decide to go back to civilian life. Either way I'll be set and at the top of my game."

Russell grinned. "That you will be."

**

Time is funny. Always around, assumed, and discernable. Felt like only yesterday when George stood in the same room getting ready for the first big day of school, carefully dressed in the clothes selected the night before. Ablutions and breakfast rushed through. Backpack on, hair combed, shiny new lunch box in hand. The tight squeeze of Russell's hand as the elementary school came closer into view, filling rapidly with a thousand-other smiling but nervous little people. Lastly, Russell remembers watching his child's final, brave, hesitant turn of the head before waving goodbye. Little heads of children all escorted into the building whose job it was to frame and mold all the tiny little brains. Doris cried like a baby that day. A prequel for what was to come.

The time had arrived. The bewitching hour here. Instead of being a few safe months away, when George's date to leave became weeks, those same weeks swiftly turned traitor and became days. Days turned to hours and hours turned to right now. Russell stood, leaning in the doorway of George's bedroom. He had prepared for this moment. He'd be ready when the time came, he told himself, but now his child was leaving and he still had so much that still needed to be said.

TIGHT ROPE

"All packed?"

"I think so," answered George distractedly, zippering up the large, sturdy, green canvas tote purchased from the Army Navy store weeks before.

"Your mom's fixing you some breakfast."

"It smells great, but I don't think I have time."

"Make her happy. It's going to be a long time before she'll be able to shove her famous dry oatmeal down your throat."

George smiled. "Not sure I can fake it this time. My stomach's been acting up, feeling sort of jumpy."

"I can understand that, but don't hurt your mother's feelings. This transition is going to be tough enough. Just have her wrap it up for you to take. Then dump it in the trash first chance you get—but out of eyeshot. Deal?"

George chuckled. "Will do."

Russell made a concerted effort to keep this morning's conversation light and breezy. He'd promised himself days leading up not to be one of those selfish parents who dumped a bunch of heavy sentimental crap on their kid's shoulders before leaving, rushing to the rescue with the telling of quotes, antidotes, and earth-shattering claptrap. Nevertheless, the few words he'd managed to say had all sounded forced and contrite as if on the way out of his mouth they got caught in his throat before finally breaking free.

"Dad?" The sound of George's voice shook Russell alert. "Remember, I'm not going to be able to write that often, at least not until basic training is over. From what I've heard, they make us write one letter home to let our folks know we arrived, and then that's pretty much it until graduation."

Russell understood.

"I mean, I'll try and all, but Mom…you know how she gets and—"

"I know," replied Russell, solemnly. *Boy, did he ever.* "But did you remember to do what I asked?"

"I did." George replied, standing up, taking a full two steps over to the bed to pull a wad of letters from underneath the pillow. A small stack of already individually enveloped letters, all neatly tied with bakery string. "Here. One for each week I'll be gone. Like we agreed."

"Good job," said Russell impressed. "Your mother will love this. I'll leave one under her pillow every Sunday. Try to start her week off with a smile or as much of one as we can squeeze out of her until you're back," he said, winking.

George's eyes began to glisten. It was time to get going.

Russell caught George's expression. "Come here you."

George marched over and stood before Russell, face to face, although be it a full head shorter.

"You know I love you, right?" Russell fought back the quiver in his voice.

George nodded, rapidly blinking back the avalanche of tears. "I love you too, Daddy," she whispered throwing her arms tightly around her father's neck. Small tear droplets no longer able to be held in cascaded across her dewy, soft cheeks as she burrowed her head into the protective shoulder of her father. "I promise to make you and mom proud."

"We already are, Princess…so proud…so-so proud…"

**

TIGHT ROPE

A sudden loud crash caused Russell to bolt straight up in his daughter's bed. His body was covered from a sticky sweat and his pillow damp from dreaming the same conversation over and over again. Quickly he threw on a robe and dashed out to see where the commotion had come from.

He noticed immediately the bedroom door was ajar and the bed made, which indicated Doris was already awake and about.

"Doris! Are you alright?" he shouted, but no response. There was never a response. Promptly descending the steps two at a time, he abruptly stopped halfway. Over the railing from the open side facing the living room he clearly understood what had happened.

Pieces of shattered glass littered the top of the coffee table. Some splintered onto the area rug and outer floor. A corner of the now broken wooden box was missing altogether, as Doris, in a daze stood over the table, holding the remnants of the once framed triangle container in her two brittle shaking hands.

"Ah, Doris…what happened now?" Russell gently asked his wife, still not expecting her to answer. The dropped crumpled dust cloth on the floor said it all. Russell walked down the remainder of the stairs, careful to slip on a pair of house shoes before entering the living room.

"Here, give me that." Russell lifted the broken, splintered case from his wife's clasp. "Don't worry, you go sit on the couch. I'll clean it up," Russell guided Doris away from the glass smatterings. "Watch your step now…careful…yes, yes, it's all right…don't worry, accidents happen. Nothing to fret over."

Surprisingly cooperative, Doris sat perched on the couch and thankfully out of the way, providing Russell with a small reprieve long enough to grab the broom and dustpan from the hall closet to begin sweeping up the mess. Then turning his attention over to the area rug, he grabbed the vacuum and glided it deliberately over the same spots three and four times to make absolutely sure there weren't any slivers of glass left scattered about to step on. One couldn't be too careful…

Taking a quick peek over at his wife, Russell couldn't mistake the sheer hollowness clouding over her eyes and face. *Of all things to break*, he begrudgingly thought. "I'll get this fixed," he proclaimed. "I'll bring it over to the mall. I think they still have one of those framing places in there…some sort of a kiosk thing, what's it called again? Starts with a 'B' I think. I don't know. I'll figure it out," Russell continued, talking to the air.

"Maybe I'll have them use Plexiglas instead of real glass this time. We'll never have to worry about this happening again."

Russell heard himself and detested how he babbled on and on whenever he spoke to Doris, but years of one-sided conversations could do that to a person. Forced them to fill in the long, vacant gaps with silly talk. Yet, try as he might, he couldn't seem to stop himself. Couldn't bear to live in total silence, even if the only audible voice heard was his own.

Doris slipped off her tattered old slippers. Placing the once decorative couch pillow under her head, she proceeded to curl up on the couch, turning her head to face the back of it and away from Russell's view.

Russell picked up the folded afghan and carefully covered her withered body. "Try to get some rest, Doris. It's all going to be okay. I'll get it fixed right as rain, you'll see."

But unbeknown to Russell, Doris wasn't the least bit concerned about the stupid broken frame or the damn shattered glass or any of the other incessant chatter Russell seemed determined to make her nuts with. Day in and day out, the man

TIGHT ROPE

never shut the hell up. Always had some idiotic thing to say as if she were too stupid to see what was going on for herself. Always assuming somehow that her lack of conversation with him meant she was batty or something.

While Russell continued rambling on, Doris' mind traveled elsewhere, waiting impatiently for him to return upstairs to shower before slipping her arm underneath the couch cushion to grope for the familiar shape of the knife nestled where she had last left it. Once her fingertips were able to stroke the sharp blade, her peace and tranquility would return and all in the world would be right again.

**

Russell had a long day ahead of him if he wanted to put into motion the next part in his plan, but time was running out. Before he knew it, Fat Mouth would be standing at the podium serving up her swill on a plate with Joe Public lapping it up, no questions asked and begging for seconds—but not if he could help it.

A short while later, he came back downstairs fully dressed and grateful to find that Doris had remained on the couch sleeping. He softly walked down the hall closed his office door, then plopped onto his chair fully prepared to boot his faithful computer up, and more than ready to get his morning email written and underway. Afterwards, he'd compose his next gift's letter and get it ready for delivery. All on schedule…all part of the bigger plan.

Notes and photos gleaned from his search the night before were stuffed in his drawer. Eventually, he knew he'd have to discard all the accumulated evidence, but for now there was little danger of discovery. Even if Doris nosed around, she'd have no clue what it was all about.

Russell stretched. His neck felt stiff. The pillows in George's room weren't as firm as the ones on his own bed. *This old machine takes forever.* The computer burred and screeched until all the programs loaded before grinding to a noisy halt. *Maybe when this is all over, I get myself a new one. Something fancy with all the bells and whistles.* Like a maestro ready to compose, Russell wiggled his fingers, cleared his throat and began to type.

Dear Black Bitch,

Hope you enjoyed the little gift I left on your stoop. I can't begin to tell you how much pleasure I took leaving it for you, or rather your father. He is your father, right? One never knows with you people. Anyway, my only regret was not being there to see the expression on your face. You know how much I enjoy surprising you, but no matter. Your next present is going to rock your socks off! I can guarantee you'll wish you could swing in the wind…but look at me, ready to give away the big secret. Can't have that, can we? No. See you sooner than later, and remember to keep the lights on for me.

Russell read the email over a few more times, checking for typos and effect, making sure the haunting veiled threat met with his approval before pushing send. He was ultra-proud of the way he was leading her on with his clever clues and innuendos, feeding them to her in bits and pieces, a little at a time to scare the be-Jesus out of her. Feeling rather accomplished and in need of something hot to drink, he stretched his stiff legs before standing to leave his cave when a soft knock at the door startled him.

"Doris?" he asked, already assuming she wouldn't answer back. Instead of getting up, Russell rolled his chair the two feet to the door and opened it a crack. "What do you want?"

TIGHT ROPE

Expressionless, Doris handed her husband a steaming hot cup of coffee along with a small plate containing a well-buttered roll. She turned and shuffled her way back to her couch, back to wait.

"Oh, geez, thanks," Russell called out after her. "You're a lifesaver."

Without missing a beat, Russell used his foot to close the door, slid back over to his desk and proceeded to rip a healthy bite off the fresh roll, stuffing large mouthfuls worth, and barely chewing his load before swallowing. Naturally, he followed his gorging by gulping a big swig of the strong, somewhat bitter brew. Although hot, Russell had to hand it to Doris—for once in her miserable life, her timing was right on the money.

CHAPTER 21

Eugene Underwood

FREELANCING CAME WITH ITS PARTICULAR set of perks. As far as Eugene was concerned, nothing beat the flexible hours, the ability to work wherever or for whomever he wanted, and the idea of not being stuck in some ratty office with a bunch of other jerks or worse, being forced to share some crummy cubicle, languishing behind a desk, counting away the hours until closing time. Being his own boss, Eugene controlled the jobs he took on as well as which clients he decided to work for. He especially appreciated not having anyone lurking around the corner, ready to pounce or micromanage him to death—or worse, try to make him adhere to a slew of arbitrary rules. Eugene despised clients who were under the false impression that their money meant they got to call the shots and tell Eugene how to do his job—*like I'm some Goddamn landscaper or something...*

Clients *like the asshole from the Bronx* didn't have upstairs what it took to appreciate the level of skill necessary to successfully conduct a clean termination; how each step, from start to finish, had to be meticulously planned, with no detail, no matter how small, ignored or glossed over. They expected Eugene to then add some idiotic theatric monologue, more at home in some B-rated movie for posterity and revenge, but this held no place in Eugene's repertoire and frankly, he resented the infringement.

"I want that prick to suffer. Beat the living shit out of him until the prick wets his pants."

Over the years, Eugene had worked exceedingly hard never to let his body language betray his thoughts or giveaway his inclinations, but clients like this guy irked his last nerve. "I prefer in and out. Clean kill. Less chance of getting caught or making mistakes."

"What? You can't torture him a bit? What the hell am I paying you for?"

Eugene ran his thumb over his forefinger, a trick he'd learned way back when to calm down. "You're PAYING me to kill him, not establish a meaningful relationship."

"Meaningful relationship? Get outta here. I'm not asking you to hump the guy, just fuck him up first. Wind him a little. Make him puke up his last meal."

Eugene's face revealed no emotion as he forcibly kept his upper body rigidly still, sliding both his hands safely into his pockets.

"And ya know what? Before you finish the bastard off say my name. I want him to know his last breath came from me…something like, 'Ah…Ghost bids you a final farewell.'"

"I'm not saying that," replied Eugene, in full monotone.

"Too corny? Okay, then at least whisper my name when you cut his throat. Can you at least do that much?"

"It's going to cost you extra."

"You can't be fuckin' serious," replied Ghost, incredulously.

"*Au contraire, mon frère.* Trust me, I don't do stand up."

Nobody told Eugene how to take care of his business—*ever*. He'd kill the bastard but on his own terms, extra money or not.

Freelancing also provided one more perk Eugene particularly enjoyed—money. He got to keep all the profits, which for him was quite the incentive. His bread and butter. The brilliant taste of freedom smeared across the palette of his existence. But of course, nothing is ever all or nothing; he had to allocate time to fit in the required legwork. Hitting the pavement, scrounging up clients, and developing projects meant occasionally wearing a few hats…or in his case, weapons.

Since Eugene prided himself on not having much of a personal life, he never found an issue distinguishing between home and work life. The two blended seamlessly. Having no wife or kids to support also meant no guilt for working long and crazy hours. And in the event the workload slowed or didn't come in steady, feeding one mouth, instead of two or three, remained a bonus. Not having personal interests outside of maintaining a comfortable existence with an occasional good beer and some tasty grub worked for Eugene, and balancing downtime and his career proved to be a breeze.

For some in the business, being their own boss meant the risk of getting shorted for a job well done. Not so for Eugene. He was his own debt collector, accountant, and enforcer. His reputation on the street supported this assertion more than adequately.

Eugene opened his wallet. Rent was due soon, but he wasn't concerned. Keeping the cut from those inept idiots had left him more than enough to live comfortably for at least the next two months. More than enough time to scope out a new lead or two. The city offered guys like him plenty of opportunities if one knew where to look.

The cooling temperatures outside helped. For most people, this meant long months of shivering, increased heating bills, and heavier jackets and scarves, but for Eugene, this opened a plethora of options. Everything from an increased selection of weapons to choose from to the less conspicuous ways to hide his tools of the trade. For the most part, guns were plain cumbersome. Some were outright weighty. Now, as the weather changed, donning a jacket or bulky sweater, or even wearing many layers, wouldn't be viewed as anything out of place. Much less of a headache to contend with should he decide to grab a few quick jobs to pad his pockets for the leaner months.

Without anything pressing on his agenda, Eugene decided to take a stroll, get the lay of the land under his belt. That last client made the recent job sound like a simple in and out deal, and it probably would have been if Eugene hadn't depended on those local yokels for assistance. Be that as it may, he had the time now to walk, take a few mental notes, and possibly avail himself of meeting with new potential clients. Checking his phone, he scrolled through the list of numbers, all systematically labeled in such a way that if any bystander got hold of it, the contact list would indicate nothing but a collection of random restaurants, a couple of car washes, and a bar or two. But for law enforcement, should they ever get their sticky fingers on the list, once they broke his code, it would be a treasure trove of information—a real *Who's Who* register of names of some of the most nefarious gangsters and bosses residing in the metropolitan area.

But Eugene was a pro. He made sure to creatively insert the

names to make detection more difficult. Anthony's Rub & Shine, Shorty's Ribs and Dibs, Carmine's Car Wash, and his all-time favorite, Big Papa's Bergen Beer Belly. Named after Big Bergen, a taller than shit Scandinavian he'd done some work for some years back, he still threw a job or two Eugene's way occasionally, specifically when faced with a problem "which needed a *final* solution." *Those were the best kinds.*

But Eugene never bothered worrying about whether or not his phone got lost, confiscated, or even of the possibility of his getting caught. Living on the fringe of society had taught him a long time ago that the life he lived came with certain risks. Eugene accepted how in many ways, fringe living meant one didn't exist or at least not in the ordinary sense of the word. A sort of "interminable isolation," not necessarily anti-society but anti-conforming. A life which had no use for social security numbers to connect him to his work, no bank accounts or credit cards, and not even a real driver's license, although the records dating back to his juvenile detention fiasco, while sealed, positively still existed. No way of getting around that. However, since then he prided himself on being able to successfully slip through the many cracks and crevices of his existence and still come out swinging and on top.

Up to now, every item he possessed contributed to his carefully designed façade. Tools for hire, gear for concealment. Nothing off the beaten path and nothing remotely mainstream, except his attire. Clothes at all times had to blend in. Despite the fact his career depended on complete discretion and the ability to camouflage, Eugene held little to no regard for society or their bombastic rules. He was certainly clever enough never to use his primary (but still disposable) cell to make unnecessary phone calls. Throwaways, or what were called "burners" in the trade, were purchased for exactly this purpose. Prepaid devices like these were bought with cash. No contract and with one purpose, they were promptly disposed of. Throwaways amped up privacy, making it harder to be tracked, easier to conduct illegal activities, and keeping hackers, unsolicited texts, and annoying telemarketers at arm's length. The objective being to leave nothing behind which could then be traced back to him. Too risky.

Eugene noticed a bar already open for business. For the past half-hour, his stomach had done nothing but complain, grumbling loudly every chance it got. *It couldn't hurt to grab a quick bite.*

Quickly, he darted across the street, playing cat and mouse with oncoming traffic. Without thinking, he shoved the heavily ornate wood door open with his shoulder. He was promptly reminded how this probably wasn't the smartest move. "Ah," he moaned, forgetting how sore his arm still was at the elbow.

Once inside, he was pleasantly surprised by the classy décor. Wooden floors, dim lighting, and clientele in three-piece suits. More of a restaurant slash bar type place than strictly a bar; clearly a step up from his usual choice of dive.

"Good afternoon, sir. One?" Asked the rail-thin young woman sporting bow tie, white shirt, and black slacks.

"Yes."

"Follow me," directed the efficient maître de, grabbing a menu.

Eugene stood where he was, making no attempt to follow, which she picked up within two seconds.

"I prefer to sit at the bar."

"Oh, sure, absolutely. No problem. Feel free to pick a stool. Someone will serve you shortly."

Eugene's eyes darted around the long, narrow room, similar to an alley between city buildings, but ascetically friendly. Big, heavy wooden tables lined the floor. Detailed carpentry abounded, including the backsides on all the leather seating. Unlike his usual joint, this bar was clean, giving off a somewhat subdued, relaxed feeling.

Inside sat a diverse crowd. At one table, a few college-aged kids nursed beers, laughs, and nachos, while at another table on the far side of the room, a few suits, probably from the bank next door, grabbed a quick bite. They drank what appeared to be trendy shots. *Figures.*

From what Eugene could tell nothing seemed out of the ordinary, nor did he recognize any familiar faces. Nevertheless, he selected a seat facing the entrance keeping his back facing the wall, as was his policy. Always watch to see who enters and exists, no matter where you park your ass.

"What can I get you?" inquired the young, welcoming bartender with the deep baritone voice, sporting thick-rimmed glasses, a dark black V-neck T-shirt and blue jeans, which highlighted his rippled muscles. His long, twisted dreadlocks were tied off to the back, defining his well-groomed goatee and flawless, stellar smile.

"Beer."

"From the tap?"

"Yeah."

"Need a menu?"

"Not if you have roast beef."

The young man chuckled. "We sure do. How do you want it? Hot or cold?"

"Cold in a sandwich. Lettuce, tomato, no onion, Thousand Island dressing on the side."

TIGHT ROPE

"Rye, wheat or Keiser roll?"

"Keiser."

"Fries or onion rings?"

"Fries."

"Anything else?"

"Not for now."

"Coming right up."

Eugene appreciated the efficiency of the bartender. No superfluous chatter. He couldn't stand small talk, especially when he was trying to eat.

The only other patron at the bar was an older gentleman seated two seats over, a bit crumpled in his attire, but by no means derelict.

"Another," ordered the old man rudely, wiggling his empty beer bottle in the air.

As the bartender passed the old man, his jaw tightened. Not necessarily enough for most people to take notice, but Eugene wasn't most people.

The grumpy old man perched on his stool made a big display out of reading the newspaper, only glancing up periodically to peer disapprovingly at the television screen between bites of his sandwich. "Damn lying politicians," he muttered to no one in particular. Eugene made no attempt to acknowledge or reply to the sudden outburst.

"I swear, nothing but a bunch of whack jobs," offered the rather verbose, shoddy man. "Our country has too many problems, I tell ya."

Eugene remained aloof, not wishing to encourage the old sod to engage him in his recalcitrant chatter.

The bartender placed a paper napkin on the bar and then

plunked the refill in front of the old man. The bill housed in its leather casing was also left with defiant finesse. Again, not with enough enmity to illicit attention, but certainly more than enough to field his protest. Eugene smirked, enjoying the exchange.

The older man's attention slipped back to his plate as he managed to consume one last considerable mouthful without choking to death before overdramatically wiping his mouth with a napkin. Once done, he crumpled and tossed it on top of the now empty dish, but not before vociferously clearing his throat. Pushing his plate forward with a flourish, he indicated to the bartender with his pointer finger he was finished.

Everything with this guy is a melodrama, thought Eugene. *What a character...*

Grabbing the check, the old man adjusted his glasses and gave the numbers a once over. "Damn shame it is," he grumbled at full volume. Reaching into his back pocket, he had to dig for his wallet, pulling out with it a small container of dental floss. Now *this* little ditty caught Eugene's discreet attention.

What brand is that? wondered Eugene.

The older man tucked a twenty and a five-dollar bill inside the leather check holder and then began counting out his change, unconsciously lip-syncing each added amount as he went along. "Forty-five, forty-six, forty-seven…Fifty-eight…" until satisfied.

"You know, I can still remember when a beer and sandwich cost no more than a few bucks. This is as much as my water bill," he announced, stealing an affable glance in Eugene's direction. "Highway robbery."

Eugene simply looked away, taking another swig of his beer, as though no words had been spoken to him at all.

"By the time, I pay for the meal, I might as well have shopped

TIGHT ROPE

for the week."

Eugene, who continued to eye up the dental floss, forced an ingratiating smile across his tight lips. "Mind if I grabbed a piece of that? I feel like I have something stuck."

Strange request but the old guy slid the small plastic container towards Eugene anyway. "Help yourself."

"Appreciated."

The bartender reappeared. "Excuse me, Sir," he asked Eugene, "did you want coleslaw on the side?"

The old guy stared at Eugene waiting for his response, all up in his business.

Eugene quickly nodded a *no* and then pointed to the television and blurted, "Out of a country of millions, you'd think both parties could have come up with a better selection than these guys." In truth, Eugene didn't much care whose asses sat in the White House or any other house for that matter. To him, all politicians were con artists, out to make a buck like the next guy. All he wanted at the moment was something to distract the old guy's attention long enough from the floss now in Eugene's possession. As expected, his efforts produced the desired result.

Russell's eyes immediately darted up to the television screen, never noticing the more than average length of dental floss being appropriated and subtly wrapped around Eugene's agile fingers.

Pretty strong—taut ...

"Personally, I'm happy than hell the Black guy is out. I don't care what other people say, I'm still not convinced he was born in the United States."

Eugene snapped the string firm to make sure—*a good enough substitute for fishing line in a pinch, for sure.*

"About time everybody woke up and voted like they had

some God damn sense. Now we'll finally get our country back."

Eugene slid the container back over but not before discreetly pocketing the floss. "Thanks."

"No problem. I carry it with me everywhere these days. Food is always getting caught in my dentures, especially anything with seeds. Those damn little buggers lodge in any hole they can find. It drives me nuts."

The friendly bartender returned carrying Eugene's beer and plate. "Here you go. Enjoy. Need anything else?" he asked.

"Ketchup. And toss me a few extra napkins."

"You got it," he replied pleasantly, heading towards the kitchen, and picking up the check holder from the old bastard at the same time. "Have a nice day," he grumbled mechanically at the old reprobate, intentionally ignoring him yet all too keenly aware of the hatred waffling in his direction.

Russell never bothered to reply or acknowledge the subtle brush-off. Instead, he stood up, readied himself to take his leave, but as he passed Eugene, he bestowed on the quiet stranger one last parting piece of wisdom. "Mark my words, if we're not careful, more "Afro-Americans" will be running the country," Russell jutted his stubble chin deliberately in the direction of the seething bartender. "You can count on it."

CHAPTER 22

Nour Ibrahim

TWO MORE DAYS UNTIL THE *rally and I'm stuck perched over the throne at two in the morning, not sure whether to throw up or take a shit.* The rest of the Ibrahim home continued to slumber. Nour had fallen asleep less than an hour earlier after having practiced her speech, and memorized as much of it as possible, only to be jarred awake by the sensation of sharp spasms slicing through her gut. Curled up in a ball, writhing under the blanket in pain until the call of nature summoned. Doubled over, she made the mad dash to the bathroom, trying to stay as quiet as possible as she felt her way in the dark, which of course produced one stubbed toe, a banged knee, and a messy mishap in her pajamas.

Earlier in the evening when she had returned home from the doctor's, her mother was all too anxious to hand her a scribbled message from none other than Dr. Khan, herself. "Don't forget to make the appointment with Dr. Frank." The "or else" was implied.

Tightlipped, Nour was pissed off. Doctor Khan had played

dirty. *If this woman wasn't such a close friend of my mother's and an excellent physician, I'd report her ass!*

Needless to say, Dr. Khan's so-called "timely reminder" of course created the expected effect with Nour's mother, immediately plying her with a barrage of questions about her health, who Dr. Frank was, and why she needed to make an appointment to see him "ASAP."

"He's a gastroenterologist."

"What's wrong?"

"I'm fine."

"If Aliyah is sending you to a gastroenterologist, you must not be fine. "

"It's only a precaution. A few tests."

"You look sick. Maybe you should sit."

"Stop. I'm okay."

"When's the last time you ate?"

"Ma! STOP!"

"Don't tell me to stop," snapped her mother. "You stop being so secretive all the time. I'm your mother and I have every right to know what's wrong with my own child. And for the record, you can tell Dr. Khan or Dr. Franklin, I don't care about those HIPPA-DIPPA laws either." When upset or under eminent duress, Mrs. Ibrahim tended to rhyme acronyms at will.

"Frank."

"Huh?"

"Dr. Frank. You called him Franklin."

"Don't play smartass with me. You knew what I meant." Nour hated when her mother got pushy. "What did Aliyah say?"

"She didn't."

"Stop being so secretive! What did she tell you she thinks it

TIGHT ROPE

is?"

"She didn't." Mrs. Ibrahim shot Nour the infamous death glare.

"At this point, she doesn't know and she refuses to guess." Nour pulled her hijab off and freed her hand from the clip. "By the way, she wanted me to ask you, does anyone in the family have irritable bowel syndrome, ulcerative colitis or Crohn's?"

Mrs. Ibrahim crossed her arms defiantly. "Not that I am aware of. I'll have to ask your dad when he comes home, but don't think I don't know you still haven't answered me."

"Sorry, what was your question again?" Drained, Nour didn't feel like arguing.

"What is wrong with you? Better yet, what do you THINK is wrong with you?"

"My stomach. It hurts. A lot."

"Period pain?"

"No. Nothing like that."

"Where does it hurt?"

"Over here," Nour pointed towards her intestines. "And I can't stop going to the bathroom. It's crazy."

"Maybe it's nerves? You've been under a lot of stress recently…"

"That's what I thought, but Dr. Khan thinks it's more than that. She told me she's not saying stress can't trigger whatever this is, but she thinks there's an underlying issue. Something else."

"I see."

"Don't worry. *Insha'Allah*, I'm going to be fine."

"What day do you take the tests?"

"I scheduled them for early next week."

"Next week? Why so long?"

"It was the earliest they could fit me in," replied Nour, shoulders drooping.

"And until then? What are you supposed to do?"

"Until then I deal. What choice do I have?"

That curt answer did *not* please her mother *at all*. Nour quickly tried to clean up her attitude. "Although, now that you asked, I wouldn't turn away a bowl of your homemade chicken soup if you offered."

Mrs. Ibrahim bent over Nour, worry plastered across her face. Leaning closer, she kissed her daughter's forehead, gently testing for temperature. "Stop keeping everything bottled up," she said, her feelings still miffed. "You don't always have to do everything on your own. I'm here for you. Your dad is here for you, but you need to trust us."

"I do." Nour reached up to hug her mother. Her mother's neck held the comforting scent of lavender soap and love.

"Let us be your parents."

Nour pulled her mother in closer, nuzzling her face into her mother's warm embrace. "Would you go with me to the tests next week?" she whispered.

The reply came in the form of a tight embrace.

For a moment, all the stress of the world lifted as Nour allowed her mind to be cosseted by her mother's protective embrace. If only she could reveal the rest as easily, but for so many reasons, it wasn't something she felt ready to disclose. The thought of burdening her parents with this level of "crazy" seemed irresponsible, even downright cruel.

She couldn't do it…not yet, anyway. After the rally, when all the madness calmed, she'd come clean. Take the time necessary to become physically healthy again. Perhaps make a few changes in

TIGHT ROPE

her personal goals and private life. Until then, she had to stay focused on a few things: delivering the best speech possible, keeping a meal or two in, and not accidentally shitting herself in public. And sadly, her focus wouldn't necessarily follow that order.

CHAPTER 23

Russell Tetler

LUNCH AT THE BAR HAD been quite the indulgence and at those exorbitant prices, it would most likely remain a rarity. Not surprisingly, the sandwich left Russell feeling full, although the inviting plate of cookies and carafe of coffee left by Doris on the kitchen counter seemed a perfect finishing touch. *As much as this nutty woman never speaks to me, she certainly always makes sure I eat. That's gotta count for something.*

With less than two full days left until the big showdown, Russell referred to his To-Do list. From the missing check marks, he ascertained that most of the list had successfully been tackled. The remaining preparations all centered around one issue: Doris.

Russell understood that what he was about to do was risky. If he got caught or killed, besides the social security, life and medical insurances, Doris would be on her own for the first time in her life. Since chances weren't leaning in his favor, Russell felt obliged to make sure she'd be financially okay.

TIGHT ROPE

Russell decided when he'd first got the idea to enact justice for George's untimely demise, the best course of action in terms of securing Doris would be to leave all the necessary paperwork, including his Will, in a folder on George's bed. Russell felt certain this was the only place she'd find it quickly enough. If he left it on a counter or in a drawer like any normal person, she'd probably toss it out or never look inside. Russell still reeled over the time Doris had hoarded all their mail for over two months, crammed inside a cookie tin, including quite a few outstanding bills, one cut-off notice from the electric company, and the updated bankcard he'd applied for. He only found out when everything started getting shut off and when his bankcard was declined while standing in line to pay for gas. Furious, he fussed at the bank and over the phone to the bank and electric company, only to find out the fault was Doris's. When asked, what compelled her to do such a thing, she only shrugged a pathetic *I don't know*, never taking her eyes off the television set. Now he *and only he* retrieves the mail.

Too bad Doris doesn't have any other family or friends nearby who could be here for her when the news about what I did arrives. Lord knows, she isn't the sharpest tool in the shed, nor a Cracker Jack decision-maker. Shoot, she hasn't gone food shopping alone in over two years.

Look at her…what happened to the girl I once married? Once so full of life and boundless energy, and a real beauty to boot. I can still remember how Doris loved to dance. How she'd swayed in my arms, resting her chin in the crux of my neck, always smelling like a mixture of fresh breezes and lilac.

I used to enjoy watching how excited she'd become about decorating the house, changing all the pillows and blankets on the beds to honor each new season. Back then Doris ran our home to perfection, or at least close to it – until George died. That's when everything changed. She changed. I changed. And together our life never recovered.

The Tetler home was mortgage-free. The ten-year old car was as well, although unfortunately once Russell met his fate, whatever direction it ultimately took, the vehicle was destined to rust away, corroding to destruction. Doris neither knew how to nor had any inclination to drive.

Russell made sure not to leave any credit card debt, and the balance on his coffin and burial plot were paid in full with cash, the receipt in the folder.

Anything I'm forgetting?

Russell bit into the second cookie. *Ah! Chocolate chip with walnuts*, his ultimate childhood favorite. The coffee still tasted on the bitter side but the sweetness of the rich chocolate chips more than compensated. He greedily grabbed for another.

Oil burner—full. Topped off last week.

Cable—paid through the year.

Car insurance—paid through the year.

Electric company—auto pay right from the account.

Pantry—canned food, paper products, and pasta galore filled the narrow shelves. Russell had a hell of a time filling this inconspicuously. Not wanting to raise suspicion and have Doris notice him dumping food into the house all at once, he did so in drips and drabs. If she could hide mail, what would she do with a bunch of cans?

Russell wracked his brain, trying to recall if there was anything, anything at all he could have forgotten to pay, fix or replenish before Saturday...

Ah-HA! The security deposit box at the bank. I'll have to remember to leave the key in the folder, labeled. Granted, the only items kept stored in the darn bank box were a few pieces of Doris's jewelry, gifted from her deceased mother. There were also their passports, most probably expired, and a deed to a piece of land Russell's dad had left him someplace upstate. Oh, and a few silver coins he'd manage to collect over the years, something he'd hope to gift to Georgie when the time came. He wasn't sure of their total net worth, but probably enough to have helped put a deposit on a new home. Now, he had no idea. *Not my problem anymore.*

Russell poured a second cup of the hot brew into his mug, leaning back in his chair a lot more tired than he'd assumed, a bit queasy, too. *Concentrate.*

Once I fire, the police will be on top of me, but if by some miracle I make a getaway, it won't be long before the shooting gets traced back to me, unless...

On the television, hotshot forensic teams took less than forty-five minutes to solve the crime. In real life, how was he supposed to know? While Russell was a bit of a pill to swallow, he'd never willfully broken the law before, not that he could remember.

Uck, my stomach. Skin shining with sweat, he placed a hand on his forehead. *Gotta be either the flu or food poisoning. Probably that overpriced sandwich.* "I can't afford to get sick," he moaned. Tomorrow was Friday. Final day before the rally and Russell Tetler's last chance to send his final "gift" to Fat Mouth. *This one was a real doozy!*

Sheesh, even my gums hurt. Russell poked around inside his mouth with his finger, attempting to find the source from where the sudden tenderness stemmed from. Had he had the wherewithal to use an actual tissue instead of a finger, he would have seen blood.

So, tired... The fatigue was gradually gaining on him. *But first, another email, I need to make sure this Black troublemaker knows her time on this planet is coming to a close.* Russell felt like utter shit and needed to hurry up so he could call it an early night. Grabbing a tissue, he coughed up a wad of bloody phlegm.

Dear Black Bitch:

"Tick-tock goes the clock. It's time for you to go to bed. Tick-tock goes the clock. Put down your sleepy head."

I like nursery rhymes, don't you? Humpty Dumpty, Ring Around the Rosy or even London Bridge Is Falling Down. They all sound so sweet, playful, and innocent. Children love them. But in reality, they are dark, haunting and cruel. Stories laden with hidden meanings, but guess what all three have in common with you? Can you guess? Need some help?

Hint: #1: All the King's horses and all the King's men couldn't put Humpty Together again.
Hint #2: Ashes, ashes, they all fall down.
Hint #3: London Bridge is falling down, falling down, falling down. London Bridge is falling down, my fair lady.

Ah, but did you know this next verse from London Bridges existed?

"Set a man to watch all night,
Watch all night, watch all night,
Set a man to watch all night,
My fair lady."

Have you guessed? No worries if you can't. All in good time. All will be made clear. You can count on it.

Not bad, he mused and cracked up, which only served to send him off into an uncontrollable raging coughing fit. For whatever reason, his throat had begun to feel scratchy. His stomach burned and his head began pounding. Between fighting the onslaught of exhaustion and the sudden dizziness, Russell wasn't sure what to do next. A chill caused his body to shudder, leaving both his hands stiff and icy cold. Strangely, so were both his feet, despite the socks and slippers. Chilled to the bone and achy, all he wanted to do was curl up in his bed under a heavy blanket and sleep whatever this was away.

Without checking the email for spelling mistakes or typos, Russell pushed SEND. Waited a few seconds until his email was safely on its way before closing up his computer for the night. Next, he reached over to shut off the single light, closed his office door, leaving his empty cookie dish and drained mug right where they were. With slow, deep breaths he took small lethargic steps, one at a time, dragging his body upstairs, his stamina all but depleted.

On the middle stair, Russell's stomach lurched then seized, causing him to clutch across his belly expelling a grunt in sheer pain. His breath came out in short uncontrollable spurts. Gripping the banister for stability, he remained hunched over and stationary only long enough to fight off the wave of lightheadedness before finding the reserve to stiffly climb the remaining stairs towards the bathroom to puke his brains out.

To Russell's credit, he did in fact make it to the toilet bowl, but by the mere fact *someone* had forgot to flush at last use, made his small victory all the less appealing.

Rocking back and forth on his knees, head over the bowl he kept repeating the same phrase over and over again. *Food poisoning. It's gotta be. Damn sandwich.*

**

From her well-situated position on the couch, Doris could still hear the entire upset as it played out upstairs, and grinned satisfactorily to herself. For so long she had yearned to cause Russell the level of pain and anguish he had dosed upon her. Her plan, as far as she was concerned, was going beautifully, never better. And as a matter of fact, when Russell stood gasping for air on the stairs, it took all the resolve and restraint she possessed not to hoot aloud. She saved the day by clasping her hand over her mouth…silently laughing it up with shameless glee, excited for phase two to kick in.

Instead of checking on him, Doris stayed exactly where she was, feigning sleep. Squirming with impatience, while she waited for Russell to finish up. The symphony of writhing and moaning sounds emanating from the bathroom sounded pretty brutal, which only served to bring her even more unabashed joy.

Finally, after what felt like an eternity, Russell emerged. Face haggard and begging for death under his breath. Doris listened intently for the familiar sound of their bedroom doorknob closing before making any rash attempt at creeping into his office for a peek. However, the minute the coast was clear, she gingerly padded her way into the kitchen, purposely opening and closing a few drawers, the fridge, a cabinet or two, and all to create the familiar noises Russell was accustomed to hearing. If Russell happened to be listening, he'd think Doris was doing her usual nightly mope and walk.

A few minutes in and satisfied Russell was out cold for the night, Doris silently crept into his office. As suspected, the plate which held the poison-laden cookies was empty, as was the mug. The carafe remained on his desk. Pulling out a pair of plastic gloves hidden in her bathrobe, she quietly grabbed all three items and took them over to the kitchen sink, mindful to pour out the remaining ingredients from the carafe before placing it along with the other two items already soaking in extremely hot soapy water. Then she lifted them out and loaded them, one-by-one into the dishwasher. She drained the other side of the sink, and made sure to re-rinse it again for good measure. Lastly, Doris poured an ample amount of bleach over all the dishes before closing the dishwasher door and pushing ON.

Normally, Doris never would have barged into Russell's office, even to retrieve empty dishes without Russell's prior consent. He'd made his position abundantly clear from the start—she wasn't welcomed inside. But for her plan to work, she'd have to be careful not to leave a trail, making sure to get rid of the evidence or at least the evidence he didn't consume.

Doris was counting on Russell feeling so deathly ill, he'd never notice the dishes missing, or if he did, he'd be way too sick to care. The risk for entering his lair seemed low and worth it. Doris smiled. *A bunch of missing dishes will be the last thing on his miserable mind. Day three, here we come.*

CHAPTER 24

Maryam Quiñónez

THIS DINNER HAD TURNED INTO what could only be described as "a polite disaster."

What the heck was Mami thinking?

Normally, Maryam wouldn't have judged a man solely on looks, but last night her mother's so-called "match made in heaven" severely tested this theory. Putting to the side the obvious issue around Hector not being Muslim, which for Maryam was already a deal breaker, he also apparently smoked like a chimney. While admittedly handsome, she almost gagged as soon as the man entered the house. His clothes reeked. And if this wasn't enough to cause her to run for the hills, his misogynistic pandering and miserably failed flirtations most certainly did. Unfortunately, while physically escaping hadn't been a viable option at the time, gagging into her napkin under the glaring intense stare of her mother had.

"NO. No way, no how. I adamantly refuse to see him again."

"But he's so good looking."

TIGHT ROPE

"He smelled like an ashtray."

"I don't understand you. He has a good job, drives a nice car, graduated from college, never married before. No kids either."

"He also makes sexist jokes and is addicted to cigarettes. His skin is already showing signs of premature aging. Matter of fact, how old is he? He looks ten years older than my father."

"Twenty-nine."

"Twenty-nine! Seriously Mami! He looks older. No, you need to stop!"

"He's a good man."

"He's an *old* man."

"Not old—mature…and trust me, you of all people need a mature man in your life. Not some young boy who hasn't had a taste of the real world."

"Still not interested."

"You're not getting any younger yourself."

"Neither is he, obviously."

"You don't want to stay single forever."

"I don't plan to."

"Maria!"

"Maryam! IT'S MARYAM!"

"NOT to me you're not!" And with that, her mother stormed out of the room, stomping away and slamming her bedroom door firmly shut behind her. Next, a deliberate and distinct clicking of the lock, and a few seconds later, the unmistakable whimpers of her mother sobbing into her pillow.

Shit! Now she's crying. Resolved to set things right, Maryam tapped softly on her mother's bedroom door. "Mami, *por favor*, can I come in?"

More sobs.

"Please unlock the door. *Yo quiero hablar contigo.*"

"Go away. I have nothing to say to you."

Maryam stood steadfast. "Please, we need to talk…I didn't mean to upset you."

"You only care about yourself, Maria."

Maryam pressed her forehead to the door exasperated, counting down from ten. Once again accused of selfishness. It never ceased to annoy her.

"No matter how much I try, you are never happy," moaned her mother for effect.

"That's not true."

"*¡Ahora me estás llamando mentirosa!*"

"I would never call you a liar!"

Maryam waited, listening for a response, but only more sobbing. "Seriously, I know…you were only trying to help. But just because I thought Hector smelled like an ashtray doesn't mean I don't love you for trying."

Inside the room the crying abruptly stopped. Less than a moment later, the lock clicked and the door opened. Her mother's damp, tear-streaked face peeking through a slight crack. "He did stink."

Maryam belly laughed. *Ya Allah, I love this crazy woman, despite how nuts she makes me.*

**

Over the past few days, Maryam's mind and heart had taken solace in a place her parents, especially her mother, would have never understood or agreed to. How could she explain how he had left such an indelible mark on her heart? How a young man from a

TIGHT ROPE

deli, whose name she didn't even know, could have caused such a strong and lasting impression, not so much by what he did or said, but by the way he carried himself. Quiet yet resolved, as if he encased his place in the world and enjoined it, unlike her, always searching but never quite satisfied.

It also didn't hurt that Maryam thought him attractive as well. His well-groomed face, athletic build, dark, penetrating eyes, thick eyelashes, and mesmerizing cheekbones were now the culprits of her distraction and daydreaming. So much so that at work, even Dr. Khan, normally too busy for small talk and office romances, felt the need to say something.

"Hello, paging Maryam Quiñónez. Will Maryam Quiñónez please come back to reality?"

Maryam shook herself alert. "Sorry, what?"

Doctor Khan laughed. "Are you all right?"

"I'm fine, why?"

"Because you've been distracted all day."

"Me?"

The doctor stared playfully. "Yes, you. What's the deal? I know it's Friday, the weekend is in reach, but we still have the rest of the day to get through."

"Sorry. I have a lot on my mind. I'm fine…nothing to worry about. What can I get for you?"

Dr. Khan had known Maryam for quite some time; she'd interned for her while going through nursing school, and the doctor was thrilled when she finally convinced her to leave the ER to work for her, but lately Maryam seemed unfocused. Bordering on distracted and chatty, as if she were in—*OH!*

"Maryam. May I ask you a question?"

"Sure."

"Are you in love?"

"WHAT!" Maryam yelped. "Me? Ah, ha, ha...you're so funny, No, no, no... Why would you even say something like that? Sheesh, I know I've been a bit, um, sidetracked and all, but in love? That's ridiculous."

"You *are* in love!" Dr. Khan laughed, grinning from ear-to-ear. "Who's the lucky fella?"

"Nobody! I swear."

"Spit it out!"

"There isn't anyone."

"Nonsense."

"Seriously, he's nobody," she gasped at the sound of her comment. "OH! Well, I mean he's somebody, not an actual nobody, but..."

When Dr. Khan smiled, her dimples looked ten times deeper.

"He doesn't even know I exist."

Dr. Khan rolled her eyes to the ceiling and crossed her arms over her chest amused. "I doubt that very strongly."

"It's true. He barely acknowledges when I'm around."

"Not buying that either. One, you're gorgeous and I doubt he's blind, and two, you make an impression on everyone you meet, so—"

"Not on him. He hardly looks at me, and doesn't say anything to me except to take my orders."

"Orders? As in he's a waiter?"

"No, as in the son of the deli owner–at the place around the corner."

"The halal spot? Next to the laundry mat?"

"Yeah. That's the one."

"Ah huh. So, what's his name?"

"I have no idea. All he does is salaam me and take my order."

"Salaam you and take your order…got it."

"Stop teasing."

"No small talk, only 'mayo, ketchup or mustard, Miss' type of conversation."

"Yeah," nodded Maryam emphatically. "Very business-like."

"Business like."

"Oh, my God…"

"I believe you!"

Maryam blushed. "Oh, all right, fine." She was dying to tell somebody about him, anyway. Why not Dr. Khan?

"Listening!" Dr. Khan drew up a chair and sat perched at its edge, positioned in anticipation.

"He's so handsome. Tall, well, taller than me. Definitely stays in shape— runner's body, lean and muscular. Raven jet-black hair, a prominent chin. He wears his beard low and he's got a mustache that's shaped like this," she said, indicating a goatee with her fingers. "And his eyes, *Aye*—his eyes. Dark, brooding eyes, full lips…he has this way of smiling that makes you want to melt."

For the next ten minutes Maryam prattled on to Dr. Khan about every word the young man of her dreams had said, or rather didn't say, but seemed like he would have said, under different circumstances. Instead of the usual doctor-nurse professional barrier, they were two women stripped of rank and file, gushing together like high school girls holed up in the bathroom sharing secrets and crushes.

"So now what?"

"So now what, what? What do you mean?"

Dr. Khan smirked and rolled her eyes. "I mean are you going to tell him how you feel or spend your entire income on deli for the rest of your life?"

"I don't know. What if he's married?"

"Did you see a ring?"

"No, but maybe he doesn't wear one because he works with food."

Dr. Khan chuckled. "Works with food, so no wedding ring—that's a new one. Sure. Okay…maybe you're right."

"No. Or *maybe,* he's one of those guys who hates jewelry. They do exist, you know. My dad is one of them and isn't shy to say so. But he wears his wedding band or my mother would have his head."

"*Or,* he could be single and attracted to you," added Dr. Khan, "but too shy to say anything and doesn't know how to approach you."

"Do you think so?" asked Maryam hopefully.

"I do, but I caution you to take your time about this. Make sure he's practicing his Islam before you rush off and do something you'll regret."

"That's true."

"Talk to him, get to know how he thinks. See if his words and behavior match his beliefs."

"That makes a lot of sense."

"Of course, it does. Why rush into anything? Take your time."

"Okay…"

"Observe him for a while."

"Observe, how?"

"Glad you asked." Dr. Khan whipped out her prescription pad, ripping off a single sheet. "You can start with this," she said playfully, turning the pad over to write. "I have to get back to work before we get backlogged, but I need you to pick this up for me."

TIGHT ROPE

She handed the scribbled slip of paper to Maryam. "I'm starving."

"Turkey on rye, mayo, lettuce and tomato?" Murmured Maryam confused as she read off the slip of paper.

"Correct. And don't forget the pickle. I can't eat a turkey sandwich without my pickle…and ask Diane and Kathy if they want anything. Lunch is on me. My treat."

CHAPTER 25

Zaid Ali

TODAY WAS FRIDAY, *JUMU'AH,* congregational prayer. But since his father hadn't yet returned to the shop, the usual Friday arguments were temporarily placed on hold. And while Zaid hadn't necessarily missed the petty arguments and daily doses of embarrassment only his father could deliver, in a strange, bizarre way, he still had to admit, working the store alone had not only been chaotic, but lonely. Breaks were few and far between. This in turn also meant his prayer had to be delayed as he single-handedly waited on customers. Often times Zaid wound up combining his noon prayers, something he never did when his father was around. They'd take turns making prayer in the back, undisturbed, while the other manned the store and cash register.

"I'll come to the store so you can go pray *Jumu'ah.*" Mrs. Ali was Zaid's only relief.

"Are you sure?"

"Of course, I'm sure."

TIGHT ROPE

"What about Baba? Who'll be here with him?"

"I'm not a child," bellowed the irritated voice from the other room. "I can take care of myself."

Mrs. Ali rolled her eyes at her son conspiratorially. "Yeah, okay then," she fought back a chuckle. "Like I said, I'll cover for you."

Zaid wouldn't have openly admitted it, but after yesterday's fiasco, he didn't feel like going to the masjid…or anyplace. Still too embarrassed about the way he failed to handle the two jerks in the store yesterday, he felt like being alone.

Once the store had cleared out of customers, Zaid had spent the rest of that day mindlessly going through the motions. Restocking shelves, taking inventory, and washing off counters, but his heart wasn't in it. His mind was stuck hopelessly on rewind, playing the humiliating scene over and over again. *Bad enough I let that guy step in at all—like some great white hope and savior. Riding in on his horse and chariot to save the day. Protect the helpless heathens at all cost.* Thank Allah, "she"—still "she" since he hadn't had a chance to catch her name before she left—hadn't noticed. *Maybe my father's right. I am stupid.*

The Prayer would be starting in fifteen minutes. *Where's Mama?* He wished for once she'd show up on time, at least on Fridays.

Door chimes clanged and in entered Mrs. Ali. "*AsSalaamu'alaikum,*" she called out pleasantly, a bit out of breath. "I'm here. You are now officially free to go and repent."

"*Wa'alaikum Salaam,*" replied Zaid giving her a warm embrace and kiss.

"Anything I need to know? Do?" she inquired, hanging her coat on the hook and swapping it out for an apron.

"No. I've already taken care of most of it. The lunch hour craziness is pretty much finished, so from now until around four or five, it should be pretty slow going, but I won't be long, promise."

"Take your time. It feels good to get out of the house and away from your father for a little bit. He's driving me nuts. 'Get me this, bring me that, rub me here, sit next to me, read the paper to me.' A regular pain in the—"

"Read him the paper? What's wrong with his eyes?"

"Nothing! Absolutely nothing. He's being ridiculous."

Zaid laughed quietly. "Sounds like Baba."

"Yesterday he wanted me to sit in the living room and watch television with him…to 'keep him company' he said. Like I don't have other things to do with my life."

"He's bored and used to being here. Then again, even when he's here, he mostly sits and finds shit to gripe about."

"Well, there you are. Nothing has changed then." Mrs. Ali placed her handbag in the backroom, locked it in the cabinet drawer and returned to the front. "I'm ready. Now go. Get out of here. And make sure you pray to Allah I don't strangle your father."

Zaid grabbed his jacket, placed a kiss on his mother's cheek goodbye, and bolted out the door.

"And Zaid? Watch your mouth."

**

Mrs. Ali slid one of the metal stools resting in the corner up to the register to relax, surprised how badly she needed time away from the house. Especially from her husband and his endless list of demands. *Such a big baby and an even worse patient.* *"Salma! I need some*

TIGHT ROPE

tea." "Salma, my neck hurts." "Did you remember to call the doctor to make my appointment?" "What time is Zaid coming home?" "What are you making for dinner?" No wonder Zaid has complained about him the way he has.

Truth was, since her husband's attack, she'd felt increasingly harried and less motivated. The vulnerability of being covered and Muslim never quite left the forefront of her mind for too long, and on those few times it did, she'd be quickly reminded by a callous slur or comment. Even the short walk from home to the store felt dangerous. As if at any moment somebody with a cross to bear or a point to make would lurch out from behind a building or perhaps a parked car and assault her. A pair of trailing footsteps triggered alarm as much as the stranger who mistakenly bumped into her, making her recoil in defense. There wasn't any single incident, but rather a long succession of reminders, indicating the tide and attitude of the country was returning to a time of unbridled bigotry. The kind which encouraged some to yell or scream, or even maul someone different…someone like her. Each day brought with it another smirk or cutting remark. A head sticking out of a vehicle yelling threats of her deportation or death. Everything she'd thought she'd escaped by coming to this country had now become the new norm, and culminated into one unnerving reality.

The chimes on the front door clanged. Her body automatically tensed. Being alone in the store made her edgy. A customer.

The beautiful Muslima stepped the rest of the way in, a paper clenched in her hand, eyes darting about, obviously searching for something…or someone. Mrs. Ali was no slouch and never missed a beat. "May I help you?" she asked, a slight smirk of a smile, causing her single dimpled cheek to concave.

The two women locked eyes and a thousand wordless emotions were shared.

"*AsSalaamu'alaikum*," Maryam said meekly. "My office lunch orders." She indicated the list by waving it in the air like a white flag.

"*Wa'alaikum Salaam*," replied Mrs. Ali, already popping off her perch. "Wonderful." She reached over the counter for the paper.

Although polite, the young woman seemed distracted. Her eyes darting around the store. *Maybe she assumed somebody—Zaid—would be here to help her.* Perhaps a romance was blossoming under her nose. If not, a little shove from her wouldn't hurt. She looked down at the paper. "Turkey with mayo, extra pickles…okay…two-roast beef on rye…and a pastrami sandwich with coleslaw on the sandwich?"

Maryam laughed, "Yes, that's it."

"How about I put the slaw to the side so it doesn't soak up the bread?"

"That would be fine, thank you."

Undoing a button on both arms, Mrs. Ali rolled up her sleeves, ready to tackle the order.

"My son, Zaid, is the sandwich maker in the family." Name dropping 101. Mrs. Ali couldn't resist. "I mean, I taught him so I'm obviously better, but nobody knows that except you, now."

Maryam's face lightened as she laughed again, appearing more at ease.

"But he's at *Jumu'ah* right now," she added, stealing a glance to see if that piece of information registered, and pleased to see that it certainly did. *So, she is here to see my boy.* "Are you new in the area or do you only work around here?"

"I live close enough, but I work across the street. I'm a

nurse."

"A nurse! How nice! Your family must be so proud of you."

Maryam nodded. "Yes…"

"Do you have children?" If Zaid had been a fly on the wall and overheard the interrogation taking place on his account, he would have melted into the cement flooring from embarrassment. But he wasn't here and Mrs. Ali kept plowing ahead, undeterred.

"Me? Children? Oh no. I'm not married yet."

Perfect answer. "Ah, well that makes sense then. You're a career girl. Who has time for a husband and children when you are busy building a career."

"Not necessarily," Maryam offered gently. "I believe a woman can have both, if she finds the right man. Although with any relationship each person has to adjust and make concessions for it to work."

Maryam couldn't see the big smiling grin plastered across Mrs. Ali's face. She liked this girl. "Did you want extra pickles with all three orders or only the one?"

"Only the one, thanks." Maryam looked at the time. Zaid's mother might be a better sandwich maker but she was certainly slower.

"Are you pressed for time," asked Mrs. Ali, a plan formulating already in her head, "because if you are, when my son gets back, I can have him run the entire order over for you. You only work right across the street, right?"

"I wouldn't want to put him out…"

"No problem. He'll be back shortly anyway. We do this all the time for customers in a rush!"

No, they didn't.

"That'll give me a chance to finish up your order and you can scoot back to your job on time. Here, write down your name, address. Oh, and your phone number in case we need to reach you."

"Thank you so much." Maryam jotted the required information before handing the slip of paper back to the older woman. "I appreciate this. *Shukran!*"

"Oh, think nothing of it. It's our pleasure."

**

Running late, Zaid had only enough time to perform wudu and get in line, missing out on the *khutbah* entirely. The front rows were already full, but he was able to squeeze into the second row from the back, next to a tall brother wearing military khakis and— *GAWD no! The soldier from yesterday? He's MUSLIM? Oh, man, fuck my life. Astaghfirallah, astaghfirallah, astaghfirallah.* Zaid couldn't believe it. *Why is it that whenever you royally screw up your life, Allah then has to make you repeat the process until you finally get it right?*

The two men locked eyes for a split second. Zaid nodded. The soldier nodded back. Shoulder to shoulder, foot to foot, it was time to leave everything else behind and pray.

As soon as the prayer ended and *Sunnah* prayers were complete, Zaid turned, anxious to leave, but before he could completely pull off his getaway, a large white hand tapped his shoulder. In a sturdy, but kind voice the man *salaamed* him. With nothing left to do but return the greeting, the two men shook hands.

"About yesterday," Zaid stammered.

"Yeah, I wanted to speak to you about that too," replied the Adonis looking muscular man. "Look, can we step outside for a minute? So, we can talk?"

Great. He's not finished with me. "Sure." They met up in the parking lot after putting their shoes back on.

"My name's Shane McCormick."

"Zaid Ali."

"Nice to meet you, Zaid. Look, bro, I just wanted to apologize for acting the way I did yesterday."

Wait, what? Is he apologizing to me? Now Zaid was truly confused.

"But it's those kind of fools, they piss me off. I've had to deal with those types before, in and out of the military. I guess when they started disrespecting the sister I lost it, but I shouldn't have stepped on your toes the way I did. It came off all wrong."

Somewhat taken aback, Zaid went to speak, but his throat was dry and parched. "Brother, you're not the one who did anything wrong. I did. I punked out."

Now Shane looked equally surprised. "Not like I gave you much of a chance." Shane shook his head and kicked at some invisible pebbles with his boot. "From my experience those kinds of guys are cowards, but together they become bold. But if they smell fear or see the slightest hesitation, they'll pounce like a bunch of hyenas. Trust me. Still, I act before I think. It's gotten me in trouble before."

"And I tend to think and forget to act altogether," Zaid said ashamed.

"Well, I wanted to apologize." Shane stuck out his hand. "We cool?"

"Like I told you, man, nothing for you to apologize for," but Zaid shook the hand and a slight Muslim brother embrace anyway. "You did what you needed to do. I respect that."

For all of Shane's natural and military enhanced brawn, he seemed rather reserved and a bit shy as he bit his bottom lip. "Listen, I have to get back to work…"

"Yeah, me too."

"Catch you around?"

"*Insha'Allah*." Zaid turned to leave and then stopped. "Shane, if you're not busy later, stop by the store. I'll make you one of my famous sandwiches. We're open 'til six."

"Sounds great. If I don't make it, I'll come by tomorrow."

"No can do. Tomorrow I'll be at the rally."

"This one," asked Shane pointing to the poster behind the masjid's encased outdoor information board.

"Yeah."

Shane took out his cell phone and snapped a photo of the poster. Gave Zaid a thumb's up and the two men parted. Each still unsure of the other, but the imaginary wall between them began to crumble.

**

"YOU DID WHAT?" *As if today wasn't stressful enough…*

"Relax," chastised his mother. "You're going to give yourself a heart attack one of these days."

"I'm gone for less than an hour," Zaid muttered under his breath.

"Oh stop. The customer was in a rush and I felt bad for her. What's the big deal anyway? *Ya Allah*. Run her order across the street. The exercise will do you good."

"Since when do we do deliveries?"

"Since right now, so keep your coat on and get a move on.

Ya Allah. Here's the order, here's her information, and here's the receipt. Go."

The last thing Zaid wanted to do was run deliveries, especially after *Jumu'ah*, but he had learned long ago not to bother bucking his mother when she had already made up her mind about something.

"Fine. Whatever." He grabbed the bag and papers from her.

"Wait."

"What?"

"Go comb your hair."

"What?"

"Your hair," said Mrs. Ali, nose scrunched up, pointing to his head. "You look…messy."

"What are you talking about, *messy*? I practically ran back to the store to relieve you."

"And pour some oil on too," she teased, waving her hand by her nose, feigning faint. "Some African musk."

Zaid couldn't figure the crazy woman out. "Comb my hair and soak my body in cologne…to make a food delivery?"

"Yes. You represent the family business. Nobody wants a sloppy, smelly delivery man."

Zaid stood, incredulously at a loss for words. "Pick your battles," he mumbled to himself while heading to the back room. A few minutes later he emerged tidier and smelling delicious.

"Okay. *Alhamdulillah*, much better. Now go," ordered his mother sniffing behind his neck. With one quick peck on the cheek, she was already shooing him out the door.

"I'll be back in a few minutes," he called over his shoulder, *salaaming* his mother.

"I'm fine here. No rush. Take your time." As soon as Zaid

was out of sight, she cupped her hands and made a prayer, a small but powerful *dua*. "*Ya Allah*, help my boy find the right woman. If she's the one, then bless him with success. If she's not, protect him. Ameen."

**

"Where's the food?" asked Kathy from behind her computer screen. "I'm so hungry."

"It's being delivered," replied Maryam, rushing to the ladies' room to fix herself up. "When the delivery guy comes, yell back for me? I need to pay him."

"No problem."

Maryam scooted to the Staff Only bathroom and rushed to check her face and hijab in the mirror.

"Tell me everything."

"AH!" Maryam shrieked.

"And don't leave out any details." The voice belonged to Dr. Khan.

"You scared the *shi*—out of me!"

"Don't change the subject. Spill the beans, and where are my pickles?"

"Nothing happened and the food is getting delivered."

"Did you speak to him?"

"He wasn't there. I did meet his mother though. She said he was at the masjid."

"Ah! Of course, *Jumu'ah*. But hey, great sign—he prays."

Maryam shrugged. "I guess you're right. I was hoping to see him and get to talk to him though."

"You said you met his mother? What was she like?"

TIGHT ROPE

"What do you mean?"

"Towards you…"

"Towards me?"

"Was she rude? Polite? Curt? Warm? Nice?"

"Oh, nice. Very nice, actually. Helpful. She's kind of funny."

"Awesome. His mom likes you. Another good sign."

"I was a customer, of course she was nice."

"I'm sorry, but have you met her husband?" replied Dr. Khan, eyes wide, and both hands crossed over her chest.

"That's true."

"Besides, she's sending her son to deliver your order, right?"

"Yes, but they deliver for all their customers in a rush."

Dr. Khan rolled her eyes to the sky. "Um. No, they don't."

"That's what she told me."

"Yeah, and if they did, I would have had them making deliveries all along, but they don't do them and I know that for a fact because I inquired just recently."

"Oh. You mean?"

"Yes. Now kindly get yourself ready to meet your Mr. Hotness."

"She mentioned his name: Zaid. At least I got that much information."

"Then get ready for Mister Hotness, Zaid, who better remember to bring my pickles."

**

All of a sudden, we're making deliveries. Correction—I'm *making deliveries. Next, she'll have me doing singing telegrams.* More annoyed than anything else, Zaid planned to drop the food off and head straight back to the store where he could finally be alone to sulk in his humiliation. *Which door is it? 101…102…104… Ah! Here we go, 105.*

"Can I help you?" asked Diane, Dr. Khan's office manager.

"I have an order for Maryam Quiñónez."

"No problem. She's expecting you. Let me ring her up." The receptionist pointed in the direction of an open seat. "You can wait over there."

"Thanks."

Less than a minute later Maryam appeared. Diane nodded over to where Zaid sat, his face staring off in another direction altogether.

"Oh, *AsSalaamu'alaikum*," she said, pretending to be surprised. "Thank you for bringing my order."

When Zaid looked at Maryam, his expression could only be described as stunned, but he reined it in fast. *Who would have thought the order would turn out to be hers? That sneaky, conniving, beautiful mother of mine, that's who.* Maryam Quiñónez…finally a name to go with the face.

"How much do I owe you?"

Zaid had to pull out the receipt to check. "Oh, um…Thirty-one, seventy-five," he replied. "You might want to check your order to make sure it's all there. If anything's missing, I can always bring it over."

Maryam handed him two twenties. "Keep the change."

"Ah, thanks," Zaid said, relieved, realizing he had forgotten to bring change with him.

Maryam peered into the bag to check the order, making sure Dr. Khan's extra pickles were inside. "Looks like your mom took care of everything."

"My mother?" *Oh, God, that's right, she met my mother.* "At the

TIGHT ROPE

store. You met my mother at the store." *Shut up moron.*

"I did. She's nice."

"I like her too." *Shit!*

Maryam laughed. "You're funny. Like her. I can see where you get it from."

"Yeah, she's a regular comedian."

Maryam waited hoping he'd say something else, but when he didn't, she did. "Well, I better let you get back."

Zaid nodded that he agreed but made no move to leave.

"Thanks again for delivering the order. We appreciate it." Diane and Kathy, as well as the doctor, were all standing behind the desk watching and grinning. *Yes, yes,* they all nodded in exaggerated agreement. "Thank you," they chimed in, almost in unison.

"Well, I better get going." Zaid turned to leave.

"Let me walk you out," Maryam blurted out. "The halls can get a bit confusing."

Zaid almost let it slip that he comes to the same building two to three times a week with his father for physical therapy, but stopped himself in the nick of time. "Sure, that would be great."

Dr. Khan mouthed *Go!* Maryam nodded in assent and closed the office door behind her, her heart beating a mile a minute, but grateful she hadn't embarrassed herself—*yet*.

Together the two walked, silently side by side along the lengthy hall. Zaid was ready to open the stairwell doors when he finally got up the nerve to speak. "Maryam? I was wondering if you'd like to have lunch with me tomorrow? On Saturday. Which is tomorrow."

Maryam laughed again. "That sounds great, but maybe we can grab a bite to eat after the rally tomorrow? I already told my friend

I would go."

A friend? I knew it. She's intended. "Yeah, sure. Afterwards is cool." he said, less enthusiastically. "Will your friend also be coming?"

"To the rally? No, Nour's one of the speakers."

"Of course. Nour! The sister in the poster—"

"Yep. The one you said you heard speak."

"Right, I did." *Not a guy*—sheer relief. "Great, great speaker."

"I'm really looking forward to hearing her."

"Me too." Maryam's smile was irresistible. "What time were you planning on going?" he asked casually, mesmerized once again by her enchanting brown eyes.

"I'm pretty sure it starts at one, but I want to get there a half-hour early so I can find a place close to the stage. How about we meet at the entrance by 12:30? If that works for you—"

She wants me to meet her? "Yeah, sure. Perfect. I will be there." Zaid didn't realize he kept bouncing on the heels of his sneakers. "Well, I gotta get back."

"Of course. I better get back inside too. You have my number?"

"I do—and your name, finally."

Maryam shot him a coy smile. "Well then, you're all set. I'll see you tomorrow, *Insha'Allah*."

"*Insha'Allah*, you will indeed." The remainder of Zaid's day flew by in a haze. A glorious, wonderful, and full of possibilities haze.

CHAPTER 26

Russell Tetler

COVERED IN A SICKLY, SWEATY film from being racked with hours of spasms, Russell spent the entire night running to the bathroom. Exhausted from so much movement, he at one point contemplated pulling his covers into the tub, but the stench assaulting his senses caused Russell's head to spin all over again. At least so far, this morning he hadn't felt much like vomiting again. Perhaps whatever was attacking him was on the way out. After last night, there wasn't a whole lot more to give to the cause.

A hot shower and some strong as hell hot, black coffee—*if he could keep it down*. Hopefully that would do the trick and clear the webs from his head. He needed his wits about him; today was the big day. No amount of food poisoning or flu, whatever this bug was that'd gripped him, would interfere with his well laid out plan.

It was already eight o'clock, but the house was unusually quiet this morning. Had Russell not known for a fact Doris never left the house unescorted, he would have sworn on a stack of hotel bibles she wasn't home. She was probably exhausted. *She hadn't even bothered to come upstairs to bed, but who could blame her with all the racket I made?*

Russell assumed Doris had probably camped out on the couch, eventually falling sound asleep as she did many other nights. But even still, it startled him when the loud knock at the bedroom door came. *Damn it!* Russell's heart raced. *Why in hell does she have to bang like that! I'm not deaf or nothing!* When he opened the door a crack, he found Doris standing wide awake, still dressed in the same attire from the night before, holding a hot cup of black coffee and two slices of dry toast.

"Why thanks, Doris. You're a real-life saver." Russell meant it. Accepting the cup and plate from her, he signaled his appreciation with a wink. Then out of habit closed the bedroom door with his foot. He had to kick at it twice to get it to actually close, spilling hot coffee on his hand.

"Damn it!" He yelled. "DORIS!"

Doris heard his plea for help but turned right back around and headed downstairs, hardly able to contain her excitement as she waited for the next round of Russell's agonizing pain to set in.

**

By eleven, Russell was dressed, fed, and ready to begin his day. His weapon and other necessary paraphernalia were secured underneath his coat. He'd made sure to brush his teeth, and then as an afterthought, decided to check his daughter's room one more time to make sure the paperwork was still where he'd placed it. Then for good measure, he strolled around the house one last time, conducting a mental inventory.

TIGHT ROPE

Oddly enough, if the shit hit the fan, which Russell sort of suspected it would, he knew he wouldn't miss this place or Doris. Those warm and fuzzy feelings had vanished years ago. Buried deep below in the earth and contained in the same grave George occupied. No matter what the outcome of today's quest, once Russell set into motion what needed doing, he'd finally have the long-awaited justice that he hungered for. He didn't much care what else happened.

"Now listen up, Doris," Russell began to say, but his intestines began twitching and rumbling. "I'm going to go out a take care of a few things. Not sure when I'll be back so don't worry about making dinner for me tonight, okay? Just take care of yourself."

From the couch, Doris's eyes never wavered from the TV screen. She'd heard every word, but frankly, she didn't give two fucks. She'd already double dosed him full of poison via his morning cup of brew, so for today, her job was done.

"Well, okay then, Doris," Russell said softly, squeezing her shoulder. "I'm going to head out now."

Oh, shut up, shut up, shut up, and leave already. My God, what's with all the long, drawn out goodbyes?

Customarily, Russell would have put on his shoes and coat and left, sometimes forgetting to say goodbye to Doris altogether, and certainly without all the added drama to boot. The more he spoke, the more Doris wanted to scream and spit at him, but since she refused to speak a single word to him since George's funeral, she'd be damned to hell in a hand basket, if she'd start talkin' to him now, no matter how much Russell tortured her with his sniveling adieus.

CHAPTER 27

THE IBRAHIM FAMILY

Mrs. Ibrahim

THE WORLD HER DAUGHTER MOVED and survived in had proven once again to be cruel and unforgiving. Nour was a catch—brilliant, beautiful, kind, highly educated, held a steady career, and had a strong Islamic grounding—but in the end, none of that mattered to these horrible people. Not one damn bit. In bigoted eyes, the minute her baby girl's skin color came into play, she was seen as not good enough, easily discounted, and ultimately devalued. The thought of her daughter spending her life alone worried her.

"Haven't you ever thought about getting married?" she'd asked Nour, hoping they'd finally discuss the matter seriously.

"Of course, I have. Someday, just not right now."

"When then?"

Nour didn't appreciate the inquisition. "When I meet the right guy."

"And how, pray tell, will you pull that off when you're holed up in an office or on some stage screaming into a microphone?"

Nour winced. She didn't appreciate it when her mother likened her social activism to *screaming into a microphone*. "Listen, can we discuss this later? I'm really tired and have a long day tomorrow."

"That's what you always say. Don't blow me off. I'm being serious."

"Nobody's blowing you off."

"Listen to me, Nour. Before you know it, you'll get so set in your ways that no man will be enough for you."

"Read that in one of your magazines?"

Her mother shot her a warning dagger. "Don't."

"Sorry. I shouldn't have said that," corrected Nour, contritely. "But I refuse to settle."

"Who's telling you to settle? What I am saying is that you need to become more available. Open yourself up to the possibilities and be willing to try."

Nour heard the hurt in her mother's pleas, her need to protect. "Let me first get through this rally. When it's over, *Ya Allah*, I promise, we'll go out for tea and discuss the absence of my love life."

"Love life? How about we discuss the absence of friends as well?"

"Touché."

**

An email from work *pinged* Nour's cell, but once her exhausted head hit the pillow, she was out like a light and didn't hear a thing. An earthquake could have shaken the entire building and she still would have slept right through.

The homemade chicken soup her mother force-fed her had hit the spot and settled her belly enough to give her a chance to grab a much-needed hot shower without needing to keep her head over the toilet. The pulse of hot water soothed the achiness away, and lulled her body into a state of peacefulness long enough to hit the sheets and catch up on some sleep. However, the phone's *ping* did not go unnoticed by another, more alert and worried set of ears.

Not wanting her daughter disturbed under any circumstance, Hafsa anxiously tiptoed into her daughter's bedroom and snatched the phone off Nour's night table before it could ping again. She slipped the phone into her bathrobe pocket with the full intention of leaving it outside the bedroom door on the hall table until morning.

Adjusting the blanket gently to cover her baby girl's shoulders, she bent and placed another soft kiss on her sleeping daughter's cheek, but instead of leaving, she remained, still. She felt the need to watch her child sleep, much as she had done when she was small. Her mind flooded with a gush of unexpected memories and troubled uncertainties.

I remember when you would have turned to me first. When you would have looked to me for comfort and reassurance. Shared with me all your sadness and fears…but that time is over, I guess. Your life doesn't include me anymore. Instead, you keep everything bottled up inside, doling out only PG tidbits here and there like I'm too fragile to hear the truth.

A lone tear slid down her cheek. Silently closing the door behind her, she wasn't halfway to the kitchen before that damn

TIGHT ROPE

device went off again.

"*Ya Allah*, why can't they leave her alone? Everyone needs to rest," mumbled Mrs. Ibrahim clearly annoyed. "No wonder the girl is ill." Pulling the phone from her robe to turn it off she caught the beginning thread of Russell's next threatening message displayed on the screen.

"*Astaghfirallah!*" she exclaimed, stunned. "What? Who is this?" Unable to peel her eyes away her feet began shaking with nervous energy. Pacing the hall back and forth, the adrenaline in her body reached full mother bear protective mode.

Where are you? She wanted her husband to hurry up and get home from the masjid already. This wasn't something to keep to herself. *Damn it! If only I could have seen the rest of what the message said.* Without the password, though, she knew she was flat out of luck. Half tempted to wake Nour and demand some answers, she turned towards her daughter's room just as the sound of keys at the front door changed her mind.

"*AsSalaamu'alaikum*," greeted Qasim, kicking off his shoes. "Sorry I'm late. I stayed to speak with the Imam about next week's school fundraiser," he said hanging his coat on the hall rung.

"*Wa'alaikum Salaam*," she responded tersely. "We've got a problem." Panic made her voice quiver.

"What happened?" he asked, now equally on high alert, his eyes darting between his wife's ashen face and the phone being waved impatiently above her head.

"Someone's threatening our daughter. I read it on her phone."

"Threatening Nour? Who?"

Unable to utter another word, she rushed into the safe embrace of her husband's arms. "I knew it," Hafsa cried, burying her face into his chest weeping. "I knew somebody would try to hurt our baby..."

Qasim plucked the phone from his wife's death grip, and pushed the display. The same threatening words reappeared on the screen. A single vein on the side of the man's forehead swelled. His eyes narrowed and mind raced. Reaching out, he pulled his wife tightly to his chest, soothingly, protectively. Had anyone else observed the embrace, they would have seen the unmistaken manifestation of unadulterated hate pulsating in the eyes of a father ready to battle to the death.

**

Outside, the dark night air turned to a hazy filament of morning light through the closed bedroom curtain. The time had arrived. Nour peeled away the sweat-soaked sheets. Her once strong, young, invincible body now betrayed her, keeping her chronically swathed in a blanket of pain. She sought to muster up the strength to sit upright. However, not all her body parts were in agreement. The back of her calf protested, first with the beginnings of a throbbing dull ache. Gingerly, she stretched both her legs under the sheet, forcibly pointing her toes outward, but as soon as she did, the rear of her leg twitched and tightened into a knot, readying itself to go into a full force spasm. Bracing for the onset of pain, Nour gripped her pillow and squeezed it, unaware of how tightly her lips were pressed together. Spasms, one right after the other, tore through her lower limbs until, eventually, stopping altogether. This wasn't the first time. Only yesterday the same dull ache had rudely awakened her, but today the knotting pulsated in her lower back. Panting feverishly, chilled and spent, she shivered uncontrollably. Nour picked up the pillow and pressed it over her

TIGHT ROPE

face. Writhing and out of breath, she wept soundlessly.

Whatever was going on inside of her, it was winning, parasitically taking over what had only a short time before been normalized bodily functions, leaving her defenseless and besieged. *I have to get through today…*

On a big day like today, the usual run of the mill nerves would have been the culprits responsible for threatening Nour's resolve, but this morning a succession of sharp shooting spasms in her gut vied for the position.

Another wave of shooting pain vice-gripped her insides, sending her running to the bathroom, dry-retching. Crouched on her knees, head over the throne, an acidic sting of bile rose up and out of her throat for the nineteen thousandth time. Overnight the pain had worsened, repeatedly awakening her from a sound sleep and sending her dashing full speed to the bathroom.

In a few hours, she'd be expected on stage, standing with microphone in hand, in front of thousands of people eager to hear her as well as a line-up of advocates…if she could ever get her ass out of the bathroom. Repeated retching had left her throat raw. At one point during the early morning hours she began spitting up droplets of blood. Her behind hadn't faired any better. Coming and going, she felt like an absolute train wreck. *The glamorous life I lead…*

"What is wrong with me?" she grumbled groggily, gripping her stomach, hunched over. "I'm so tired." Nevertheless, sick or not, hurling or not, crapping or not, Nour would have to find some way to get herself cleaned up and halfway presentable, ready to do her job. Shuffling back to her bed, she reached out for her phone on her night table, but it wasn't there. *Weird…I could have sworn I put it here.*

Trying not to awaken either of her parents, she slipped out of her room and tiptoed past their bedroom. First stop the bathroom. After determining it wasn't there she walked to the kitchen. Much to her chagrin, both her parents were not only wide awake, but seated at the kitchen table slouched over their tea, obviously in the middle of a serious conversation. One she had clearly interrupted.

"*AsSalaamu'alaikum*," greeted Nour. "I didn't know you two were already up."

In unison, her parents *salaamed* her back, their faces strained. Without uttering a single word, her father slid Nour's phone across the table, staring into his daughter's face, unblinking.

"Ah! Just what I was looking for." As Nour reached out to snatch it, her father's hand beat her to it, covering hers with his. *Okay...* "What's going on?" Nour squinted, unsure why her father's face looked so grim, but before she had a chance to inquire, another sharp gut pain ripped straight through her insides. Nour bolted full speed from the kitchen to the bathroom.

"Nour!" her mother yelled after her, startled by the sudden outburst. "What's the matter?" she hollered, snatching the phone off the kitchen table and following her daughter to the bathroom. "What's wrong?"

Nour barreled into the bathroom, slamming the door behind her. With one hand cupped over her mouth, she loosened the tie to her pajama bottoms with the other, barely making it in time.

"NOUR!" Mrs. Ibrahim pounded the door with her fist. "Answer me!" But all she received in reply were her daughter's retching and groaning. "Let me in! This instant!"

"What the hell is going on?" Mr. Ibrahim asked, having joined his wife at the bathroom vigil. "Just go in. Don't ask her for permission."

"I can't. It's locked."

TIGHT ROPE

"Nour!" he shouted. "Open this door." He firmly twisted the handle but with no success. "Let your mother in."

"I...I can't," Nour finally muttered, her voice scratchy and faint. "I'm...sitting"

"What does she mean sitting?" whispered Mr. Ibrahim, exasperated.

His wife shot him a look, rolled her eyes and shook her head.

"Oh. OH." Mr. Ibrahim threw his hands in the air in surrender. "This is between you and your daughter."

"Call for an ambulance while I try to talk to her," said Mrs. Ibrahim loud enough for Nour to hear.

"NO!" Yelled Nour emphatically. A second later, the lock clicked open. Mrs. Ibrahim shot her husband *the look* and shoved her daughter way in, pushing the door shut behind her.

"You need to go to the hospital."

"I can't."

"You can and you will."

"I'm fine."

"FINE? Look at you..."

"It's just nerves."

"Nour, if you don't stop this madness—"

Nour pulled the cord of her robe tighter around her body. Leaning in over the sink, she braced herself on the counter with the palms of both hands. "Mommy..." Beads of sweat dripped from her hairline. "I...need you...to support me," she sputtered. "Please..."

"Support you?" Incensed, Mrs. Ibrahim pulled Nour's phone from her pocket, practically shoving it in Nour's face. "You want *my* support? Then start by telling me who the hell this person is who's threatening you!"

"What?" Nour retched. *Not again.*

Mrs. Ibrahim stepped behind her daughter now slumped over the toilet, soothingly rubbing her back, waiting for this next wave to end. Almost in a whisper she pleaded, "Don't *what* me anymore. Trust goes both ways. If you want me to support you, then you need to trust me."

Nour began to cry. "I...I...don't know," replied Nour.

"What don't you know?"

"They never sign their names."

"They? Oh, baby, how long has this been going on?"

"Mommy, I—"

Mrs. Ibrahim slammed her fist on the bathroom wood door and roared. "HOW LONG?"

Nour flinch. "A few weeks."

"And you never thought to tell us?"

"I didn't want to worry you."

"Are you out of your damn mind! You have someone threatening you and you say nothing? As if we can't take it? Are you joking right now?"

"Please stop yelling at me."

"You're lucky I'm not choking you! Damn it to hell, Nour! You don't think."

Nour rinsed out her mouth with cool water. Silence tended to be the wisest course of action.

"Who else knows about this?"

"Nobody."

"Nobody?" Her mother shook her head in disgust. "Not even the police? You didn't even file a complaint? NOTHING?"

Nour shook her head no.

"*Ya Allah!* What is wrong with you?"

TIGHT ROPE

"I can't do this right now. I need to get ready to go."

"Correction, young lady, *we* need to get ready to go."

"What?"

"You heard me. Either we all go or nobody is leaving this house."

Fine. If they want to follow me around, be my self-appointed bodyguards, so be it. Tugging a hand towel from the ring she pressed it firmly over her face, drawing in a long deliberate breath from under the cooling damp fibers. Reluctantly standing as straight as presently possible, she shook her head, staring back at her abysmal reflection in the bathroom mirror. "We leave in forty minutes."

From the other room, Mrs. Ibrahim heard her husband's voice conversing into the phone using an especially hushed forceful tone. "As many as you can get, brother… At one, but I want everyone there earlier… Yes, that works. *Shukran*, Brother Shane. I really appreciate this. *Ma'a Salaam.*"

CHAPTER 28

Russell Tetler

THE CHOICE TO TAKE MASS transit with a gun strapped to his waist wasn't necessarily Russell's brightest claim to fame, but on a day like today, this particular decision would prove *not* to be his worst either. After much consideration, he didn't want to find himself in the position of having to worry about parking the car or trying to retrieve it afterwards, in the event he was lucky enough to make a clean getaway. At one point, he'd contemplated renting a car, but then he would have had to use a credit card in his name to secure it. Hence the mass transit he suffered through now.

The problem with busses was that they were long, bumpy, sardine cans, and depending on whether or not the bus was full, the response from the suspension system could be the difference of a relatively smooth ride or one that jostled the brain cells out of commission. Either way, for Russell, this ride from hell couldn't end soon enough.

Russell went over the plan in his head. If by some miracle of

TIGHT ROPE

miracles, he escaped undetected, he'd hide in plain sight in some nearby dive, restaurant or bar, depending on how far he got. Once inside, he'd casually order a drink, and pretend to read a newspaper or menu nonchalantly like any good old senior citizen would do while an all-points bulletin was out looking for him.

"Us old folks can easily blend, cause we're the invisible people," he told his barber one visit. "We never get noticed unless of course we're walking too slowly across the street and then watch out! Blasting horns for days." Russell used to also joke that he could run butt naked on the highway in broad daylight, and all that would happen to him would be fifteen minutes of YouTube fame, and a free one-way trip to the local loony bin.

Russell checked the time. He still had over an hour and a half to get there and find a place to stand. His poor selection of sweater, scratchy as heck, had already begun to leave a small annoying welt on the back of his neck. Stretching, it took all he had not to scratch at it. *A present from Doris.* Russell berated himself, *I should have remembered.* Using his finger to stretch and distend the collar, he attempted to draw the fabric farther enough away from his already irritated, blotchy, red neckline.

Russell jerked. The temperature on the bus felt stifling and hot all at once, but in reality, if anything, the bus temps were a bit cool. The heat taking over him came from the poison traveling through his system, making its way into his gut and other vital organs. The additional bumps on the road and sudden jarring stops did little to help.

Reaching up, he wiped the sweat dripping from his forehead with the back of his hand. *Even my eyeballs hurt,* he thought miserably, closing them from the glare of light stabbing his retinas through the bus window. The heavily made-up lady sitting too close to him, doused in a gallon of cheap perfume, wasn't making the trip any easier. If only he could shove her nasty ass off the seat as far away from him as possible. *I should spring for a cab...* Russell stole a peek. *No, too far. It'll cost a fortune.*

They stopped. *Oh, God, more people,* more bodies crunched into the moving sardine can. Rows of people all pressed together, tilting in unison with each sharp turn or pothole. Outside the bus, traffic snarled to a dead still. *You've got to be fucking kidding me.*

His stomach lurched again. Clearly the need for an emergency bathroom run was upon him as a gripping pain ripped through his gut and burned. Using a mangled tissue from his other pocket, he swiped the sweat accumulating under his hairline. *Shit. Let's go already!* He'd begun to feel a bit light-headed. Bleeding in the brain was known to cause confusion.

A tightening in his chest made inhaling difficult. *I gotta get off this bus.* Pulling the cord repeatedly to alert the driver, he shoved his way through the compressed collection of straphangers until making it to the back-door steps. When the bus finally lurched to a halt, he leapt off, gasping for air. Eventually, he hailed for a cab. *Fuck it.*

As Russell struggled to the rally with the intention of ending someone's life, his own weakening heart muscles protested. Rolling down the cab's window helped some, but as fluids filled both lungs, an irregular heartbeat occurred, and the more oxygen he managed to gulp, the more he coughed. None of this discomfort mattered enough; the rancorous old man's stubborn agitation battled to realize his final goal.

CHAPTER 29

The Rally

THE STAGE SEEMED AWFULLY SMALL compared to the amount of bodies expected to use it. The long hours of marketing the event had worked. Many more people had come than even Nour had expected. Although folks were on edge, they were also anxious to make a connection. A rally such as this one did just that. A conduit of like minds gathering in hope, despite the repressive swamp infested cabinet of white hoods now in charge. Somehow faith managed to endure in the hearts of those willing to say *enough*.

If Nour weren't already feeling nervous, she'd surely be feeling it now. Stepping up to the stage, she greeted the three other speakers and introduced her parents, both on high alert, but cordial enough. Then she made her way over to a few of the stagehands to express her gratitude, eventually making the rounds over to the music group booked for the event. An amazing string and drum group called Red Line.

Red Line had a reputation for being brazenly vocal about the election results and had gained instant notoriety for their political leanings, as well as a laundry list of cancellations. Black Listed—the usual punishment doled out for those entertainers or reporters unwilling to goose-step in line with the current White House administration— they were the latest casualties of the new wave of McCarthyism á la The White House.

Including Nour, there was a total of four speakers in the line-up. The decision had been made that she would open, which only made sense as the newest member on the political stump. Truth be told, she assumed most of the audience were coming to hear the voices of the other three, better known, more seasoned speakers, but this didn't matter in the slightest. It had been an honor to be included amongst these heavy-hitters. She looked forward to hearing and learning from them as well.

The crowd filled quickly with many faces. People young and old, of every complexion, some with families, children and babies in strollers, grandparents sitting on lawn chairs with grandkids cuddled on their laps. College students lugging backpacks stood in small groups, leaning on whatever they could find, while other more resourceful folks sat on blankets and plastic bags. Nour recognized a few familiar faces in the crowd, people from the community. Directly in front of the stage, a wall of security amassed: men from the masjid. A tall, strikingly handsome Muslim man near the steps waved knowingly to her father and nodded. *Brother Shane?*

Interspersed in the crowd were undercover police. Nour couldn't spot them individually, too far from the crowd, but she tried to anyway. Scanning the crowd, she wondered which set of eyes belonged to *him*.

Threats…hopefully, that's all they were. Words to scare her silent. Maybe he was just another Internet warrior, a bolder bully on the keyboard. A random coward who loved nothing more than to harass anyone he didn't agree with, and make an absolute nuisance of himself behind the protection of a screen.

Then again, Shadow might be the kind who lives for Armageddon, and praying for a race war since the election. Those people Nour feared the most. Judging by the frowns both her parents wore, they shared the same grave concern. *The sooner this is over, the better.*

"Ten minutes," yelled one of the stage hands.

So many people...

"Five minutes."

Faces everywhere...

"Three minutes. Take your seats, everyone."

Bismillah.

"One minute."

The crowds stood ready. The noise level rising to a deafening decibel, fueling the mounting adrenaline pumping through the crowds. *Time to get this party started.* Red Line began playing a powerful, rhythmic drum piece, a perfect call to attention.

Once the pulse of the drums died down, Nour stepped stoically to the podium and the crowd went berserk. The energy in the air was electric. People yelling and shouting, "RESIST! RESIST!" Only Nour's parents knew how hard their daughter was fighting back her nervousness. But what nobody knew was the extent of the excruciating pain now searing through her gut.

Nour tapped the microphone three times. The crowd immediately quieted. All eyes were focused on her, ready to hear her speak.

SAHAR ABDULAZIZ

AsSalaamu'alaikum and Greetings!

The crowd roared.

Thank you all for coming out today. We have an incredible lineup of some of the most powerful voices of our generation, gathered here together as one because we know and understand the opponent we face!

The crowd roared again.

These are homegrown, adversaries. Residing inside our borders, of the brown shirt variety, and you know exactly who I mean.

The crowd cheered again. One man yelled, "We sure as shit do!"

We understand that as a nation descendant of immigrants and slaves, all with various beliefs and complexions, we can never look away or ignore those who perpetrate hate and fear. Pretending that what they say or encourage others to do is nothing but political differences colliding. No! I am here to tell you, that we can never view hate speech as mere rhetoric or political scheming or pandering. We can never make excuses for bigotry and hate, because the minute we do that, the enemy wins, and the stakes are too high now to ever let hate be permitted to win again.

The people clapped and hollered in agreement.

Today we have some of the most trusted and honored fighters of our century gathered here to share their thoughts, their direction, and their hopes for a better future that includes all of us, as one extended human family! We—

TIGHT ROPE

Nour never had the chance to finish before a single haunting gunshot rang out from the crowd. Within seconds, screams of shock and horror rippled through the crowd, sending people diving for cover. "She's hit!" a voice wailed, referring to Nour. "GET DOWN!"

Feet pummeled the sidewalk, a stampede in every which direction. People crashed into one another, all in search of cover. Children were swept protectively up into the arms of their terrorized parents, while others simply crouched on their knees, draping the remaining half of their bodies over the strollers, forming human shields. Others bolted, seeking shelter behind trees, or elbow crawling under benches for cover.

"GET ON THE GROUND!" Shane ordered. "You, over there, DOWN!" Bystanders dove for cover, with some running from one end of the block to the other seeking safety. Hysterical mothers screamed out the names of children lost in the frenzy, or pushed asunder by those trying to escape. Horrified screams sliced through the air, piercing the stench of the panic-choked throng. On stage from behind the podium and surrounded by a host of dazed onlookers including her parents, Maryam, Zaid, and Shane, Nour rocked side to side, clutching her stomach in agony, curled in the fetal position.

"Is she shot?" cried Mrs. Ibrahim.

"You—call for help," ordered Shane to another man standing nearby.

"She's breathing," said Mr. Ibrahim.

"Give me space!" Maryam's hands searched frantically for evidence of a bullet wound. "Are you hit?" she asked. Nour only moaned.

"Back up," ordered another voice, quite possibly Zaid's.

"Give her room to work."

Shane had already corralled his security force. "You two," he said, specifically at a couple of Muslim brothers blocking the stairs, "keep everyone away." To the nearest security guard already with his ear pressed to his phone, while cupping the other to hear. "Call an ambulance!"

Within minutes, law enforcement set up physical barriers to exclude unauthorized personnel from the scene while establishing paths of entry and exit so medical personnel could get to the victim without contaminating the crime scene. Moments later, a team of medics joined Maryam. Sheer mayhem ensued all around them, but nobody hovering over Nour seems to notice or care. All concentration and concern remained intently focused on the coiled, writhing body.

"*Ya Allah*," whimpered Mrs. Ibrahim. "Nour, baby, I'm here. It's Mommy. I'm here, sweetheart." Qasim drew his wife to him, giving the medics room to work.

"Everyone, BACK UP! NOW!" Police on the scene joined the security detail currently ushering the frenzied mob lingering near the stage. A reporter from one of the television stations stood off to the side, already on the air.

"I'm standing where only moments before, a single terrifying shot rang out. Police say the suspect pulled out a handgun and fired one shot towards the stage where activist Nour Ibrahim was speaking. Whether or not Ibrahim was the target is still unknown. However, medics took Ibrahim to the hospital under guard, but the extent of her injuries remains unclear. So far, no further information about the suspect is available. Police say they are using every resource available to identify and arrest the suspect, and urge anyone with any information to call 555-123-4567."

TIGHT ROPE

Later on, a bystander, another off-duty RN who stayed behind to help, noted to the reporter the eerie feeling of seeing a bunch of abandoned belongings scattered about the lawn area that had only a few minutes prior been filled with people. Each item left behind told a terrifying tale of its own. A set of car keys, a stroller with nothing inside but a milk-filled sippy cup, abandoned blankets. During the search police retrieved an abandoned throwaway cell phone. They hoped it would lead them to the identity of the shooter.

"I heard fifteen people, seven of them children, were hurt in the rush," said the reporter.

"It could have been worse," the stunned nurse whispered, a lone tear sliding down her already smudged stained cheek. "A real bloodbath."

CHAPTER 30

Eugene Underwood

HE PREFERRED KILLING AT CLOSE range, specifically not more than ten feet away, but preferably at arm's length. If and when the opportunity presented itself, even closer… *much, much, closer*. The closer the better. The more intimate, the more delicious.

Eugene's never understood when guys new to the business became all nervous and sweaty, some even trembling. One time, he remembered watching a first-timer practically pass out from holding his breath.

"Here, dry your hands," Eugene instructed, handing the kid a paper towel.

"Thanks. Guess I'm a bit nervous."

"No shit. Couldn't tell."

Face flushed, the young man wiped his hands. Searching for a place to toss the used crumpled paper towel, he caught Eugene staring at him in disgust.

"Sorry." He stuffed the used towel in his pant pocket. Not too smart leaving evidence lying around …

"Look," said Eugene, never bothering to hold back the contempt in his voice, "is this your first job? Doing this?"

"Yeah, but I can handle it."

Figures. My luck. "What are you called?"

"What am I called?" Again, the young man appeared confused.

"For Christ's sake, your name, you imbecile. What-do-I-call-you?"

"Waldo."

"WALDO?" Eugene held back a grunt. "You're fuck'in kidding me, right?"

"I wish."

Someone's parents had a sense of humor. That or they hated the kid. Eugene cupped his face. "… Okay, WAL-DO, well, I don't want you passing out on me so listen up. Take a deep breath in, and release a silent yell. *Silent* being the operative word here. Hard as you can. Make even the slightest noise and I swear I'll kill you myself."

The young man did exactly as he was instructed.

"Good. That'll kick your killer hormones in and get you ready to take care of business. Now, I want you to take another deep breath, but this time grab your stomach like this," Eugene showed him how to lift his diaphragm. "Okay, now bend over."

Waldo bent over.

"Okay, now straighten up."

Straightening up, the young man's face registered amazement. "That worked!"

"Of course, it did. And if you get nervous again, rinse and repeat. Now shut the fuck up and get ready. I think I see our mark coming."

Particularly intriguing to Eugene were brutal torture techniques and final life extinguishing plans devised to handle any unanticipated situation that could arise in his line of work. He took a great deal of pride on being ready for any unforeseen event or mishap. Actually, he marketed his expertise using the motto, "I get shit done right the first time no matter what happens, and I do mean, *no matter what happens.*" Crude, a tad sophomoric, but brutally to the point, and so far, he'd had a lot of success pitching it.

For example, there were times when Eugene found himself in the unfortunate situation when he'd be forced to kill in a precariously small space or behind a thin-walled office, or even perhaps out in the open where any bystander could, by happenstance, wander by and discover what he was up to. However, no matter where Eugene ultimately carried out his lethal operations, he did so with an unhinged yet harnessed proclivity for instant human obliteration. His reputation on the street for getting the job done right the first time preceded him, and kept open many doors of opportunity. Unfortunately, the whack-jobs he'd recently contracted for some of the smaller jobs failed to impress, leaving him seriously disappointed. The more people involved, the greater the potential for screw-ups, and the more screw-ups that occurred, the more headaches for him. Not cool. This level of incompetence couldn't go unanswered. In his mind, he still had unfinished business with those three bozos from the botched grocery job. Just thinking about it made him mad, and anybody on the street who had ever worked with or for Eugene Underwood knew: *You don't fuck up the job. You don't half-ass the job. And whatever you do, you finish the job or else.* The "or else" part wasn't hyperbole.

The process of weapon selection tended to calm Eugene

TIGHT ROPE

down. To date, his favorite was none other than the military style garrote. Nothing more than a flexible wire attached to a small wooden handle, it was an excellent and silent tool to use when exterminating a life. One pulled, taut motion, and done. Easy to keep concealed and super inexpensive to replace. On the rare occasion when Eugene's garrote wasn't handy, perhaps due to an unanticipated kill, he found many other perfectly acceptable materials could be substituted with just as much deadly precision. So far, he had used everything from nylon guitar strings, a telephone cord, cable wires, your everyday household rope, but without argument, his all-time favorite—fishing line. All perfectly legal items one could carry on their person without fear of arrest.

**

Hands shoved casually in his pockets, head bowed low, Eugene made no prolonged eye contact as he strode away. Slipping undetected from the hysterical throng of people, but never once losing sight of Flossy, who was currently attempting to make a run for it. He appeared to labor through every breath, stopped occasionally, and evidently had difficulty keeping his balance. At one point, he almost got sideswiped by an irate cabbie for crossing the road too slowly between lights. The old codger weaved back and forth, either drugged, drunk, or completely out of his mind.

Eugene followed Flossy at a safe distance as he staggered over to the other side of the street, appearing to scan for a place to stop and hide, presumably without the fear of getting run over. Pressed flatly on the side of a building's brick wall for support, the guy was sweating pellets. All of a sudden, he lurched forward at the waist gripping his gut, violently dry hurling, and giving off the most disagreeably loud wrenching curdle Eugene ever heard. Blurred by ambulance sirens and bleeping police cars from around the corner and directly across the street, people passed him without turning around, lost in their own worlds, oblivious to the guy. Everybody, that is, except for his executioner.

This guy's utterly pathetic—one more, sorry fuck-up in a long line of sorry-ass fuck-ups. Eugene snarled, not entirely sure if he felt more insulted or furious. The Call of the Sociopath controlling Eugene's decision-making process could no longer bear waiting. *That's it! I've had it.*

Allowing himself no extra time to lollygag or second-guess, which was never his style to begin with, Eugene instantaneously reached the coldblooded decision to personally put an end to this fool's life. Not only was this imbecile a personal insult to all those who did this kind of skilled labor for a living, but also to him personally. As far as Eugene was concerned, it was high time somebody sent out a clear and uncompromising message to stop all this amateurish, pussyfooting nonsense—once and for all. However, to successfully pull this off, he'd have to move swiftly because in all likelihood, the police weren't far behind, most definitely out in force, in search of this careless jerk-off.

In a controlled yet calculating manner, Eugene pressed his back flat to the buildings brick wall to think for a few seconds, while instinctively reaching into his pocket for his weapon and gloves. Using his teeth to hold the garrote and his knees to grip his gloves, he summarily whipped off his windbreaker and turned it inside out, then put it back on, silently zipping it closed. Reaching to grab his gloves, he slipped each one on making sure to tug the leather grip snuggly around each of his fingers. Lastly, he removed the weapon from his clenched jaw and made his move.

TIGHT ROPE

The air filled with a kinetic yet frantic energy. The manhunt was on. Blaring sirens, people scrambling for cover, sounds of crying and the stench of fear penetrated the air. Some police assembled, while others were already hitting the pavement. With the added police presence, Eugene would be painstakingly cautious to avoid getting caught, but he wasn't the least bit deterred; if anything, he enjoyed the challenge. He fed off it.

Edging his way far from the unfolding scene he quickened his steps, never losing sight of his target, and pausing only long enough to calculate each subsequent tacit move, which would inevitably bring him closer to his target and his kill. Gloriously short and sweet, he softly approached, step by silent, murderous step.

Lightheaded and still somewhat hunched over, Flossy appeared unable to secure his bearings. Oblivious to his surroundings as the sharp stabbing pain inside of him began to burst, he was blissfully unaware of his impending death. So intent on his own retching, Russell never noticed when the expertly looped, razor-thin wire circled over his head from the back. Yanked hard and tight, it choked the life out of him in one exacting motion.

Russell collapsed on the pavement, his head smacking onto the concrete in a lifeless broken doll thump.

Eugene stepped back to admire his work, pleased he'd been able to pull it off without getting covered in blood. Stealing a quick peek around to ensure no one nearby was watching before he began wiping the wire clean with the unsoiled corner edge of Russell's flannel shirt. Once spotless, he pocketed the garrote. Leaning over, Eugene used his gloved thumb to lift each of Russell's eyelids, checking for any lingering sign of life.

Negative. Both eyeballs rolled back.

Though difficult with gloves on, he felt for a pulse as well. Then bent in closer to hear for a breath. *Another negative. Excellent.*

Assured his target was no longer a living, breathing member of society, Eugene dragged the lifeless body by the feet behind the over-filled dumpster before taking another quick peek around, keen not to leave any incriminating evidence—nothing that could be traced back to him before finally taking his leave. Just to make sure, quite a few blocks later and clear out of the vicinity of the crime, he handed a homeless man pushing a shopping cart filled to the brim, his windbreaker.

"Thanks," called the toothless man after Eugene.

Nothing like a job finally well done. Eugene rubbed both his hands together, coolly strolling away from Russell's dead corpse as if it was another ordinary day in the neighborhood. Nonchalantly, he headed in the direction of his new favorite pub to celebrate a job well done. Fifteen minutes later, he arrived, pleased to see the same pretty maître de greeting him as he stepped into the foyer.

"Good afternoon sir, and welcome back. Will you be needing a table today?"

"No table necessary. I'll head over to the bar. I know my way."

The young woman smiled and called after him. "Have a nice lunch."

The television over the bar was already turned to a sports channel where a heated panel discussion about players refusing to stand for the anthem was currently being waged.

"It's disrespectful and dishonors the men and women who fought and gave their life to protect this country," admonished the latest bottle blond panelist.

"The people who fought for this country fought for The

Constitution to be upheld, for freedom of speech, freedom to protest. This is his form of protest. How is that disrespectful? It's his constitutional right as an American."

"Right, he and his fellow players are all so oppressed as they collect their millions from the same country they seem to love criticizing."

"First off, I resent your implication that their money is some big favor. Those players earned those millions, it wasn't donated to them. Secondly, he never denied being one of the privileged few, but what he is saying is that until everyone gets a fair shot, he can't sit by and stay quiet. Look, it's no secret people are suffering, especially People of Color. There's a disproportionate pipeline from the street to the prisons in effect. People are getting shot for minor traffic violations. All he wants to do is constitutionally draw attention to these kinds of flagrant inequities. And so, what if he does it on his knee and it itches your pseudo-neocon sensibilities? Bottom line is, there's nothing—no kind of protest that he or any person of color could do—that would meet with your approval."

"And what exactly will him bending on his knee and disrespecting the flag do to change any of that?"

"It's got us talking."

Breaking his own rule, Eugene chose the stool directly facing the screen to sit. The place was practically empty, but then again, it was still early. A moment later the same friendly bartender from the other day came from somewhere in the back and greeted him like he was an old pal.

"Afternoon, sir. What can I get for you today?"

"Good afternoon. You know what? I'm starving. How about a beer from the tap, a roast beef sandwich on rye—onion, lettuce, tomato, Thousand Island dressing—a side of fries, coleslaw, and a pickle."

"Coming right up," replied the bartender.

"Do me a favor?"

"Sure thing."

"Change the channel to the news."

The bartender switched to a national news station already in the middle of covering the story. "Good enough?"

"Perfect."

"Authorities believe the suspect responsible for today's shooting is a man, quite possibly in his late 60s. However, police will not confirm if this photo being circulated, taken by a bystander, could possibly be the gunman. In this photo—unfortunately it's a bit blurry— the alleged shooter is taking aim and fires. I'm not sure if you can see, we're trying to pan the camera closer." The reporter brings her cell phone closer to the camera lens.

"Okay, you can kind of see a figure of a man lifting something that has the shape of a pistol. In this next photo taken only moments later, the victim, Nour Ibrahim, had already fallen to the ground behind the podium. You can see people standing, shocked, some ducking and taking cover. Pure pandemonium broke out after the gun fired."

"Brooke?" asked the newscaster located in the actual studio, "How many shots were fired?"

"Police so far have confirmed only one shot. No further information about the suspect is available. However, police are cautioning that the shooter is armed and dangerous. If you see anyone fitting the description, do not approach; call the tip line. They also want the public to know that they are using every resource available to identify and arrest the suspect, and urge anyone with any

TIGHT ROPE

further information or possibly photos to call—"

With expert form, Eugene never flinched, smirked or smiled. He didn't give off any decipherable acknowledgment or interest about the story being reported. *Wait till they find the present I left them...*

CHAPTER 31

Doris Tetler

BACK HOME A TORN OPEN bag of caramel popcorn rested on Doris's lap. Sticking her hand deep into the back corner of the container, she managed to scour out a handful of extra kernels. Mindlessly, she shoved the small gooey morsels of deliciousness into her mouth. Bored and restless, she snatched the remote control, rapidly pressing the buttons and jumping from station to station until landing on a worthwhile show. Lately, most of the crime fiction and forensic investigation shows, along with their bane background music compilations designed to raise the hair on the back of her neck, failed to keep her attention. *Psychological thrillers, my ass!* They'd become too predictable. *Nothing but one long monotonous blob of bleary nothingness.*

The thrill of watching other people's mind-numbing, lackluster murders had lost some of its oomph. Not only that, but Doris felt she had gleaned all she could about how to commit the perfect crime. Now, for her, these television programs were

TIGHT ROPE

nothing more than a conglomeration of one dreary, sloppy murder after the next, so she decided to go in search of something new; something that offered more entertaining gore, and preferably a hell of a lot more information. *Something with a little pizzazz for God's sake! Doesn't anyone have any imagination anymore? At least when I plot to bump somebody off, I do it with genius and style!*

Doris swore to the heavens above and the hell which, in all likelihood, awaited her below, that once her own diabolical escapade had come to its final conclusion, she'd seriously have to take the time to reevaluate her viewing selections or at the very least, start a letter campaign. It was high time somebody complained to the networks, who wrongly assumed that reruns and dreary forensic shows were all the viewing public was worth. Doris continued pushing the buttons on the remote.

Hmmm, Cooking with Granny, Lawn Care on a Budget, Tabernacle and You, news, news, more news. *Screw that*, but something on the last station caught her attention. Maybe it was the name. *Nour Ibrahim*…it sounded remotely familiar. Curious, she pushed the button back to the station just passed.

"Police are saying that the suspect; a man in his late 50s early 60s pulled out a handgun and fired one single shot at the stage where community activist Nour Ibrahim was speaking. For now, police aren't sure whether or not Ibrahim was the actual target; however, she has been taken to the hospital under police protection. As of now, the full extent of her injuries remains unclear. So far, no other information about the shooting suspect is available. Police have confirmed that they are using every resource available to identify and arrest the suspect, and urge anyone with information to call—"

SAHAR ABDULAZIZ

Ah, now I know why the name sounded so familiar. That's the girl Russell's always yammering on about—says he can't stand her. Froths at the mouth anytime she's on the screen. Can't imagine what she did to piss him off so bad, but she sure got under his skin, which frankly, made Doris like her already.

Watching news wasn't something Doris normally gravitated towards when she had sole control over the television, especially since Russell the Mindless Drone basically watched nothing else. His news obsession felt like sheer torture; endless hours of the same dreary information delivered in that irritatingly monotone practiced Ken and Barbie voice all newscasters used. It was enough to make a person go nuts, *but maybe that's the objective after all. Tell the news events in such a way to force us listeners to tune it out or stop paying attention in the first place. Then get us flipping from channel to channel in search of entertainment only to wind up right back where we started from.* Doris popped another handful in her mouth. *And to tell the truth, it's not like it matters anymore which station you land on either, except of course if you prefer your news delivered to support your own particular political leanings.* Doris shook her head, ready to chuck the remote across the room.

All them fancy stations claiming to deliver the real news...talking for hours, sometimes days, about things nobody in their right mind gives a crap about. Then, when some folks go all mental over it, fed up to the point they start arguing and screaming back at the screen like Russell does, then there's a problem! Little do the morons realize they're sneaking the real news in, behind all that other stupid stuff, like the rise in parking tickets or ducks crossing the highway, or something equally as dumb. Doris tore open the bag the rest of the way and licked the inside clean, coughing uncontrollably when by mistake she inhaled a single uncooked corn kernel.

With nothing else worth keeping her attention, Doris decided

TIGHT ROPE

to follow the shooting to see where that went. Leaning back on the couch cushion, lifting her vein-lined legs unto the coffee table, she grabbed for the next snack bag, popping it open so she could continue shoving fistfuls of the overly salted and under caramelized popcorn into her mouth. Doris chuckled. *Boy oh boy, wait until Russell finds out somebody shot that Ibrahim girl. Then again, by the time he finds out, he'll probably be too close to death himself to give a shit.* Poetic justice.

For the remainder of the day, Doris dozed in and out. She hadn't slept well, if at all, the night before as Russell serenaded her by puking his guts up. A few times she caught herself retching alongside with him. Not out of sympathy, *no never that*, but purely a physical reflex. Same type of thing used to happen when George was a small child. Like any other kid, she'd inevitably catch a cold, be it the sniffles or a cough, and Doris would nurse her so attentively that when her child had a hard time breathing in through her stuffed nose, Doris would take in deep breaths for her. If the child coughed, she'd cough along with her, as if by some maternal osmosis, she'd help release whatever ailed her sick child. It never worked.

After hours of exhausted TV viewing, Doris went upstairs to bed. Pulling the blanket over her shoulder she adjusted the pillow under her head just the way she liked it. It wasn't long before she began to drift off.

Still halfway between dreaming and awake, her mind wandered back to that day from hell when the news arrived about her daughter. How she couldn't process what was being said to her, hoping for a miracle that somehow, it was all some big, ugly mistake. At any moment, she'd be profusely apologized to for being made to feel so upset, and her daughter would come barreling through the door, unharmed, and rushing into her mother's warm embrace, never to leave again.

But for Doris, no such miracle transpired and the news was exactly what they delivered: a nightmare of unspeakable standings. *Unspeakable*, yes, good word for it because that's when Doris decided she could no longer use her voice to express how she felt. For her, words caused nothing but pain, heartache, and despair. They sliced through her like a knife and left a wound so deep, so foreboding, that nothing and nobody could ever begin to repair it. The words left long and ugly scars, and healing from their infliction felt unthinkable, like a betrayal. Consequently, since then, words no longer left Doris's mouth. Instead they were left adrift, dangling around in her head alone, and unable to be set free from the prison created by her wounded mind.

Prayers meant nothing either. Just another jumble of meaningless words as far as Doris was concerned. Never again after that day would she ever pray. Angry at herself for all those fruitless hours spent in worship on her knees, heart exposed, begging, beseeching…and all for naught. "Oh, Dear God, please bring my baby home to me safe and sound." "God, please protect George from harm." "Please don't let anyone hurt my baby girl." "Dear Lord, I pray to You and only You, don't let my George be dead."

She pleaded with God to make those military-suited visitors stop talking, but there they were, saying all those awful, terrible things that couldn't be true. "I prayed to You. I begged You to make them stop lying to me, to make them stop telling me my precious baby girl is dead."

And then in an instant, the tiny, hopeless voice inside of Doris died along with all her faith, turning forever mute. No longer would she allow herself to believe, care or want from anyone or anything else ever again…not when someone so much a part of her being could be stolen so needlessly from her life.

**

Late that evening, closer to eleven, there was a succession of heavy, menacing knocks at the front door. The window in Doris's bedroom facing the street appeared alit with flashing lights. In actuality, there were three vehicles parked on the curb, but only one had their flashers on. Nevertheless, it made for quite a light show.

Naturally, Doris at first assumed she was still asleep, off dreaming her nightmare once again, back on the couch as she listened to the messengers of death on that terribly chilly, gloomy afternoon. The day when the clouds above her heart drew heavy and dark, when a deafening clap of thunder tore through the heavens and lightening lit up the entire dim sky. The day when a burst of monsoon-like rain fell uncontrollably to the earth, her cohort, lamenting alongside her for their mutual, terrible loss.

Unaccustomed to having visitors, Doris, who was now fully awake, became quite startled by the ruckus taking place on her front stoop, and apparently down her entire block. Apprehensively slipping on her robe and slippers, she managed to scamper her way to the door, detecting the sound of police radios in the background. Another round of incessant pounding.

Drawing the curtain slightly away she snuck a quick glance. Doris counted three police people standing on her stoop, two men and one woman.

"Mrs. Tetler? I'm Officer Hamilton," a voice loomed. "This is

Officer Marsh and Victim Advocate, Connie Lance. May we come in?"

No response.

"Please open up the door," ordered the officer civilly, waving a slip of paper.

Doris did as she was instructed, unbolting the top lock first and then the bottom, opening the door widely enough to pluck her head out. The lights from the police car were blinding. Glancing around, Doris noticed a few nosey neighbors craning their necks to see what was going on. A passerby across the street pretended to be waiting for his dog to poop, while others made no pretense at all. A throng of people she barely recognized gathered, all drawn to the unveiling horror like flies to shit.

"Mrs. Tetler?"

Doris nodded.

"Doris Tetler?"

Doris furrowed her brows, a bit annoyed, but with her head, indicated another "yes."

"Ma'am," said Officer Hamilton, all three individuals duly presented their credentials. "May we come inside?"

Doris pursed her lips, clucked her tongue, but begrudgingly moved off to the side, out of their way, pointing the three in the direction of her living room.

"Why don't you come sit with us, Mrs. Tetler." The advocate offered Doris use of her own chair using that all too familiar fake friendly intonation in her voice. Doris never trusted those types.

Both officers chose the couch, while the Advocate sat on the chair directly facing the chair where they indicated for Doris to sit. Without delay, Officer Marsh, the lead person whose job it was to deliver the bad news, spoke candidly, plainly and to the point, but surprisingly without being blunt or unsympathetic. Doris appreciated his style more than the advocate's phony friendliness.

"We are sorry to have to inform you, Mrs. Tetler, your husband, Russell was killed in what we suspect was a mugging. He was found this afternoon unresponsive. The paramedics attempted to revive him but without success." Marsh was careful not to divulge too many details about what they suspected Russell of doing prior to the mugging to see what, if anything, Doris would reveal. "We are actively trying to apprehend the suspect or suspects. Your husband's personal effects are at St. Peter's Hospital."

As Marsh spoke, the advocate and Officer Hamilton remained quiet, astutely studying Doris, and monitoring her for any adverse reactions. Much to their mutual surprise, it hadn't taken long for those quirks to show up in full-unadorned fashion.

Doris fixed her robe, pulling then knotting the cord tighter around her waist. Adjusting her posture, she fixed her back upright in her chair, and began fiddling with her fingers. One of the cuticles on her pinkie had annoyed her all day.

"Mrs. Tetler? May I call you Doris?" asked Marsh, avoiding the joint side-glances of his colleagues. Doris didn't reply, too busy using her teeth to tear at her skin. "Do you understand what I am telling you? Your husband was found dead."

Total silence.

"He was attacked."

The room waited. Doris bit her cuticle off, and spit it out over her shoulder. She then began to blow on her finger in quick bursts where the new exposed skin stung.

"Mrs. Tetler? Do you understand what Officer Marsh is telling you?" the advocate asked, trying her hand at getting the woman's attention.

Damn condescending bitch. I heard you. I'm not deaf. Doris folded her hands in her lap and crossed her feet at the ankles, much like she'd done that day seated on the cold, metal, white folding chair at George's funeral. However, at that funeral she'd wept, her tears refusing to stop. She'd never forget how frozen her body felt. Like ice. Or the way her head pounded like never before. No amount of painkiller or sleeping pills brought any relief. Tonight, she felt none of those emotions, except perhaps a crushing sense of disappointment. *Stupid old fool…went and got himself killed before my poison had a chance to work. That bastard stole even his death from me.*

Undeterred, Doris rose to her feet. For the first time in years she found her speaking voice. "Would anyone like a cup of coffee or tea?" Her voice came out a bit too raspy. Clearing her throat, she added, "I also baked some wonderful chocolate chip cookies." Without bothering to wait for a reply or see their reaction, Doris took off towards the kitchen. The advocate leapt to her feet to follow, but after she turned the corner she stopped. Doris was standing in front of the open refrigerator putting on a strange shade of dark lipstick, using a glass jar as a mirror. Then, just as casually, she leaned into the fridge and began laughing. At first the sound came in short clips, more of a chuckle, but then turned bone chilling. A sort of dry cackle, so eerily piercing, that both officers in the other room jumped to their feet in alarm.

"What's she doing?" whispered Marsh in a low voice at Lance.

"She's laughing." Silently mouthing her answer in return, palms in the air, shaking her head utterly stunned. As an advocate, Connie Lance had attended many death notifications during her career and had witnessed plenty of people reacting differently to grief, but this was a first even for her. From experience, she found most people, after hearing devastating news, sought out comfort and a shoulder to cry on. Others passed out, so she made it a practice to inform family when they were seated; much easier to grab hold of and risked less of a fall. Still, other people fell silent or sat shocked in utter disbelief, too upset to speak. Of course, there were those few who became hysterical, physically lashing out at the police for delivering the bad news. A few times she'd witnessed outright denial, but uproarious laughter?

"I don't think this one's all up there," murmured Hamilton to Marsh.

Marsh tended to agree. "All the more reason to give her some extra time to process what we're saying. Everyone deals with grief his or her own way. Trust me, I've seen plenty of strange reactions. Besides, there's no need to rush this. We've already got the gun Tetler fired, a clear match to the bullet pulled from the podium, as well as two eyewitnesses who placed him at the scene. Now all we need is the motive to tie this case up."

"And why somebody killed him afterwards," added Hamilton. "Fluke? Wrong place at the wrong time?"

"Yes, that too, and who, but you know, to be honest, I'm still not convinced this was a one-man job." Marsh jotted a few notes and observations on his pad. "The warrant says we can search the place, but maybe the wife will give us permission to search. I would rather not have to be limited by it, so let's play this cool for now."

Hamilton agreed. "I'm glad we had Connie tag along on this one."

"Who you telling?"

From the kitchen, Connie Lance watched Doris prepare the coffee tray: three filled mugs, three spoons, three saucers, and three napkins. Connie wanted to point out to Doris that she was short one setting, but thought to stay silent and observe instead. Sometimes silence reveals more about a client's personality than anything else.

Doris reached into a cabinet and pulled out a cookie jar. "Cookie?" she asked rather pushily, wearing a stare that said she wouldn't take no for an answer.

"Thank you." The nosy bitch accepted the cookie and then felt compelled to take a bite under Doris's watchful glare of approval. "Delicious."

Doris grinned. "I only use the freshest ingredients," she said, filling the serving plate with enough cookies for each of her guests to have two. She wanted them sick. Not dead. Lastly, sugar and cream were added to the tray.

"Let me get that for you," offered Connie gently, popping the remainder of her cookie in her mouth to free up her hands, but Doris wouldn't release her firm grip.

"These were Russell's favorite cookies, you know. Chocolate chip. He liked nothing better than a hot cup of coffee and a plate of chocolate chip cookies." Doris wore a strange expression that would later be described as a "malevolent smile."

Doris reentered the living room, placing the serving tray on the coffee table. She handed each officer a cup and saucer. "One for you and one for you." Then she handed one to Connie as if the four of them were gathered together for a Mad Hatter Tea party as opposed to a homicide. On the side of each saucer, Doris placed two cookies. "There you go," said Doris, taking her seat, again crossing her hands and ankles, her back perfectly erect. "Now, where were we?"

Officer Hamilton made a practice of answering all questions and concerns as many times as family members asked, and did so with as much empathy and delicacy as he could muster. Despite the strange and unexpected kitchen outburst, he patiently continued to explain to Doris what would happen next: the need for body identification, the subsequent police investigation, and the possibility of criminal justice procedures. Doris listened, never interrupting or asking any questions.

"Do you have any questions, Mrs. Tetler?" Connie interjected, wanting to make sure Doris understood what was being said, but Doris disregarded her, gesturing for Hamilton to continue.

"Do you drive, Mrs. Tetler?" asked Officer Hamilton, swallowing a rather large bite of his second cookie.

Doris shook her head.

"That's no problem. We can arrange to have someone drive you to the medical examiner's office, if you have no transportation."

"That would be lovely. Thank you," replied Doris, blinking.

That would be lovely? Marsh grimaced. Something besides this woman's strange behavior was unsettling. Despite his many years delivering death notifications, this had to be the weirdest of them all. Nevertheless, he had a job to see to. "Mrs. Tetler, we would like to have your permission to search your husband's personal belongings. We're hoping to gain insight as to why somebody might have wanted to hurt him."

Doris stared. Her elation well hidden. She could have given the officer a million reasons why somebody would have wanted to hurt Russell with her name prominently placed at the top of the list, but instead, she remained silent.

"Mrs. Tetler?" Connie asked. "Are you okay?"

Doris gazed straight ahead, sneering at nothing in particular. Marsh shot Connie a perplexed look.

"Do you need something to drink?" asked Connie sympathetically. "Perhaps some water?"

Doris continued to stare.

"Ma'am, do we have your permission to do that?" inquired Marsh more directly.

"Permission?" Doris appeared confused, finally making eye contact with Marsh.

"To search your husband's personal belongings–" Marsh repeated.

"Oh, of course," said Doris. "Absolutely!" Doris practically hopped to her feet. "Follow me." Scooting past everyone she headed directly for Russell's office. Once satisfied that the gang had successfully trailed behind, she flung open the door. "You're gonna want to start in here."

Officer Hamilton shot Marsh a look, suggesting they forge ahead. Once inside the small room, Hamilton sat down at Russell's desk, turned the computer on and waited. Soon enough a prompt appeared. "You wouldn't happen to know the password, Mrs. Tetler?"

"I sure do." Doris grinned. *Russell thought he was so damn smart.* Bending over, she slipped her hand under the desk." She groped around for a tiny piece of paper she'd seen him tape underneath. "Ah, got you." Jubilantly, Doris read it off. "Capital 't,' then lower case, i–g–h–t, no space, capital 'r', lowercase o–p–e. 'TightRope.'"

CHAPTER 32

The Hospital Visit

THE NEWS HAD BEEN PARTIALLY correct. Nour was brought to the hospital under armed police protection, but *Alhamdulillah*, not because she'd been shot. Allah had other plans. A second before the gunman pulled the trigger, the excruciating pain from a complete blockage in Nour's intestine caused her to collapse to her knees. When she crumbled, everyone naturally assumed she'd been hit, including Russell. The timing couldn't have been more perfect.

The emergency small bowel resection surgery to remove the diseased portion of Nour's intestine had lasted four hours and had gone well. It wasn't until the evening of the next day that the surgeon came into her room to speak directly with her. Up to that point, she'd only come by periodically to check on her sleeping patient, allowing the highly-trained nurses to keep her charge as comfortable and out of pain as possible.

"Thankfully, you had enough healthy small intestine so I was able to do a procedure called anastomosis, where I was able to staple the ends together," explained Dr. Owen. The doctor took out his pen and began writing.

"I don't understand. Why?"

"You have Crohn's Disease. Your small intestine was almost completely blocked. What about gut pain? Once inside I found fistulas, small holes."

"Terrible pain."

"Have you experienced any night sweats?"

"Yes."

"Fever and no appetite recently?"

"Yes. All of that."

"How about nausea and vomiting?"

"I couldn't stop, but I thought I had a flu."

The doctor smiled. "No flu, but you were dangerously ill."

"So, I'm okay now? You removed the Crohn's?"

Dr. Owen pulled up a chair and laid her clipboard with her patient's notes across her lap. "Most people who have this surgery fully recover. In no time at all, you should be able to go back to doing your normal activities, and most kinds of work."

"Okay, great." Nour felt better already. "Is that it?"

"I had to remove a large part of your small intestine. You may find that you will experience loose stools or have issues getting enough nutrients from the foods you eat, but I'll have a nutritionist come up to speak to you."

"Sounds good."

"Yes, however, the surgery isn't a cure—it's a fix."

"But I thought you said you cut it out."

"I removed the damaged areas of your intestine, but you may need ongoing medical treatment or possibly further surgeries."

"For how long will I need medical treatment?"

"Forever. Crohn's Disease is a chronic condition."

Nour blew out a deep breath, barely able to contain the tears. "When can I go home?"

"Normally I'd keep you here for three to seven days, but since this was an emergency operation, it may be a bit longer. Let's watch and see, okay?"

"When can I begin to eat real food again?"

"Are you feeling hungry?"

"A little."

"Well, that's a good sign."

"I dreamt I sunk my teeth into a slice of hot cheesy pizza."

"Ah, well, not so fast. Today is only day two since the surgery. Tomorrow, if everything goes well through the night, I'll order you clear fluids. After that, we'll start to introduce thicker fluids, and then soft foods. See if we can get your bowels moving again. Until then, your IV will supply you with all the nutrition your body needs."

"You have officially given new meaning to having a bagged lunch," teased Nour, who tended to use humor to handle stress.

Dr. Owen smiled. "You bet. No taste but it does the job. Do you have any other questions, concerns before I go?"

Nour shook her head. She actually did, but for now they were best unasked. She needed time to sort this all out.

"If you think of anything else, either ask the nurse to contact me or, if it can wait, we'll chat again tomorrow. Until then, I'll have the nutritionist sent to speak with you, and I'll also have a gastroenterologist come in to explain Crohn's."

"Thank you."

"Take care of yourself. Get some rest, and try not to worry.

You're going to be fine."

Nour couldn't wait to be alone to cry.

**

On the day after the surgery, Maryam snuck into Nour's room and found her sound asleep. The only noise came from the machines still hooked up to her body. Reluctant to disturb her, Maryam left a vase of flowers on the night table with a note. Her flower arrangement paled in comparison to the many others filling every available shelf space and windowsill. There were so many deliveries that at one point Mrs. Ibrahim asked the nurses to give them away to other patients, although she did request to keep the cards and letters that accompanied them.

As promised, the nutritionist, as well as the gastroenterologist, each came to speak with Nour during the week. Maryam stopped by with Dr. Khan; they brought along pamphlets on Crohn's disease. Her parents were thankful for the information, but Nour felt a bit overwhelmed.

"You don't have to pretend that you're okay with all of this," insisted Mrs. Ibrahim. "You're allowed to be upset." The two women were alone in Nour's hospital room having tea together. Not the hospital's microwavable Lucifer swill, which closely mimicked lukewarm bathwater, but a real cup of steaming hot brew purchased at the coffee shop around the corner.

"I'm fine."

"No, you *look* just fine, but inside, we both know better."

Nour nursed her delicious tea. Every sip symbolized another step closer to feeling normal again, or at least a *new normal*. Tea was exactly the kind of medicine she needed to awaken her numbed senses—especially taste—which had taken heavy fire under the barrage of IV pumped medications traveling through her system. "Thank you for bringing this...so good."

Mrs. Ibrahim's heart grew heavy watching her daughter struggle. "On a lighter note, your friend, Maryam—she really cares about you."

"I really like her too." Nour adjusted the pillow behind her head.

"I'm glad to see you have such a nice friend."

"See! I told you I wasn't a total social misfit," teased Nour.

Mrs. Ibrahim smiled, relieved to see Nour's sense of humor return. "Which brings me to my next question, smart mouth."

"I'm all ears."

"Who's the gorgeous, Muslim guy standing sentry at your door?"

"My who?"

"Oh, don't you dare start to lie to me, young lady. He's been practically camped out at the hospital since you got here. I want a name, rank, file number. Who's his mother? And what are his intentions?"

"*Wallahi*, I have no idea who you're talking about."

"I see. Pleading the fifth. Okay, then that leaves me no choice. You're forcing me to interrogate your father."

"Dad? Dad knows him?"

"Apparently so."

"You're being serious right now?"

"Of course, I am. You think that young man would be standing out there without your father's okay?"

"Are you sure he's not just a police officer?"

"I'm positive."

"How do you know he's Muslim?"

"He salaams me. My goodness, for someone so smart, you sure can be dense sometimes."

Nour was intrigued. Then horrified. "*Wallahi*, I have no idea who you're talking about, but if he's as gorgeous as you say and Muslim, please don't let him see me like this!"

Mother and daughter shared a laugh. Nour lowered her voice. "Is he outside my door right now?"

"He was when I came in."

"What if he comes inside?"

"He's not going to come inside."

"Just hand me my scarf on the chair. Just in case."

"I don't think you need to worry about this right now." Mrs. Ibrahim handed Nour the scarf smirking.

"How do I look?" asked Nour.

"Lopsided. Here, let me help you."

Mrs. Ibrahim adjusted and pinned the hijab properly. "There. Much better."

Then the mood in the room turned somber. Nour broached the subject that everyone thus far danced around and brushed off. "Mom, it's time you told me what happened. Everyone's been tiptoeing around it and I keep getting told *later*. Now is later. I need to know. Everything."

Mrs. Ibrahim had anticipated questions. Nour wouldn't be her daughter if she didn't ask, but it still didn't make the delivery any easier. Next to her chair she had a satchel filled with clippings collected from various newspapers. "You're a grown woman, and you have the right to know. But hear me out first."

"All right."

"You just had major surgery. You're slowly regaining your

health and strength. The added stress from diving into all of this right now won't do you any good. With that said, I know I'm talking to the wall, so here are all the news clippings I could find about him. It's not everything, but it should give you what you're looking for." She leaned in closer to the bed, taking her daughter's soft, much thinner hand in hers. "No matter how much digging you do, you might never know all the whys."

"I know."

"Get stronger first. Give yourself time to feel healthier. All of this is in Allah's hands now. But no matter what, keep in mind, that guy is never going to bother you again."

"Did he have any family?"

"*Astaghfirallah*!" Mrs. Ibrahim grimaced. "The papers said a wife. The court placed her in a mental institution."

"A mental institution?" Nour pulled herself up. "Why?"

"Are you ready for this?" Mrs. Ibrahim handed her daughter a glass of water. "She poisoned the police."

"WHAT?" Nour almost spat.

"Wait, I was listening to one news report and it gets weirder. Turns out the cops who came to question her the night of the shooting, started feeling sick a few hours later, but of course, nobody suspected anything. They probably thought they had the flu, but it wasn't that at all. One officer got so sick that he had to be taken by ambulance to the ER."

"This is nuts!"

"Yup. The crazy lady fed them cookies laced with rat poison."

"This is insane."

"Sure is. And the papers this morning reported that it was the same poison found in the husband's body."

"Oh, my God."

"Like something straight out of a horror movie."

"That's terrible! Will they be alright?"

"Yes, *Alhamdulillah*, but here's the craziest part, if you can imagine crazier."

"I'm not sure if I can take much more."

"I can stop."

"Don't you dare!"

Mrs. Ibrahim chuckled. "One newspaper wrote that there was so much poison already in the husband's body, that if the—whoever it was, they're not saying yet—anyway if that nut job hadn't killed him, the poison definitely would have."

"*Ya Allah*. This is so sick…and beyond evil. I can't, I don't even know how to respond to any of this."

"Serves his damn ass right."

"Umi!"

"You heard me and this is why I'm telling you to leave this alone, just for a few more days. After that, I won't stop you."

There were a few soft taps at the door and then a head peeked in. "*AsSalaamu'alaikum*! You're awake! *Alhamdulillah*," Maryam exclaimed. "Can I come in?"

"*AsSalaamu'alaikum*, of course," said Nour and her mother in unison.

"Perfect timing." Mrs. Ibrahim stood. "I need to get going anyway but I'll be back later. Do you want me to get anything for you?" she asked. "More tea, maybe?"

"Tea would be great, but, actually, I feel disgusting. Could you bring me a few, you know…?"

"I gotcha," winked her mother knowingly. "See you later, ladies." Playfully she leaned in to give her daughter a kiss on the cheek. "And remember, I'm leaving this satchel in the locker over there. It's your call, but for once, be kind to yourself."

"Nice seeing you again, Mrs. Ibrahim," said Maryam. Both women hugged, *salaamed*, and then the room fell still. "You're looking better."

"Thanks."

"You gave us all quite a scare. OH!" Maryam snapped her finger. "Before I forget, Dr. Khan told me to tell you that she'll be in later to see you as well."

"Oh great."

"No worries. She doesn't plan on lecturing you until you get out."

Nour grinned. "By the way, I want to thank you for checking in on me the way you have and looking in on my parents. It means a lot to me."

"Oh stop. *Alhamdulillah*."

"And also for the information you dropped off. I knew next to nothing about Crohn's. I guess I'm getting a crash course now."

"It's manageable. However, like anything else, you're going to have to stay on top of it. One thing is for sure, you can't go on ignoring your pain or make excuses for not taking care of yourself. This is an autoimmune disease. If you don't face it, it will force you to, as you can plainly see."

"I'm trying not to get depressed about it, but I'm so…"

"Angry?"

"Very."

"Resentful? Pissed?"

"All of that."

"You have a right to be."

"My mother said the same thing."

"Did she? Well, she was right. Who wouldn't be? But

remember, you have a strong network of people behind you who love and adore you, and we're all here to help you navigate through this. You're not alone."

"It's not only this disease…it's all of it. The hours of preparation, the planning, the energy…everything that went into making this rally happen, and then this. In the end, it feels like it was all for nothing."

"How do you figure?"

"Well, for starters, I got shot at."

"Yeah. Okay. I'll give you that. That sucked."

Nour grimaced. "Then there's the fact that the rally was cancelled. All those people who came will probably never go to another protest rally again."

Maryam smirked and crossed her legs. "I'm surprised at you," she said, whisking away an imagined smudge of dirt from her skirt.

"What's that supposed to mean?"

"It means I'm shocked. What little faith you have in the rest of us."

"Wha–?"

"Yes, *this* rally was cancelled, but read this." Maryam pulled from her handbook a small pile of news clippings. "Nobody is running away or giving up. We can't afford to. Especially not now. The stakes are too high."

Nour's face drew confusion.

"Don't believe me? Look!" Maryam insisted, dropping the clippings on Nour's lap. "Read it for yourself. *Iqra* sister, because you obviously know not."

One headline read, "Civil Rights Activist Stands for Justice in the Face of Hate." Another one read, "Shot but Not Silenced!" and another, "Social Activist, Nour Ibrahim Faces Hate and Wins."

TIGHT ROPE

"I...I don't understand." Nour's heart raced. Her eyes glanced furtively over the articles. *Could this be true?*

"People are mobilizing, Nour. They're not backing down. Nobody's backing down, especially not after the community saw you stand up, despite all the hate thrown your way. And look, read this; other communities are starting to join us. They see how far these fascists will go to silence us and they know they're next." Maryam knew she should probably quit, but couldn't. There was no way in hell she was going to let her friend wallow in bed thinking she failed.

Nour began tearing up.

"Here," Maryam handed her a tissue to wipe her eyes. "Deathly sick, you still stood on stage knowing you had a lunatic stalking you—and you think your bravery isn't energizing? Pu-leaz, give me a break! Hate didn't win—not even by a long shot."

It was all too much. The guilt, the pain, the uncertainty, the apprehension, the feelings of disappointing others...the damn burst open, and despite the physical discomfort, Nour cried the angry, healing tears of a warrior.

Maryam, never one to hold back, wept along with her. Two women, two sisters, and in the end, friends. After a few minutes, after eyes were semi-dried and noses blown and wiped, Maryam broke the silence again. "Look, for what it's worth, for a while, you're going to feel off your game, but I promise, you'll find your flow again, if you listen to your body."

"And if I don't?"

"She'll make you listen!" The two friends laughed. "Seriously though, Crohn's is something you're going to have to come to peace with."

"I don't know where to begin."

"You've already begun. What you're going through, all these jumbled emotions, they will eventually lead you to a new norm. Before you know it, you'll learn how to manage your days, gauge your energy levels, know what foods work and don't. I'm not sure if you know this, but this disease reacts differently for each person so there are no set rules."

"The nutritionist mentioned it."

"Oh good, you spoke to one. Excellent. See! You're already on your way. Trust me, soon you'll manage your symptoms like a pro. You'll even learn how to embrace the good days and fly past the bad, but it takes time. *Sabr.*"

"You sound so confident."

"Of course, I do, because you have me." Maryam smiled widely.

Nour playfully sucked her teeth. "And what about work? What am I supposed to do about that, oh wise sage?"

"People with Crohn's can work. You may have to adjust your hours or the kind of work you do, but let's face that hurdle once you get home and back on your feet, and see how you feel. Who knows, maybe you'll be able to pick up where you left off without a problem. You might even be able to work from home or find a part time job or something. There's so many opportunities to explore, but for now, I suggest you shelve it."

Too exhausted from trying to figure it all out, Nour agreed. "Fine. Consider it shelved, but I do have one more extremely important question for you."

"Shoot." Cupping her mouth in horror, Maryam instantly realized what had just stupidly slipped out. "Shit, I'm sorry. I didn't mean to say that."

Nour cracked up. Her belly was still intensely sore. Any

sudden coughing, sneezing or laughing were major no-no's so she tried not to laugh too hard, but failed miserably.

Mortified, Maryam blushed. "Okay, let me rephrase that. What is your question?"

After finally gaining her composure, Nour tried as calmly as possible to speak. "My question is this: who's the gorgeous hunk I heard was standing guard outside my door?"

EPILOGUE

ONE YEAR LATER

Doris Tetler–Morgan Valley Psychiatric Center:

APPARENTLY, A FEW OF THE residents on the floor came down with a mild case of food poisoning. Needless to say, when the patients demanded to know what happened, like clockwork, Doris felt compelled to incite panic. She announced to the other patients that in no uncertain terms, they were all being poisoned and systematically exterminated one by one. Of course, the head nurse sternly tried shushing Doris, but she was too late to quell the mounting panic or sway the hyperbolic hysteria breaking out everywhere.

One patient, a young man suffering from severe paranoia who spent most of his days heavily medicated, began pouring his milk and scooping his mashed potatoes into a plastic plant. Another patient stood on a chair with his mouth wide open and drooling. Banging his head with one hand, he started spitting wildly, all the while arguing with someone…presumably Satan. However, before taking center stage, he had successfully, and out of view of the staff, pocketed a nice number of plastic utensils and crayons, which he planned to use as future weapons.

A few of the serener patients wept, insisted they were eternally doomed, and swore they could feel the poison already starting to work. Doris's annoying roommate, Maya, an extremely paranoid schizophrenic suffering with multiple personalities, became so terrified that she began hollering a symphony of colorful obscenities, only somewhat muted by the wastebasket over her head, worn like a helmet. "They're trying to kill us all!" she warned, handing out plastic spoons. "Slit your wrists, quick! Let the poison drain out of your system before it's too late!"

At this point, the entire place turned into a mad house with patients biting and scratching one another, all trying to escape. And while the bedlam continued, Doris remained seated. Her ankles crossed. She kept both of her hands folded on her lap with fingers clasped tightly together. Thoroughly entertained, she chuckled, unequivocally enamored with the absolute hysteria she'd awakened.

Eventually, all the residents were properly corralled and safely skirted back to their rooms, but not without a ton of coaxing and dragging. Many needed to be sedated. A few, like the devil-worshipping plastic utensil collector, had to be physically restrained on top of being heavily medicated for his own safety when an attendant found him attempting to pluck out one of his eyeballs with a spoon to appease his demonic voices.

Once back in their room, the skirmish between Doris and Maya had only just begun. For months, the two women fought over the stupidest things. Whether the lights remained on, the length of time one took on the toilet, and the latest World War –

Maya's incessant talking. Maya and her band of schizophrenic, merry voices refused to shut up. Intermittently she'd be plain old Maya, whimpering, sniveling, and cowering in the corner. This personality Doris could ignore, but at other times, Maya's more aggressive personalities would emerge. Some of them would curse and prance about, especially the one called Gretchen. That personality was a total psycho-bitch who loved nothing more than having to be physically restrained by the male support staff. Instead of fighting them off, she'd groan in pleasure, egging them on, and daring them to fuck her. She'd practically have an orgasm on the floor.

But it was Lily's personality that pissed Doris off the most. Lily was a child, an irritatingly whiny, grating child, probably no more than five or six years old, who for no apparent reason loved to sing songs. Annoying songs. Nursery rhymes in particular and all–damn–day. Doris pleaded with Lily to give her break, but the obstinate little brat would only become louder and more aggravating. Doris complained to the staff, but true to form, they never followed up, and Doris grew more indignant.

"Ring around the Rosie, pockets full of posies. Ashes, ashes—"

"SHUT THE FUCK UP, LILY, will you?" Doris yelled, incensed. "I can't think with all that racket you're making."

"I don't have to listen to you. You're not my mother!" Lily stuck her tongue out and wagged it at Doris to make her point.

"Oh, for fuck's sake."

"I'm telling that you're cursing at me."

That was the last straw. Doris had finally had enough. She hauled off after Maya…or Lily…whoever the hell she was, and grabbed a nice-sized clump of her hair. "I'm gonna do a whole lot more to you if you don't shut the HELL up!"

Little did Doris comprehend the unbridled wrath about to come hauling down in her direction by way of Gretchen, who was not only a psycho-sex maniac but Maya's number one protector-personality. The same personality who materialized whenever Maya's deviant father came sneaking into her bedroom at night wearing nothing but a bathrobe and a hard-on. Since then, whenever Maya, Lily, or any of the other weaker personalities felt threatened, Gretchen would resurface with a vengeance, and she didn't take shit from anyone, especially when things got physical.

"Take your filthy hands off me, bitch," hissed Gretchen, grabbing Doris's wrist and twisting until she was able to force Doris to free her hair.

Doris yelped as a searing pain shot through her arm, but somehow, she still managed to land a hard slap.

Rubbing her red cheek, Gretchen's face contorted into a strange mixture of anger and pure ecstasy. With a wicked smile, she licked the blood trickling from her split lip.

"I see. You wanna dance, you miserable old bitch? Let's dance."

At the time, Doris hadn't a clue which personality she was currently speaking to, nor did she care, which was her final fatal mistake. "Go to hell, psycho," she spat.

"You first."

Gretchen lunged towards Doris like a linebacker, shoving her backward into the bathroom, pinning her shoulders against the wall, and kicking the door closed behind them.

Later that evening, a nurse making rounds found Maya on her bed wrapped like a mummy in a bedsheet, swaying to and fro, and moaning, "She warned her…she warned her…"

"Warned who?" asked the nurse, glancing toward Doris's empty bed.

"She shouldn't have grabbed Lily."

"Maya! Where is Doris?" the nurse demanded. Maya pointed her tongue at the closed bathroom door.

"Doris?" the nurse yelled. "It's time for your medication." Pushing the unlocked door open, she gasped. "Holy SHIT!"

On the bathroom floor, covered in a pool of her own congealed blood, lay Doris. Her dead eyes bolted wide. Her battered arms flung wide apart. Sharp glass shards from a smashed bathroom mirror littered the tiled, cold, stony floor beneath her blood-soaked body. One of the bigger shards used to slice her throat had been also commissioned to carve a short message into Doris's chest, which read, "And they all fell down."

The significance of the gory engraved message continues to remain a mystery.

Eugene Underwood

EUGENE NEVER GOT CAUGHT FOR Russell's murder, but that alone wasn't the impressive part. Fringe living afforded him a wide expanse to retreat and continue on his chameleon lifestyle, an existence which others only imagined or read about.

Within hours of the murder, he had taken off, on his way to another city, once again blending seamlessly into the vast surrounding landscape, a passing silhouette lurking in some alleyway and waiting for the right moment to extinguish his next target.

No, the truly remarkable part about Mr. Eugene Underwood came in the form of his ability to compartmentalize his acts of violence without guilt, shame, or remorse. He was perfectly comfortable butchering one moment and contemplating opening up a bar the very next—not that he was serious or anything. Although, should one ever be passing through some obscure town or city and happen past a pub called, *The Garrote*, they may want to think twice before entering.

Nour Ibrahim

THE CROHN'S HAD PROVEN to be one large, excruciating, learning curve for not only Nour, but for those around her as well. Delegating her energy and fighting back fatigue had become two crucial survival skills, along with learning how to pace herself, not something that came naturally to the go-getter, but now she had no choice. Something had to give, and despite the fact that Nour wanted to remain self-sufficient, she finally had to learn how to ask for and accept help. This aspect of living with a chronic disease turned out much harder than expected, especially as she tried holding tight to the life she had. Nonetheless, whenever she made the mistake of stepping out of her body's comfort zone, a sharp physical rebuke soon followed, sometimes laying her up for days at a time.

It hadn't taken long before Nour realized that going into the office full time would no longer be physically doable. Thankfully, the job—astonishingly under Sherri's insistence—had allowed her to network from home part time. This schedule worked out extremely well. Sherri was beyond thrilled with Nour's output. Projects were not only finished on schedule but meticulously composed and organized.

The speech she never finished delivering at the rally got

published online and went viral. After that, offers for her speech writing skills kept flowing in. She could hardly keep up. While it saddened Nour that she couldn't physically be on the front lines in the struggle any longer, her pen most certainly was. But best of all, working from home spared her from having to listen or be subjected to anymore narrow-minded, xenophobic, intolerant 'watercooler talk' morons.

Besides what she handled for the company, Nour started a blog, something she had wanted to do but never found the time. She wrote about her disease. People reading her blog touted her as brave, but she didn't feel brave. More like drained, and at times, afraid. The relentless push-pull of the chronic disease systematically chipped away at her fortitude and often left her questioning her self-worth.

Her writing drew in a large audience, a steady readership, and even a few select advertisers. Nour found, however, that no matter how hard she toiled or succeeded, the real challenge came from the way she judged and viewed herself. Her self-reproach and frustration from constantly having to contend with depleted energy levels took its toll. While the surgery had indeed saved her life, the doctor had been brutally honest when he told her it was far from being a cure. On many days, despite the persistent gut pain, she had to force herself to get out of bed and move. Just 'showing up' took courage and tenacity. Thank goodness, she had the steadfast support of her parents, the close friendship of Maryam, and most of all, the unwavering shoulder of Shane to lean on. Her strong, dependable, fine as hell, great listener, and husband extraordinaire.

"I'm so frustrated," she said. "As if my body and I are at war. How am I supposed to work like this?" Nour periodically held pity parties, with her husband the only invited guest.

TIGHT ROPE

"One day at a time, hon." Being in the military stationed across the country, this wasn't the first-time Shane had to console his wife through a computer screen.

Nour crossed her arms over her chest like a petulant toddler sent to the corner. "Easy for you to say."

"You're seriously beautiful when you pout."

Nour exhaled. "Hush up…I'm being serious," she pleaded. A thin smirk eked out from the corner of her mouth.

"So am I."

Nour glanced at her husband's face staring back at her. His grey-steel, blue eyes smiled back reassuringly. "I don't mean to lash out at you, but how could you possibly understand? Look at you! Your body works perfectly. You're some bigshot, well-oiled, trained machine. While I, on the other hand, spend most of my days stuck at home trying to figure out what to eat, so fatigued that most of the time I need to take a nap right after taking a nap. It's ridiculous."

"I'd give anything to nap next to you right now…"

"Stop it."

"Curled up behind your soft, rounded—"

"Seriously, you need to stop."

"Never."

"Then change the subject." Nour missed him terribly.

"Okay, well, if I must. Onto other, less motivating topics."

"Such as?"

"Such as have you begun packing yet?"

"Yes, but why?"

"Because I spoke to my commander. He said my transfer should be approved anytime now, and if all goes as planned, I should be cleared to go, maybe by the end of next week."

Nour's face brightened. Now here was the news she'd been waiting for! Besides wanting to join her husband in California, for all the obvious reasons, the move to warmer temperatures would be a welcome reprieve after the last harsh winter in New York. "I'm almost done," she said, somewhat exaggerating. In truth, she'd barely started but with what little she planned to bring, besides her clothes, packing would take her less than an hour or two. "Only a few more boxes." *And that pile of files in the corner.*

"Once I get my orders and all the dates are set in stone, I'll buy my plane ticket. I'll have two weeks off. That'll be more than enough time to bring your stuff to my parent's house so the movers can pick up everything from there to haul out."

Nour couldn't wait. The weeks had dragged by slowly, each day leaving her missing Shane more and more. She started to relax. Soon they'd begin living their life together under one roof. And then she remembered. "Ah, you know, I'll have to fly back out here sometime within the next month or so."

"Already? Wow, when is Maryam due?"

"She's thirty weeks."

"*SubhanaAllah*. That went fast."

"Only for you," laughed Nour.

Shane remembered Zaid and Maryam's wedding day. How excited Mrs. Ali looked. Cloud nine couldn't have competed with that woman, although the rapport between her and Maryam's mother seemed a bit less complimentary. There were many strained smiles, overly courteous responses, and an apparent tension between the mothers lingered, but thankfully not to the point of disruption. This was pretty much the same way his mother behaved the first time meeting the Ibrahim's.

Funny enough, Mr. Ali tried to stay detached to the bitter end,

TIGHT ROPE

adamantly refusing to participate in any of the wedding preparations. But once the stunning bride entered the room on the arm of her beaming father, something happened. Shane saw it when he caught Mr. Ali studying his son's face. There must have been something he read or detected in his son's expression because at that very moment, his facial expression transformed and softened. Shane felt relieved to see some of the harbored pretenses evaporate, as one protected border melted away...at least for that single capsulated moment in time.

"Hey you," teased Nour. "Hello? What are you thinking about?"

Shane shook his head, "I'm sorry, my wandered for second. What were you saying?"

"I was saying that Maryam has finally admitted to driving Zaid crazy. One minute she's laughing, the next hysterical crying. She told me he caught her washing shoelaces the other day."

"Shoelaces?" interrupted Shane. "Why shoelaces?"

"Nesting, probably. Women will sometimes do that when they're getting ready for their baby to arrive...or so I'm told."

"You know, Mrs. Nour McCormick, we're going to make beautiful children together, *Insha'Allah*."

Nour rolled her eyes playfully. "Oh really? And why is that, Mr. Shane McCormick?" This wasn't the first time they'd had this discussion, but in truth, it never got old.

"Because I brilliantly married the most gorgeous woman on the planet."

That maddening rush of longing engulfed her. "Definitely change the subject!"

Shane laughed with the same warm smile which captured Nour's heart only a year before. "Okay, fair enough, but once I have you all to myself, there will be no more changing subjects on me."

"Deal."

"I wonder how my brother Zaid is really holding up these days. I owe that guy a phone call." The last time the two men were together, they never did get the chance to finish their conversation.

"I'm still thinking about joining the military." Zaid glanced up and caught Shane's reaction. "Probably Reserves."

"Why's that?"

"I want to do my part."

"Okay…"

"I want to protect my country. Give something back."

"Those are all good reasons," Shane agreed good-naturedly.

"I hear a "but" coming."

"— *but*, are they *your* reasons?"

"What do you mean by that?"

"I mean—and please don't misunderstand me, I'm not saying there's anything wrong with what you said—but just don't kid yourself."

"Who's kidding? I'm being totally serious. This isn't something I just pulled out of the air. I've been thinking about doing it for a while."

"Absolutely. It's your decision. And I told myself the same things when I got ready to join."

"So, then what's your point?"

"My point is, it's complicated."

"So, you're telling me you regret your decision now…"

"No, not necessarily. But like they say, hindsight is 20-20."

"And?"

"And military life and marriage isn't an easy combination, for starters. Divorce rates among military marriages is high for a reason."

"You and Nour seem to be handling it fine."

"We are, but remember, she met me already serving. Military life was already part of the package. Personally, my brother, I think you're underestimating how important you are to the people who count on you and need your protection here now more than before."

"I've thought about that."

"Not to mention the fact you're a married man, now. It's not a decision you get to make on your own anymore. Maryam should have a say."

**

Nour leaned her chin on her curled fists. "Maryam told me Zaid is busy running the store. Oh, but get this, his father renamed it."

"Renamed the store? To what?"

"Ali & Son."

"You're kidding, right?"

"I wish I was. Maryam said Zaid hates it, but doesn't have the heart to tell him. Especially not after the big deal his father made out of making him a partner. Oh, but on a good note, she did mention that he's going back to college. I think she said he's already taking some night courses or will be soon."

"*Alhamdulillah*! Did she say to study what?"

"I think she mentioned political science."

Shane needed to hang up. "Okay, love. I gotta get back to work, but please finish up that packing and I'll keep you posted on my end."

"*Insha'Allah.*"

"I love you, Nour McCormick…*AsSalaamu'alaikum.*"

Nour stood up to stretch. As promised, she'd finish packing in the morning. In the far corner of her room, a massive pile of personal folders from her job tormented her. *I should have thrown them all out like Sherri said.* Without giving it much thought, she lifted the entire stack and walked it over to the garbage bag, but just before she was ready to dump it all in, a small piece of rope dropped onto her foot, still tied in the shape of a tiny noose.

"ACK!" she screeched, jumping clear back and practically knocking over her vanity chair. *Tetler's last "gift."*

Nour remembered hearing stories from family and community members about how lynching crimes were commonly used against African Americans, especially in the south where Whites in hoods thought nothing of torturing or burning a Black person at the stake. Far too many hanged for supposed "lesser offences:" a Black man accused of looking at a White woman or for "giving lip'" to a White man. Lynched bodies were left swinging from a tree to instill terror and spread fear, used as a cruel and inhumane reminder to those who mistakenly believed they deserved humanity.

Nour shuddered. Some of those same perpetrators who'd committed these lynching's were still alive today, never having been brought to justice. The fact they got to live out the remainder of their lives as if nothing they did had any consequence remains a national travesty in a long, hauntingly dark history of travesties.

Although dead, Tetler's twisted souvenir still managed to induce terror. Angrily, Nour snatched the rope off the floor and flung it at the garage bag. "Enough!" she avowed, but before even having the chance to collect her thoughts, her cell phone *pinged*. "Now what!" There, prominently displayed on the screen was a single bone chilling message.

"I won't miss."

"You may not control all the events that happen to you, but you can decide not to be reduced by them." – Maya Angelou

ACKNOWLEDGMENTS

"O you who believe, be maintainers of justice, bearers of witness for Allah, even though it be against your own selves or (your) parents or near relatives—whether he be rich or poor, Allah has a better right over them both. So follow not (your) low desires, lest you deviate. And if you distort (justice) or turn away from (truth), surely Allah is ever Aware of what you do." (Qur'an 4:135)

I would like to express my deepest gratitude to the many individuals who had supported me through the writing of this book, especially to those who had encouraged me to continue when really, all I wanted to do was quit.

Thank you, Djarabi Kitabs Publishing for your unwavering support and bravery. When initially presented with this book's manuscript, you never once hesitated, welcoming TIGHT ROPE [and me] with open arms. I am truly and forever grateful.

SAHAR ABDULAZIZ

Thank you to those who have assisted me in editing, proofing, and design. Layla Abdullah-Poulos, my amazingly brilliant content editor, Hend Hegazi, my talented and gifted editor, Kayla Weir, my incredible proofreader, and Joshua Jadon, my clever and artistic cover designer. TIGHT ROPE shines because of your collective efforts and skills. My deepest respects.

I want to also thank my Lady Writers, Evelyn Infante, Kelly Jensen, Susan Moore Jordan, Catherine Schratt, and Laurel Wilczek. These incredible writer-friends have allowed me to bounce ideas off of them for countless hours. I extend to each and every one of you many hugs for reading and offering both comment and insight, but most of all, friendship and support. Thank you also to my dearest Sistah-friends, Tiffani Velez and Manal Moustafa for your insight and suggestions. I treasure you all–

To my family…what can I say when 'Thank You' doesn't feel like nearly enough for all that you do? Therefore, I will humbly remain grateful for your steadfast belief in me and in the path, I have chosen to journey. I love you all–

Lastly, I pray that this small effort is pleasing to Allah. Ameen.

"O mankind! We created you from a single (pair) of a male and a female, and made you into nations and tribes, that ye may know each other (not that ye may despise (each other). Verily the most honored of you in the sight of Allah is (he who is) the most righteous of you. And Allah has full knowledge and is well-acquainted (with all things). (Qur'an 49:13)

GLOSSARY OF TERMS

Abeed [abed]: A derogatory term in Arabic meaning "slave"
Afwan: You're welcome
Alhamdulillah: All praise is due to Allah
Allah: The one and only God
AsSalaamu'alaikum: May peace be upon you
Astaghfirallah: I seek forgiveness from Allah
Baba: Father
Bismillah: In The Name of Allah
Habibi: Friend, my love, sweetheart [depending on use]
Hafiza [h]: "Guardian" or "Memorizer" of the Qur'an
Halal: Permissible
Hijabis: Slang for women who wear hijab
Humar: Derogatory term: idiot, fool, stupid
Insha'Allah: "If it pleases Allah"
Jumu'ah: Friday, Friday prayers
Khutbah: Lecture or sermon
Ma'a Salaam: Used to say 'Goodbye'
MashaAllah: "Allah has willed"
Masjid: Place of worship
Muslim: One who submits to Allah
Qur'an: "The recitation" The central religious text of Muslims
Ramadan: 9th Lunar month, Month of fasting
Salaam: Peace
Sahabah: The companions of the Prophet Muhammad [PBUH]
Sheikha: A woman respected for her piety and religious knowledge
Shukran: Thank you
Shahadah: The Muslim profession of faith
SubhanaAllah: "Allah is perfect"
Wallahi: "I swear to Allah"
Wa'alaikum salaam: And peace unto you
Umi: Mother
Ya Allah: "My dear God"

Proof

Made in the USA
Columbia, SC
23 May 2017